Novel Grounds
FOR murder

Novel Grounds
for murder

HICKORY HILLS COZY MURDER MYSTERIES

CAROLYN MAPLEWOOD

Copyright © 2024 Carolyn Maplewood

All rights reserved. This book or parts thereof may not be reproduced in any form, stored in any retrieval system, or transmitted in any form by any means – electronic, mechanical, photocopy, recording, or otherwise – without prior written permission of the publisher.

Jacket art: Raelynn Carter

This is a work of fiction. Names, characters, places, and incidents either are the product of the author's imagination or are used fictitiously, and any resemblance to actual persons, living or dead, business establishments, events, or locales is entirely coincidental.

carolynmaplewood.com

ISBN:9798344037615

DEDICATION

For my momma, who has been gone nearly a decade now, yet somehow, is still here with me on every page.

CAST OF CHARACTERS

Welcome to Hickory Hills!

Meet the lively townsfolk of this small Missouri town—some you'll love, some you'll loathe, but all of them bring life, laughter, danger, excitement, and just the right dash of intrigue.

Josephine "Josie" McCarthy

Owner of the local book café and everyone's favorite accidental detective, Josie has a knack for finding mysteries—or perhaps they have a knack for finding her. Clever, determined, and always ready to dig a little deeper, she balances brewing the perfect cup of coffee with uncovering the secrets hidden in her quiet little town.

Caleb Barlow

The newest addition to the Hickory Hills police station, Caleb is grumpy and no-nonsense, with little patience for meddling civilians—especially Josie. He initially finds her interference frustrating, but it doesn't take long for him to realize her instincts are sharper than expected. Now, the two make an unstoppable (if unofficial) crime-solving duo, though Caleb isn't quite ready to admit it just yet.

Harriet "Hattie" Atwood

Josie's fiercely protective older sister and loyal partner in crime-solving, Hattie, is as bold and vibrant as the art she creates. Recently widowed and with her son off at college, she's navigating an empty nest and rediscovering herself through her artistic passions and spontaneous adventures in her beloved camper van, *Captain Vantastic*.

Eloise Jackson

Retired NYPD detective turned beloved baker. Eloise is the grandmother everyone wishes they had. She may serve up cookies and muffins with a smile, but her detective skills are sharp as ever. A mentor to Josie and the town's resident wise woman, she's never far from the heart of any mystery.

Holly Rousseau

Josie's best friend since forever, Holly, has a gift for making people feel at ease. With her warm heart and genuine interest in helping others, she often finds herself in the middle of the town's conversations—though never as a gossip. Whether she's at Eloise's bakery or her daughter's salon, Holly "accidentally" overhears bits of information that prove valuable to Josie's investigations. Always with the best intentions, she's the town's unofficial confidante, making her an invaluable ally in uncovering the truth.

Professors Konstanze "Stanzi" & Max Meyer

Stanzi and Max, longtime friends of Josie, are well-respected professors often on leave from teaching to focus on their research and publications. When they're not immersed in their academic pursuits, they enjoy hosting lively game nights at their Victorian home and frequently embark on research trips that seem to take them all over the world.

Rhett & Emma King

The adventurous couple every small town needs. Emma, Hattie's childhood bestie, has a free spirit and a love for anything thrilling, while her teddy bear of a husband, Rhett, keeps things grounded with his woodworking and calm demeanor. Together, they round out Josie's group of misfits.

Nikki Rousseau

Holly's daughter and the queen of Curl Up and Dye, where haircuts come with a side of town secrets. Her salon is a hub for gossip, making Nikki a valuable (though sometimes unwitting) ally in Josie's sleuthing efforts.

Anders Rousseau

Holly's husband and Nikki's father, Anders, is the tech wizard behind the scenes. When the clues need digital deciphering, Anders is your guy—always ready to help Josie and Holly dive into the world of computer forensics, whether they ask for it or not.

Dr. Graham Emerson

Holly's father and an esteemed university professor, Dr. Emerson's quiet wisdom and academic pursuits make him a respected figure in town.

Sheriff Declan Sturdy

Caleb's boss, a steady-as-an-oak ex-military man who plays the "good ol' boy" card when it suits him—but don't be fooled. Declan misses nothing, and his calm exterior hides a sharp intellect. He's more than happy to let Josie and Caleb run with their hunches, but he's always one step ahead of the game.

Claire Greene

Josie's frenemy who loves to stir the pot. Claire might butt heads with Josie and Holly, but beneath the prickly exterior lies a potential ally. Whether she's helping or hindering is often anyone's guess.

Sam Keppleford

The charming newcomer, Sam, has been turning heads ever since he started renovating that big, old mansion on the outskirts of town. He's friendly and fun and just here to enjoy the quiet life.

Hank Granger Sr., Hank Junior & the Granger Boys

The hardware store crew—three generations of friendly, dependable locals. Need a tool or a tip for fixing something? Hank Sr. and his brood are the ones to ask.

Connie Fontaine

Hickory Hills University's retired theatre professor and a town treasure, Connie, loves to spin a dramatic tale, and when she's not rehearsing a local play, she's stirring up scenes with her sharp wit and love for a bit of gossip.

Arthur "Artie" Blackburn

Owner of Artie's Garage, he's a slippery car repairman with a less-than-stellar reputation. Not exactly a model citizen, but still, he's part of the town's tapestry.

Gayle Murphy

Owner of the town diner and always ready with a smile. Need a good meal or a side of small-town news? Gayle's got you covered.

Granny Clara Belle, better known as "Smokin' Belle."

The no-nonsense owner and pit master of the Hickory Smoke BBQ Shack. Her brisket is as legendary as her gruff exterior, but she's a softie for anyone with a kind heart and a healthy appetite.

Tiffany Boggs

The receptionist you love to hate and a self-appointed town bully. Don't cross her—or do if you want to rile her up. Either way, Tiffany leaves an impression.

Tony Castelli

Tony is the deli king of Hickory Hills. With his slogan, "Where Flavor is King," Tony rules his deli with a warm smile and an eye for quality. His sandwiches are as unforgettable as his booming laugh.

Derek "Dex" Foster

A local boy who took a wrong turn in life, Dex got caught up in a bad crowd years ago and landed himself in some trouble. He's back in town now, trying to leave his criminal past behind—but whether Hickory Hills will welcome him back remains to be seen.

Vance "Van" Atwood

The late husband of Hattie and father of Zeke. Though he's no longer around, his legacy lingers in Hickory Hills—and in the hearts of those he left behind.

Ezekial "Zeke" Atwood

Hattie's son, off at college on a football scholarship, Zeke's rarely seen around town. But even from afar, he's protective of his mom and always ready to step in when needed.

Captain Vantastic

Hattie's beloved and quirky camper van is as colorful and full of personality as its owner.

Roy McCoy

Roy McCoy, the owner of McCoy's General Store, is as steady as the sunrise and just as comforting. With his signature flannel shirt and warm smile, Roy starts every morning at Novel Grounds, savoring Eloise's muffins and a steaming cup of coffee—predictable, dependable, and quietly adored by everyone in town

Willa Mae Turner

Owner of the pie shop on the square, Willa Mae's pies are as beloved as her outgoing, larger-than-life personality. She loves to be where the people are and is always where the action is! A devoted Agatha Christie fan, she fancies herself a local Miss Marple, and though her advice is often unsolicited, it's always well-meaning and wrapped in her signature charm.

Henry "Teddy" Theodore

The heart of Hickory Hills for as long as anyone can remember, a beloved mechanic with a warm smile and a generosity that's as legendary as his garage.

Christopher "Bear" Theodore

He is Teddy's grandson and shares his grandfather's warmth and kind nature. Their favorite pastime is quiet mornings spent fishing by the river

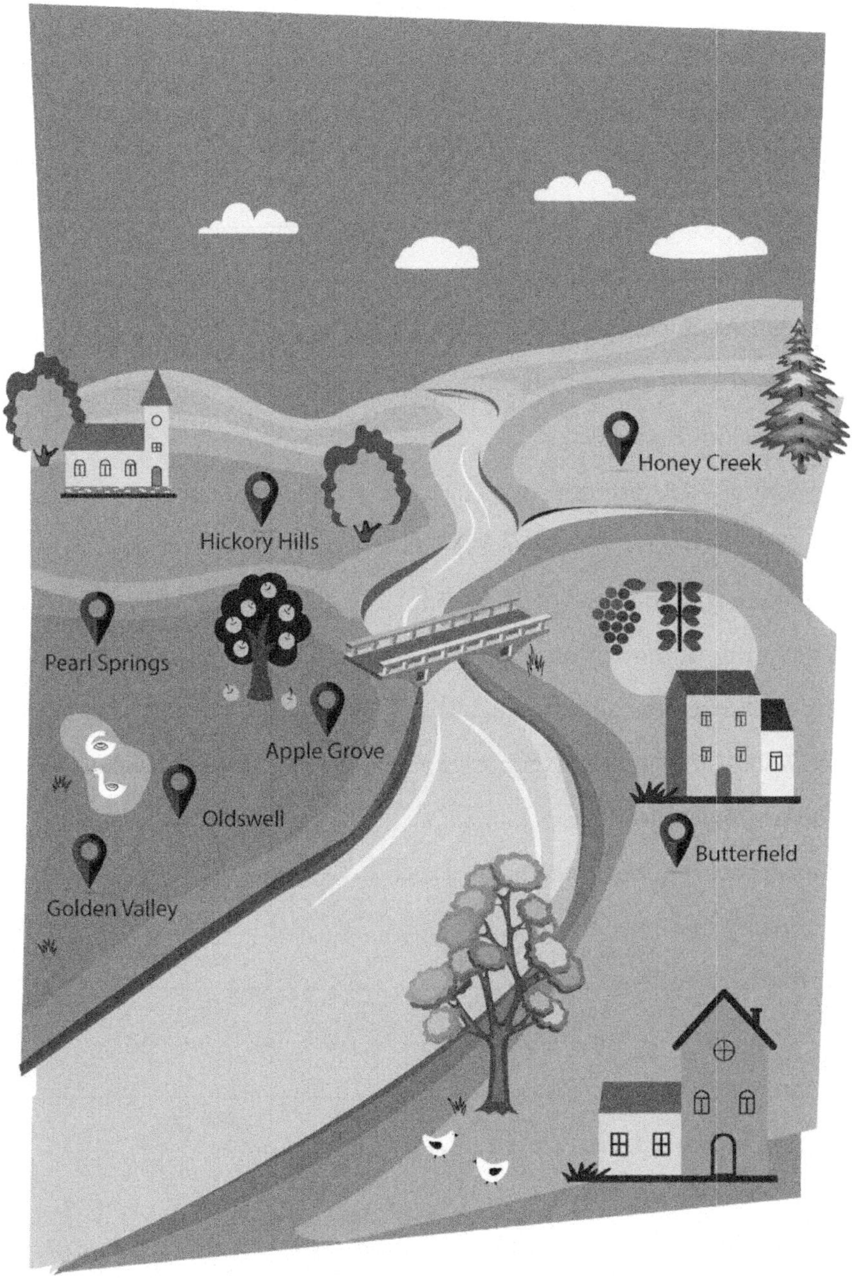
Honey Creek
Hickory Hills
Pearl Springs
Apple Grove
Oldswell
Butterfield
Golden Valley

Contents

1 muffin to hide 1
2 spilled beans 13
3 brewed awakening 27
4 a shot of suspicion 38
5 a murder most novel 56
6 a recipe for suspense 64
7 lattes, lies, & lockups 78
8 apples, accusations & a ghost 89
9 cappuccinos & clues 111
10 brewed lies & tattered pages 128
11 espresso shots & double-crossed plots 145
12 whodunit, a double shot of drama 154
13 gathering at the farmhouse 170
14 clues, coffee, & chemistry 176
15 a whole latte lies 184
16 locked in suspicion 195
17 espressoing doubts 199
18 grinding down the truth 212
19 storm in a coffee cup 220
20 masquerades & macchiatos 233
21 dark roast, dark secrets 241
22 steaming ahead, case closed 247

ACKNOWLEDGMENTS

To my sister, Karen,
Thank you for being my sounding board and biggest cheerleader, for supporting my dreams, for always knowing exactly what to say when I needed it most, and for patiently putting up with all my chatter about plot twists, characters, and those dreaded deadlines

1 muffin to hide

I PARKED MY OLD JEEP Grand Wagoneer in the back lot of my book café and hopped out. The Jeep might be old, but that faux wood paneling and cream exterior were a chef's kiss. Every time I slid behind the wheel, those honey-colored leather and corduroy seats offered the coziest hugs. Simple, timeless, reliable—just how I liked things.

Mocha, my smoky black Goldendoodle, was in the backseat, her curly fur brushed out as if she'd just come out of the dryer. Her big, intelligent brown eyes looked out at me as I opened the door. She bounded out with a soft thud and sat patiently at my feet as if waiting for my permission to tackle the day. She knew the routine by heart, which was more than I could say for myself some mornings.

A crisp breeze nipped at my nose as I tilted my head up, taking in the autumn morning. The towering hickory pecan tree above rustled, sending a cascade of golden leaves fluttering to the ground in delicate spirals. Mocha, of course, tried to catch them mid-air, snapping at them like a playful toddler. "You get 'em, Mocha," Sometimes, I wondered if she was more human than dog.

The university stood above us, perched on the bluff overlooking the town. Its ivy-covered, chateau-like buildings glowed pink and gold in the rising sun, casting long, sleepy shadows across the quiet streets. The town, still slumbering, had a peaceful hush about it.

The familiar scents of fallen leaves and freshly baked muffins greeted me as I walked toward Novel Grounds. My best friend, Holly Rousseau, stood by the back door, balancing a precarious stack of boxes. Her face lit up in a warm smile as she juggled the boxes in one hand in an attempt to wave.

"Morning, Holly!" I called out, picking up my pace as I noticed the muffin boxes wobbling dangerously.

"Hey, Josie! Here's today's muffin delivery from Eloise," she said, her grey-green eyes sparkling with their usual excitement. I rushed to grab the top half of the boxes before they toppled.

"Thanks," she exhaled, relieved. "I don't think Eloise would be too happy with me if I ruined yet another batch of muffins!"

I laughed, falling into step beside her as we walked through the backroom. The comforting scents of coffee grounds and the earthy notes of old books greeted us. The plush carpets beneath our feet softened the creaking of the old wooden floors. I flipped on the lights, and the soft glow illuminated the familiar scene: warm, cozy, welcoming. Mocha trotted along, her fluffy tail wagging enthusiastically as she inspected every nook with fresh curiosity.

I took a moment to appreciate the book café—a dream I'd built from scratch after years of planning. It was more than a business; it was my corner of the world, my little sanctuary. The café's charm lay not only in its cozy nooks and crannies but also in its blend of old-world style and modern-day comfort. Customers would soon be settling into their favorite corners, sinking into overstuffed chairs, and sipping on literary-themed coffees in delicate blue and white floral porcelain cups.

Of course, the French cream-colored bookcases, my prized find at an estate sale, added the perfect touch of elegance. Each shelf was filled with well-loved classics and modern favorites, inviting patrons to lose themselves in a good story and hopefully purchase a book or two. Together, the books, the coffee, and the muffins make Novel Grounds a little haven—a slice of comfort in the bustle of life.

Holly set the boxes down on the counter, pausing to open one. The rich aroma of baked apples, cinnamon, and caramel filled my senses. She closed her eyes and inhaled deeply. "These pecan caramel apple muffins are like a warm hug on a chilly day! Oh. My. Lands. The buttery cinnamon crumble, that drizzle of pecan caramel icing—it's pure gooey goodness."

"And don't even get me started on those chocolate peanut butter swirl muffins. They're my kryptonite," I said, tucking a loose strand of hair behind my ear and smiling at her enthusiasm. There was something contagious about Holly's reactions to food.

I slipped on my apron, decorated with whimsical pins shaped like books and coffee cups, and began brewing the morning coffee. The smell of fresh grounds hit the air as I scooped them into the filter. Mocha let out a soft bark from her corner, her tail thumping against the floor. She stared at the muffin boxes like they held her life's purpose.

"Patience, girl," I laughed, walking over to rub the top of her velvety head. "You and me both."

"I think I've put on fifteen pounds since I started helping Eloise at the bakery," Holly said, her light brown curls bouncing as she arranged the muffins in the display case.

"Yeah, me too," I said with a grin, filling another coffee filter with fresh grounds, "And I don't even work at the bakery. Just having these muffins here at Novel Grounds feels like a calorie commitment." I hit start on the machine, which groaned to life before bubbling and hissing like it was just as tired as we were.

Holly laughed, glancing over her shoulder at me. "You're impossible."

"Impossible, but not wrong," I teased, wiping a stray crumb off the counter. "If I ever stop fitting into these jeans, it's your fault. You and Eloise."

She rolled her eyes, though a smile tugged at her lips. "Oh, please."

"Those muffins are going to fly off the shelves today," I said, adjusting my new blush-colored glasses. I'd picked them out for a touch of sophistication, although I wasn't fooling anyone—not in my old jeans, scuffed cowboy boots, and berry-colored sweater. The look basically *screamed practical first, stylish second.* I pulled the shot lever on the machine and watched the dark espresso flow into the metal pitcher.

"Honestly, I don't know how Eloise does it," I said, shaking my head at the perfectly golden muffins Holly was arranging in the display case.

"You know," she said, winking at me, "you really should take her class. There's always room for another Muffin Maestro in this town."

In reply, I just gave her a look. The rich, nutty aroma of espresso filled the air as I grabbed a tall glass and tossed in a handful of ice cubes. "Okay, Holly," I said, grinning. I'm feeling creative today. I'm making you an iced caramel apple latte with extra ice—something that screams fall but still satisfies your year-round addiction to cold coffee. Because apparently, you like to live dangerously."

Holly glanced up from the muffins, her eyebrow arching. "Caramel apple? Is that even a thing?"

"It is now," I said, pouring freshly brewed espresso over the ice. The cubes crackled softly as the heat met the cold. "You're about to experience autumn in a cup. Trust me."

She watched, amused, as I added a pump of caramel syrup and then a shot of apple flavoring. I topped it off with cold milk, drizzled caramel sauce over the ice, and gave it all a swirl with one of her favorite blue-and-white striped straws—because best friends notice things like that. "Ta-da!" I declared, sliding the drink across the counter to her. "Warning: it may cause an uncontrollable urge to buy pumpkins and flannel shirts."

Holly took a sip, her eyes widening as a satisfied hum escaped her lips. "Okay, this is... amazing. Why have I been drinking plain caramel lattes like a sucker?"

"Because you've been living a life of unfulfilled potential, and I just fixed that for you," I teased, grabbing another towel. "You're welcome," I said, smirking as I wiped a stray crumb off the counter. "Next time you're at Eloise's bakery, tell her I've raised the bar on fall flavors."

"Oh, I'll let her know," Holly replied, her grin widening. "But if I start drinking these every morning, I'm holding you responsible for the next fifteen pounds."

I laughed, shaking my head. "Deal. I'll buy us both bigger jeans. You know, just in case."

Holly rolled her eyes, her laughter bubbling up as she arranged the last of the muffins in the display case. "Oh, the drama!"

I smiled and grabbed a tall glass for me. The familiar bubbling hiss of the coffee machine filled the brief pause. "Speaking of drama," I said, tossing her a sidelong glance, "let's be real. If I took that muffin class, the only thing I'd be mastering is how to set off the fire alarm. Muffin Maestro? Ha! More like Muffin Mayhem."

"Well, speaking of mayhem," Holly said, her tone shifting just slightly, "it sounds like the whole town's been in it lately."

I stilled, topping off my latte with a final stir. "Mayhem?" I asked, leaning on the counter as I sipped my drink. "What's going on?"

Holly's gaze drifted toward the front window, her playful expression dimming ever so slightly. "Oh, you know—small-town drama. Nothing you haven't heard before." She shrugged, but the way her fingers fidgeted with the edge of the napkin that was wrapped around her drink told me there was more she wasn't saying.

There was always more to the story with Holly. She had a way about her—warm, approachable, the kind of person people felt comfortable with, whether she was arranging muffins or trimming bangs at Curl Up and Dye. It wasn't just that she listened; she truly cared. And maybe that's why everyone in Hickory Hills told her everything. She wasn't one to gossip, but trust me, she always knew exactly what was happening around town.

"Small-town drama," I repeated, giving her a knowing look. "Let me guess—this is about Artie?"

It had to be about Artie Blackburn. Ever since he'd taken over Teddy's garage, it seemed like Hickory Hills couldn't go a day without mentioning him—and rarely in a good way. My sister, Hattie, and I had already had our own run-in with him, and we weren't the only ones. Artie had a knack for rubbing people the wrong way, like sandpaper on a sunburn.

Holly raised her brow as she sipped her iced latte. The blue-and-white straw swayed slightly when she sat it down on the counter. "You know me too well," she admitted after a beat. "It's just... there's something off about the whole thing. Artie, Teddy, all of it."

Her voice dipped just enough to tug at my curiosity. I leaned forward, resting my elbows on the counter. "Off how?"

She hesitated, glancing at me like she wasn't sure if she should keep going. But we'd known each other too long for her to hold back. "Teddy's not himself, Josie. You've seen it. I know he's getting older, but there's something else going on. You think he really sold the garage to Artie on his own terms?"

My mind flicked back to the last time I'd seen Teddy in the café. He'd been quieter than usual, his hands trembling as he reached for his coffee. When I asked how he was doing, he'd brushed me off with a gruff, "Just getting old."

"I don't know," I said, wiping the counter with a slow, deliberate motion, more to give myself time to think than anything else. "Teddy hasn't been the same since Dex got out of prison. You remember that whole mess, right? Pretty sure everyone in town does."

Holly nodded, her lips pressing into a thin line. "Yeah. That was bad."

Bad was an understatement. Teddy had taken Dex under his wing back in the day and treated him like family, only to have Dex betray him in the worst way. When Dex got caught stealing cars, it wasn't just Teddy's reputation that took a hit—he nearly got Teddy's son dragged into the mess, too. It was the kind of betrayal you didn't just bounce back from.

"You think Artie's another Dex?" I asked softly, more to myself than to her.

Holly didn't answer, but the silence spoke volumes. Everyone wondered the same thing, but no one wanted to say it aloud. Hickory Hills might be small, but secrets had a way of growing into something bigger when left unchecked.

"Well," I said finally, forcing a little cheer into my voice, "whatever's going on, we'll figure it out. This is Hickory Hills—secrets don't stay buried forever, especially not in this town."

Holly smiled, though a flicker of worry lingered in her eyes. "You're probably right. I just hope whatever's going on with Teddy works out. He's been good to everyone for years, and seeing him like this..." She trailed off, then waved it away. "At least we've got these lattes to brighten our day." She raised her glass in a toast.

I chuckled softly, tapping my glass against hers. "As long as I'm not part of the drama, I'm happy to just make coffee and mind my own business."

Holly gave me a knowing smile. "You? Stay out of the drama? Josie, somehow, it always finds you."

"Maybe so," I said with a laugh, but her words hit closer to home than I cared to admit. I glanced out the window at the quiet street outside, the golden morning sun glinting off the shop windows. Hickory Hills looked as peaceful as ever, but appearances, especially here, could be deceiving.

Holly broke the moment, sliding the last muffin into its place in the display case. "I still can't believe Eloise started making these back in New York when she was a detective."

"She says it's a science," I said, sipping my drink. "And frankly, I'm not questioning a retired detective who can bake like that. I heard it was her way of solving cases—baking, I mean. I can just picture her in one of those retro aprons, solving mysteries and making pastries."

"Yep. Whenever she hit a dead end, she'd retreat to her kitchen, whip up something sweet, and bam! Next thing you know, she's solved the case," Holly said, her grin widening. "Said it was the only way to get her brain to stop obsessing over the details."

"Must've been a sight," I said, picturing a younger Eloise, apron over her polyester suit, stirring batter with one hand while jotting down clues with the other. "Imagine criminals being taken down by detective work and a side of blueberry muffins."

Holly chuckled, shaking her head. "Some say Eloise solved her toughest case with nothing but a muffin recipe and a hunch." She shot me a grin. "Criminals probably didn't know whether to run or stay for dessert."

I let my gaze linger on the rows of muffins, each one perfectly golden and topped with just the right amount of crumble. "And now, here we are—her muffins are legendary in a whole new way. Thirty years ago, she left New York to care for her mom in rural Missouri and look at her now. Baking was her calling all along."

Holly took another sip of her latte and then gave a thoughtful nod. "It's like she brought a piece of her past with her—mixing years of detective work into every batch. Maybe that's her secret ingredient."

"Exactly," I said, smiling as I looked at the beautifully arranged display. "Now she's sharing her baking secrets with the rest of us."

Holly turned to me with a playful wink. "So, when are you signing up for her class?"

I laughed and shook my head. "Still not taking the class. I'd rather leave the muffin magic to the professionals."

Mocha had settled contentedly on her dog bed in the corner, keeping a sleepy eye on the growing activity in the café. She was my faithful little shadow, always watching, always ready to comfort.

The book café bustled with warmth and camaraderie as bleary-eyed college students filtered in, preparing for their early shifts. The day was just beginning. Hannah arrived first, setting up the book displays with practiced ease, while Logan restocked the shelves with syrups, sugar, and cocoa powder. Their quiet, efficient movements were a comforting rhythm in the café's daily routine. Before long, the morning rush would begin, and our little slice of small-town paradise would buzz with life again.

I paused by the window, watching the town square come to life. The courthouse sat like a steadfast anchor in the middle, its old brick façade giving Hickory Hills classic Americana charm. As the county seat, we always have our share of traffic—especially on court days. But this time of year, the students from Hickory Hills University kept the cafés and shops buzzing, their hopeful energy swirling through the crisp autumn air like the leaves underfoot.

I noticed the other shops were fully dressed for fall—plump pumpkins and silly scarecrows decorated every entrance, while garlands of orange and gold leaves and hand-tied wreaths hung from every storefront door. The sight sent a little pang of guilt through me. The fall decorations I'd bought weeks ago were still untouched in a box in the backroom. I'd meant to put them up days ago, but every time I thought about climbing that ladder to hang the garlands, a knot of hesitation twisted in my stomach.

I wasn't afraid of heights—well, not exactly, but there was a definite... unease. My mind flashed back to the last time I had to climb up to hang something—a cheerful summer banner. My legs had wobbled the whole time like I was on a tightrope rather than an eight-foot ladder. I had been so close to delegating the task to one of my college workers, but something stubborn inside me had insisted I do it myself. It's not that I had to control everything—okay, maybe a little—but this café was my pride and joy. I wanted to be the one to make it shine.

I glanced over at the ladder leaning against the back wall. Maybe today was the day I'd finally conquer that little fear and hang those garlands. After all, it wasn't like I was scaling a skyscraper—just a quick climb. Easy enough.

The distant chime of the clock tower reminded me it was almost opening time, and the comforting scent of Willa Mae's pies drifted in from down the street. I flipped the "Open" sign, making a mental note to check in with Teddy later. He wasn't running the garage anymore, but he had a right to know what Artie Blackburn had been up to.

I unlocked the door and stepped outside, soaking in the breathtaking display of trees lining the square. Heavy with crimson, orange, gold, and russet leaves, their branches seemed to be holding their breath, waiting for the slightest breeze to set them swirling to the ground. A familiar swell of pride filled my chest as I looked up at the sign attached to the brick building, boldly proclaiming Novel Grounds.

But standing there, taking in the scene, I could feel something was brewing. The winds of change weren't just stirring the leaves; they were gathering strength, swirling through Hickory Hills, and I sensed that life here was about to get a lot more complicated.

The first in line were the familiar faces of Konstanze and Max. As she liked to be called, Stanzi always brought a dash of old-fashioned charm to the café with her stylish vintage flair, sparkling blue eyes, and brightly dyed red hair. Her retro dresses, often paired with statement brooches and scarves, made her stand out. Beside her was Max, tall and thin, with his thoughtful gaze peeking out from behind round, dark-framed glasses. His rare but stunning smile lit up his face, adding to the quiet charm of their quirky companionship. Originally from Germany, their British accents—picked up from years of living in the UK—only made them more endearing. They both taught at the university where Holly's dad, Dr. Graham Emerson, was a professor, and they often popped in before their classes.

"Morning, Stanzi! Morning, Max!" I greeted, grabbing a marker from behind the counter. "The usual for you two?"

Stanzi nodded with a smile. "Yes, and an extra latte, please."

"You got it." I scribbled the order onto the cup. As always, the two looked like they'd stepped out of a time machine from the 1940s, perfectly styled but somehow effortless.

Stanzi turned to Holly, who was arranging muffins in the display case. "I'm seeing Dr. Graham Emerson at our faculty meeting today," she said with a knowing smile, "so I thought I'd bring him a latte."

Holly chuckled. "Make that a *Murder on the Orient Expresso* for Dad. He's into all the fancy drinks now—espresso, chocolate syrup, whipped cream, crème de cacao, and chocolate curls. Anything sweet and chocolatey." She grinned. "Discussing anything juicy today?"

Stanzi and Max exchanged a look. She sighed. "Budget talks, as usual," Stanzi replied, rolling her eyes. "But I'm going to push for more funding for my languages, literature, and archaeology classes."

Holly handed Max his black coffee and a box of muffins. "Smart move bringing treats to the meeting. Good luck!"

Just then, Tyler, one of our college baristas, ambled over with Stanzi's two to-go coffees, a soft smile brightening his face. His man-bun was securely in place, and a to-go cup in each hand. Tyler had a gentle, squishy demeanor that endeared him to everyone—one of the true gems of our café.

"Here you go, Professor Meyer," Tyler said cheerfully, handing over the drinks. "One plain latte and one Orient Expresso."

"Thank you, Tyler. I'll see you in class later," Stanzi said, her voice warm as she took the drinks.

Tyler nodded, a little shy. "Uhm, righto, Professor," he said before returning to his station. Despite his busy college schedule, Tyler always brought his A-game, ensuring every customer left smiling.

"Stanzi, we need to get going, or we'll be late," Max urged gently. Already halfway to the door, he looked back at his wife, who was still busy with her bag.

"Yes, yes, I'm coming!" Stanzi muttered, hurrying to catch up. Just as she reached the door, she paused and grabbed Max's sleeve, her eyes lighting up with excitement. "Oh, I almost forgot! You're all still coming to game night at our place tonight, right?" she called out over the hum of the café chatter.

Holly's face lit up immediately. "Wouldn't miss it! Especially after last month's twist ending," she grinned.

Every month, my friends and I chip in for a subscription to a mystery puzzle box game—part escape room, part detective work. We gather at Stanzi and Max's old Victorian house, tea and snacks at the ready, poring over cryptic clues, encoded messages, and mind-bending riddles. It quickly became one of my favorite traditions. "Isn't tonight the new mystery box?" I asked, already feeling the familiar spark of excitement build. I'd been looking forward to it all week.

Stanzi nodded eagerly. "Yep, it arrived yesterday. Max wanted to open it early, but I made him wait." She shot him a playful look.

"I would've just peeked," Max said with a mischievous smirk.

"Sure you would've," Stanzi teased, rolling her eyes, tugging at his sleeve.

"Good thing you didn't," Holly said with a laugh. "I live for that moment when we all see the clues for the first time. You know, before Max solves half of it within ten minutes."

He chuckled, clearly used to the ribbing. "Tonight's box is rated extra challenging—lots of puzzles and some out-of-the-box thinking required. My favorite."

Smiling, I added, "Perfect. I'm already picturing a sleepless night of decoding cryptic ciphers and piecing together evidence. Nothing says 'relaxing' like solving a fake kidnapping."

"I hope this one's as tricky as the last," Holly said, rubbing her hands together. "That encoded message last month took us hours!"

"Only because someone," Stanzi chimed in, grinning, "refused to believe the perpetrator had an alibi."

Holly threw her hands up. "Hey, how was I supposed to know the clue was hidden in the 'innocent' witness's letter?" she laughed.

"We'll be there," Holly confirmed, her eyes sparkling with anticipation. "No way I'm missing it."

"Neither am I," I added, "Something is soothing about unwinding with puzzles... even if Max does make it impossible to win."

Stanzi laughed as she slung her bag over her shoulder. "Well, that's why we keep him around—for his genius, not his charm."

I chuckled with her, my gaze drifting back toward the counter as I went over to wipe down one of the tables. The chatter of the café buzzed around me, but a low murmur from a nearby table caught my attention.

Two regulars were deep in conversation by the window. Their voices were hushed, but their tones were sharp enough to catch my ear.

"Did you hear about Gayle's car? Stalled on the highway two days after she had it 'fixed' at Teddy's old place," one of them said, shaking her head.

"Same old Artie," the other replied with a bitter edge to her voice. "He's running that garage into the ground. People say he's been cutting corners since Teddy sold it."

"Sold it? Is that what they're calling it?" the first woman muttered, her voice dropping even lower.

I strained to hear more, but the two women stood up, their conversation fading as they headed for the door. The morning breeze carried their words away, leaving me standing there, still wiping the same spot on the table, lost in thought.

What had really happened at that garage? Why did it feel like no one was willing to talk about it openly? Maybe it was just my overactive imagination. But then again... maybe it wasn't.

2 spilled beans

IT WAS MID-MORNING—usually my favorite part of the day. The early rush had come and gone, leaving the place peaceful as university students shuffled off to their first classes. This quiet was my reset button, a time to catch my breath and clear my head before the lunchtime crowd poured in. But today, tension clung to me like static. No amount of deep breathing or wiping down tables helped. I gave the counter a half-hearted wipe and forced myself to focus.

The back door swung open with a familiar whoosh. In breezed my sister, Hattie—a whirlwind of energy. It was hard not to smile when she was around. "Yoo-hoo, where is everyone?" Hattie called. Her voice was filled with its usual brightness.

"We're upfront, Hattie!" Holly called from behind the counter, grinning at the sight of my sister.

Hattie, my only sibling and ten years my senior, always knew how to make an entrance. Her creative spirit practically shimmered from her bright blue eyes, framed perfectly by her spiky white pixie cut. Today, she was dressed in one of her signature colorful bohemian outfits. It was impossible not to notice her.

Outside, her vibrant camper van, Captain Vantastic, sat parked in its usual spot, drawing the eyes of every passerby. Painted with bold swirls of color and whimsical designs, it was like a traveling art project—cheerful and impossible to miss. I chuckled, recalling the little adventure we'd had two weeks ago.

"Hard to believe we were chasing down a flying tire in the town square not too long ago," I said.

Hattie snorted, shaking her head as we both laughed at the memory. "Right? That was quite the scene—Mocha barking, me sprinting after those runaway lug nuts like it was a relay race. What a day!"

That incident had ended with us taking Captain Vantastic to a more reputable mechanic after a disastrous stop at Artie's garage. Since then, Hattie had flown off to visit her son, Zeke, at the University of Alabama. Now, with her van finally fixed, and back in town, she waltzed into the café like she owned the place—which, in a way, she kind of did.

Hattie grabbed one of the blue-and-white porcelain cups from the counter and poured herself a coffee with her usual dramatic flair, pinky raised like she was trying out for a tea commercial. "And voilà! The artist fuels her brilliance," she declared, striking a pose.

I smirked as I handed her the cream. "Careful, Hattie, your caffeine addiction is showing."

"Caffeine addiction," Holly chimed in from behind the muffin display, "is a perfectly acceptable coping mechanism in this town. Especially after the last couple of weeks that Hattie's had."

Hattie tilted her head toward Holly with mock seriousness. "You're not wrong." But as she stirred her coffee, her usual sparkle dimmed for just a second. It wasn't obvious, but I caught the tiny flicker of hesitation. Hattie was hiding something.

"Zeke was so disappointed he didn't get to see you," she said finally, her voice breezing past the moment.

"Trust me, I missed him too," I replied, leaning on the counter. "Did he get the books I sent?"

Hattie waved me off with a dramatic flick of her wrist. "Oh, he got them. But between football practice, classes, and dodging starstruck sorority girls, he hasn't exactly cracked them open yet."

Holly laughed softly, balancing a fresh tray of muffins as she joined in. "Zeke? The star linebacker who's probably too busy signing autographs to read? Color me shocked."

"Right?" Hattie said with a theatrical eye roll. "He said something about squeezing in the reading on the team bus. Honestly, the kid can't sit still unless it's to binge-watch Ted Lasso."

I snorted. "Well, those books are supplemental reading for his classes, not inspiration for halftime speeches. So as long as he glances at them before his next essay, I'll call it a win."

Hattie grinned at that, but her stirring slowed, her eyes dipping to her cup. "Before I left, I had a... chat with Artie. About that flying tire incident."

I raised my eyebrows and made a face at her. "Oh boy. Here we go."

Her lips pressed into a dramatic line that practically screamed, prepare for drama. "He had the nerve to blame me for *his* mistakes. Me!"

"What?" I asked, the word coming out louder than I'd intended.

"Oh yeah." Hattie's tone dropped to a simmer, her spoon clinking against her cup as her stirring grew more aggressive. "Apparently, I overloaded the van and should've checked the tire pressure before I left the shop. Can you believe that? Like it's my fault the lug nuts came loose."

Holly gasped, putting a hand on her hip, her voice dripping with mock indignation. "Let me get this straight—he messes up and then blames you? Is this his way of advertising 'Tires Gone Wild'? Feel the adrenaline rush as your tire takes an unexpected solo adventure! Bonus: enjoy the low, low price of fixing your car's alignment and all the other damage done to your vehicle when it slams into the pavement!"

I laughed, even as my protective instincts kicked in. "Tire pressure? That's the excuse? Tire pressure has nothing to do with lug nuts coming loose. If Artie had done his job, Hank Junior wouldn't have had to chase a runaway tire through the square like some slapstick comedy routine."

"Exactly!" Hattie said, throwing her hands in the air. "I told him as much. I may or may not have also reminded him that one more mistake like that, and he might need to start applying to carnivals as a one-man clown act."

I raised a skeptical brow. "Oh no. What exactly did you say?"

Hattie took a slow, deliberate sip of her coffee, clearly milking the suspense for all it was worth. "Don't worry. I kept it professional... mostly."

She had that familiar glint in her eye, the one that always meant she was dying to drop a bombshell when the timing was just right. Whatever it was, I had a sinking feeling it was going to be big.

"Artie called me this morning," she finally said, her voice deliberately casual. "Said he wanted to 'discuss things'—after hours."

My coffee cup froze mid-air. "After hours? That's... strange."

"Strange?" Holly cut in, leaning over the counter. "Try slimy. What does he even mean by 'discuss things'? That sounds like code for something shady."

"I don't like this, Hattie," I said, setting my mug down with a clink. "The way things have been over there... it's not the garage Teddy built. Not even close."

"No kidding," Holly muttered, lowering her voice as she reached for a muffin tray. "Hank Granger, Senior, was going to sue after his truck broke down right after Artie 'repaired' it. But then he dropped the whole thing. Said it was a 'misunderstanding.' Since when does Hank Senior just let things go?"

"Or Gayle Murphy," I added, leaning closer. "Her car stalled on the highway two days after Artie supposedly 'fixed' it. That garage is a mess, Hattie. And Artie's at the center of it."

"It's not just the cars," Holly said, her voice dipping conspiratorially. "Mrs. Milgram told me she saw him arguing with someone outside the garage late one night. And the next day? That guy? Gone. Left town without a word."

The coffee in my stomach churned. I turned to Hattie. "You're not actually going to meet him, are you?"

Hattie was tough, but even she had her limits. I could tell by the way her fingers drummed nervously against her cup that this was one of those moments.

"I told him no," she said, but her voice wavered just slightly. "But you know me—I don't back down easily."

"Hattie, don't go," I said firmly. "I mean it. Artie's bad news, and whatever he's planning, it's not worth it."

She gave me a small, lopsided smile—the kind that was supposed to reassure me but only made me more worried. "I wasn't planning on it, Josie."

"I'm serious, Hattie. This guy isn't just some slimy mechanic. He's dangerous."

She hesitated momentarily, swirling the last bit of coffee in her cup like it held the answers. "You might be right," she said, voice softer than usual. "But I can't just sit here and let him get away with it either."

"That's not what I'm asking," I said, lowering my voice and leaning closer, trying to reach that logical side of her—the side that sometimes got buried under all that artistic, act-first-think-later impulse. "Just be smart about this. Please."

She gave me a small nod, but doubt still flickered in her eyes. Without another word, she drifted over to her favorite spot by the window, coffee in one hand and her sketchbook in the other.

Hattie settled into the chair, her pencil hovering above the blank page like it might bite her. She wasn't scared—Hattie didn't do scared. But shaken? Definitely.

I watched her for a moment, raising an eyebrow. "You know, staring it down won't make the words magically appear," I teased, folding my arms.

She didn't respond. She just kept staring at the page. Classic Hattie. With a shrug, I headed toward the book section, letting the hum of the café and the scent of coffee settle my nerves. She'd work it out—she always did.

Of course, that's when my brain decided to wander to the one story I didn't want to get lost in—Dex. Or Derek Foster, as his mother probably still called him when he forgot her birthday.

It's been over twenty years, but Hickory Hills still treated Dex like he had a "Wanted" poster stapled to the bulletin board at Town Hall. It didn't matter that he'd served his time. Mrs. Huxley still crossed the street when she saw him, and Hank Senior grumbled like a storm cloud whenever Dex stepped into the hardware store. Everyone seemed to be waiting for him to screw up again, like the man was a ticking time bomb.

And then there was Teddy. He wasn't the same after Dex went to prison, but how could he be? People whispered that there was more to the story than we ever knew, that maybe even Teddy had some skeletons rattling around in that old garage of his. I wasn't sure how much of that was truth and how much was just small-town gossip growing legs.

Now, with Artie running Teddy's garage, it felt like Dex's shadow was stretching longer than ever. And those cracks in the town—cracks everyone liked to pretend didn't exist—were starting to show again.

I shook my head, pushing the thought aside. One mystery at a time. My top priority was keeping Hattie from jumping headfirst into whatever mess was brewing.

A burst of cold air yanked me from my thoughts as the door swung open, bringing with it the familiar clunk of Rhett's boots on the hardwood floor. He strolled in with Emma, greeted by the usual chorus of cheerful hellos from the regulars. The scent of sawdust and fresh-cut pine clung to his red-and-black checkered jacket, like he'd just stepped out of a lumberjack ad.

"Mornin', y'all," Rhett said, his country drawl thicker than normal. "I'll take my usual coffee, please. And, uh, toss in one of them chocolate peanut butter muffins while you're at it."

I handed him his to-go cup and muffin, grinning as he took them. "Thanks a bunch, Josie. You want me to bring that shelf by tomorrow?" he asked, pausing at the door. "Should fit that space near the front window."

"That'd be great, Rhett," I said, grateful for his handiwork. "You'll be at game night tonight, right?"

"Oh, we'll be there," Rhett said, tugging at his jacket. "Headin' to the woodshop now. See y'all later!"

Emma chimed in as he reached for the door, a mischievous grin spreading across her face. "We're ready to win—Rhett's been practicing."

Rhett chuckled, tipping his head toward a group of regulars as the door swung shut behind them. "Don't believe her. I'm just there for the muffins."

"Sure you are," I muttered, watching him go.

Emma unwound her bright blue tartan scarf, leaving the collar of her tweed riding jacket popped up, her whole preppy-equestrian vibe so perfectly curated she could've cantered straight out of a Ralph Lauren catalog. She leaned in with a twinkle in her eye, dropping her voice like she was about to spill a juicy secret. "You know, Rhett acts all humble, but I caught him looking up mystery box game tips online. He's been strategizing for game night."

I stopped mid-laugh. "Rhett? Strategizing? For game night?"

"Oh, yeah," Emma said, grinning wider. "He's got that whole 'aw, shucks' routine down to an art form, but don't let him fool you—he's got a competitive streak a mile wide."

I shook my head, already picturing it. "I bet he's got a notebook tucked away in his tool shed. 'Operation: Outsmart the Girls' scrawled across the top in all caps."

Emma's laughter bubbled out as she leaned closer, like we were swapping state secrets. "Wouldn't put it past him. Rhett's basically a golden retriever in human form, but the second you bring out a puzzle? Boom. Sherlock Holmes with a redneck drawl."

I snorted, nearly choking on my coffee. "Redneck Sherlock Holmes? Now that needs to go on a T-shirt."

Emma grinned. "He'd probably wear it, too."

I shook my head, still laughing. "Someone's gotta keep things interesting, I guess. It wouldn't be game night without Rhett overanalyzing the clues like it's a matter of national security."

She arched an eyebrow at me, smirking. "Please, Josie. You're the real puzzle master. Last time, you cracked that cipher before Rhett could even open the instruction booklet."

I shrugged, letting a smug smile creep onto my face. "Years of reading mystery novels, what can I say? And maybe a little small-town charm. You know, the kind where I sip my coffee innocently while secretly solving everyone's problems between sips."

Emma laughed, "If you ever go pro, just promise you won't use your powers to crush us all at game night."

These game nights at Stanzi and Max's old Victorian house had become my lifeline. A little bubble of comfort and connection that felt immune to whatever chaos might be brewing in Hickory Hills.

Their home was more than just a setting—it was a character in its own right. Cozy and inviting, with well-loved bookshelves stuffed full of classic novels with worn spines leaning against one another like old friends. Vintage curios dotted every surface, each with a story Max would gladly tell if you asked. The air always smelled faintly of tea and freshly baked Victoria sponge cake, a Stanzi specialty. And the warm glow of antique lamps cast everything in a soft, golden light.

It was like stepping into the pages of an Agatha Christie novel—or maybe a snug corner of a British countryside manor—complete with mismatched armchairs draped in floral cushions and a fireplace that crackled merrily, even if the weather outside didn't call for it.

And then there were the puzzles. The challenge of a new mystery box always sets my brain buzzing. Tonight's game promised a kidnapping case full of ciphers and clues that would keep us wracking our brains for hours. I couldn't wait. There was something so satisfying about gathering with the gang, teasing Rhett about his not-so-secret strategy notebook, and piecing together answers one clue at a time.

Stanzi and Max's game nights weren't just fun—they were grounding. The laughter, camaraderie, and lighthearted competition all reminded me why I loved this little group of ours so much.

Emma leaned on the counter, her smile bright. "So, how's the planning for Novel Grounds' big autumn murder mystery party coming along?"

I returned her smile, though her question stirred a tiny knot of anxiety in my chest. The party was shaping up to be our biggest event yet, and while I was excited, there was always that nagging voice in the back of my mind whispering about what could go wrong. Still, with friends like Rhett and Emma pitching in, I knew it'd be a night to remember—one way or another.

"Oh, it's coming together. I'm nearly finished with the script. Connie's been helping me fine-tune it."

Emma's eyebrows lifted knowingly. "Ah, Connie. The legend herself."

Connie was Hickory Hills University's beloved retired theater professor. Even in retirement, she remained a cornerstone of the university and the community, always willing to lend her creative expertise.

Grinning, I said, "She's practically written the handbook on dramatic flair."

Emma laughed softly, but then her tone shifted, becoming just a touch more curious. "By the way," she said, leaning in slightly, "I've heard some strange things around town lately. Any chance that will make its way into this year's script?"

I tilted my head. "Strange things? Like what?"

She shrugged, tugging her scarf a little tighter. "Oh, just... you know how it is around here. Gossip races faster than Hank Granger's souped-up tractor at the Fourth of July parade. But I'm sure it's nothing compared to the drama you're cooking up for tonight's puzzle box."

I slid her drink across the counter—her usual: The Cheeky Donkey, a rich mocha latte with a nutty surprise inspired by Sancho Panza's loyal and dependable donkey, Dapple. Steam curled above the almond milk and espresso, the dark chocolate and hazelnut aromas blending into cozy perfection. Emma took it with a smile as I swiped her debit card.

"Well," I said, handing the card back with a grin, "I think I'll leave the town gossip out of the script—don't need to accidentally start a riot at the party. But Eloise is baking her triple chocolate brownie muffins and pumpkin chocolate chip muffins."

Emma's eyes lit up as she took a sip of her macchiato. "Food that good might make everyone forget about solving the mystery entirely. Honestly, I'm just here for the food at this point."

I laughed. "Fair. But I'm not covering for you if you sneak two muffins while Rhett's distracted by a cipher."

"Deal," Emma said, holding up her cup in mock toast. "Now, do you need help with decorations or anything?"

I sighed. "Actually, I still need to hang the fall garlands outside. I keep telling myself I'll get to it, but somehow the day keeps getting away from me." I glanced out the window, seeing yet again that the rest of the square was decked out with autumn wreaths and orange lights. My shop was lagging behind, and it showed.

Emma gave me a sly look. "You know, you could always ask Logan or Rhett to do it for you. Rhett could probably hang them up without even using a ladder."

I snorted. "Oh, I know. But I feel like I should just handle it myself."

Emma tilted her head, intrigued. "Any particular reason?"

I hesitated, fiddling with the edge of my apron. "I guess... I just want it to look right. And maybe because I need to prove to myself that I can do it. You know, just me, the garlands, and a trusty ladder."

Her eyes narrowed playfully. "You, a ladder, and autumn decorations? Sounds like the beginning of a Hallmark romance movie. Maybe that new handsome deputy will rush in and sweep you off your feet?"

I rolled my eyes, laughing. "More like he'll have to peel me off the pavement if I fall. Heights and I aren't exactly on speaking terms."

Emma smirked, but there was kindness behind it. "Well, if you change your mind and decide the garlands can survive Rhett's 'artistic touch,' let me know. Otherwise, just be careful. We can't have the reigning riddle queen taking a tumble before game night."

"Don't worry," I said, waving her off. "I'll be fine. It's not like I'm scaling a skyscraper. Just a few steps up a ladder. What could possibly go wrong?"

Emma raised her cup in a mock toast, her tone teasing. "Famous last words, Josie. Famous last words."

I rolled my eyes, laughing with her, but before I could come up with a witty retort, Willa Mae caught my eye and waved as she darted over, mug in hand, her rich dark brown eyes twinkling with excitement. Her warm brown skin glowed under the café lights, and her ever-present energy seemed to light up the space even more.

"I'll be providing my famous chocolate pecan pie," she announced, sipping her coffee. "Josie, I'm so excited for this year's mystery! I'm coming as Miss Marple. I've got the fluffiest cozy knit cardigan, a perfect floral dress, the ugliest sensible shoes, and the cutest classic hat."

"That's going to be fantastic, Willa Mae!" I said, grinning. "I'm so glad you're on board."

We watched as Holly danced over to the counter, swaying to Ella Fitzgerald playing overhead. "Hey, Emma! Hey, Willa Mae! Come sit with Hattie and me."

Both women waved at her at once, and Willa Mae added, "I'm telling y'all, this year's *Death by Chocolate: The Pumpkin Plot* is going to be even better than last year!" Looking over at Holly, she said, "I've got my Miss Marple costume all ready." She linked arms with me as we all meandered over to the cozy corner where Hattie was sitting.

Holly mimed adjusting an invisible bowtie as we walked. "I can't wait to see everyone's costumes. I'm thinking of going as The Doctor." She shot me a sly look. "What about you, Josie?"

Instead of answering, I started humming the *Doctor Who* theme. Holly and Hattie joined in without missing a beat, and we made a very off-key trio. You'd think we'd get some strange looks from the other customers, but they were used to us by now—our impromptu outbursts had become part of the Novel Grounds charm.

Emma, however, shook her head at us quizzically. "I'll never understand how people get so wrapped up in a show," she said, though her tone wasn't unkind.

We all burst into laughter, and I finally replied, "To answer your question, Holly, I think I'll go as Nancy Drew. I've got a vintage plaid skirt that's perfect for it."

Emma took a sip from her mug, her eyes twinkling. "That's so fitting for you, Josie. I can't wait to see what role you've got up your sleeve," she teased, nudging me with her elbow. "Knowing you, you'll be the clever detective solving everything."

I smiled. Clever detective. If only it were that easy. Sure, I could string together clues and red herrings for a party, but in real life? The pieces didn't fit so neatly. There was no script, no carefully plotted twists—just... people. People with secrets, fears, and messy motives. Right now, I felt less like Nancy Drew and more like someone flipping through a book with too many missing pages.

"Okay, not to change the subject, but...changing the subject," Emma said, snapping me back to the moment. She settled into a seat next to Hattie, setting her mug on the side table. "I hope this year's party has just as many surprises!" She flashed a mischievous grin.

Mocha, who had been napping at Hattie's feet, perked up at the sound of Emma's voice. She stretched lazily before resting her head in Emma's lap. Emma grinned and playfully booped her on the nose. "Well, hello there, Mocha!"

"I'm sure it will," I replied, my gaze drifting around the café as I mentally ran through my never-ending to-do list. "I just hope it lives up to everyone's expectations."

The mention of last year's party brought a wave of nostalgia. It had been a huge hit—especially with our book drive and literacy programs—and I couldn't help but feel a twinge of doubt creep in. Could I outdo myself this year? This time, we were raising funds and collecting toys and non-perishable food donations for the holiday gift and food drive, and I wanted everything to go off without a hitch.

Holly, ever the bubbly one, jumped in with her usual enthusiasm. "Josie, you know everyone's going to love it! And those pumpkin mochas? Pure genius. People will be talking about them for months!"

"Thanks, Holly," I said, glancing around at my friends and the small crowd that had gathered. Her encouragement was like a shot of espresso to my confidence.

Hattie raised an eyebrow, her lips curving into a smirk. "I wouldn't worry about it. Josie's never been one to disappoint in the surprises department. Remember last year's plot twist? Who saw that coming?"

Emma laughed, shaking her head. "Definitely not me! I'm still not over the fact that Willa Mae was the mastermind all along. I was convinced it was going to be Rhett."

Sam, the new guy in town, leaned forward with his usual easy smile. His longish blonde hair, styled just right, and that cowboy charm had already made him the darling of Hickory Hills. "Well, I can't resist a good mystery," he said, flashing a playful wink. "Especially when there's chocolate involved. Count me in, Josie—I'll be there with bells on."

He leaned back, his fingers tapping on the arm of the chair. "Besides, I could use a break from all the dust at the old place. This renovation project is no joke."

Holly chimed in with a grin, "You're really tackling that old antebellum mansion on the edge of town, huh? That place has been empty for years."

Sam shrugged, his smile still easy. "Yep. Thought it'd be fun to breathe some life back into it. Something about that house just felt... right, you know?" He threw in another wink. "Maybe I'll host the next mystery night when it's done."

"That house?" Willa Mae said, her eyes narrowing just slightly as she sipped her coffee. "I heard it's full of creaky floors and things that go bump in the night. You might end up with more mysteries than you bargained for."

Sam chuckled. "Well, I'm all about the mysteries. Keeps things interesting."

Willa Mae grinned, shifting her attention back to me. "Back to last year's party, Hattie's right, that twist was amazing!"

Roy, the owner of McCoy's General Store, paused mid-stride, clearly intrigued by the conversation. He had a bag of muffins in one hand and a knowing grin on his face. "Oh, I couldn't help but overhear, Willa Mae. That twist with the art and jewel thief? Brilliant, Josie!" He took a bite of an apple muffin and gestured with his bag, which looked suspiciously full of Eloise's baked goods. "I'm telling you, Josie, that was some clever stuff."

"That was so cool!" Holly agreed, beaming. "It added such a unique twist to the mystery."

Sam leaned back, folding his arms across his chest, his smile never wavering. "Where do you get these ideas, Josie?" he asked, his tone light.

We were all huddled together in Hattie's favorite nook near the big, picturesque window—Holly, Hattie, Emma, Willa Mae, Roy, and Sam. Holly perched on the edge of the seat next to me. Her animated chatter about the murder mystery party filled the small space. The soft afternoon light from the window highlighted the comfortable mess of notebooks, coffee cups, and scattered papers, making it feel like our own little corner of the world.

As I explained the inspiration for this year's plot, I noticed Sam wasn't really paying attention. Sure, he laughed at the right moments and nodded in all the right places, but his focus wasn't on me—it was on Holly. His gaze followed her movements with an intensity that made my stomach churn. When she leaned forward to adjust the apron strings around her waist, his eyes lingered—not in a leering way, but like he was filing something away. When Holly glanced his way, his expression instantly shifted into that easy-going smile, but I could've sworn his eyes had narrowed for a split second.

"You've got quite the imagination," Sam said, finally turning back to me. His tone was still friendly, but there was an edge to it.

I forced a smile. "Guess that's what happens when you grow up devouring mystery novels."

Sam drummed his fingers on the arm of his chair, "Real life ever creep in, though? Do you borrow from what's happening around here... or just use Eloise's old cases?"

"A little real life sneaks in now and then, but last year's was actually inspired by one of Eloise's old cases. Something about a ghost thief swiping a priceless artifact from a museum."

Sam leaned in, "Ghost thief? Now that's intriguing."

Meanwhile, Holly was oblivious to Sam's strange behavior. She was busy chatting with Willa Mae and Roy about costumes for the party.

I steered the conversation back to the party. "I'm juggling a little bit of everything—decorations, catering, drinks. Some college theater kids and volunteers are helping out. We're raising funds for the holiday gift and food drive, so I want it to be perfect."

"That's incredible," Sam said, leaning forward enthusiastically. "It sounds like you've got everything under control."

And, of course, Holly chose that moment to tune in. "Great! We're still looking for more volunteers if you're interested," she exclaimed, practically bouncing.

My instinct said no, but my practical side said I needed all the help I could get. I hesitated for a split second, but Sam didn't.

"Absolutely," he said, nodding eagerly. "Happy to help however I can."

I plastered on a smile, my mind racing. Why did I feel uneasy? Sam had been nothing but charming since he got to town—helpful, friendly, that cowboy-next-door vibe everyone loved. Maybe I was overthinking it. Stress and all the weirdness swirling around Artie could make anyone paranoid. Right?

Still, something about him didn't sit right.

I made a mental note to ask Eloise about him later—she always had a way of picking up on things I didn't. For now, though, I had to stay focused on the party. The community was counting on it, and with my friends behind me, I was determined to make it unforgettable.

But my thoughts drifted even as Holly and Sam dove into a conversation about decorations. Artie, Hattie, Sam... it was probably nothing. Just small-town gossip and a little too much caffeine.

Probably.

3 brewed awakening

THE BELLS JINGLED SOFTLY above the door as I tried to focus on something more productive, like the party-planning to-do list, but when Caleb walked in, everything else vanished. Decorations? Charity drive? Nope. Just scruffy jawlines and piercing blue-green eyes. Somehow, that familiar jingle of the bells seemed so much louder. And the air shifted the second he stepped inside.

He was the newest addition to our town's police force—and, okay, the not-so-secret focus of my current crush. I tried to remind myself that I had more important things to do, like planning this party. But as soon as he crossed the threshold, that familiar rush of nerves hit me just like every other time. He'd been stopping by every day for weeks.

I straightened, pretending I hadn't noticed him the second he walked in. Something about Caleb—this effortless mix of rugged and refined—always caught my attention. His eyes briefly met mine, and my stomach did a small somersault. Classic. I smoothed down my apron to busy my hands. At almost forty, Caleb had this quiet confidence that made people pay attention without him ever needing to say much. It was both calming and, at the same time, slightly unnerving.

My gaze flicked up to his stubbled jaw, a little scruffier than usual, like maybe he'd been too busy to shave. The lines of his face looked a little sharper, more tired, but he carried himself with the same steady assurance. I wondered if something was on his mind—maybe a difficult case. He always seemed to carry a weight that no one else could see. And for a moment, I found myself lost in those rugged lines of his face that made him look more effortlessly handsome—if that was even possible. My fingers itched with the sudden, absurd urge to reach up and trace the rough stubble, to feel the texture against my fingertips.

I quickly dropped my gaze but bumped into one of the baristas in my flustered retreat. The tray of coffee and muffins flew out of his hands and hit the floor with a loud crash. Perfect.

The café filled with the sharp sound of shattering porcelain.

"Great," I muttered, kneeling to clean up the mess while my mind played back the ridiculous urge I'd just had. What was I thinking? I've barely said two words to Caleb, and here I was fantasizing about tracing his jawline like some lovesick teenager. At least he hadn't noticed... I hoped.

As I wiped up the coffee, a shadow loomed over me. Holly crouched down, her voice brimming with mischief. "There he is, Josie," she whispered conspiratorially.

Of course, Holly would pick this moment.

I glanced over, and sure enough, Caleb was ordering at the counter. My heart did its usual unhelpful flip, but I focused on wiping the floor instead of sneaking another look.

"Don't think I didn't notice how you practically dive-bombed to the floor when you saw him," Holly teased, nudging me. "Josie, you can't keep letting him walk in here without saying more than two words. You're thirty-six, not sixteen!"

"I do talk to him," I said, shooting her a look. "I say 'hi,' he says 'hi,' we talk about the weather. You know, normal adult conversation."

Holly rolled her eyes. "Sure. Riveting stuff. He's been coming in every day for weeks, Josie. Either he's really into black coffee, or—"

I cut her off as I stood, tossing the soaked napkins into the trash. "Don't start."

Holly just grinned and nodded toward Caleb, who was just taking his coffee—black, no frills, no fuss from Tyler. "I'm just saying, you see him at church every Sunday, you see him here, and still... nothing. Come on, Josie. Make a move before someone else does."

Cue Claire, striding in with her usual confidence and perfectly practiced smile. "Well, well, well," she drawled, her honeyed tone sounding both sweet and cutting. "Looks like someone's trying to impress the new deputy with her barista skills. Got a special brew just for Caleb, Josie?"

My stomach twisted as Holly stiffened beside me.

"Some of us don't need to play games to get attention, Claire," Holly said sharply, but Claire ignored her, zeroing in on me.

"I'm just teasing," Claire said, flipping her blonde hair over her shoulder with practiced ease. Her gaze flicked to Caleb at the counter, then back to me. "I did hear he's single, though. Better make your move before the competition heats up."

Before I could find my voice, Claire turned her full attention to Caleb. "So, Caleb," she said with a smile so polished it could've blinded someone, "are you coming to Josie's big murder mystery party? It's supposed to be the event of the season."

I felt my cheeks heat, but Caleb, ever composed, sipped his coffee and nodded. "I'll be there. Sounds... interesting."

His answer was casual, but my face burned anyway. Claire, of course, wasn't finished.

"Trying to impress the new guy, Josie? Hope the party goes better than your love life," she tossed over her shoulder as she grabbed her latte and sashayed toward the door.

Seriously, Claire?

Holly leaned in, giving my arm a comforting pat. "Don't let her get to you," she said, her voice low.

"I'm trying," I muttered.

Caleb was now headed for the door.

But Holly wasn't done. "Hey, Caleb!" she called, her tone deliberately bright. "You should volunteer for the party. We could use someone with real detective skills!"

Caleb's gaze shifted to Holly, then to me. Something in his expression softened. "I'd be happy to help," he said quietly. The sincerity in his voice caught me off guard. "Just let me know what you need."

A small, warm, and sincere smile reached his eyes, but there was still a trace of something else there—a quiet weariness like he was carrying more than anyone realized.

"Thanks," I said, keeping my tone casual even though my heart was doing acrobatics. "We can always use more hands."

Claire, sensing she'd lost this round, shot me a final smirk before disappearing out the door. I let out a breath I hadn't realized I'd been holding.

Caleb gave a small nod. "See you around," he said before heading out.

As soon as the door closed behind him, Holly spun toward me, grinning like she'd just cracked the case of the century. "See? He's totally into you, Josie. Did you catch the way he looked at you?"

I rolled my eyes, though I did a tiny flicker of hope. "Maybe. Or maybe he's just being polite."

"Polite, my foot," Holly shot back, folding her arms. "That man has been coming in here every day for weeks, and today, he just happens to swoop in and defend you from Claire's nonsense? Please. The man's interested."

I bit my lip, Holly's words spinning in my head. Maybe she was right. But then again, Caleb had this way of staying just... out of reach. Guarded, like someone who didn't let people get too close. And that only made him more intriguing.

Holly finished loading muffins into the display case, her movements brisk but practiced. She wiped her hands on a towel and slung her bag over her shoulder. "All right, I'm off. Gotta help Nikki at the salon for a bit. Don't forget to work on those decorations!"

"Tell Nikki I said hi," I replied with a quick smile.

"Will do!" Holly flashed a grin, her eyes dancing with her usual spark. She paused by the door, throwing a wave over her shoulder. "Bye, bestie!"

"Bye, Holly!" I called after her, the soft chime of the doorbell trailing behind her as she disappeared into the afternoon.

The door clicked shut behind her, and the café instantly felt quieter, like someone had dimmed the lights just a bit. Holly had that effect—leaving a space buzzing with her warmth and energy long after she was gone. I glanced at the display case she'd just finished stocking, rows of perfectly arranged muffins.

I smiled to myself, shaking my head. That was Holly—always in motion, always bright, like a firefly in constant flight.

I watched her bounce down the sidewalk, curls bobbing with each step. She was off to Curl Up and Dye, where Nikki managed things like a pro, even though she was only eighteen—managing a salon and taking college classes part-time? That girl had drive.

It always amazed me how Holly and Anders had built this life together—marrying right out of high school, having Nikki at nineteen, and still managing to keep their family thriving. They'd been high school sweethearts, but not the kind you'd expect. No football player and cheerleader here—Holly and Anders had bonded over their mutual love of books, British television, and everything nerdy.

Back in high school, while everyone else was at the big games, Holly and Anders were probably tucked away in the library, swapping novels or discussing the latest sci-fi show. They had their own little world, built on inside jokes, Doctor Who marathons, and a shared obsession with solving puzzles. They'd even formed a book club for 'geeks only' at Hickory Hills High—just the two of them and a few others who preferred stories to sports. That's how their love had grown, slow and steady, like the turning pages of their favorite books.

With his quiet intellect, Anders was always more comfortable around technology and books than people. He was the kind of guy who could hack together a computer system from scratch and troubleshoot it in minutes—a real tech whiz. Holly used to joke that the only way to pull him away from his screen was by dangling a mystery novel in front of him. He'd always been that way, ever since they were kids.

Now, Anders was the go-to guy for fixing any tech issues in Hickory Hills. Computers, security systems, you name it—if it had a circuit board, Anders could fix it. Even Eloise had once called him up to help install a security system for her home bakery, and of course, he'd rigged it up with all sorts of high-tech bells and whistles that only he understood.

But despite his genius with computers, Anders had always had that gentle, bookish side too. He and Holly were a perfect match—both loved getting lost in other worlds, whether through books or the endless rabbit holes of obscure documentaries. They'd passed that love of learning on to Nikki, too. Now, she was juggling her career and school like a seasoned pro.

I admired Holly and Anders. They'd figured out how to make their quirky, book-filled life work, even with the curveballs that came their way. Sure, they were busy, but the kind of busy that came from living a life full of love, laughter, and a healthy dose of nerdy obsessions.

Holly helps at Eloise's bakery in the mornings. Eloise refuses to use the kitchen at the back of Novel Grounds, and so after lending a hand at the home bakery, Holly delivers the muffins to the café in the wee hours. Then, she helps me for the rest of the morning before rushing off to spend her afternoons at the salon with Nikki. Anders, meanwhile, is always tinkering away with his latest tech project, usually holed up in his office, probably knee-deep in code or building some elaborate security system for a client. Each doing their own thing, but they always come together at the end of the day, just like they did back in high school.

As Holly disappeared from view, a small pang of longing stirred inside me. She had this wonderfully messy, beautifully nerdy life—a family that loved her, work that made her feel useful, and a daughter who was already making her mark on the world. And here I was, standing in my cozy café, feeling... well, a little bit envious.

But I had my own life, my own path. Holly, in her infinite wisdom, would be the first to remind me that everyone's story unfolds in its own time. And I had to believe that mine was still unfolding, too. With a sigh, I turned back to the café, ready to tackle the next task on my to-do list.

Connie Fontaine breezed into the café like a gust of eccentricity, her white curls bouncing under a deerstalker hat. She was waving a neon pink pipe around, sending tiny bubbles into the air as if it were the most natural thing in the world.

"Ah! The game is afoot, Josie!" she declared loudly, her voice carrying through the café with the kind of booming theatricality that only Connie could pull off. Heads turned, amused smiles flickering across familiar faces. No one was surprised—Connie had been making grand entrances for as long as anyone could remember.

Connie's entrances were always a spectacle, but today, she'd outdone herself with the bubble pipe. "Connie," I said, fighting back a laugh, "you realize Sherlock never smoked a bubble pipe, right?"

She paused dramatically, inspecting the pipe with the serious expression you'd expect from an Academy Award-winning actor. "Nonsense!" she exclaimed, puffing out a few more bubbles. "Sherlock would've loved this upgrade. It's positively... effervescent!" She tapped her magnifying glass against her chin like she was pondering the mysteries of the universe.

"Well, if you're done sleuthing, how about helping with the decorations?" I suggested, fully aware I was feeding into her antics.

With a gleam in her eye, Connie immediately strode toward the decorating table like a detective on the verge of solving a case. The students crafting decorations burst into laughter as she held her magnifying glass up to the crepe paper. "Aha! I see it now—the culprit behind the crooked banners!" she announced with the drama of someone solving a high-stakes mystery.

I shook my head, smiling. "Connie, you're a natural," I called over, laughing as I returned to the counter to help with orders.

Despite her 82 years—she'd celebrated that milestone last spring—Connie had more energy than people half her age. She was sharp, spry, and carried that ever-present mischievous glint in her eye. Time had only added depth to her charisma, and her theatrical spirit had grown even bolder with age.

As the head of Hickory Hills University's theater department for nearly fifty years, Connie shaped countless young actors, playwrights, and directors, teaching them the craft of theater and the art of living life like it was the performance of a lifetime. Even in retirement, she guest-directed student plays and occasionally popped into drama classes to share theatrical wisdom—on her terms, of course. She was adored by the café's regulars, especially the university students, who hung on her every word, whether she was quoting Shakespeare or spinning wildly creative takes on Agatha Christie.

When I moved back to Hickory Hills over a decade ago, fresh off being left at the altar, I wasn't sure of anything. My future felt like a blank page I didn't know how to fill. But one thing I did know: I needed a fresh start, something that felt like home again. With her endless energy and uncanny ability to see people straight through, Connie helped me believe that dreams could become a reality.

I still remember the day I first mentioned my idea for the café. At the time, the pain of rejection and betrayal felt overwhelming, like the whole wedding disaster had shattered more than just a day—it had broken my belief in love, trust, and myself. I'd fled to the old farmhouse I'd inherited, but the hurt followed me there, lingering like a shadow. For months, I drifted, trying to figure out what came next.

One afternoon, while I was sitting alone in the corner of Gayle's Diner, Connie swept in like a gust of energy. Without so much as a hello, she plopped down across from me, dramatically waving her arms as if performing for an audience. Formalities weren't her style.

"Now, Josie," she began, her tone leaving no room for argument, "you've been moping long enough. It's time to pick up the pieces and create something beautiful with them."

At the time, I didn't know what she meant. I was too buried in the hurt, too tangled in the memories of being left at the altar, wondering what was wrong with me. But Connie, in her way, saw right through the walls I'd built.

"What if," she said, leaning in with that signature gleam in her eye, "you did something you've always wanted to do? Something bold. Something you."

That's when the idea for the café began to take root—a place where I could combine my love of books, coffee, and community. It felt like the kind of fresh start I'd been searching for, a chance to create something meaningful and finally leave the past behind.

When I told Connie about it, I was hesitant, barely believing it could be more than a dream. She listened, her sharp eyes never leaving mine, and when I finished, she leaned back with a grin.

"Josie, darling," she said, her voice full of conviction, "you have to do it. Don't you know the world is waiting for what only you can offer?"

Her words stuck. At a time when I felt broken and unsure of my worth, Connie reminded me I wasn't broken—just bruised—and that I still had something to give.

Her support was a lifeline. Whether she knew it or not, her encouragement kept me afloat. With her—and Hattie's—help, I threw myself into making the book café a reality. It became more than a business; it became a place of healing. Every cup of coffee, book shared across a table, and moment of connection was a step toward rebuilding myself, stronger than before.

"Josie, darling!" Connie called, pulling me out of my thoughts. She was standing on a chair now, adjusting one of the banners with exaggerated care. "Does this banner scream 'mystery and intrigue,' or is it merely whispering 'mediocre party'?"

I stifled a laugh. "Let me see." I walked over, studying the banner. "Oh, it's definitely screaming 'mystery,' Connie."

"Good!" she declared, hopping down with surprising agility for someone her age. "It's all in the angle, you know. Theater is about presence, even in the smallest details. The same applies to party décor!" She raised her hands dramatically, then swooped toward the table where more students were working, her enthusiasm infecting everyone around her.

"Connie, you're always the star of the show," I said, unable to resist teasing her.

"Well, darling," she replied, winking, "when you've been in this business as long as I have, you learn a thing or two about stealing the spotlight."

When I'd asked her to help with the murder mystery party, she'd thrown herself into the project with the energy of someone putting on a Broadway production. It was Connie's idea to layer the script with a play-within-a-play structure, drawing from some of her favorite mysteries and Agatha Christie's best twists. She even insisted on teaching the volunteers how to 'embody' their characters through voice and movement, just like she'd taught her students in the old days. As she wove some ribbons into the decorations with a flourish, I felt gratitude for her presence in my life.

The rest of the afternoon buzzed along, the café humming with energy as preparations for the murder mystery party kicked into high gear. Volunteers fluttered between tables, hanging streamers, arranging decorations, and laughing at Connie's antics as she draped herself in crepe paper like a makeshift scarf. She was in rare form as usual, drawing giggles and applause from the student helpers.

Across the café, my attention shifted to Teddy and his grandson, Christopher—or Bear, as most people called him—setting up decorations in the bookstore section. Seeing them here, mingling in the chaos of last-minute prep, brought a wave of relief. But it didn't untangle the knot of worry that had been sitting in my chest for weeks.

I still remember how Christopher became "Bear." He was just a scruffy kid tagging along with Teddy at the garage when someone joked that, with his messy hair and oversized clothes, he looked more like a bear cub than a kid. The name stuck, just like "Teddy" had for Henry. The Theodors and their nicknames were practically a town tradition by now.

I walked over, trying to push aside the worry. "How've you been, Teddy?" I asked, adding extra warmth to my voice. "I miss our talks."

Teddy looked up from his work, his kind eyes lifting, though they didn't have their usual spark. "Ah, you know me—keeping busy in my home garage." He paused, glancing around the bustling café with a fond smile. "But nothing beats being here with you, Josie."

His smile widened just a little, and for a moment, I caught a flicker of the old Teddy—the one who always had a story, a chuckle, and advice that could steady even the worst day. "I'll never forget when you were convinced you'd wreck your engine just trying to change the oil."

I laughed softly, the memory clear as day. "I was determined to get it right, even though I had no clue what I was doing."

"And look at you now," he said, his tone tinged with wistfulness. "Still just as determined with everything you take on." His gaze swept the café, lingering on the streamers and decorations. "This murder mystery party's going to be fantastic, by the way."

"Thanks, Teddy," I said, glancing around at the volunteers. "I couldn't do it without everyone's help." My eyes drifted to Bear, who was hanging streamers nearby, his movements slow and deliberate. He looked thoughtful—maybe too thoughtful. "Hey, Bear—how's the first semester going?"

Bear gave a small shrug, his focus staying on the streamers. "It's okay. Still figuring things out," he muttered, his voice quieter than usual.

"Totally normal," I said with a smile, hoping to ease the tension. "I didn't have everything figured out at your age either. Life's a journey—you don't have to know all the answers right away."

Bear nodded but didn't look up. His usual spark was missing, and his jaw set tightly as he worked spoke volumes. Normally, Bear would've been cracking jokes or making everyone laugh, but today? He seemed weighed down. Whatever was pressing on Teddy felt like it had settled on him, too.

Nearby, Connie was battling a particularly stubborn piece of crepe paper, her dramatic flair still intact. As she yanked a streamer into place, she suddenly winced and pulled her hand back. "Oops! Got myself good!" she announced, holding up her finger where a thin line of blood appeared. "Hold on, let me grab a band-aid."

I reached for a napkin to help, but my attention snagged on Sam, standing just a few feet away. His face had gone noticeably pale, and his usual easygoing demeanor had vanished, replaced by something tight and uncomfortable.

"You okay, Sam?" I asked, handing Connie the napkin but keeping my eyes on him. His posture was stiff, his shoulders drawn back like he was bracing himself.

Sam swallowed hard, forcing a weak smile. "Yeah, yeah, I'm fine," he muttered, though his voice lacked its usual smooth confidence. "Just... never been a fan of blood." He stepped back, his eyes darting away as though looking anywhere but at Connie's finger.

I handed Connie a Band-Aid. She wrapped it around her finger with a dramatic flourish. "Battle wounds of a true party planner," she joked, holding up her bandaged finger like a trophy. The students around her laughed, and the café buzzed with life again.

4 a shot of suspicion

ANNOYINGLY, I COULDN'T get rid of the weird tension from earlier. Bear's distance, Sam's odd reaction—it all nagged at me, refusing to be shoved into the "deal with it later" box. But there was no time to dwell. The autumn decorations weren't going to hang themselves.

I stood at the base of the ladder, staring up at the last spot for the garlands. Beside me, Mocha sat, her big brown eyes watching me with a mix of curiosity and judgment.

"Wish me luck, Mocha," I muttered. She tilted her head, clearly unimpressed. Yep, she definitely thought I was about to reenact some slapstick comedy routine.

I sighed, sizing up the ladder like it was my mortal enemy. It's just a ladder, Josie. The building was a sight to behold, though—white-painted brick, big dark-wood windows, and that deep blue door that made everything pop. Honestly, it looked like something out of a fall postcard. Almost enough to make me forget about the ladder. Almost.

And then there was the sign: Novel Grounds Book Café. Double-sided, painted white with delicate blue flowers. Whenever I looked at it, I felt like I was running a quaint Parisian bookstore instead of a small-town café. Maybe the climb would be worth it.

I grabbed the ladder and placed a foot on the first rung. "You're not beating me today, ladder," I muttered. I could practically hear it laughing in response. *We'll see, Josie. We'll see.*

As I climbed, clutching the garlands like a lifeline, my brain dredged up *The Incident.* You know, the one everyone still talked about at reunions. Junior year of college. Lake party. Rope swing. Classic Josie. While everyone else managed a graceful splash into the water, I clung to the rope too long and crashed to the ground. Busted knee. Busted pride. Lifelong trust issues with heights.

Mocha huffed below me, breaking my spiral. I glanced down at her. "Why do I do this to myself?" She gave me a little boof—her version of "you're ridiculous."

I laughed despite myself. "You're right. It's just a ladder. No big deal."

At the top, I hung the garlands, my hands only trembling slightly. Success. Stepping down, I felt a ridiculous surge of triumph, like I'd just scaled Mount Everest.

"Not bad for someone who avoids heights," I told Mocha, who wagged her tail, clearly impressed by my survival skills.

Stepping back, I admired my work. The café looked beautiful—cozy and inviting, with the garlands framing the windows just right. For a moment, everything felt perfect.

Then Alexis, one of the college workers, appeared, balancing a tray of floral coffee cups like a high-stakes waiter. She looked frazzled, which was basically my default setting.

"Josie, sorry to interrupt," she said, shifting the tray. "But you're needed behind the counter."

I nodded, trying not to let my relief at being back on solid ground show. "Let me put the ladder away, and I'll be right there."

She lingered, soaking in the autumn sunshine. Honestly? Smart move. The crisp breeze, warm light, and smell of coffee wafting through the air made everything feel like the world wasn't so bad. Once I'd stashed the ladder, I joined her, Mocha trotting at my side. It was one of those rare, peaceful moments where life just felt right.

Alexis turned to me with a wince. "We've got a rush, and we're short-handed. Ava called in sick again."

I blinked, mentally rearranging my to-do list. "Okay, let's tackle the rush first. I'll jump in with the lattes, then we'll figure out the rest."

Pumpkin Spice Lattes: the lifeblood of fall. I tied on my apron and longingly glanced outside at the sunshine. Then I stepped into the chaos, ready to save the day one foam swirl at a time. Behind the counter, the café was buzzing with the usual 2 o'clock crowd. The sound of milk frothing, orders being called out, and conversations filling the space.

"All right, team!" I called out, clapping my hands to get everyone's attention. "We've got a rush, but we can handle it. Let's keep the drinks flowing!"

Mrs. Milgram, one of our favorite regulars, waved from her usual corner table. "Afternoon, Josie!" she called, her voice as warm as the Prairie Sunset herbal tea she always ordered.

I prepared her tea without her needing to ask and brought it over, setting the steaming cup in front of her. "Here you go, Mrs. Milgram. Fresh as always."

She wrapped her hands around the mug, sighing softly. "Thank you, Josie. You always know just what I need."

I leaned in, catching a hint of worry in her expression. "How's everything today?"

"Oh, it's my granddaughter," she admitted, her shoulders slumping slightly. "She's been struggling at school. I just don't know how to help her."

"Kids are tougher than we think," I said gently. "And with a family like yours, she's got all the love and support she needs. She'll find her way."

Her smile warmed a little as she patted my hand. "Thank you, Josie. You always know the right thing to say."

I headed back to the counter just as Hank Junior, the local hardware store owner, strolled in, looking frazzled, rubbing his temples like the day had gotten the best of him.

"Hey there, troublemaker," he teased, though his grin was tired.

"Rough day, Hank Junior?" I asked, already pouring his usual Dead Poets Society Dark Roast—strong just like him.

"Shipment came in late," he grumbled, shaking his head. "Threw off my whole afternoon."

I handed him his cup. "Here. This'll help you conquer the world—or at least the hardware aisle."

His grin softened, and he gave me a nod. "You're a lifesaver, Josie. Thanks."

But, naturally, the espresso machine chose that moment to stage its rebellion. It sputtered and hissed like an angry cat, belching steam and sending a thick fog rolling through the café.

"Uh, Josie?" Tyler called out from behind the counter, his voice tinged with panic. "I think the espresso machine is auditioning for *The Fog Part II*!"

I grabbed a towel, waving at the steam like it would somehow obey. "Don't worry! Just a minor meltdown. We've got this."

Hattie popped up beside me, helping me wrestle the stubborn window frames open to let in some crisp autumn air. She wiped her forehead dramatically and quipped, "Who needs a spa day when you've got Josie's steam room experience?"

I grinned at her, grateful for the humor. "Maybe I should start charging for this. 'Free latte with every sauna session.'"

Roy, sitting in his usual corner, peeked over the top of his newspaper and chuckled. "Josie, you've got this place buzzing again—literally." He gestured toward another bag stuffed with Eloise's muffins.

Granny Clara Belle, "Smokin' Belle" herself, nodded in agreement. "You always bring sunshine, dear. Even if it comes with a little steam," she added with a wink.

One of the college workers rushed by with a tray of muffins and grinned. "Never a dull moment, boss!"

Emma, still lingering after her earlier chat, hurried over with a carafe of coffee in hand. "Need me to brew some coffee manually?"

"Thanks, Emma," I said as I crouched in front of the espresso machine with a wrench in hand. "But first, let me see if I can talk some sense into this drama queen."

The machine hissed again, like it was taking offense.

"Alright, you temperamental beast," I muttered under my breath, adjusting a few bolts. "Work with me here."

With her usual flair, Connie appeared at my side, holding up a magnifying glass like Sherlock Holmes. "Fear not, dear patrons!" she announced in a theatrical British accent. "Detective Josie is on the case!"

The café erupted in laughter, and even I couldn't help but grin. Connie peered at the espresso machine with mock seriousness, inspecting it as though it held the secrets of the universe.

"Thanks for the backup, Sherlock," I said, tightening the last bolt. With a sputter and one last hiss, the machine whirred back to life, humming as if nothing had ever gone wrong. A small cheer went up from the café.

"There we go!" I declared, standing and wiping my hands.

Tyler clapped. "Josie saves the day—again!"

I laughed, taking a moment to soak in the café's usual rhythm: the clink of mugs, the comforting hum of conversation, and the rich aroma of freshly brewed coffee. It was chaotic, sure, but it was my chaos.

Just as I started to savor the moment, the bell over the door jingled. Dex walked in, followed closely by Tiffany and Artie. The three of them couldn't have looked more mismatched—Dex, all brooding silence; Tiffany, practically glowing with confidence; and Artie, with that oily smugness that set my nerves on edge.

But it wasn't just their arrival that threw me off. There was something in the way Dex avoided eye contact, like a man carrying a secret that was too heavy to bear. On the other hand, Tiffany was all sharp edges and biting wit, her eyes scanning the café as if calculating who she could tear down next. Artie trailed behind, his smirk never fading, but there was something else in his eyes—something dark like he knew a secret that could destroy someone.

As they entered, the air seemed to tighten. Conversations dulled as if the café itself sensed the tension these three brought in with them. I straightened, bracing myself.

"Here we go," I muttered under my breath.

Tiffany, in her usual snide fashion, leaned on the counter. "Busy day, Josie? Or just pretending to be?"

I shot her a cool smile. "It's always busy here, Tiffany. Coffee and books tend to draw people in, you know?"

She scoffed, flipping her hair over her shoulder. "Well, some of us have *real* work to do."

As she walked away, I caught a look exchanged between her and Artie—a quick, loaded glance. Something passed between them. I wonder what that was about.

As she sidled up to Artie, their conversation dropped to hushed tones. I couldn't hear their exact words, but Tiffany's expression shifted, hardening as Artie said something that made her jaw clench. His smirk grew, enjoying his power over her, and he got loud enough for me to hear.

"Keep your mouth shut, Tif," Artie hissed, his tone urgent. The chill in his voice sent a shiver down my spine. "We can't risk anyone finding out about it."

It was a cryptic snippet of conversation, but it was enough to make my stomach knot with unease. What on earth were they hiding?

Meanwhile, Dex lingered near the community bulletin board, staring at the flyers with his hands shoved deep into his pockets as though just trying to disappear. The weight of guilt hung heavy on him.

Artie swaggered over to where Hattie sat. His presence filled the room with a strange mix of arrogance and hostility. His voice was low, but I could hear enough to know it wasn't good.

"You think you can scare me, Hattie? You're barking up the wrong tree," he growled, his hand slamming onto the table, making her jump.

Hattie's face remained calm, but there was tension in her shoulders, and her knuckles whitened as she gripped the arms of her chair. She didn't back down. "It's not about scaring you, Artie. It's about making things right."

I caught Tiffany's eye from across the room—she watched the exchange intently, lips pursed like a predator sizing up her prey. Her gaze unnerved me. She wasn't just interested—she was planning something.

"Well, that's it for me," I muttered, my blood simmering. Artie had no right to come into my café and harass my sister like this. And I refused to let him ruin everyone's day. Taking a deep breath, I mustered my most professional smile and approached Artie and Tiffany.

I pulled my shoulders back and calmly and firmly said, "Hey there, Artie, Tiffany. Is there something I can assist you with?"

Artie chuckled, the sound grating like nails on a chalkboard. I ignored it and locked eyes with him. Tiffany shot me a sharp glance, but I stood my ground. My café, my family—they meant everything to me, and I wasn't about to let these two disrupt that. Not today.

Before things could escalate, Sam, with his easy smile and laid-back charm, strolled over. "Hey there, folks! What seems to be the problem?"

he asked, his voice carrying that calm, unassuming confidence that usually diffused tension.

I could see Hattie relax slightly at the sight of Sam, grateful for the distraction.

Artie, always quick to shift gears when it suited him, plastered on a strained smile. "Ah, Sam, my man! What's the latest buzz around here?" His attempt to act casually felt forced like he was trying to cover up the confrontation he had just stirred up.

Sam chuckled good-naturedly, slipping smoothly into the conversation. "Oh, you know how it is in a small town. Never a dull moment," he replied casually. Then, he reached into a plain white bakery bag stamped with the *Novel Grounds* logo. "Speaking of, Eloise's famous pumpkin chocolate chip muffins just arrived. Holly dropped off the latest batch this morning, and I snagged a few to share."

That piqued Artie's interest. His hand twitched toward the bag, though his expression remained wary. He knew these muffins well—everyone in town did. Holly and Eloise's treats were legendary, and Artie had a soft spot for them like the rest of us. Tyler appeared from the back with a fresh coffee for Artie, blissfully unaware of the tension.

"Here you go, Artie," Tyler said warmly, placing the steaming cup down in front of him. Then, with a quick glance at the clock on the wall, his expression shifted slightly. "Oh man, I've got to get to Professor Meyer's class now," he added, his tone hurried as he pulled off his apron and slung it over his shoulder.

Tyler rushed to retrieve his book bag and then gave a quick wave to the rest of us before making a beeline for the door, his backpack slung across one shoulder. "See you tomorrow!" he called over his shoulder, leaving just as the tension in the room seemed to thicken.

As Artie reached for his coffee, another figure stepped forward—Dex. He had been skulking in the shadows, his posture tense, but now he approached our group with a small bag in hand, offering a sheepish smile.

"Hey, Artie," Dex said, his voice a little stiff, clearly trying to keep things casual. He held out the bag toward Artie. "I, uh... I grabbed this for you earlier. Thought you might want something to eat."

Artie's eyes narrowed, his eyes flicking from the bag to Dex's face, suspicion evident in his expression. The two men had never exactly been close, and Artie's guarded nature made him even more wary than usual. He glanced at the bag for a moment longer before snatching it from Dex's hand.

"Thanks, I guess," Artie muttered, ripping open the bag to find a breakfast sandwich wrapped in wax paper. He unwrapped it slowly, still eyeing Dex as if waiting for some catch. "What's the occasion?" he added, a hint of challenge in his voice.

Dex shrugged, his hands stuffed deep into his pockets. "No occasion," he said, his eyes darting away. "Just thought you might be hungry."

Artie snorted, but he took a bite of the sandwich anyway, chewing slowly. He was still eyeing Dex like he didn't quite trust the gesture, but hunger won out over suspicion. He washed the bite down with a sip of the coffee Tyler had just dropped off.

Now Artie had both the sandwich from Dex and the muffin from Sam, which he eyed more warily.

Sam, still smiling, clapped Artie on the back a little too hard, his tone too cheerful. "Don't forget the muffin, buddy. Best pumpkin chocolate chip in town. You'll be back for more, I promise."

Tiffany's frown deepened, and she looked at Sam suspiciously. "What are you up to?" she asked, her voice dripping with skepticism.

Sam met her gaze with that same easy smile. "I'm just making sure everyone's taken care of," he said lightly. His eyes flicked toward me for the briefest of moments, something unreadable passing through them.

Before Tiffany could press him further, Sam wrapped things up with a final pat on Artie's shoulder. "Well, I better get back to my coffee. See you around, Artie. Enjoy the muffin!"

With that, Sam returned to his seat, sipping his coffee like nothing had happened. As Artie took another bite of the sandwich from Dex, he glanced warily at the muffin again. Then, with a small shrug, he took a bite of it, too, washing it down with the fresh coffee from Tyler.

After they left, Dex lingered by the bulletin board, staring at the flyers like they held the answers to life's toughest questions. His shoulders slouched, and there was a heaviness to his posture. But whatever weighed on him wasn't just Artie and Tiffany's awkward drama. Dex looked like a man wrestling with ghosts—ones that refused to stay buried.

"Hey, Dex," I called softly, stepping out from behind the counter.

He turned slightly, his tired eyes meeting mine. "Hey, Josie." His voice carried the same weariness I'd been noticing lately like every word had to push through a wall of regrets. His hands stayed shoved deep into his jacket pockets as if anchoring him in place.

"You doing okay?" I asked, keeping my tone casual but kind.

His eyes flicked to me, startled by the question. "Yeah... just dealing with some things," he muttered, his gaze shifted toward the photo of Teddy on the wall. It was from back when things were simpler. His voice wavered just enough for the guilt to slip through. "Been thinking about reaching out to Teddy, but... I don't know, Josie. I messed up. I don't think he'd want to hear from me."

There it was—raw, unvarnished pain. Dex wasn't a man who said much, but when he did, it carried weight.

"Teddy wants to see you," I said, keeping my voice steady like it was an unshakable truth. "It's not too late, Dex."

He nodded, the tiniest flicker of hope breaking through, but he didn't reply.

I shifted gears, sensing he needed a break from the heavy stuff. "What can I get for you today? Something strong? Double espresso to fuel all that brooding?"

His lips twitched—almost a smile. "Just a black coffee, Josie." He pulled some cash from his wallet and dropped it on the counter.

"Coming right up," I said, shooting him a reassuring smile as I grabbed a cup. While I poured the coffee, I glanced at him from the corner of my eye. Dex was a mystery, sure, but mysteries always came with layers—and I had a feeling he wasn't all bad.

I handed him the cup, and he gave me a small, grateful nod, slipping his change into the tip jar. "Thanks," he said, his voice softer now.

As he headed for the door, I called after him, "Hey, Dex?" He stopped, glancing back. "It's never too late to fix things," I added.

He hesitated, then gave a small nod before stepping out into the fading sunlight.

Nearby, Matt, one of my newer hires, paused mid-wipe in the reading nook. He frowned as something shiny between the cushions caught his eye. Fishing it out, he held up a delicate heart-shaped locket that glinted in the lamplight.

"Hmm, a locket," he muttered, inspecting it briefly before tucking it into his apron pocket.

I watched as he deposited it in the lost-and-found box behind the counter. Sunglasses, scarves, bookmarks, and other assorted things were always left behind.

"Whew, what a day," I sighed, rubbing my temples as I took in the café's quiet hum. Satisfaction mingled with exhaustion.

Matt slung his bag over his shoulder and headed for the door, giving me a quick nod. "All set, Josie. See you tomorrow!"

"Thanks, Matt," I called after him with a tired smile. "Don't forget to email me if you can't find your costume for the party!"

As the door jingled shut behind him, I turned to the volunteers, who were gathered near the counter, their faces bright with anticipation. The energy in the room shifted from tired to excited, and before I knew it, I was grinning.

"All right, everyone, listen up!" I said, clapping my hands to get their attention. "I've got updates on the murder mystery party, and I promise they're good."

The group leaned in as I launched into party-planning mode. "We've got decorations to finish, clues to plant, and plenty of treats to prep," I said, ticking off tasks with an animated gesture. "And, just so you know, I've already conquered my fear of heights and hung the outdoor garlands." I paused, smirking. "So no ladder-wobbling rescue missions needed this year!"

That got a laugh, and my sister Hattie, who was helping organize the clue cards, chimed in, "What, no dramatic midair garland battles? Josie, I'm almost disappointed."

"Don't worry," I shot back with a grin. "I'll find some other way to keep you entertained."

"Please don't," one of the college students quipped, balancing a tray of leftover muffins. "We don't need you breaking your neck before the big night."

"Noted," I replied with mock solemnity, raising my coffee cup in a toast. "Here's to keeping all my limbs intact!"

The volunteers chuckled, and the lighthearted banter eased any lingering tension. I could feel the excitement bubbling up as I laid out the rest of the details.

"With all of your help, this year's party is going to blow last year's out of the water," I said, my voice brimming with confidence. "And if not, we'll distract everyone with Eloise's pumpkin chocolate chip muffins. Sound like a plan?"

"Always," Holly replied, grabbing one of the aforementioned muffins off the tray. "It's a foolproof strategy."

As the meeting wrapped up, the café buzzed with the low murmur of conversations and the comforting clinks of porcelain cups. Volunteers lingered in small groups, chatting over the last muffins and coffee before heading home.

I leaned against the counter, watching it all with a satisfied smile. Despite the occasional hiccup and my unresolved nagging unease, seeing everyone come together was nice, almost comforting.

Eloise stood near the counter, unusually quiet, her poofy gray hair catching the warm glow of the overhead lights. She looked like the picture of a sweet grandma, but anyone who'd ever met her knew better. Beneath that cozy exterior was a retired New York detective who could outwit anyone in town, myself included.

"Eloise," I said, stepping closer, "what's going on? You look like someone just told you the muffin tins are made with icky Teflon."

Her lips twitched, but her expression stayed serious. "Oh, Josie, if only it were that simple." She placed her hands on her hips in her signature no-nonsense stance. "Some hotshot from FMR Foods—Blake, their marketing guy—dropped by this morning after Holly left to deliver the morning muffins. And guess what he wanted?"

"Let me guess," I said, already bracing myself. "A lifetime supply of pumpkin chocolate chip?"

She snorted. "I wish. No, he wanted to buy all my muffin recipes. Offered me a fat check, like I'd just hand over my babies to some corporate suit."

My jaw dropped. "Wait, what? He thought you'd just sell him your recipes?"

"As if!" Eloise's eyes narrowed, her indignation sharp enough to cut steel. "I told him exactly where he could stick his check. Nicely, of course." She added this with a cheeky grin, but the tension in her shoulders betrayed her frustration.

I laughed. "I would've paid to see that."

"Oh, it gets better," she said, leaning in conspiratorially. "When I said no, he got pushy. Real pushy. Like, practically foaming at the mouth. My spidey senses were screaming louder than a fire alarm."

My smile faded. Eloise's instincts were rarely wrong, and if she thought something was off, it probably was. "You think there's more to it?"

"Absolutely," she said, lowering her voice. "No one gets that desperate over muffins unless there's a lot of money—or something bigger—involved."

My attention snagged on Tiffany, who was hovering too close, pretending to browse the bookshelves but sneaking glances our way. Her eyes flicked between Eloise and me like she was trying to eavesdrop without getting caught.

Eloise noticed her too, her gaze sharpening. "You've got good instincts, Josie," she murmured, her voice barely audible. "You're going to need them around that one." She gave a subtle nod toward Tiffany.

I resisted the urge to look directly at her. "She's been sniffing around a little too much lately," I whispered.

"Mark my words," Eloise said, her voice edged with steel. "That girl's got secrets. And people with secrets? They get dangerous when they're cornered."

Before I could respond, Tiffany inched closer, her footsteps a little too loud, like she wanted us to know she was there. She lingered near the bookshelf, holding a random novel upside down. Not exactly subtle.

I raised my voice slightly, hoping to throw her off. "What do you think Blake will try next, Eloise? Guys like him don't take 'no' for an answer."

Eloise chuckled, though her expression stayed serious. "Oh, he'll try something, all right. Desperation makes people reckless. I'd bet my best Krav Maga move that FMR Foods is tangled up in something bigger than muffins."

Tiffany edged even closer, practically hovering over us now. Her eyes narrowed as she tried to catch every word, her cover officially blown.

I turned to her with my best polite-but-don't-push-it smile. "Did you need something, Tiffany?"

She blinked, clearly caught off guard. "Oh, um, no," she stammered, fumbling with her bag. "Just remembered I need to pick up my dry cleaning." She turned on her heel and practically sprinted for the door, leaving a trail of awkwardness in her wake.

I cleared my throat, the question that had been nagging at me since earlier bubbling up. "I wanted to ask you about Sam."

Her head tilted slightly, her detective instincts switching on in an instant. "Sam? What about him?"

I tried for casual, even though I knew Eloise could see right through me. "I don't know. He's been... weird. You've known him longer than I have. What's your take?"

Eloise folded her arms, her expression sharpening as if she were sorting through mental case files. "Hmm. Funny you should mention that. I've noticed some odd behavior, too. Little things, but nothing I can pin down just yet."

"What kind of odd?" I pressed, leaning against the counter.

She lowered her voice, glancing around like she was about to share classified intel. "He's been asking a few too many questions. About deliveries, schedules, that sort of thing. Could just be his way of trying to fit in, but..."

"But it feels like more," I finished for her, my stomach tightening again. "I've noticed him hovering around the café a little too much. Like he's paying attention to things most people wouldn't."

Eloise nodded, her gaze thoughtful. "Could be nothing. Or it could be something. People show their cards eventually," she added, her tone brisk and sure, like a veteran detective stepping back into the field.

"Retired detective mode kicking in?"

She grinned, giving me a wink. "Always, sweetheart."

Her smile faded just a bit, replaced by something more serious. "But you trust your gut, Josie. Don't brush this off if it's bothering you."

I nodded, grateful for her support. "Thanks, Eloise. I'll keep an eye on him."

"Good," she said firmly, her eyes sweeping the room one last time like she was mentally cataloging potential red flags. Then, her face softened, her usual warm demeanor returning. "Good. Now, enough of this serious business. We've got bigger priorities."

"Bigger than suspicious guys and a snooping Tiffany?" I teased, trying to lighten the mood.

"Absolutely," Eloise said, deadpan. "Morale. And muffins. Always muffins."

I laughed as she patted my hand, her grip stronger than you'd expect from someone her age.

The café buzzed with the last scraps of energy from the volunteers as they began to disperse. Emma gave an enthusiastic wave, her energy practically lighting up the room. "See you later, everyone!" she chirped. "Hattie, Josie, Eloise—I'll see you at Stanzi's and Max's for the big mystery box reveal!" She practically skipped out the door, her excitement contagious.

On the other hand, Hattie seemed to be halfway out the door already. Her mind was clearly elsewhere. "I'm off to get tacos," she announced, her voice breezy but unnecessarily loud. "I'll bring them to game night!"

Eloise gave me a knowing look. "Tacos. She'll probably show up with one half-eaten and the rest mysteriously missing."

I grinned, shaking my head. "Classic Hattie."

Eloise chuckled, nudging me lightly. "All right, Josie. I'm heading out, too. Keep your eyes open—and your muffins guarded."

I laughed. "Always."

As she strolled out the door, I saw Hattie zipping up her jacket with all the urgency of someone late for a flight. Her movements were quick and jittery, like she had too much caffeine in her system, though I knew it was just Hattie being Hattie—impulsive and always on the verge of her next wild idea.

"You look like you're planning a heist," I said, leaning casually against the counter, arms crossed.

"Tacos," she replied, her grin a little too wide, her voice a little too bright. She slung her bag over her shoulder, her fingers fiddling with the zipper. "What? You think I'm plotting something?"

I shook my head, my tone light but teasing. "Tacos, huh? What kind of tacos require that much nervous energy? Are they endangered?"

She rolled her eyes dramatically, but her hand lingered on the door handle. "Just tacos, Josie. Not everything has to be a mystery."

"With you, everything is a mystery," I shot back, tilting my head and narrowing my eyes. "Hattie, if you're heading to Artie's shop..." My voice softened slightly. "Just don't do anything crazy, okay?"

She paused for half a heartbeat, her fingers frozen on the door handle before recovering with a breezy laugh. "I told you, it's tacos. You worry too much."

I gave her a skeptical look, but she was already halfway out the door, her tone far too casual as she added, "I'll try to make it to game night. You know I can't resist a good mystery."

"Don't try—just be there," I said firmly, calling after her. "Max and Stanzi are counting on you. And if you bring tacos, make sure they actually make it to the table."

She hesitated, her hand resting on the doorframe as if weighing her next move. But then, with a quick wave, she disappeared into the fading evening light.

I watched her go, the golden hues of the town square painting the scene like a postcard. Hickory Hills looked so peaceful, all warm light and cozy charm, but something about Hattie's hurried departure didn't sit right. It wasn't just tacos—this I knew for sure.

Mocha padded over, her tail wagging as she nudged my leg. "What do you think, girl?" I asked, scratching behind her ears. "Is this a tacos kind of thing or a 'Hattie's about to get herself in trouble' kind of thing?"

She let out a little huff, her version of an eye roll, and flopped down at my feet. "Yeah, that's what I thought," I muttered.

Turning back to the café, I handed off the closing duties to Alexis, one of my college workers, who was wiping down the counter. "Think you can finish up here tonight? I've got a few errands to run."

Alexis gave me a thumbs-up. "Got it, boss. Go save the day or whatever it is you do after hours."

"Thanks, Alexis," I replied with a small grin, grabbing my keys.

A few minutes later, I was driving through the dimming streets of Hickory Hills, Mocha sitting happily in the backseat with her head out the window. The crisp autumn air smelled faintly of leaves and earth, but the unease in my chest refused to lift.

"What are you up to, Hattie?" I muttered, gripping the steering wheel tighter as I turned onto the road leading to Artie's shop.

As I pulled up, my stomach sank. Hattie's van was just speeding out of the parking lot, her tires kicking up a cloud of dust as she rounded the corner like she was running from something—or to something.

"Hattie, no," I groaned, fumbling for my phone. I dialed her number, but of course, it went straight to voicemail.

Mocha let out a concerned little whine from the backseat, and I sighed, slumping against the wheel for a moment. "Don't worry, Mocha," I got out and leaned into the window of my Jeep, giving Mocha a quick scratch behind the ears. "Stay here, girl. This'll only take a minute. Probably."

She tilted her head, giving me a look that screamed bad idea, human, before letting out a low, concerned whine.

"Yeah, I know," I muttered. "I've got a bad feeling too."

The cool evening air hit me as I stepped out. The sun had long set, leaving the world cloaked in shadows and the faint glow of streetlights. The garage loomed ahead, its familiar smell of motor oil and grease greeting me as I approached. Normally, the place would be buzzing with clanging tools and revving engines. Tonight? Dead silent.

I took a deep breath, trying to shake the growing unease curling in my gut. "Artie?" I called, my voice cutting through the eerie quiet. "It's Josie!"

Nothing.

The silence pressed down harder, thick and unnatural, like the air itself was holding its breath. I hesitated at the door, glancing back at Mocha, who was now watching me like a particularly judgy gargoyle from the backseat. "Great pep talk, thanks," I muttered, before stepping inside.

The dim light cast long, jagged shadows across the shop floor. Everything looked normal—toolboxes neatly stacked, cars parked in their bays—but my instincts were buzzing. Something was wrong.

"Artie?" I called again, my voice softer this time.

A faint rustling came from the back office. I froze mid-step, my pulse quickening. "It's probably just a raccoon," I whispered to myself. "Or... not."

I crept toward the sound, the smell of new tires and motor oil getting stronger. When I reached the office, I hesitated, one hand hovering near the doorframe.

And then I saw him.

Artie was slumped over his desk, utterly still. The sight of him—motionless, lifeless—made my stomach drop. I took a step closer, the metallic scent of blood hit me before I even registered the dark, sticky pool spreading across the papers beneath his head.

"Artie?" I choked out, even though I already knew he wasn't going to answer.

The torque wrench lying a few feet from his chair made everything horribly clear.

My knees felt weak, but I forced myself to stay upright, to think. I fumbled for my phone, my hands trembling as I dialed 911.

"911, what's your emergency?"

"There's been an... accident," I managed, my voice barely steady. "At Artie's car repair shop. He's... he's dead."

The dispatcher's voice was calm, asking for details, but her words blurred together as I stared at the scene before me. Artie, the blood, the wrench—it was too much.

After hanging up, I stood there, frozen, as the weight of what I'd just walked into settled over me. My mind raced with questions: Who would do this? Why?

I took a shaky breath, trying to calm my racing thoughts. My eyes swept over the dimly lit space, searching for any sign of what had happened—or who had been here. Everything looked eerily normal. Too normal.

Then something caught my eye.

A small glint on the floor near one of the garage bays.

I frowned, stepping closer, my cowboy boots scuffing against the concrete. At first, it looked like just another stray bolt or nut, the kind of thing you'd expect to find in a repair shop. But as I crouched down, my stomach twisted.

It wasn't a bolt.

It was a bracelet.

Not just any bracelet—Hattie's bracelet.

The turquoise beads gleamed faintly in the flickering overhead light, their magnetic clasp undone. I stared at it, my heart sinking. She wore it nearly every day. It wasn't just a piece of jewelry; it was the last gift Van had given her before he passed. She treasured it, always twisting it absently around her wrist whenever she was deep in thought.

And now, it was here, lying on the cold concrete floor of Artie's garage bays.

My breath hitched as I crouched lower, staring at it like it might somehow explain itself. Why is this here? My pulse quickened, the questions hammering in my mind. Did she come here? Did she see something? Did she—

No. No, there had to be an explanation. Maybe she dropped it earlier, before any of this happened. Maybe it fell off when she was... I don't know, passing through. Except Hattie didn't just "pass through" places. If she was here, it was for a reason.

My fingers hovered over the bracelet, trembling slightly, but I didn't pick it up. Not yet. My gut told me this wasn't something I should disturb.

That's when I heard the voice.

"I wouldn't touch that if I were you."

I froze, every hair on my neck standing on end. Slowly, I straightened and turned, my heart pounding against my ribs.

Caleb stood in the open bay door, his figure framed by the shadows of the night outside. His expression was unreadable, his eyes sharp as they flicked from me to the bracelet on the floor.

"Caleb," I said my voice barely above a whisper.

His gaze lingered on the bracelet, then drifted past me toward the office in the back. "Josie," he said quietly, his tone steady but tense. "What's going on here?"

5 a murder most novel

"CALEB, WHAT ARE you doing here?" I asked, my voice barely above a whisper.

The moment the words left my mouth, I regretted them. Of course, he was here—he was a cop, for crying out loud. But seeing him in the dimly lit garage, his expression unreadable, threw me off balance. And as if my heart wasn't already racing from, you know, the dead body, it decided to skip an extra beat just for Caleb Barlow, who somehow managed to look sharp even in a setting that reeked of motor oil and bad decisions.

His eyes scanned the garage before settling on me. "The better question is, Josie, what are you doing here?" His tone wasn't harsh, but it carried just enough authority to make me feel like I'd been caught sneaking into the cookie jar.

I shifted my feet. "I was looking for Hattie," I said, aiming for matter of fact. "She hired Artie to fix Captain Vantastic, but he botched it so badly one of the tires flew off and landed in the mayor's rose bushes." I attempted a shaky laugh. "She wasn't exactly thrilled about that."

Caleb crossed his arms over his chest, "And you thought she'd come back here to complain? Alone? At night?"

"Well, she's always been a little... direct," I admitted, folding my arms.

"But she was here because Artie *asked* her to come in after hours. I just... had a bad feeling." My gaze dropped to the turquoise bracelet on the floor. "And now, I don't know what to think."

Caleb followed my line of sight, his brow furrowing when he saw it. "That's hers, isn't it?"

I nodded, my throat dry. "She wears it every day. It's the last thing her husband Van gave her before..." My voice faltered as the weight of the situation pressed harder.

Caleb crouched to study the bracelet without touching it. "If it fell here, she was in the garage bays," he said, his voice calm and measured. "She didn't make it to the office." His eyes flicked back to me. "Unless she dropped it in a hurry—or during a struggle."

A struggle. The word hung in the air like smoke, heavy and suffocating. I opened my mouth to argue, but nothing came out.

"Josie," Caleb said gently as he stood, his gaze steady on mine. For a moment, I saw the conflict in his eyes—Caleb, the cop, and Caleb, the man who seemed to care about me. "You said she was furious. If she came here angry, things could've escalated."

"No," I snapped, sharper than I intended. "Hattie's impulsive, but she's not a killer."

"People do stupid things when they're mad," he replied evenly, his tone maddeningly calm. "You know that."

"And I know my sister," I shot back, my arms tightening across my chest. "She wouldn't—she couldn't—do something like this."

He didn't argue, but the flicker of doubt in his eyes stung worse than any words could've. My mind spiraled. Was I defending her blindly? Had I ignored signs something was wrong? Hattie was fiery and unpredictable, sure, but a killer?

No. Not Hattie.

I shook my head like the motion could banish the thought. "She's probably halfway to game night with a bag of tacos," I muttered, more to myself than to Caleb.

He didn't laugh. "When did you see her van?"

"Just before I came in," I said quickly. "But that doesn't mean—"

"Doesn't mean what?" Caleb cut in, his tone firm. "That she didn't come here angry? That she didn't..." He hesitated, his jaw tightening. "Josie, you need to let me do my job."

The words hit harder than I wanted to admit. Caleb was right—but that didn't mean I would sit back and do nothing. "Fine," I muttered, stepping back with more sass than grace. "Do your job, Officer Barlow."

Naturally, my heel caught on a crack in the concrete, and I stumbled. Arms flailing, I grabbed the nearest thing to steady myself—Caleb.

Specifically, Caleb's arm. His very solid, very muscular arm.

For one absurd second, I forgot how to move. My hand was wrapped around what felt like a steel beam wrapped in a Carhartt jacket, and my brain short-circuited. Was he flexing? No, that would be ridiculous. Unless...

"Careful there," Caleb said, his voice tinged with amusement.

I glanced up, cheeks blazing. He was trying so hard to keep a straight face, but I caught the flicker of a smirk tugging at his lips. His eyes sparkled just enough to confirm my suspicion—he knew exactly what I was thinking.

"You good?" he asked, his voice steady and infuriatingly self-assured.

"Yep. Totally fine," I said, yanking my hand back like his arm was on fire. "Thanks for the save."

"No problem." His smirk deepened just slightly, his gaze lingering for a beat before he slid effortlessly back into cop mode. "Maybe watch your step next time."

"Oh, I'll be sure to do that," I shot back, my tone breezy despite my racing heart. "Wouldn't want to damage your very impressive... law enforcement muscles."

His lips twitched, and I could tell he was fighting a grin. "Noted. You should go check on your dog."

I huffed and turned toward the door, desperate for fresh air anyway. "Mocha," I muttered, stepping outside. "It's official. I've lost it."

Mocha's head popped up in the Jeep window, her tail wagging furiously. I opened the door, and she hopped down, prancing around me like I was her favorite person in the world—which I probably was.

"Hey, girl," I murmured, crouching to scratch her ears. She gave a happy little woof, oblivious to all the drama. "You wouldn't believe the mess in there. Or how distracting certain arms can be."

She tilted her head at me, pure judgment in her eyes.

"Don't give me that look," I laughed, rubbing her floppy ears. "It's not like I asked to be rescued by Mr. Broody Biceps."

Mocha wagged her tail, unimpressed with my excuses. I sighed, leaning my forehead against hers. "You're the only one who gets me."

She gave me a reassuring nudge.

As I turned back facing the garage, Caleb was speaking to another officer. His shoulders were tense, but his voice was calm. He caught my eye briefly, his expression softening slightly.

And yep, I was definitely sure he'd been flexing.

"All right, back in you go," I said, opening the door. She hopped in, settling down with a happy sigh as if her work here was done.

The cool night air had cleared my head a little, but the tension crept in again as I walked back to the garage. Caleb was speaking to another officer, his posture all business, his voice low and firm as he gestured toward the scene. I hesitated near the entrance, watching him from a distance. He looked like he was carrying the weight of the entire investigation on his shoulders.

I stepped inside, the hum of the crime scene buzzing around me—officers murmuring, the shuffle of movement, the coroner's arrival. But all I could focus on was the bracelet and what it meant.

Caleb spotted me lingering by the door. He excused himself from the officer and walked toward me, his expression softening—just a fraction.

"Josie," he said, his voice low and steady, his eyes locked on mine.

"Well, um," I stammered, suddenly hyperaware of how close he was standing. He smelled like woodsmoke and cinnamon rolls—warm and unfairly distracting. And now all I could think about was cinnamon rolls. Great. I was flustered, hungry, worried about Hattie, and standing at a crime scene. Really hitting all the life goals tonight.

"I want to hear your theories," Caleb said, his tone professional but gentle, like he was trying to coax something out of me.

The heat rushed to my cheeks. "Theories," I repeated, clearing my throat and taking a tiny step back. Focus, Josie. Dead body, not dreamy deputy.

I pointed toward the wrench, just a few feet from Artie. "The blood's smeared—like the strike came from an angle," I said, mimicking the motion of a swing. "Whoever did this hit him from behind. He didn't see it coming."

Caleb's brows furrowed as he glanced at the wrench, then back to me. "Quick," he murmured, his tone thoughtful. "Whoever did it didn't allow him to fight back."

"Right," I added, my confidence growing as I pushed through the awkward tension. "But look at the prints on the wrench—they're smudged, like someone tried to wipe them clean. Whoever it was panicked after the fact."

Caleb nodded, his lips quirking in the faintest hint of a smile. "You've got a good eye, Josie. Been watching a lot of crime shows?"

"Just years of reading mystery novels," I shot back, grinning despite myself. "That, and knowing people. They're not as complicated as they like to think."

His chuckle was low and brief, but his eyes stayed serious as they flicked back to the scene. "It fits. No defensive wounds. If the hit came from behind... maybe Artie trusted the person."

A chill ran down my spine. "You think it was someone he knew?"

Caleb's jaw tightened. "Maybe. But we can't jump to conclusions."

I nodded, glancing around the garage again, searching for anything that might help. "Those footprints," I said, pointing to a patch of oily marks near one of the cars. "They're too small to be Artie's. Whoever did this stepped in the oil spill."

Caleb followed my gaze, his brows drawing together. "Good catch. We'll need to cast those." He turned back to me, his expression unreadable. "But I've got to ask again—why were you here, Josie? Were you following Hattie, or did you expect to find something?"

My stomach twisted. "I wasn't following her," I said quickly. "I just saw her van leaving and thought something might be wrong. I didn't expect to find..." I gestured toward the scene, swallowing hard. "...this."

Caleb's sharp gaze didn't leave my face, and I felt like he was dissecting every word I wasn't saying. "Did Hattie tell you what her meeting with Artie was about?"

"No," I admitted, my voice quieter now. "She's been stressed, but she wouldn't say why. I didn't think it was... this serious."

His posture shifted, his arms crossing tightly over his chest. After a moment of silence, he spoke again, his voice quieter but firm. "Josie, is there anything you're not telling me? If you know anything, you need to tell me now."

My heart pounded. I wanted to tell him everything, but what was "everything," exactly? "I don't know anything for sure," I said, my voice barely above a whisper. "But I know Hattie didn't do this."

Caleb studied me, the weight of his gaze making it hard to breathe. Finally, he sighed, his expression softening. "I get it. You're worried about her, but you've got to let me do my job. You're too close to this."

"Too close?" I snapped, frustration bubbling up. "Caleb, she's my sister. What do you expect me to do—sit on my hands?"

"I'm not saying that," he replied, his tone gentler now. "But if you get too involved, you could make things harder for both of us. Let me do my job, Josie."

The words hit harder than I wanted to admit. He was right, but that didn't make stepping back any easier. "Fine," I muttered, stepping back with a little too much attitude. "Do your job, Officer Barlow."

After rinsing the bowl and fork from my hastily eaten pasta salad, I sighed heavily. The weight of the day pressed down on me, and I started pacing. Mocha padded beside me, her nails clicking softly on the hardwood—a sound that usually brought comfort but tonight felt like a countdown. The familiar creaks of the old floorboards, the ones I'd grown up hearing, couldn't settle my racing thoughts. The uncertainty hung over me like a wet blanket—stifling and inescapable.

I stopped by the kitchen window, staring out into the stillness of the night. Mocha nudged my leg, sensing my unease. The moon spilled silver light over the fields, a peaceful contrast to the storm in my head. The distant call of a loon echoed, lonely and searching, and it struck me: sometimes, we're only echoes of the people we used to be. Where was Hattie? Why hadn't she come home?

Her explanation about going to the car shop didn't sit right. Something wasn't adding up. I checked my phone again, hoping for a message or a call. Nothing.

As I wandered through the quiet farmhouse, the usual coziness felt hollow without Hattie's presence. The house, once our sanctuary, seemed too big, too quiet. Her fierce loyalty and protective nature had always comforted me, but now they left me wondering—how far might she go?

I thought back to our last real conversation a few weeks ago. She'd been sitting at the kitchen table, twirling Van's old football ring around her finger, staring at it like it held the answers to every question.

"I thought life would look different by now, you know?" she'd said softly.

"What do you mean?" I asked, though I already knew.

"Van and I... we had plans." A faint smile had flickered across her face, then disappeared. "We were supposed to travel the country and visit every state park after Zeke went off to college. The empty nest thing was supposed to be our time, Josie. But now..." Her voice trailed off, and she tucked the ring back into her pocket, her gaze distant.

"You still have time, Hattie," I'd said, trying to sound hopeful. But we both knew it wasn't the same. The day Van died had torn her life apart, and no amount of well-meaning words could piece it back together.

She shrugged then, the impulsive spark in her eyes flickering to life. "Maybe," she said, standing and grabbing her keys. "But now I'm doing things my way."

At the time, I hadn't thought much of it. Hattie had always been a free spirit. But now, as the hours dragged on, that conversation replayed in my mind, louder and sharper. Maybe she wasn't just running from her life but chasing something.

Her decision to take early retirement had baffled me, too. She'd loved her teaching job, adored her students. But then again, she'd loved Van more. Buying that travel van had been her way of keeping their dream alive, even if it was just her now. Still, the abruptness of it all... It didn't feel like her. Or maybe it did, and I'd been too wrapped up in my own life to see it.

Sinking into my favorite thinking chair—the one that spins so I can change my view with a slight shift of weight—I tried to find the clarity that usually came in this spot. But tonight, no amount of turning could untangle my thoughts. The soft cushion cradled me, but even that comfort couldn't quiet the storm in my head.

Mocha curled up at my feet, her warmth a small solace against the chill in the air. My mind kept circling back to Hattie—where was she? What was she thinking? Memories of happier times surfaced—late-night talks, shared secrets, the way she'd always been the rock I could lean on. But now, everything felt uncertain, and the fear that something was terribly wrong clawed at me. Could she be hurt? In trouble? Or... worse?

The clock on the wall ticked away, each second dragging into an eternity. "Oh, Hattie," I whispered to the empty room. "What have you done?"

A sudden chime shattered the silence, and I lunged for my phone. My heart raced—but it was just a group text from our closest friends. They'd heard about Hattie and were headed over. Relief washed over me. At least I wouldn't be alone with my spiraling thoughts.

I set the phone down, still feeling the worry in my chest but grateful for the company. The minutes dragged on as I paced the kitchen, glancing out the window every few seconds for headlights. Mocha whined softly from her spot on the rug, her big eyes tracking my every move.

Finally, the crunch of gravel in the driveway broke the quiet. Rhett's old pickup rumbled to a stop, and I saw Emma and Eloise stepping out with him. The weight of the silence lifted slightly as they approached the house.

The front door creaked open, letting in a rush of cold night air as they entered. The warmth of the house seemed to pull them in, wrapping them in the soft light of the living room.

Emma wasted no time, pulling me into a hug. "We're here," she said firmly, as if sheer determination could fix everything.

Eloise, ever the practical one, placed her hands on her hips and scanned the room. "All right," she declared. "Let's get to work."

6 a recipe for suspense

EMMA STOOD AT THE COUNTER MAKING COFFEE, the soft hum of the brewing pot blending with the scratch of Eloise's pen and the occasional creak of the settling house. Every sound felt magnified in the stillness. Then, I heard the faint crunch of tires on gravel.

Eloise glanced up from her notes, Emma turned toward the window, and Rhett pushed back his chair with a quiet scrape. Even Mocha perked up, her ears twitching as headlights swept through the front windows, casting long beams across the walls. Finally. The rest of the gang was here.

I hurried to the front door, pulling it open just as Holly, Anders, and Nikki stepped out of the car. Max and Stanzi's SUV rumbled to a stop behind them, its headlights slicing through the growing gloom.

Holly wasted no time, wrapping me in a hug the moment she stepped inside. Her usual cheery demeanor was nowhere to be found—her face was tight with worry. "Any word?" she asked softly, though we both knew the answer.

I shook my head, swallowing the lump in my throat. "Nothing."

The kitchen, once warm and familiar, had become our makeshift command center. Eloise remained at the helm, her laptop open, maps spread out across the table. The coffee cups, some still steaming, were forgotten amidst the chaos. The quiet weight of the room pressed down on all of us as the minutes dragged into hours.

We'd already spent the night combing through town and calling every familiar contact: Hattie's old neighbors, the regulars at Novel Grounds, even the police station. Still, nothing. It was as if she'd vanished into thin air, leaving only our unease behind.

Exhaustion clung to us, but no one was ready to give up. Rhett sat slouched at the table, trying to project steady calm, though his fidgeting hands gave him away. Holly paced the length of the kitchen like a restless tiger, her steps growing quicker with every passing minute. Even Eloise, typically a bastion of composure, stared blankly at her untouched coffee.

The front door creaked open again, and Max's familiar voice drifted in, polished with his usual British charm but strained with worry. "Any news?"

"Not yet," I replied, my voice flat and hollow. Anxiety had wrung it dry.

Max headed straight for the coffee pot, his practicality a stark contrast to Stanzi, who was already pacing like Holly, her heels clicking in sharp staccato across the floor. "We need to stay rational," Max said, his words calm but his tense shoulders betraying him. "Hattie's smart. She wouldn't do anything reckless."

"Wouldn't she?" Stanzi muttered, her sharp gaze darting around the room. "She's been off lately. You said so yourself, Josie." She crossed her arms, her tone accusatory, though I knew it wasn't aimed at me.

I sighed, running a hand through my hair. "I know. Something's not right. Even when she was off chasing her next adventure in Captain Vantastic, she always checked in. Like clockwork. I don't know what to do."

Thunder growled in the distance, low and ominous, as the wind rattled the windows. The whole house felt restless, like it, too, could sense Hattie's absence.

Rhett leaned forward, his steady voice breaking through the tension. "Should we call the police again?"

I hesitated, torn between protecting Hattie and the growing fear that something had gone terribly wrong. "Let's give her a bit more time," I said, though even I didn't believe myself. The uncertainty cracked my voice, and Holly shot me a sharp look.

"How much more time, Josie?" Holly's pacing stopped abruptly. She turned toward me, her fingers tugging at a loose thread on her sweater. Her voice wavered. "What if something's really wrong?"

"She's Hattie," Anders cut in, leaning against the counter with his arms crossed, trying too hard to sound nonchalant. "She always lands on her feet. She probably just needed space."

Holly's eyes narrowed, her hands trembling slightly as she stepped toward him. "Space? She wouldn't just disappear without telling us, Anders. Not like this." Her voice cracked, and for a moment, her usually bright, cheerful eyes shone with raw fear. "What if she's in trouble? What if—"

"And what if you're overreacting?" Anders shot back, his jaw tight. "Running around in a panic isn't going to help anyone. Let's wait before jumping to the worst conclusions."

The room went quiet except for the faint rattle of the windows as the wind picked up. Holly stared him down, her mouth opening and closing like she wanted to argue but didn't have the words. Nikki stepped forward, her voice soft but firm. "We've waited long enough, Dad. What if she's hurt? Or worse?"

"Then we'll deal with it," Anders replied, his voice low but resolute. "But until we know for sure, panicking won't change anything."

Holly let out a frustrated breath, turning back to me. "Josie?"

I shook my head, feeling the weight of everyone's eyes on me. "I don't know," I admitted quietly. "I don't know what to think. But this... this isn't like her."

The room fell into an uneasy silence, broken only by the faint ticking of the clock and the occasional creak of the old house. Outside, autumn leaves swirled in the growing storm.

Eloise finally looked up from her notes, her calm voice slicing through the tension. "All right. Enough guessing. Let's focus. Where haven't we checked yet?"

Max nodded, his practical demeanor kicking in. "And who else can we call? Someone has to know something."

Stanzi resumed her pacing, muttering to herself in clipped, frustrated German, while Holly sank into a chair, her head in her hands. Rhett rubbed his temples, looking like he was carrying the weight of all of us.

I glanced at Mocha, curled up in the corner, her dark eyes watching us quietly. She whined softly, and I crouched to scratch behind her ears. "I know, girl," I murmured. "We'll find her."

But even as I said it, the knot of worry in my stomach only tightened.

The sudden crunch of gravel outside snapped all our heads toward the door.

"Wait... is that—?" Holly's voice cut off mid-sentence as I darted to the front door and yanked it open, heart pounding.

Hattie's camper van rolled into the driveway, tires grinding to a stop. Relief surged through me so quickly that it almost knocked me over, but it was tangled with something darker—fear, worry, and the sharp edge of frustration. "She's here!" I shouted over my shoulder, my feet already flying down the porch steps. The screen door slammed behind me, but I barely registered it.

Hattie climbed out of the van, her face pale and exhausted. I hugged her before she could even take two steps, holding on tightly as my emotions crashed over me in waves. Relief. Anger. Fear. She was here. She was safe. But why hadn't she called?

"Where have you been?" I mumbled into her shoulder, the scent of her familiar vanilla shampoo almost undoing me. I pulled back, my hands gripping her arms, and my voice cracked as I continued. "We've been searching all night! The police think you're involved in Artie Blackburn's murder!"

Her eyes widened in shock. "Murder?" Her voice broke on the word. "I don't understand... I wasn't... I didn't..." She trailed off, her face growing paler with every word.

"They found your bracelet at the scene," I said, my voice wobbling despite my effort to stay steady. "I saw your van speeding away. Do you have any idea how scared we've been?"

She blinked rapidly, shaking her head as though trying to clear it. "Josie, I don't... I swear, I don't know what you're talking about. I went to

Artie's, yes, but murder? I didn't even see him!"

Her voice cracked, and the confusion and fear in her eyes twisted the knot in my stomach tighter. "But your bracelet..." I started, my tone softer now, the initial anger draining away.

Hattie's hand flew to her wrist, her face stricken. "It must've fallen off. But Josie, I didn't—" Her voice broke as she grabbed my hands, her grip tight and trembling. "You have to believe me. I didn't do anything. I just wanted to talk some sense into him."

Her desperation was written all over her face, and I couldn't speak for a moment. I wanted to believe her—I did—but everything was so tangled, so unclear. Still, I nodded, my shoulders sagging under the weight of the night. "We'll figure this out," I said quietly. "Together."

She pulled me back into a hug, her arms tight around me like she was holding on for dear life. "I didn't do anything wrong, Josie. You know me."

Inside, the kitchen buzzed with quiet energy as our friends gathered around the table. Eloise scribbled notes on a notepad, Emma brewed yet another pot of coffee, and Rhett leaned against the counter, his brows knit in concentration. The tension in the room was thick, but Hattie's presence shifted it slightly—turning panic into purpose.

"Why were you really at the car shop last night?" I asked, setting a mug of coffee in front of her. "And don't give me the tacos excuse again."

Hattie winced, her fingers curling around the warm mug. "I went to talk to Artie about the money he owed me," she admitted. "But when I got there, no one answered. The whole place was dark." She sighed, rubbing her temples. "I felt stupid standing there, so I just left."

"And your van?" Stanzi pressed, leaning forward from her perch on the arm of the couch. "Josie said she saw it speeding away."

Hattie frowned, shaking her head. "I wasn't speeding. I just... I was frustrated. And embarrassed. I drove out to Pearl Springs and parked by the lake to clear my head."

"Of course, you went to Pearl Springs," Emma chimed in with a weak smile. "Where else would you go when life feels like a dumpster fire?"

Hattie let out a dry laugh. "Cheesy tacos and a good book by the lake—that's how I spent my night. Not exactly the behavior of a criminal mastermind."

The light moment didn't last long. Hattie's expression darkened as she stared into her coffee. "I sent Josie a text to let her know I wouldn't make it to game night," she said, her voice trembling. "But the signal out there is terrible. The message must not have gone through." She looked up at me, guilt etched across her face. "I didn't know until this morning. I'm so sorry, Jo-Jo."

Her words hit like a wave—equal parts relief and frustration. "You should've come home," I said softly, my voice catching. "You scared us."

"I know," she whispered. "I didn't mean to worry you. I just didn't want to tell you I'd gone to see Artie. I knew you'd be mad."

I sighed, pinching the bridge of my nose. "I'm not mad, Hattie. I'm just... I'm glad you're okay."

The room fell into silence, the weight of the situation pressing down on all of us. Mocha barked suddenly, breaking the tension as headlights flashed through the window. My stomach dropped when I saw Caleb's police truck pull into the driveway. His silhouette was stiff and imposing in the dim light, and I knew this wasn't a social visit.

"Caleb's here," Hattie murmured, her hands twisting nervously in her lap. She glanced at me, her fear mirrored in my own eyes.

"I'll handle it," I said, though my voice sounded far more confident than I felt. I stood and opened the door just as Caleb reached the porch. He was drenched in authority, from his mud-specked boots to the set of his jaw.

"Josie. Hattie," he greeted us, his voice low and steady, matching the storm brewing outside. "I need to talk to you." His eyes scanned the room behind us, taking in the worried faces of our friends. "Mind if I come in?"

Hattie nodded, her voice barely above a whisper. "Of course."

As Caleb stepped into the kitchen, the tension in the room sharpened like a blade. He glanced at the coffee mugs scattered across the table, the untouched food, and the maps Eloise had spread out. "I see you've all been busy," he said quietly.

Hattie's grip tightened on her mug. "I didn't do anything, Caleb," she said, her voice breaking. "I swear."

"I know," Caleb replied, his voice softer now. "But I need you to come with me for questioning."

The room erupted into protests. Holly shot to her feet. "Wait, questioning? For what? You can't seriously think she—"

"Caleb, this is ridiculous," Nikki said, stepping forward, her tone sharp with disbelief. "Aunt Hattie wouldn't hurt a fly."

Caleb held up a hand, his expression calm but firm. "She's not under arrest. This is just procedure. But we need to clear some things up."

Hattie's face drained of color, and my stomach flipped. "I'm coming with you," I said, grabbing my keys. My voice shook, but my resolve didn't.

Caleb gave me a long look, then nodded. "Let's go."

As we stepped into the stormy morning, the wind whipped through the driveway, tugging at our clothes and filling the silence with its restless howl. Caleb secured his German Shepherds, Remington and Winchester, in their kennel before opening the truck's back door for Hattie. She climbed in without a word, her shoulders slumped under the weight of suspicion.

I followed them in my Jeep, my friends' worried faces watching from the porch as we pulled away. This was only the beginning—I could feel it in my bones. And no matter how tangled the road ahead became, I wouldn't let Hattie face it alone.

At the station, Caleb's dogs, Remmi and Winnie, trotted to their usual corner and flopped down with their toys like it was just another day at the office. Sheriff Declan Sturdy, an old friend of our father's, greeted us with a nod. His eyes were sharp and observant. His graying hair was cut high and tight, and his neatly trimmed beard added a sense of distinguished authority. His calm demeanor made him seem like an oak tree, rooted and steady. "Josie, you should wait here," he said firmly.

I opened my mouth to protest but stopped when Sheriff Sturdy exchanged a glance with Caleb. After a long pause—and after I gave them my biggest, saddest puppy-dog eyes—Caleb let out a begrudging sigh and gave a nod. "Let her come," he muttered.

Sheriff Sturdy led me to an observation room, where I could see and hear everything as Caleb began questioning Hattie. My heart pounded as I watched, nerves on edge.

"Why were you at Artie's car shop last night, Hattie?" Caleb asked.

Hattie swallowed hard. "I went to talk to him about the money he owed me, but when I got there, no one answered. I felt silly. I thought maybe he stood me up on purpose... You know...trying to make me nervous all day just for me to show up and nobody to be there. I thought he was having a good laugh at my expense. So I left, grabbed tacos, and drove out to the lake to clear my head."

Caleb's expression didn't shift. "You didn't see him at all?"

"No," she said, shaking her head vehemently. "The place was completely dark. I stood there for a few minutes, felt stupid, and left."

He pressed her, searching for inconsistencies, but Hattie's story didn't change. Her frustration started to peek through, her voice growing sharper with each answer, but Caleb didn't let up. Sheriff Sturdy entered with the forensic reports just as I thought I couldn't take another second of it. Caleb scanned the papers, his brow furrowing before he let out a quiet sigh.

"You're free to go," Caleb said, his voice gruff. "But don't leave town."

Relief flooded through me, and I darted into the hallway as Hattie stepped out. I hugged her fiercely, holding her so tightly I could feel her trembling. "I knew you didn't do it," I whispered.

She nodded, her chin trembling as she whispered back, "Thank you for believing in me."

Behind us, I caught Caleb's low voice as he spoke to the Sheriff. "The time of death doesn't line up with when she was there. She couldn't have done it."

I exhaled shakily, but the tension wasn't entirely gone. This wasn't over—not by a long shot. When I turned back to Hattie, her eyes brimmed with unshed tears. "We'll figure this out," I told her firmly.

"Together."

Caleb emerged from the interrogation room, his expression softening when he saw me. His aquamarine eyes locked onto mine, and for a second, the tension of the last few hours melted away, leaving just the two of us in the cramped hallway. He leaned against the doorframe, his posture casual but his gaze intent. "You know," he said, his voice low, the teasing edge unmistakable, "you're not going to sit this one out, are you?"

I felt my breath catch, the smallest wobbly smile tugging at the corners of my mouth. His tone had shifted—gentler and warmer like the entire Hickory Hills Police force, and a murder investigation didn't surround us. "Just a hunch?" I asked, my voice quieter than I intended.

He stepped closer, the doorframe forgotten as he moved into my space. "Yeah," he murmured, his lips twitching, his eyes flicking between mine. "Just a hunch."

It felt like the world narrowed, the fluorescent lights above dimming, the distant hum of conversation fading. His hand brushed against my arm—lightly at first, like he wasn't sure if he was allowed to touch me. But then his fingers lingered, grazing the fabric of my sleeve, his warmth seeping through to my skin.

"Josie," he said, my name coming out softer than I'd ever heard it like he was testing how it sounded in this new way between us.

"Caleb," I whispered, and for a moment, it didn't feel like a name so much as a question.

His lips curved, his usual stoicism completely abandoned as he leaned in just slightly like we were the only two people in the world. His hand slid down my arm, his fingers brushing the inside of my wrist. It was such a small touch, but it sent a spark racing through me, and I didn't think I could step away even if I wanted to.

"Excuse me, am I interrupting something?"

Hattie's voice shattered the moment like glass hitting concrete, and I yanked my hand back like I'd touched a casserole dish straight out of the oven. My cheeks burned as I spun around to face her, only to find Sheriff Sturdy standing right behind her, his arms crossed and his bushy eyebrows raised in clear amusement.

"Oh, don't mind us," Sheriff Sturdy said, his lips twitching as if he were holding back a laugh. "We'll just wait until you two are done playing footsie in the middle of my station."

I flushed, mortified, while Caleb backed up and scowled, but the corners of his mouth betrayed him—just the slightest hint of amusement before he turned back to his work.

By the time Hattie and I stepped into Novel Grounds, the tension from the station had begun to lift—just slightly—much like the rain outside. Inside, Eloise, Rhett, Emma, and Holly were waiting. Relief swept across their faces the moment they saw Hattie. Stanzi and Max were the only ones missing. They had to get to the university to teach their classes.

"Thank goodness you're back!" Holly exclaimed, practically tackling Hattie in a hug. "I was about to draft a missing person poster. You know, the cute kind with a 'last seen angrily storming out' description."

Hattie gave a weak laugh. "Sorry to ruin your creative outlet, Holly."

Eloise stepped forward, her sharp gaze softening only slightly. "We're just glad you're okay," she said, before lowering her voice. "But there's something else... my secret recipes have gone missing."

"Your recipes?" I echoed, my stomach dropping. Hattie's eyebrows shot up, mirroring my shock. Eloise's recipes weren't just recipes—they were practically her babies. They weren't just the heart of her bakery; they were the soul of our café. Losing them wasn't just a financial blow—it was personal.

"When did this happen?" I asked, my voice tight.

"I discovered it this morning," Eloise replied, her tone clipped. "I've already reported it to the police, but let's be honest—they won't find them unless the thief turns them in with a signed confession. We'll have to figure this out ourselves."

Hattie looked between us, guilt flickering across her face. "I can't believe someone would do that. Eloise, I'm so sorry."

"We'll get to the bottom of it," I said firmly. "Whoever did this messed with the wrong café."

Eloise's lips twitched, her steel resolve back in full force. "That's the spirit, Josie. Let's show them you don't steal from Novel Grounds and get away with it."

Before anyone could respond, Hattie's phone buzzed loudly in her pocket, breaking the moment. "Sorry, I need to take this," she said, holding up a hand as she glanced at the screen. She stepped toward the corner of the room, her brow furrowing as she answered. "Hello? This is Hattie."

The rest of us exchanged glances, giving her some space while she paced near the counter. Her tone became more clipped as the conversation continued.

Holly used the opportunity to chime in. "Oh! I overheard something yesterday at the Curl Up and Dye."

Hattie, still mid-call, shot Holly a look over her shoulder. "Holly, please tell me you're not about to solve this mystery with salon gossip," she said, her hand covering the receiver.

"Don't knock the salon grapevine," Holly shot back, grinning. "Two clients were whispering about Dex. One said they saw him skulking around the car shop. The other brought up his... questionable history." She raised her eyebrows meaningfully.

"Dex?" I said, frowning. "Sure, he had that stolen car parts way back in high school, but he's kept his nose clean since then. He's even dating Tiffany, and she works at the shop. It makes sense he'd be around there."

"Maybe," Rhett interjected, his brow furrowing. "But sometimes the people we think we know best are the ones keeping the biggest secrets."

Hattie finished her call and rejoined us, her expression frazzled. "Sorry about that. Where were we?"

Eloise placed a hand on Hattie's shoulder, her tone reassuring but no-nonsense. "Let's not jump to conclusions. We'll ask around, gather some facts. Gossip isn't evidence, but it's a start."

The conversation shifted slightly as Rhett cleared his throat. "Oh, Josie, I almost forgot—I installed that new shelf for your window display this morning."

"You did?" I said, my grin returning. "Thank you, Rhett! Now I can finally put out those painted pumpkins we made."

Holly snorted. "You mean the ones with the sayings that are more terrifying than ghosts? 'No Wi-Fi,' 'Student Loans,' and 'Printer Out of Ink'? Honestly, they're scarier than any horror novel."

Laughter rippled through the room, breaking the tension for a moment. It reminded us why we were all here—this wasn't just about solving a mystery. It was about protecting what we'd built together.

As the moment passed, Hattie sighed and gestured toward her phone. "I hate to leave you all shorthanded, but Captain Vantastic needs urgent repairs. That call was the mechanic—they said they shouldn't have even returned it yesterday. Some mix-up with a new guy. I need to sort it out."

"Go," I said, waving her off. "We'll hold the fort here."

Hattie smiled, relieved. "Thanks, Josie. I'll take Mocha with me for some company."

"Mocha's always happy to hang out with you," I said, grinning. "Just don't let her eat any tacos if you swing by the taco truck."

As Hattie left to deal with her van, I turned back to Eloise, Holly, Rhett, and Emma. The lighthearted moment was already fading, replaced by the urgency of finding those recipes.

"We need to start with the obvious," I said. "FMR Foods was practically drooling over Eloise's recipes last week. Maybe they wanted them badly enough to steal."

Eloise nodded, her sharp eyes narrowing. "You should pay them a visit."

"Rhett, Emma, you're with me," I said. "Holly, can you stick with Eloise? She could use some backup at the bakery."

Holly gave a mock salute. "You got it, boss. Plus, I can keep Eloise from overworking herself."

"I heard that," Eloise muttered, already grabbing her coat. "And good luck with that."

We all exchanged smiles, but the gravity of the situation wasn't lost on anyone. The missing recipes weren't just a small theft—they were the thread tying everything together.

"Let's move," Rhett said, clapping me on the shoulder. "The sooner we start, the sooner we find some answers."

As we headed out into the crisp autumn air, my thoughts churned. Eloise's recipes and Artie's death felt connected, but the puzzle pieces weren't clicking into place. Yet.

One thing was certain: someone in this town was hiding something. And they were about to learn that Novel Grounds—and its fiercely loyal crew—didn't back down from a fight.

Two hours later, Rhett, Emma, and I stepped out of the car and stared up at FMR Foods' towering office building. The sleek, modern glass-and-chrome exterior gleamed in the sunlight, its sharp edges a stark contrast to Novel Grounds' warm, rustic charm.

"Well," Rhett said, adjusting his jacket, "this doesn't scream 'welcome,' does it?"

Emma's brow quirked. "It screams something, but I wouldn't call it friendly."

Inside, the reception area was as sterile as I'd feared. The sharp scent of Pine-Sol mingled with the faint hum of industrial air conditioning. A receptionist ushered us into a polished conference room, her smile polite but distant, like she'd mastered the art of looking friendly without actually meaning it.

Minutes later, a tall woman in a crisp suit strode in, her heels clicking against the glossy floor with military precision. Her smile was thin, and her handshake was colder than the office temperature. "Cassandra Drake," she said, her tone clipped. "I'm the Operations Manager. What can I do for you?"

I matched her handshake, trying to inject just the right balance of politeness and firmness. "Josie McCarthy. This is Rhett and Emma King. We're here to discuss Eloise Jackson's recipes—the ones you were so eager to buy but mysteriously vanished."

Cassandra's smile wavered just a hair before snapping back into place. "I was under the impression our Chief Marketing Officer had already secured the recipes." Her tone sharpened. "And now they're... missing?"

"Stolen," I corrected, leaning forward slightly. "Eloise refused to sell, and now they've disappeared. That's quite the coincidence, don't you think?"

Cassandra's mask slipped for a moment—just enough for a flicker of annoyance to cross her face. "I don't appreciate what you're implying," she said, her voice as frosty as her handshake. "FMR Foods doesn't engage in theft. We operate with integrity."

"An agreement Eloise never made," Rhett interjected, his arms crossed. "Sounds like someone got ahead of themselves."

Cassandra's jaw tightened. "Our company vets every contract meticulously. If the recipes were stolen, perhaps Eloise is holding out with this convenient 'theft' story."

"Why would she do that?" I asked, raising an eyebrow. "She's not exactly the type to fake a robbery."

"Why *does* FMR Foods need a few small-town recipes?" Emma chimed in, her voice quiet but cutting. "Surely you can whip up your own muffins without all this drama."

Cassandra's composure cracked for just a second before she smoothed it over. "Eloise's recipes represent a strong regional brand. Local flavors resonate with customers. We saw potential in incorporating them into our portfolio."

"Potential enough to steal?" Emma shot back, her words hanging in the air like a dare.

Cassandra's eyes narrowed, her polished demeanor slipping. "We. Don't. Steal," she said slowly, each word laced with ice. But her clipped tone only made her denial sound less convincing.

My phone buzzed, cutting through the tension. I ignored it at first, but then Rhett and Emma's phones started buzzing too. A chorus of alerts. My stomach sank.

"I'll take this," I said, stepping away from the table and glancing at my screen. The knot in my stomach tightened as I answered. Something else was happening—something that could complicate everything.

As I stepped into the hallway, Cassandra's cold gaze followed me through the glass wall of the conference room. Whatever was unfolding, she wasn't just a bystander. And I had a sinking feeling that Eloise's recipes were just one piece of a much larger, messier puzzle.

7 lattes, lies, & lockups

HOLLY'S NAME FLASHED ACROSS MY SCREEN, the urgent buzz making my stomach twist. "Excuse me," I said to Cassandra, stepping into the hallway to answer. "Holly, what's wrong?"

"Caleb took Eloise!" Holly's voice was high-pitched and trembling. "He stormed in here like he was on some cop show. We were right in the middle of baking muffins, Josie! He's saying she killed Artie. They're locking her up—with bars and everything! Eloise tried to explain, but Caleb wasn't listening. He had that determined, 'I know everything' look—you know the one."

I stopped pacing, gripping the phone tighter. "What? Why would he think Eloise—of all people—had anything to do with Artie's murder?"

"They found her recipe box at the scene," Holly blurted. "They think Artie stole her muffin recipes and that she snapped when she found out. Josie, this is insane. Eloise didn't do anything!"

I swallowed hard. Eloise. Cool, collected Eloise, a retired New York detective who'd probably seen more crime scenes than Caleb had dreamed of, now sitting in a cell? The thought made my chest tighten.

"Wait, back up," I said, forcing myself to think clearly. "You said Artie was trying to sell her recipes? To who?"

"That big corporation—FMR Foods!" Holly practically shouted. "Apparently, he was pretending to be Eloise's son. That's how he was going to sell them! And now Caleb thinks Eloise killed him to stop him."

The air rushed out of me like I'd been punched. This wasn't just about stolen recipes. This was a full-blown conspiracy with Eloise caught in the middle.

"It gets worse," Holly added, her voice trembling. "They found strands of her hair. Caleb's convinced she did it."

My thoughts spun like a tornado. "Hair? Holly, she bakes for a living and then delivers orders. Her hair's probably in half the homes and businesses in Hickory Hills! That doesn't prove anything."

"Tell him that," Holly snapped. "He wouldn't listen to me! Josie, you have to come. Now."

"I'm on my way," I said, my voice steadier than I felt. "Stay calm. We'll figure this out."

Hanging up, I stood frozen, my hand trembling against the phone. Eloise—our Eloise—was locked up because of some ridiculous recipe box. My mind raced, connecting dots that didn't quite form a picture yet.

Cassandra's cool gaze flicked toward me when I reentered the conference room. "Everything okay?" she asked, her voice laced with artificial concern.

"Not really," I said, gathering my bag and nodding toward Rhett and Emma. "We have an urgent matter to attend to. Thank you for your time."

Cassandra's smile barely moved, but her eyes narrowed as if she was calculating something. "I hope everything works out," she said smoothly, though her voice's tenseness said otherwise.

As we left, I glanced back. Cassandra was on her phone, her face twisted in what looked like anger—or frustration. Something about it didn't sit right with me, but I didn't have time to dwell on it now.

The drive back to Hickory Hills was torturous. Traffic crawled, and every red light felt like a personal attack. Rhett's jaw was clenched as he maneuvered into a faster lane, narrowly avoiding a horn-happy sedan.

"First, they harassed my sister, and now they arrest Eloise?" I fumed, the frustration boiling over. "What's next? Are they going to accuse Mocha of grand theft kibble?"

"Deep breaths, Josie," Emma said, her voice calm but edged with worry. "We'll figure this out. We always do."

I let out a sharp exhale. "I know. But this feels...like everything's tangled together—Artie, the recipes, FMR Foods—but we're still missing something."

Rhett's knuckles tightened on the steering wheel. "Well, then we untangle it. One piece at a time."

When we pulled into the police station, my determination had hardened into steel. Eloise wasn't just a victim of circumstance. Someone had gone to great lengths to frame her, and I wasn't about to let them get away with it.

The receptionist behind the desk blinked up at me as I marched in. "I need to see Eloise Jackson," I said firmly.

The woman hesitated, clearly uneasy. "I'm not sure Sheriff Sturdy will allow—"

"Just ask him," I interrupted, my tone sharper than intended. "Please."

She disappeared through the frosted glass doors, leaving us in the silent, too-bright waiting area. The minutes ticked by, each one stretching unbearably long. My mind churned with questions, none of them with answers.

What was Eloise thinking right now? Was she calm, mentally plotting her defense? Or did she feel the sting of betrayal from Caleb, the very person who should know better? Either way, one thing was certain: this wasn't over. Not even close.

Ten minutes later, Caleb emerged from the back, his expression a mix of exasperation and—was that concern? His eyes landed on me, narrowing slightly. "Josie," he said, his tone hovering between irritated and resigned. "What are you doing here... again?"

I crossed my arms. "Oh, just here to bake muffins and discuss small-town gossip. What do you think I'm doing, Caleb? I'm here for Eloise."

He let out a long-suffering sigh, running a hand through his hair in that way he did when he was trying to keep his cool. "You always have to stick your nose in, don't you?"

"Only when someone I care about is in trouble," I shot back, giving him my most unbothered smile. "Someone has to step up when the local law enforcement jumps to conclusions."

Caleb's jaw tightened, but I caught the faintest twitch at the corner of his mouth. "Fine," he muttered. "You can see her, but Rhett and Emma stay here."

I winked at Rhett and Emma, leaning in just enough to whisper loudly, "Guess he doesn't trust us not to meddle."

Rhett smirked, and Emma stifled a giggle. Caleb, predictably, sighed again and gestured for me to follow him.

When I stepped into the small holding cell, Eloise sat calmly as if waiting for tea to steep. She glanced up and gave me a warm smile.

"Josie," she said, her voice steady and unshaken, "I had a feeling you'd show up."

I plopped into the chair across from her, my mind buzzing with a million questions. "Eloise, what in the world is going on? Why do they think you had anything to do with Artie's murder?"

Eloise folded her hands, her calm demeanor never faltering. "They found my recipe box and some strands of my hair at the crime scene. It's bad, Josie. I'll give them that—it looks bad. But you and I both know I'd never—"

"Of course, you wouldn't!" I interrupted, throwing up my hands. "First, Hattie, and now you? What's next? Are they going to arrest me? Maybe, Rhett? No, wait, probably, Stanzi during one of her lectures at the university?"

Her lips quirked into a small smile. "I appreciate your outrage, but this is where we need to keep level heads. Remember what I always taught you: observation and critical thinking. Someone's framing me."

"Obviously," I said, leaning forward, my voice dropping to a whisper. "And I'm not letting them get away with it."

"Good," Eloise said, her tone steady and full of that quiet, unshakable confidence that had seen her through decades as a New York detective. "Now, stay sharp. Listen to what people say and what they don't say. And Josie? Don't get distracted."

I rolled my eyes. "Oh, please. When have I ever gotten distracted?"

Eloise raised a single brow.

"Okay, fine," I muttered, leaning back. "But you're lucky I haven't called the mayor to organize a full-scale protest yet."

"I'm counting on you for brains, not theatrics," she replied dryly, then laughed.

As I stood to leave, Caleb was waiting by the door, arms crossed, his frown firmly in place. "Everything okay?" he asked, his voice softer now, though still gruff.

"It will be when Eloise is out of here," I shot back, brushing past him. "Any updates on how you're going to fix that?"

Caleb's lips pressed into a thin line, but after a moment, he sighed. "I'll let Rhett and Emma see her, too. Maybe it'll help."

I blinked, surprised by the gesture. "That's... actually thoughtful of you. Thanks."

"Don't let it go to your head," he muttered, but his gaze softened ever so slightly before he left the waiting area.

I regrouped with Rhett and Emma, motioning them toward the holding cell. "Your turn," I said, nudging Rhett. "Be nice, and no bringing up conspiracy theories."

Rhett grinned. "Don't worry. I'll save those for you."

As they headed back to see Eloise, I sat down in the lobby and rested my head against the wall. My exhaustion was catching up with me, but I couldn't stop replaying everything we knew. The missing recipes. Artie's connection to FMR Foods. And now Eloise's arrest. The pieces didn't fit—yet—but they would. They had to.

Minutes later, Rhett and Emma reemerged, their expressions a mix of frustration and determination. Rhett clapped me on the shoulder. "Eloise is tough, but this isn't making sense."

"No kidding," I said, standing up and grabbing my bag. "But I'm not waiting for the answers to come to us. Let's go."

We left the station, the night air crisp and biting against my skin. Just as I pulled my jacket tighter around me, Caleb appeared in front of us, carrying a takeout bag in one hand and his car keys in the other. He had his phone pressed to his ear, his brow furrowed.

"Eloise has to eat," he said gruffly into the phone. His tone was all business, but an undercurrent of quiet concern made me pause mid-step.

Rhett leaned toward me, whispering, "Well, that's unexpected. Who knew Caleb was the nurturing type?"

I rolled my eyes, but a tiny smile tugged at my lips. "He's probably just worried she'll stage a jailhouse hunger strike," I quipped, though part of me recognized there was more to it. Caleb wasn't exactly a "show-your-feelings" kind of guy, but it was impossible to miss when he cared.

Caleb lowered the phone, catching me staring. "What?" he asked, his tone sharp, but his expression softened slightly. "She needs food if she's gonna keep her head straight."

Rhett snorted, leaning closer to me. "Guess he's not all grumpy lawman."

I ignored him, narrowing my eyes at Caleb. "So, you do have a soft side. Should I make note of this moment? Maybe get it engraved on a plaque?"

Caleb gave me a long, steady look—the kind that said you're pushing it, McCarthy—before he sighed. "Don't start, Josie."

But I caught the faintest hint of a smile as he turned and disappeared back inside.

Rhett grinned at me. "Okay, you have to admit, that was kind of sweet. Grumpy and soft—like a hedgehog."

"A hedgehog that puts my friends in holding cells," I muttered, though I couldn't help the tiny smile tugging at the corners of my mouth.

"Come on, let's grab food before you start roasting Caleb for having a heart," Emma said.

Gayle appeared at our table, her presence as comforting as the smell of fresh coffee. She tucked a stray gray curl back into her messy bun, her hazel eyes sparkling despite the late hour.

"Y'all look like you've been run over by a pick-up truck," she said, resting a hand on her hip. "What's going on?"

"It's a long story, Gayle," I sighed, leaning back in the booth. "Let's just say the last 24 hours have been... eventful."

Gayle's warm gaze softened as she set a plate of complimentary biscuits on the table. "Well, whatever it is, you'll get through it. You McCarthy girls are tougher than nails."

Rhett grinned, snagging a biscuit. "See, Josie? Even Gayle knows you're stubborn."

I gave him a side-eye glare. "Stubborn and tough are not the same thing, Rhett."

Gayle chuckled, but her face turned serious as she leaned in slightly. "If there's anything I can do, just holler. And don't forget—sometimes a slice of cake makes the world seem less messy."

Her words brought a flicker of comfort, but before I could respond, my phone buzzed. I glanced at the screen and froze.

"The alarm at Novel Grounds," I muttered, already sliding out of the booth.

"What now?" Emma groaned, grabbing her coat as Rhett tossed some cash on the table.

Gayle's expression turned worried. "Y'all be careful now, you hear? Come back if you need anything."

We hurried out into the night, my pulse hammering as we rounded the corner toward the café. As we approached, two figures bolted from the shadows, their shapes illuminated briefly by the dim streetlight.

"Is that... Tiffany and Dex?" Rhett squinted, adjusting his glasses.

"It has to be," I said through clenched teeth, my frustration threatening to boil over. "What are they up to now?"

The coffee shop door swung slightly in the night breeze, its lock clearly jimmied. My stomach dropped as we stepped inside.

The scene was chaos. Books littered the floor like confetti. A shelf had been knocked over, its contents strewn everywhere, and the bitter tang of spilled espresso clung to the air. My sanctuary—my café—looked like a crime scene.

I froze, my breath catching in my throat. Emma moved beside me, carefully picking up a book that had been flung to the ground.

"Why would they do this?" she asked softly, her voice tinged with bewilderment.

My legs felt like lead, and I couldn't speak. The stress, fear, and exhaustion from the last day finally broke through, and tears spilled down my cheeks.

"Josie," Emma said gently, wrapping an arm around my shoulders.

"We'll fix this. Together. Like we always do."

Rhett crouched down, his voice calm and steady. "This just proves we're on the right track. Someone's scared we'll figure it out."

I wiped at my face, my anger overtaking the sadness. "Scared enough to try to intimidate us. But why target me? Why the café?"

Emma frowned, glancing at the mess around us. "Tiffany's hated Hattie for years. Maybe she thinks this is some kind of petty revenge. But Dex? What's his angle?"

"Money, probably," Rhett said with a shrug. "He's always been a follower. Tiffany pulls the strings, and he goes along for the ride."

I wanted to believe it was that simple, but I knew it wasn't.

Something white caught my eye beneath a toppled chair. Kneeling down, I reached for it, my fingers trembling as I lifted it into the light.

A check.

It was made out to Hattie. The amount was for the exact cost of repairing her camper van. And the dark stains on the corner? Blood. Artie's blood.

My chest tightened as I held it up, the weight of what it meant crashing down on me. "They're framing us," I whispered, my voice shaking. "This... this is what they're going to use."

Emma's hand tightened on my arm, her jaw clenching. "Then we're going to fight back."

Rhett's voice was low but steady. "You're right. This isn't just about recipes or old grudges anymore. Someone's trying to pin this on your family, Josie. And we're not going to let them get away with it."

I nodded, determination locking into place. Whoever was behind this—Tiffany, Dex, or someone higher up—had underestimated us. That was their first mistake. And I was going to make sure it was their last.

"We fight back," I said, my voice firmer than I felt. "We gather evidence, clear Hattie's name, and expose those two for the criminals they are. This ends now."

Rhett gave a sharp nod, his jaw set. "We're with you, Josie. All the way."

Just then, the piercing wail of police sirens cut through the night, growing louder as they approached. Within moments, flashing blue and red lights painted the street, and a patrol car screeched to a halt in front of the café. Caleb stepped out first, his usual stoic expression shadowed with concern? Frustration? Maybe both?

He scanned the mess inside the café through the open door before his gaze landed on me. "Josie." His voice carried that familiar gruffness. "What happened here?"

I swallowed hard, trying to steady myself as I held out the check like it was radioactive. "The alarm went off, and Tiffany and Dex were running away when we got here. They trashed the place... and left this." My voice cracked slightly as I pointed to the check, its corner stained with Artie's blood.

Caleb took the check, his brows knitting together as he inspected it. His frown deepened, his grip tightening just slightly. "We'll figure this out," he said, his tone firm but calm. "But, Josie, you need to let us handle it from here."

"Handle it?" I shot back, the weight of the last 24 hours cracking my composure. "First my sister, now Eloise, and now this! I can't just stand by while they try to destroy our lives, Caleb."

He exhaled heavily, running a hand through his hair. "I get it, but you charging into every scene isn't helping. If you push too hard, you'll just make things worse—for you and Hattie."

The words stung, but they didn't knock the fight out of me. "So, what? I just sit at home and knit while my sister's life is falling to pieces. Not a chance."

He blinked and quietly looked at me, exasperation etched across his face. "Just... trust me on this, Josie. We'll handle it."

I hesitated, my heart pounding as I looked into his eyes. There was no denying that he was trying—trying to do his job, trying to protect me, trying not to let his emotions get in the way. But I wasn't ready to let go of the reins just yet.

"We'll keep digging," I said, refusing to back down. "We won't let them get away with this."

Rhett and Emma nodded, their determination matching mine. Caleb sighed, clearly sensing he wouldn't win this round, but he didn't argue further. Instead, he motioned to his officers to start processing the scene.

"Come on," Rhett said, gently nudging my arm. "Let's get some air."

Outside, the cool night wrapped around us, biting at my skin. I leaned against the brick exterior of the café, watching as the flashing lights cast long, dancing shadows across the sidewalk. A small crowd had already gathered, their murmured speculations buzzing like flies.

"Josie, what happened?" Mrs. Huxley, the town's unofficial gossip, bustled toward me, her glasses perched precariously on the tip of her nose. "We saw the police cars! Is everything all right?"

I smiled politely, "Just some trouble at the café, Mrs. Huxley. Nothing we can't handle."

"Well, I do hope you're not caught up in anything scandalous," she said, her tone dripping with faux concern. "You know how quickly news travels in Hickory Hills."

"Right," I said, my smile tightening. "Wouldn't want to give you too much to talk about."

Rhett snorted behind me, muttering under his breath, "Too late for that."

I ignored him, glancing back toward the café. Through the window, I caught a glimpse of Caleb. He was standing near one of the overturned shelves, barking orders to his team. But as his voice quieted, his shoulders slumped just slightly.

For the first time, I noticed something different about him. Caleb wasn't just gruff and efficient tonight. There was a weight to him, a vulnerability in how he rubbed the back of his neck or glanced toward the door as if he was carrying more than just the responsibility of the case.

"He looks stressed," Emma said quietly, following my gaze. "Do you think he's okay?"

I shrugged, my emotions too tangled to untangle. "He's probably just frustrated. I mean, I did kind of tell him off... again."

Rhett chuckled, crossing his arms. "I think he secretly likes it when you give him a hard time."

I shot him a glare, but my cheeks warmed. "Don't be ridiculous."

Inside, Caleb suddenly turned, catching me watching him through the glass. For a split second, our eyes locked. His usual stoicism cracked, and there it was again—that flicker of something softer. He quickly turned back to the task at hand, but the moment lingered in the pit of my stomach.

"What do we do now?" Emma asked, breaking the silence.

I straightened, brushing the stray hair from my face. "We don't wait around for someone else to fix this mess. We dig deeper—Tiffany, Dex,

FMR Foods... there's more going on here, and I'm not stopping until we figure it out."

"Good," Rhett said with a grin. "Because I'm not done annoying Tiffany yet."

That earned a laugh from Emma, who nodded in agreement. "If we're going to be a thorn in their side, let's make it count."

As the crowd began to thin and the flashing lights dimmed, I let their humor buoy me. The fight was far from over, but at least I wasn't in it alone. And whoever was trying to tear us down? They didn't know what they were up against.

8 apples, accusations & a ghost

THE SCENT OF FRESHLY BREWED COFFEE mingled with the sugary warmth of Willa Mae's pies as I made my way back to Novel Grounds. I was balancing a box of to-go coffees and a stack of golden-brown pies in my arms. I was trying not to spill anything while dodging sidewalk cracks. Small-town life had its perks, but level pavement wasn't one of them.

While waiting for my order earlier, I'd caught snippets of gossip about Tiffany and Dex heading out to the apple orchard. That little tidbit had nestled itself into my brain. What were they doing out there? Knowing those two, their plans likely didn't involve apple-picking and homemade donuts.

As I approached the café, I spotted Caleb leaning casually against the doorframe, his sharp eyes scanning the street. The morning sunlight caught the faint stubble on his jaw, and for a split second, I forgot how annoyed I'd been with him. He looked... tired. But not just tired. Worn down, maybe. The kind of tired that made me feel a pang of sympathy.

"Hey," he said, his gruff voice softening as I got closer. His gaze flicked to the pies and coffees in my arms, and a flicker of amusement tugged at the corner of his mouth. "You bring breakfast for the whole town, or is that just for Mocha?"

"Strictly for humans," I shot back, my lips twitching into a small smile. "Mocha's on pie probation."

"Right," he said, nodding solemnly. "She's still working off that pumpkin pie incident from last year."

I laughed despite myself. "Exactly."

His eyes lingered on mine for a beat too long, a shadow of concern crossing his face. "How are you holding up?"

I shrugged, doing my best to sound breezy. "Oh, I've had worse days."

He tilted his head, clearly not buying it. "Yeah, you're fine—except for the break-in, the framing, the stress of clearing Hattie's name, and Eloise sitting in a jail cell. Other than that, peachy, right?"

"You forgot the coffee shortage," I deadpanned, holding up the to-go box. "But don't worry—I've fixed it."

His lips twitched, but instead of firing back, his expression softened again. "Look, Josie... just be careful, okay? Trouble seems to follow you around."

I raised an eyebrow, my smile turning sly. "Trouble? Or a certain police officer?"

"Fair point," he said, his voice dropping just enough to make my heart skip. "But seriously. Keep your head on straight."

The moment lingered, his quiet concern throwing me off balance. But before I could say something I might regret—Caleb nodded. "Which brings me to an update." He straightened, his tone shifting into full-on detective mode. "You remember those footprints you pointed out at the garage?"

"Of course," I said, my curiosity immediately piqued. "What did you find?"

"We cast them," he said, lowering his voice as he stepped closer. "They belong to a woman. Size seven and a half. Cross-training sneakers—brand new, barely any wear. Same prints we found outside Novel Grounds last night."

My pulse quickened. "It's Tiffany," I said firmly, the pieces clicking together in my mind. "I knew it. She works at the garage, and I saw her running from my café with Dex. This proves she's involved."

Caleb held up a hand, his expression calm but serious. "Hold on, Josie. Yes, she works at Artie's garage, so her prints being there doesn't automatically mean guilt—it's her workplace. Of course, her footprints would be there."

"But what about the café?" I countered, frustration bubbling up. "She doesn't work here, and Rhett, Emma, and I saw her fleeing the scene."

He sighed, rubbing the back of his neck. "Look, I've investigated Tiffany and Dex. I don't think they're the ones who trashed Novel Grounds."

"What?" I stared at him, incredulous. "How can you say that? We literally saw them running away!"

"I know," he said patiently. "And I'm not saying they're innocent saints, Josie. But Tiffany comes into Novel Grounds regularly—your coffee shop is practically her second office. Those prints could've been left at any time, even days before the break-in."

"But we saw her!" I insisted, pacing now. "She was there, Caleb. Why else would she be running?"

"She could've been running because she didn't want to explain why she was out late with Dex," Caleb said, his voice steady, trying to temper my frustration. "We don't know the full story yet. That's why we have to be careful."

I stopped pacing, turning to him. "So you're saying she's not a suspect?"

"I didn't say that," he clarified, meeting my eyes. "I'm saying the footprints alone don't prove anything. We have to tread carefully—no pun intended. But yes, you should be wary of Tiffany and Dex. They're hiding something, that much is obvious. I just don't think they're the ones who broke into your café. Not yet, anyway."

I crossed my arms, trying to keep my annoyance in check. "So what's your theory?"

"I think Tiffany and Dex are wrapped up in something bigger," he said, his tone thoughtful. "Whether it's tied to Artie's murder or the sabotage at Novel Grounds, I can't say for sure yet. But there's a lot we don't know about their relationship—what they're up to, why they're working together. That's what I'm trying to figure out."

I sighed, my frustration simmering down into reluctant agreement. "So what do we do?"

Caleb's lips twitched in a faint smile. "You let me handle Tiffany and Dex. And you, Josie, focus on staying out of trouble."

I rolled my eyes, but his quiet concern softened me. "Fine. But if I find something that proves Tiffany's guilt, you'll hear about it first."

"Deal," he said, his voice lighter now. "But until then, don't go charging after her. I'd like to keep you in one piece."

I smirked, the tension easing just a little. "Don't worry, Caleb. I'll leave the reckless charging to you."

He chuckled softly, stepping back. "Fair enough. I'll keep you posted."

With that, Caleb turned and walked down the street, leaving me standing there with my box of coffee and pies—and the growing certainty that Tiffany was running out of places to hide.

Inside the Novel Grounds, the buzz of activity hit me like a warm hug. My people—Hattie, Rhett, Emma, Holly, Stanzi, Max, and a handful of my part-time college staff—were hard at work putting Novel Grounds back together. Mocha peeked out from the back office, her nose twitching at the scent of pie and muffins.

"All right, team," I called out, setting the food on the counter. "Breakfast is served! And no, Mocha, I'm still talking to the humans. You're on a strict no-pie diet."

"Thank goodness," Hattie said, swooping in to grab a coffee. "I need caffeine before I can face the horror of reshelving this disaster."

"You're welcome," I said with a smirk. "Pie for breakfast is the secret to high morale. That, and the promise of no more flying tires."

Hattie groaned but grinned. "Let it go, Josie. I already apologized for taking out the mayor's roses."

"Pretty sure the roses have forgiven you," Rhett chimed in. "But Hank Junior at the hardware store? Still not over the scratches."

"And let's not forget the mayor," Holly added, laughing. "Saw him this morning talking to those roses. Pretty sure he got misty-eyed."

The laughter lightened the room, even as the cleanup continued. Claire Greene, my favorite frenemy, was wiping down counters like she was in charge. It was the most I'd ever seen her sweat. But of course, Claire wouldn't be Claire if she didn't have some gossip to share.

"Did you hear about Tiffany and Dex?" Claire asked, her voice low enough to seem discreet but loud enough for everyone to hear.

I perked up, walking over with a coffee in hand. "What about them?"

Claire's lips curved into a knowing smile. She paused, dragging out the moment like she was delivering breaking news on live TV. "Saw them heading out to the apple orchard this morning. No idea what they're up to, but let's just say they didn't look like they were going for cider and hayrides."

Holly raised an eyebrow. "You think they're plotting something?"

Claire shrugged dramatically, clearly enjoying the attention. "Who knows? But considering everything that's happened, I wouldn't put it past them."

I exchanged a look with Hattie, who rolled her eyes but said nothing. Tiffany and Dex at Buck's Orchard wasn't exactly breaking news—half the town went there this time of year for apples, cider, and those irresistible donuts. But the way Claire said it, paired with the memory of Tiffany sneaking around eavesdropping just the other day, made me think that keeping tabs on those two wasn't the worst idea.

For now, though, there were books to reshelve, shelves to repair, and pies to eat. The bigger mysteries would have to wait—at least until the coffee kicked in.

The door chimed again, and in came more familiar faces. Pretty soon, it felt like half of Hickory Hills had descended on Novel Grounds, turning the café into a full-blown community cleanup effort. My heart warmed, even as my anxiety quietly simmered. Because if there's one thing small towns do well, it's rallying together—and spreading gossip at an alarming speed.

Old Hank from the hardware store, his sons, and grandkids showed up and offered to fix anything that might've been damaged. Gayle Murphy from the diner brought her famous sheet cakes, pineapple upside-down, and marble because, of course, she did. And Granny Clara Belle "Smokin' Belle" Thompson? She rolled in with enough BBQ sandwiches to feed the entire county. Even Roy McCoy from the general store dropped off extra cleaning supplies while Mrs. Huxley from Rustic Roost Antiques hovered nearby, catching every word like she was cataloging it for her next newsletter.

"Josie, honey, how's it all going? We're all just devastated about what happened," Mrs. Huxley cooed, patting my hand like I'd lost a beloved pet.

"I'm managing," I said with a polite smile that probably looked more like a grimace. What was I supposed to say? Oh, you know, just another day where someone tries to destroy my livelihood. No biggie!

Roy leaned in conspiratorially as he swept debris with Hank's sons. "You know," he said in a low voice like we were in some gritty detective movie, "I saw a couple of suspicious folks hanging around here last night. Could've sworn one of 'em looked like Dex."

"That boy's always been trouble," Connie Fontaine chimed in, her tone as sharp as one of her cutting remarks in the town's amateur theater productions.

Great. Exactly the calming words I needed to hear.

I kept my expression neutral, focusing on sweeping the same spot on the floor. "I'll keep that in mind."

But Connie wasn't done. Oh no. With her dramatic instincts in full swing, she leaned in closer, her voice dropping to a stage whisper. "Of course, it wasn't just Dex and Tiffany. It was Julius's ghost."

I blinked, mid-sweep. "Julius's ghost?"

Here we go.

"Oh, don't act like you haven't heard the story, dear," Connie teased, wagging a finger at me like I'd skipped an important piece of small-town folklore. "The tragic tale of Julius Montgomery—the Confederate soldier and his sweetheart, Miss Evangeline. Everyone knows his spirit still haunts the old silo north of town."

Roy rolled his eyes so hard I thought he might sprain something. "Oh, come on, Connie. A ghost? Really?"

Connie turned to him with a look that could have shriveled a lesser man. "Roy, darling, if you're going to heckle me, at least have the decency to do it after the story."

"For Pete's sake," Roy muttered, but he didn't move an inch—because, let's face it, even Roy couldn't resist the pull of Connie in full storytelling mode.

Sam leaned in, his curiosity winning out. "Go on, Connie. Don't leave us hanging."

Connie's eyes sparkled with triumph as she stepped forward, lifting her chin like the leading lady in a Tennessee Williams play. She paused dramatically, letting the tension stretch, her silver bangles chiming softly as she waved her hands like a conductor about to cue the orchestra. Her voice dipped into a low, velvety drawl, the kind that made you forget she was standing in a coffee shop-slash-bookstore and not commanding the spotlight at the community theater.

"Julius Montgomery," she began, savoring every syllable, "was a dashing Confederate soldier with eyes like storm clouds and a smile that could melt butter. Evangeline, the belle of Hickory Hills, was his one true love. They were set to marry, but—" Connie paused dramatically, letting the weight of it sink in, "—the war swept Julius away before they could exchange vows. Evangeline waited for him, of course, because that's what a proper southern lady does."

She clasped her hands together and sighed like a character in a tragic love ballad. I had to bite back a laugh—Connie really could make anything sound like a gothic masterpiece. I mean, she could make a grocery list sound like an Edgar Allan Poe poem if she wanted to. The way she held the room was pure theater.

"And then what happened?" Hannah, one of the student workers, asked from the back, clearly drawn in despite herself.

"Well," Connie said, her eyes wide with the gravity of the tale, "Julius came back. But not the way anyone expected. They say he died on the battlefield, somewhere near Boonville, but his spirit returned, wandering through the fields where he and Evangeline used to meet. One night, she saw him by the old silo—their favorite spot. She ran to him, but he disappeared into the mist just as she got close. Heartbroken, Evangeline refused to believe it. On stormy nights, she would climb to the top of the old silo north of town, hanging a lantern to guide him home. But one night—" she lowered her voice to a whisper, "—the storm was too strong. The wind knocked her off balance, and she fell to her death."

The room fell silent except for the faint scrape of a chair as someone shifted uncomfortably. Even Roy looked like he might be rethinking his skepticism.

"And now," Connie concluded, her voice a whisper steeped in tragedy, "they say her lantern still swings in the wind on foggy nights."

She let the final words hang in the air like a curtain falling at the end of a play. Her eyes darted around the room for dramatic effect.

A shiver ran down my spine despite myself. Okay, I'd give her this one—creepy. "And Julius?" I asked, half-curious, half-hoping she wouldn't take it to an even darker place.

Connie leaned in slightly, lowering her voice to just above a whisper. "Julius's ghost has been spotted ever since. Wandering around the silo, through Hickory Hills... especially when someone is hiding a secret or causing trouble. The town always says—when strange things start happening—Julius is near. Like he's warning us."

A slow, dramatic pause followed, and then she folded her hands in satisfaction, her tale complete.

I gave her a half-smile, pushing back against the creepy-crawly feeling sneaking up my spine. "So, you're saying a ghost sabotaged my café, Connie?"

She straightened up, tilting her chin just enough to look serious. "I wouldn't rule it out, Josie. Not with the silo so close. And you know what this town is like. Ghosts or no ghosts, there's always more going on than people let on."

"Well, thanks for that," I said dryly, glancing out the window as if a Confederate soldier might stroll through the town square. "But I think I'll focus on the living suspects for now."

She patted my arm, her lips curving into a knowing smile. "Suit yourself, dear. But if you see a Confederate soldier today, don't say I didn't warn you."

With that, she swept past me to grab a damp rag, leaving her audience somewhere between intrigued and unsettled. I shook my head, amused despite myself.

Still, there was always more going on than people let on. Small towns were funny like that, wrapping folklore and facts so tightly together that you couldn't tell where one ended and the other began. Ghosts weren't what worried me, though. It was the secrets people buried and just how far they'd go to keep them hidden.

"You know," Stanzi said as she walked by with a stack of books, "I overheard someone say Tiffany's been acting even weirder than usual. Like, sneaking around the back of Novel Grounds earlier this week."

I paused mid-swipe of the same spot I'd been cleaning for the past five minutes. "She was? What was she doing?"

Stanzi shrugged. "No clue, but it didn't look innocent. You think she's up to something?"

I set the rag down. "Something's definitely up….the footprints…nd now, with her and Dex at the orchard…"

The door chimed, and a small crowd of neighbors shuffled out after finishing the cleanup, leaving just our core crew—Hattie, Rhett, Emma, Holly, Max, and Stanzi. My book café finally looked like itself again: clean shelves, sparkling tables, and the comforting smell of coffee overpowering the lingering hint of cleaning supplies.

I glanced around at my friends, my determination hardening. "I think we need to head to Buck's Orchard," I said, the decision snapping into place. "If Tiffany and Dex are sneaking around, I want to know why."

Rhett exchanged a glance with Emma before nodding, his no-nonsense expression settling in. "We've done what we can here. Might as well see what they're up to."

"Agreed," Emma added, looping her arm through mine. "Let's find out what trouble they're stirring before it finds us first."

I smiled at her, grateful for her steady presence. "All right, let's go. And thank you—everyone—for helping today."

The last of the student staff, Tyler and Hannah, waved as they left. Tyler gave a thumbs-up. "Call us if you need anything else!"

As the café emptied, Holly suddenly linked arms with Hattie and

Stanzi, her face lighting up with mischief. "Looks like we're off to solve another mystery!" She struck a dramatic pose, practically twirling in place.

"Don't forget the snacks," Max chimed in. "If we're going to Buck's Orchard, we'd better stock up on cider donuts and kettle corn. Investigating on an empty stomach never ends well."

Holly gasped in mock horror. "The audacity! I'd never let us go hungry on a stakeout. Who do you think I am?"

This was my crew. My small-town, slightly chaotic, pie-fueled mystery-solving team. And despite the chaos, I wouldn't trade them for anything.

"Well," I said, brushing off my hands, "if we're done reenacting an episode of Scooby-Doo, let's get moving."

"Ruh-roh," Emma deadpanned, earning a round of chuckles.

Together, we locked up the café and headed into the crisp autumn air, the promise of cider donuts and a good mystery pulling us toward whatever answers Buck's Orchard might hold.

By late afternoon, we arrived at Buck's Orchard in Apple Grove, where the air smelled like cinnamon, fried doughnuts, and freshly pressed cider. Families were picking apples, kids zipped through the corn maze, and couples strolled hand in hand between rows of pumpkins. It was idyllic, like walking into a postcard—but I wasn't here for the ambiance. I was here for answers.

"Okay," I said, scanning the crowd like I was conducting a stakeout. "We'll grab some donuts, sit down, and keep an eye out. Blend in."

Max snorted. "Right. Because nothing screams 'blending in' like the way you're glaring at that pumpkin display."

I rolled my eyes but couldn't argue. Subtlety had never been my strong suit.

We got in line for the orchard's famous apple cider donuts, the sugary aroma making my stomach rumble in spite of my nerves. I'd just picked up my first donut, warm and golden, and lifted it to take a bite when Mocha let out a sharp bark.

Out of nowhere, a big golden ball of fluff shot by snatched the donut right out of my hand. The retriever bounded off like it had won the lottery.

"Hey!" I cried, staring at my empty hand in disbelief. "That was mine!"

Mocha wagged her tail and started play-bowing, clearly thrilled to have found a new friend in this fluffy thief.

"Maple, no!" A familiar voice rang out.

And of course, it was him.

Caleb jogged over, slightly out of breath, looking more rugged than I was prepared for in his rumpled flannel shirt and dirt-smudged ball cap. His well-worn jeans and scuffed boots didn't exactly scream "Police Deputy." He scooped up the donut thief with ease, the doggo wagging her tail like she'd done something heroic.

"Sorry about that," Caleb muttered, his voice tinged with sheepishness. "She's my grandparents' dog. Always causing trouble when she gets loose."

I crossed my arms, narrowing my eyes. "Well, I guess chaos runs in the family."

Caleb shot me a look—half-amused, half-exasperated. "I'll get you another donut. Relax."

I huffed, brushing crumbs off my jacket. "I was just about to enjoy that donut, you know."

Maple wriggled out of Caleb's arms, joining Mocha in what could only be described as a full-on doggy celebration. The two were racing in circles, their tails wagging so hard they might've flown away. Honestly, it was hard to stay mad with that much canine joy happening.

While I was distracted by the dogs' antics, Caleb slipped away into the donut hut like he had some secret backdoor deal with the staff. Moments later, he reappeared with a fresh donut in hand, holding it out like a peace offering.

"Here," he said, a small chuckle escaping. "Consider this an apology on Maple's behalf."

I took the donut, pretending not to be disarmed by the gesture—

or the way his eyes sparkled with amusement. "Fine. Maple's forgiven. This time," I said, breaking off a piece and savoring the warm, sugary goodness.

We stood there for a moment, watching the dogs frolic. "Where are Winni and Remi?" I asked, referring to Caleb's German Shepherds.

"They're back at the station," he said. "Didn't think this was the best place for them. Too many ways for them to get into trouble while I'm distracted."

I nodded, taking another bite into my donut and willing myself not to think about how distractingly good Caleb looked in flannel. Rugged and outdoorsy was definitely my thing, and on him? It worked. Too well.

Before I could spiral, I caught sight of Rhett and Emma sitting at a nearby picnic table, trying—and failing—not to laugh. Stanzi and Max weren't far behind, both watching the scene unfold like they were rooting for the leading couple in a rom-com. I shot them a mock glare, but their smirks only grew.

I turned back to Caleb, determined to stay focused. "So, what brings you here, Caleb? Did you really come all this way to supervise Maple's donut-stealing escapades, or is this just a happy coincidence?"

"Helping my grandpa," he said with a shrug. "Buck's Orchard has been in the family forever."

I blinked. "Wait—this is your grandpa's orchard?"

"Yep," he said, an almost bashful smile tugging at the corners of his mouth. "Caleb Senior, but everyone calls him Buck."

"Huh," I said, glancing around at the bustling orchard. "I've seen you here from time to time, but I thought you were just here for the donuts like the rest of us."

"I do like the donuts," he admitted, his grin widening, "but I've been helping out here since I could walk."

"Well, your grandparents' dog has excellent taste in donuts," I teased, nodding toward Maple.

Caleb chuckled, shaking his head. "She's a menace, but yeah, she knows what's good."

Mocha and Maple bounded back over, their tails wagging in synchronized joy. Mocha barked up at me, her paws landing on my leg as if she were lobbying for her own donut. "All right, you two," I said, scratching her ears. "You're lucky I like dogs."

Caleb raised an eyebrow, a teasing glint in his eyes. "And here I thought you had a soft spot for trouble."

"Only when it's cute and fluffy," I shot back. "Don't push your luck."

Rhett strolled over, clearly done pretending not to eavesdrop. "So," he said, his tone far too innocent, "are we here for donuts, or are we actually going to figure out what Tiffany and Dex are up to?"

"They're here at the orchard," I said, keeping my voice low but firm. "After what we saw last night, I'm not exactly buying the 'casual autumn stroll' excuse."

Caleb's jaw tightened, his cheek ticking like it always did when he was deep in thought—or irritated. "So, this is you *not* charging after her?"

I raised an eyebrow. "Caleb, you saw the state of my café. You know they were running from it. And now they're sneaking around here? Call me crazy, but that's a little more than a coincidence."

He let out a slow breath, his eyes scanning the bustling orchard like he could somehow spot the culprits just by looking hard enough. "It's a pattern," he admitted. "I'll give you that."

"Exactly," I said, softening just a touch. "So, what do you say? We team up and figure out what's going on?"

Rhett clapped his hands together, grinning like a kid about to start a scavenger hunt. "Perfect. Let's split up. More eyes, more ground covered. Divide and conquer." He shot Caleb a pointed look. "Don't worry, Deputy. We'll play nice."

I blinked at Rhett. He wasn't wrong, but his sudden enthusiasm caught me off guard. Caleb, however, just nodded, like the idea had already crossed his mind.

"That's actually not a bad plan," Caleb said. "If they're moving around, splitting up gives us the best shot at catching them in the act." He paused, leveling a look at me. "But we stick to pairs. No one goes alone."

I smirked. "Protecting me already? How sweet."

"More like keeping an eye on you, " he said as he turned to the rest of the group. "Rhett, Emma—you take the east side near the corn maze. Josie and I will check the cider house rows."

"And us?" Hattie chimed in, sauntering over with Holly, Stanzi, and Max in tow. She looked far too delighted, like she'd been waiting for an excuse to insert herself into the action. "Don't tell me we're sitting this one out."

Caleb sighed, rubbing the bridge of his nose like he was already regretting this. "Fine. Hattie, you and Holly cover the pumpkin patch and the picnic area. Stanzi and Max, take the hayride trail and the parking lot. And keep your phones on. If you see anything—or anyone—call me."

Hattie saluted with a dramatic flourish. "Roger that, boss."

"Don't make me regret this," Caleb muttered.

"No promises," Hattie shot back, linking arms with Holly and marching off toward the pumpkin patch. As they went, she turned back, letting out an obnoxious catcall in my and Caleb's direction. "Don't get too distracted, you two!"

Holly burst into giggles, and the two of them disappeared into the crowd, leaving me standing there with cheeks hotter than a fresh batch of cider donuts.

"Fantastic," I muttered, brushing imaginary crumbs off my jacket. "Just fantastic."

Caleb glanced down at me, a hint of a smile pulling at the corner of his mouth. "They're not wrong. Stay focused, Josie. This isn't a game."

I rolled my eyes, trying to hide the fact that I was still blushing. "Got it. No distractions. Let's go."

"Good," he said, his tone softening slightly as he started toward the cider rows. "Because Tiffany and Dex aren't harmless. And if something goes sideways, I'm stepping in."

For once, I didn't argue. Because, deep down, I agreed with him. Tiffany and Dex weren't harmless. And the knot of unease in my stomach told me we were walking straight into something bigger than we expected.

We wound our way through rows of apple trees until we spotted them—Tiffany and Dex standing near the far end of the orchard, deep in conversation with a man I didn't recognize. Dex looked as jittery as a cat in a room full of rocking chairs, and Tiffany's body language screamed defensiveness.

"Tiffany!" I called out, trying to sound firm but not aggressive.

She spun around, her expression shifting from surprise to irritation in less than a second. Her hand darted to her purse, shoving something inside before fixing me with a glare. "What do you want, Josie?"

Oh, she was annoyed. Good.

As we approached, my eyes flicked to the man standing beside them. His jacket had "Blake" embroidered on it, and the second I locked eyes with him, I had a flicker of recognition, but I couldn't immediately place him. Whatever recognition sparked in him, though, was enough to make him bolt. He turned on his heel and disappeared into the orchard, moving fast enough to leave an apple tree quaking behind him.

"Blake?" I called after him, but he didn't stop.

"Typical," I muttered, watching him vanish. My gut screamed that I'd seen him before, but I filed it away for later. There was a more immediate annoyance to deal with—Tiffany.

"I know you were near my café last night," I said, crossing my arms and leveling my best no-nonsense stare at her. "What were you doing?" Tiffany scoffed, her sneer as sharp as her tone. "I don't have to explain myself to you, Josie. You're delusional."

Dex shifted uncomfortably, looking like he'd rather be anywhere else. "We weren't anywhere near your café," he said, though his voice lacked conviction. "You're just stirring up trouble."

"Funny," I said, narrowing my eyes. "Because I'm pretty sure I saw you running."

Tiffany's gaze darted to Caleb, and for a brief moment, her mask slipped. Guilt? Panic? Whatever it was, she quickly smoothed it over with a haughty glare. "We heard noises, okay? Saw some guy in a black mask. We didn't stick around to investigate because, unlike you, we don't go looking for trouble."

My eyebrows shot up. "And you didn't think to report that?"

Tiffany hesitated, her confidence wavering for a split second before snapping back. "It wasn't our business."

Just as I was about to press further, Caleb's hand landed lightly on my arm, his touch grounding me. "Josie," he said quietly, his tone low but firm. "Let it go for now."

I clenched my jaw, frustrated, but I nodded. He was right. We weren't going to get anything out of them here. As we turned to leave, Tiffany's smug expression burned into my brain. This wasn't over. Not by a long shot.

After leaving the orchard, I returned to the café, hoping the brisk autumn air would help clear my mind. It didn't.

Thanks to my friends and the town rallying together, Novel Grounds looked spotless, but the memory of someone breaking in and trashing it still rattled me. The cheerful glow of the twinkle lights outside didn't do much to ease the lingering tension in my chest.

Inside, the café was quiet, almost too quiet. Hattie was back at the farmhouse, and my friends had gone off to enjoy their evening, leaving me alone to tackle the stock lists. I sat at the counter, staring at the inventory sheet, but my mind refused to cooperate. Every thought kept circling back—Artie's murder, Eloise's stolen recipes, and the wreckage of my café. There had to be a connection, didn't there?

I sighed and set down my pen. "You'd make a great detective, Josie," I muttered to myself. "You know if thinking in circles solved cases."

Mocha trotted over, her tail wagging like a cheerful metronome, breaking through my frustration. "At least you believe in me," I said, scratching behind her ears. Her tongue lolled out in response, clearly ready for something more exciting. "Okay, okay," I relented. "Let's go for a walk. Maybe we'll both clear our heads."

The evening air was crisp, biting at my cheeks as we stepped outside. Mocha trotted beside me, her leash jingling with each step. The twinkle lights lining the shops glowed warmly over the square, and the streetlamps painted golden pools on the brick sidewalks. Diners were heading into Gayle's, and the faint scent of burgers and pie drifted on the breeze. Normally, this small-town charm would feel comforting, but this evening it didn't.

We strolled past Artie's garage, where the police tape still fluttered in the wind like a warning. Mocha froze suddenly, her body stiffening, her ears perking up.

"What is it, girl?" I whispered, tugging gently on her leash. But she wouldn't budge. Her gaze was locked on the growing shadows near the edge of the block, and a low, rumbling growl rolled from her throat.

The air seemed colder and sharper here. The last traces of twilight had given way to a deep, inky blue, the kind of darkness that made it feel later than it really was. It wasn't even 5:30, but it felt like midnight.

A lone streetlight buzzed overhead, its flickering bulb casting uneven light on the cracked pavement. The wind picked up, rattling the leaves in the trees and sending them skittering across the ground like whispers. I shivered, and not from the cold.

"Mocha, come on," I said, keeping my voice steady as I gave the leash another tug. "It's just the wind."

She glanced at me but didn't relax, her wide, alert eyes darting back to the shadows.

From somewhere above, an owl let out its haunting call: "Who cooks for you? Who cooks for you all?"

The sound sent a chill down my spine. I shook my head, trying to laugh off the eerie tension. "You hear that, Mocha? We're being haunted by a culinary critic."

Mocha didn't seem amused. Her growl deepened, her tail stiff and motionless now.

"Okay, okay," I murmured, bending down to rub her ears. "We're going. See? Nothing scary here—just a garage with flappy police tape."

I straightened, pulling my hoodie tighter around me, and glanced over my shoulder. The street was empty, but I didn't feel like I was alone. My heart beat a little faster, though I tried to push the thought away. It was probably just my imagination—or too many late-night mystery novels.

"Let's go home," I said softly, giving Mocha one last reassuring scratch before turning us toward the square. But as we walked away, I had an overwhelming creepy feeling that something—or someone—was lingering just out of sight, watching.

And then I heard it.

Footsteps. Heavy. Dragging.

I froze, my breath hitching in my throat. Crunch, thump, drag. The sound cut through the quiet evening, like someone dragging a limp leg through the leaves behind me.

My heart hammered as I spun around, my gaze darting through the flickering shadows cast by a lone streetlight. The pavement stretched empty, but the streetlight's glow bent jaggedly, throwing unnatural angles against the cracked asphalt.

Crunch, thump, drag.

"Okay, nope. Nope, nope, nope," I muttered under my breath, tugging Mocha's leash to urge her forward. She wasn't budging. Her ears were pinned back, her growl low and steady—a sound I'd never heard from her before.

"Come on, girl," I said, trying to sound braver than I felt. "It's just the wind or... or some animal."

Crunch, thump, drag. Closer now.

My pulse roared in my ears as I whispered, "God has not given me a spirit of fear but of power and love and a sound mind." My voice wobbled, but I clung to the verse like a lifeline.

"Connie?" I called out, my voice shaky, trying to sound braver than I felt. "Is that you? You playing a joke on me and Mocha?"

Crunch, thump, drag.

I swallowed hard, my mouth suddenly dry. My instincts screamed run, but my feet refused to move. Mocha's growl deepened, her tail stiff and straight as she stared into the growing darkness.

Then I saw it.

A shadow moved just beyond the trees.

My breath caught as I squinted, trying to make out the shape. It was faint, barely visible in the dim light, but it was there—a man. His silhouette was strange, his clothes old and tattered, like something pulled straight out of history.

And then it clicked.

No.

It couldn't be.

"Julius?" I whispered to no one, the name escaping my lips before I could stop it.

The figure stepped forward, slow and deliberate, his face pale and drawn, his uniform shredded. A Confederate soldier.

It wasn't real. It couldn't be real. It was just a story, right? Connie's ridiculous ghost story, nothing more.

The figure raised an arm, pointing straight at me. His movements were slow like molasses and as deliberate as a chess player moving their final piece.

Ice wrapped around my chest. Mocha barked again, frantic now, her leash jerking so hard it nearly ripped from my hands.

"Run," my brain screamed, but my feet stayed frozen.

Crunch, thump, drag.

Finally, adrenaline kicked in. I turned and bolted, Mocha surging ahead beside me. My breath came in short, panicked gasps as my feet pounded against the pavement.

Behind me, the sound followed. Crunch, thump, drag.

It was relentless, keeping pace no matter how fast I ran.

"God is my refuge and strength," I whispered between gasps. "A very present help in trouble." The words came out like a lifeline, pulling me through the thickening dread.

Mocha barked again, yanking me forward, her leash taut as she propelled me toward the safety of the square. My legs burned, but I didn't dare slow down. The sound was right there, haunting me with every step.

Crunch, thump, drag.

When Gayle's Diner's glowing lights finally came into view, I almost sobbed with relief. The hum of laughter and conversation from inside spilled out into the square, wrapping me in its warmth.

I skidded to a halt, my chest heaving as I looked over my shoulder.

The street was empty. Silent.

Just the faint rustle of leaves in the breeze.

"Thank you, Jesus," I whispered, the tension in my body easing as I bent to scratch Mocha's ears. Her barking had subsided, but her eyes still darted toward the darkness behind us.

"See? We're fine. Totally fine," I told her, mostly to reassure myself. "Just... maybe next time, let's take a different route."

Mocha huffed, her leash slackening as she nudged me toward the diner. The bright lights and familiar faces were a welcome distraction from the weight still pressing on my chest.

Normal. Everything looked normal. People laughed, shopped, and ate fries at Gayle's like the world hadn't just tilted sideways.

Mocha, completely over the drama, wagged her tail, looking up at me as if to say, "What's the hold-up, Mom? Let's get back to our cozy spot."

But before I could fully convince myself everything was fine, that little voice of doubt whispered at the back of my mind. Had I really seen him? Julius? Or was it just the shadows playing tricks on me?

As if the night couldn't get any more complicated, my eyes landed on the one person with a knack for showing up exactly when I wasn't in the mood for company.

Caleb.

Of course.

He was leaning against the door of my café, arms crossed, his casual confidence as irritating as it was... attractive. Mocha, the traitor, perked right up and started wagging her tail like she'd just spotted her favorite person in the world. I groaned under my breath. "Seriously? You're supposed to be on my side."

Caleb straightened when he saw me coming, his broad shoulders shifting off the doorframe like some sort of patient, gruff guardian angel. He didn't say anything at first. He just waited with that unreadable, assessing look of his. Mocha's wagging tail picked up speed. Fantastic.

"Josie," he said finally, his low voice carrying that mix of gravel and warmth that was starting to make my stomach flip way too often. "What are you doing?"

Mocha practically dragged me toward him, clearly expecting belly rubs or some kind of reunion fanfare. Caleb, ever the softie when it came to dogs, crouched to give her a quick scratch behind the ears, his expression softening in a way I refused to find endearing. Nope. Not falling for it.

"What am I doing?" I echoed, crossing my arms. "Oh, just out for an evening jog. You know, cardio."

Caleb raised an eyebrow, his skepticism cutting through my sarcasm like a hot knife through butter. "You. Jogging."

I shrugged, trying to play it cool. "Gotta work off all those donuts from the orchard." The second the words left my mouth, I winced. An evening jog? Seriously? When have I ever jogged? Why couldn't I just be normal for five seconds?

"You don't jog," Caleb said flatly, his eyebrow still firmly arched.

"Okay, fine," I admitted, yanking lightly at Mocha's leash to keep her from rolling over for belly rubs. "I'm... investigating. Happy?"

"Investigating," he repeated, standing and crossing his arms in a way that made him look far too in charge for my liking. "Alone. At night. After your café was broken into?"

"I can handle myself," I shot back, mirroring his stance even though I knew I looked more like an annoyed librarian than someone intimidating. "Besides, you were the one who said Tiffany and Dex were sneaking around. I'm just... following up."

"Following up," he echoed again. "By yourself. In the dark."

"Yes, Deputy Obvious," I said, rolling my eyes. "I wasn't aware I needed permission to walk around my own town."

Caleb sighed, rubbing the back of his neck. "Josie, your café was trashed. You don't know who's behind it or what they're capable of. You can't keep charging headfirst into these situations."

"I'm not charging," I argued, though even Mocha gave me a side-eye like, You totally are. "I'm... strategically gathering information."

He gave me a long, tired look that said, how do I keep getting roped into this? Then, with a shake of his head, he stepped closer. "You worry me more than I'd like to admit, you know that?"

That one landed like a sucker punch. His tone wasn't scolding—it was quiet and honest, and it hit me in a way I wasn't prepared for. My chest tightened, and I forgot how to string words together for a second. What was I supposed to do with that? Laugh it off? Pretend I didn't hear it? How he looked at me—like I was somehow equal parts reckless and impossible not to care about—was throwing me off balance.

"I prefer to call it problem-solving," I said, my voice softer now, though I threw in a shrug for good measure. "Besides, I've got Mocha. She's practically a guard dog."

Caleb glanced at Mocha, who was currently sprawled on the sidewalk, her tongue lolling out as she basked in his attention. "Yeah. Terrifying."

"She has her moments," I said defensively, though my lips twitched into a smile despite myself.

Caleb sighed again, his gaze softening just enough to make my heart do that annoying flutter thing. "Just... be careful, okay?"

"I always am," I said breezily, even though we both knew that wasn't true.

"Sure," he muttered, stepping aside to let me unlock the café door. "Because you're the picture of caution."

I shot him a look over my shoulder. "I'm careful when it counts."

"Uh-huh." His voice was laced with doubt, but his eyes held that same steady concern that always threw me. "Just promise me you won't do anything... Josie-ish tonight."

"Define 'Josie-ish,'" I said, narrowing my eyes.

"Running into danger. Sticking your nose where it doesn't belong. Ignoring every warning sign," he listed, ticking off each point on his fingers.

"So... problem-solving," I said, grinning as I stepped inside. "Got it."

Caleb just shook his head, but I caught the faintest hint of a smile tugging at his lips before the door clicked shut behind me.

The familiar warmth of the café wrapped around me as the weight of Caleb's words lingered. He cared. That much was obvious. But why did it feel like there was something else in how he looked at me tonight?

"Focus, Josie," I muttered, shaking off the thought. There was a mystery to solve—a tangled web of Tiffany, Dex, Eloise's stolen recipes, and my vandalized café. And I wasn't about to let feelings for Caleb—or whatever this weird tension was—distract me.

Still, as I moved through the café, turning off lights and locking up behind me, I glanced out the window one last time. Caleb was still there, leaning against his truck, watching like he wasn't quite ready to leave.

I sighed. Great. Solving this mystery was going to be hard enough without my traitorous heart getting involved.

9 cappuccinos & clues

IT WAS SUCH A GLORIOUS AUTUMN DAY that I couldn't resist rolling down all the windows on the drive into town. The breeze carried the crisp, earthy scent of fallen leaves and wood smoke, and the hills blazed with crimson, orange, and gold—like someone had spilled a giant bowl of Fruit Loops across the countryside. In the back seat, Mocha darted from window to window, her floppy ears catching the wind as she barked at every passing cow. Her sheer joy was infectious.

At least one of us wasn't spiraling into overthinking.

I tightened my grip on the steering wheel. My book café had been ransacked. Eloise was sitting in jail for a crime I knew she didn't commit. Tiffany and Dex were acting shadier than usual, and let's not even start on that bloody check with Hattie's name on it. And then, of course, there was the ghost. Or whatever that was.

I groaned. My life felt like one of those whodunit novels I sold at Novel Grounds, only with fewer clever clues and more unanswered questions. Oh, and one very frustrating, very handsome police deputy who told me to "be careful" like I was some delicate flower. Caleb. Why did my thoughts always come back to Caleb?

Mocha barked again as we passed another herd of cows, her tail thumping against the seat. I chuckled. "You're loving this, aren't you, girl?" Her tail wagged even harder, her enthusiasm unwavering. At least one of us had life figured out.

The café came into view, nestled in the heart of Hickory Hills. The square was alive with the hum of small-town life. Autumn wreaths and garlands framed the warm red-brick and stone storefronts, their vibrant hues glowing in the golden afternoon light. The smell of cinnamon and pumpkin drifted through the air. It was picture-perfect.

After parking in the back lot, I stepped inside Novel Grounds. The place was running like clockwork, and my student staff was handling the morning rush like pros. Holly was a baking whirlwind, practically a one-woman muffin factory, as she whipped batter, rotated trays in and out of the oven, and kept the display case fully stocked. The kitchen smelled like apple-cinnamon heaven, but I also noticed the determined set of her jaw and the faint smudge of flour across her forehead.

"Holly, you're amazing," I said, sliding another tray of muffins her way. "Are you sure you're not secretly powered by coffee and pure willpower?"

She shot me a grin, though her movements didn't slow. "Just doing what I can, Josie. Eloise would do the same for us if the roles were reversed."

I leaned against the counter, watching her expertly flip a batch of muffins onto the cooling rack. "Yeah, but Eloise also knows how to pace herself. You're one burnt-out baker away from setting off the fire alarm. Again."

"That was one time," Holly said, waving her spatula at me like it was an extension of her arm. "And it barely smoked."

"It smoked enough to have the fire chief personally request that we stop experimenting with maple bacon muffins."

"Okay, fine," she conceded with a laugh, brushing flour off her apron. "But this time, no bacon. Just good ol' dependable apples and cinnamon."

I crossed my arms, raising an eyebrow. "Still, maybe take a breather? Sit down? Drink some water that isn't secretly iced coffee?"

Holly snorted. "You sound like Nikki."

"How is Nikki doing, by the way?" I asked, switching gears. "Holding down the salon solo?"

"Oh, you know Nikki—she's probably rearranged the whole place by now and turned it into some trendy new concept salon without asking." Holly laughed as she set another tray into the oven. "She texted me earlier. Said everything's running smoothly. Translation: I'm not allowed to come back because she's running the show now."

"She takes after you," I said, reaching for a dish towel to help wipe the counter. "Quick-thinking, steady under pressure. And I mean that as a compliment. She's lucky to have a mom like you."

Holly paused for just a second, her face softening with a hint of pride before she waved me off. "Nah, she's like her dad. Cool under pressure, always thinking ten steps ahead. Me? I'm more of a 'fake it till you make it' kind of gal."

"Sure," I teased, nudging her shoulder. "That's why you've got this place running like a five-star bakery in between running a salon and keeping half the town from falling apart."

"Someone's gotta keep you out of trouble," she quipped, flashing me a wink. "Speaking of which, shouldn't you be off solving mysteries? You've got this. Go. Do what you need to do. I'll keep things running here. Besides, Caleb's probably sitting at his desk right now, waiting for someone to deliver snacks and meddle in his day."

"First of all," I said, holding up a finger, "it's not meddling. It's investigative charm. Totally different."

Holly smirked. "Right. And second of all?"

"Second of all," I continued, grabbing a box of muffins and two cappuccinos, "I'm going to take your advice. But only because you're about five seconds away from turning into a muffin yourself."

She laughed, shooing me toward the door. "Go! Save Eloise. Or solve the case. Or at least annoy Caleb enough to loosen him up. Just don't come back until you've got some answers—or a good story."

I saluted her with the coffee cups, trying to keep the grin off my face. "Yes, ma'am. Just promise me you'll take a break before you pass out in a pile of apple peels."

Holly rolled her eyes, but the smile on her face told me she appreciated the concern. "Go, Josie. Before I assign you kitchen duty."

With a wave and a mental note to check in on her later, I pushed open the door to the café, letting the crisp autumn air hit me. Mocha trotted at my side as I balanced the muffins and cappuccinos, ready to tackle the next step.

Let's be real: if Caleb was going to insist on keeping me in the dark about this case, I wasn't above trying to bribe him with baked goods and caffeine. Muffins had a way of loosening lips, and if they didn't, well, at least Eloise would have something comforting while she waited for me to figure out how to clear her name. Win-win.

Balancing the box and cups, I pushed the door open with my hip and stepped back into the crisp autumn air. The police station wasn't far, and the crunch of leaves underfoot was oddly soothing. I didn't exactly have a plan—when do I ever? —but showing up with snacks seemed like as good a start as any.

As I neared the station, muttering to myself, Mocha trotted happily at my side. "Okay, Josie, what's the game plan? Walk in, charm Caleb with small talk, and hope he accidentally reveals classified information. Sure. Foolproof. What could possibly go wrong?"

Just as I was starting to second-guess myself, I spotted Connie Fontaine down the street. And, of course, she was in full detective mode. Her deerstalker hat was perched at a jaunty angle, and she had a magnifying glass in one hand as if she'd wandered straight out of a community theater production of *The Hound of the Baskervilles*.

I slowed, unable to resist watching her latest performance. Connie crouched low to inspect something on the sidewalk. One hand was outstretched dramatically as if she'd discovered a clue that would blow the whole case wide open. Whatever she was doing, it was peak *Connie Fontaine*.

"Morning, Connie!" I called, unable to resist.

She spun around with the flourish of a Broadway star hitting her cue, her deerstalker hat slightly askew and her magnifying glass raised dramatically. "Ah, Josie!" she exclaimed, her voice booming as if she were addressing a packed theater. "Just the leading lady I needed to see!"

I chuckled, bracing myself for whatever scene she was about to create. "Let me guess—you've cracked the case wide open?"

Connie dropped the magnifying glass with an exaggerated gasp and pressed a hand to her chest, eyes glinting with excitement. "Oh, my dear, the plot has thickened like an overcooked gravy."

"Do tell," I said, playing along.

She glanced around, lowering her voice to a stage whisper. "It's about Artie," she said, drawing out his name like it was some sort of dark secret. Then, leaning in so close, I could smell her *Chanel Number 5* hand cream. She added, "I have it on impeccable authority that Christopher Theodor stormed into the car shop just days before Artie's... untimely demise."

I frowned. "Christopher...I mean, Bear? I didn't even know he had any beef with Artie."

"Oh, darling," Connie said, "It wasn't just a beef. It was a full-blown roast. The poor boy believed he was going to inherit the shop! Thought it was practically his birthright. Imagine his heartbreak—his betrayal! He accused Artie of swindling his sweet, unsuspecting grandfather out of the place. It was epic, Josie. The kind of drama you usually need a stage and a spotlight for!"

"He thought he'd inherit the shop? Since when?"

"Since forever!" Connie declared, throwing her arms wide like she was revealing the final act of a play. "And when Artie told him otherwise, he left in a fit of rage! Rage, Josie! You could feel it in the air—a simmering, Shakespearean betrayal!" She clutched her chest and staggered back a step as though she were about to faint.

Mocha tilted her head at Connie, clearly trying to decide whether to bark or join in.

"Let me get this straight," I said, biting back a smile. "You think Caleb needs to know about this because Bear's... dramatic exit is evidence?"

"Evidence of motive!" Connie said, her voice ringing out like the final line of a murder mystery. She shook my arm for emphasis as though I were the key to justice itself.

I bit my lip to keep from laughing, "Thanks for the tip, Connie," I said, trying to sound appropriately grave. "I'll be sure to let Caleb know."

She let go of my arm with a satisfied sigh and gave me a regal wave. "No need to thank me, dear. 'Tis my civic duty. And rest assured—if I uncover more dark deeds, you'll be the first to know." She tipped her hat with a dramatic bow, her magnifying glass raised like a sword, then marched off, scanning the sidewalk for more "clues."

As she disappeared around the corner, Mocha let out a happy bark, clearly amused by the whole thing. "She's something else, isn't she?" I said, scratching behind her ears.

I started walking again, shaking my head as a grin tugged at my lips. Connie might be completely over-the-top, but there was something endearing about her flair for the dramatic. If this whole Artie mess were a play, she wouldn't just star in it—she'd rewrite the script to make sure it ended with her taking a bow to thunderous applause.

The station hummed with its usual mix of voices, radio chatter, and the occasional ring of a phone. Mocha trotted beside me, her leash jangling and tail wagging. Caleb was hunched over paperwork, looking impossibly focused. His German Shepherds, Remi and Winnie, lounged nearby, both giving the room their signature "don't even think about it" stares.

When Caleb finally glanced up, his sharp blue-green eyes locked onto me, and for a split second, his stoic expression softened. Recognition? Relief? I couldn't tell, but it threw me off just enough to make me glad I had Mocha as a distraction.

"Hey, Josie," he said, his voice low and just a little rough like he hadn't spoken in hours. He sat up straighter, his eyes flicking to the box of muffins I was holding.

"Hey," I replied, smiling at him. "I come bearing snacks. Thought you might need reinforcements for all that paperwork." I set the box on his desk and, for reasons I will never understand, added a ridiculous Vanna White hand flourish. Good grief, Josie.

To his credit, Caleb didn't comment. His lips twitched, though, and I was pretty sure he was fighting a grin as he reached for a coffee. "Thanks. You didn't have to."

"No big deal," I said quickly, tugging Mocha's leash as she sniffed a little too close to his chair. "Figured you could use a sugar boost."

As he sipped the cappuccino, I caught the faintest hint of a smile. "Appreciate it." His voice softened, but that guarded look of his didn't completely leave.

I shifted on my feet, desperate to break the silence before it got awkward. "So, uh… any updates on the case?"

His expression tightened, and just like that, the wall was back up. "Still working through it," he said, setting his coffee down. "Evidence points one way, but it's not adding up."

"How so?" I leaned in slightly, curiosity bubbling up.

He hesitated, his fingers drumming on his desk. "Eloise is the prime suspect," he said, frustration creeping into his tone. "Her recipe box was at the scene, along with hair fibers. I know you don't want to hear it, but—"

I held up a hand, cutting him off. "Do you really think she did it? For crying out loud, she's a retired detective. Does leaving all that evidence behind sound like Eloise to you?" I put my hands on his desk and leaned in, "And come on, Caleb, She's 70 years old. Do you really think Eloise bashed a man on the head with enough strength to kill him? You can't seriously believe that."

His eyes flickered with a familiar frustration, but there was something else—respect, maybe.

"You know just as well as I do," he began, crossing his arms even tighter, "that *frail 70-year-old lady* is a pistol-packing mama who could probably take down half this department if she felt like it."

I opened my mouth to argue, but he held up a hand. ""She's tougher than half my department" So, don't give me that *'she's too old and fragile'* routine. You know better."

I stared at him for a second, half impressed, half annoyed. "All right, fair point. She's tough, no question. But that doesn't make her a murderer, Caleb. Just because she *can* doesn't mean she *would*."

Caleb's jaw clenched, and for a moment, I could see the inner tug-of-war he was fighting. "I get it," he said, his voice dropping to that softer tone that always caught me off guard. "But the evidence is what it is. If she's being framed like you think, then we need to prove it. But I can't ignore the facts we've got right now. Josie, you're not looking at the bigger picture."

He rubbed the back of his neck and sighed, "There's a process—rules to follow. You think I like this? Holding her in custody?" His voice dipped, quieter but no less firm. "I don't like it, but my hands are tied."

For a moment, I just stared at him, surprised by his honesty. I'd always thought Caleb's by-the-book nature was just who he was—strict, immovable. But now I saw it was more than that. He cared—maybe too much—and sticking to the protocol was his way of keeping things steady.

"You're frustrated," I said softly.

His eyes met mine, sharp and unyielding. "You think I enjoy this? Josie, I know she's probably innocent, but the court doesn't care about gut feelings. Evidence matters."

I softened, catching a flicker of the weight he carried. "I get it," I said gently. "I know you're doing your job, and honestly, you're good at it. But Eloise didn't do this. We both know that."

He didn't respond right away; he just gave a slow nod, as if he was still turning it over in his mind. "I'm looking into other leads. But until something new breaks, I'm stuck."

"Well," I said, straightening, "maybe I've got something to help with that."

Caleb raised an eyebrow, clearly skeptical.

"Connie Fontaine," I said, trying not to grin. "She's been sleuthing. Apparently, Bear Theodor stormed into Artie's shop a few days ago, furious. Thought the garage was his inheritance and accused Artie of swindling his grandpa."

Caleb leaned back, his brow furrowing. "Bear? Didn't know he had a claim to the place."

"Neither did I, but Connie swears she's got a source. She even said it looked like they were about to come to blows. That's got to be worth looking into, right?"

He tapped his pen on the desk, thoughtful. "It's a lead. I'll follow up. Thanks, Josie."

"You're welcome," I said brightly, feeling an odd mix of satisfaction and nerves under his steady gaze.

Mocha chose that moment to start nosing around Caleb's desk, probably looking for snacks. I tugged her leash gently, smiling as she wagged her tail in pure, oblivious joy. "Well, I'll let you get back to it," I said, backing away. "Real police work and all."

He held my gaze, and tension hummed between us—not the usual bickering tension but something quieter, heavier. It felt like we were two people staring at the same puzzle from opposite sides of the table, both frustrated that the pieces didn't fit.

"All right," he said finally, his voice low and deliberate. "I'll keep looking, but you"—he pointed a finger at me, his eyes narrowing just enough to be serious—"keep it clean. No sneaking into evidence rooms, no badgering witnesses. Got it?"

I raised my hands in mock surrender, a grin tugging at the corner of my mouth. "Wouldn't dream of it."

Caleb smirked—an actual, honest-to-goodness smirk—and it threw me off just enough to almost trip over Mocha's leash.

"You're not half-bad at this detective thing yourself," he said, and for a second, it almost sounded like a compliment.

"High praise," I quipped, fighting the heat creeping up my neck. "But actually, Caleb... Eloise needs to know she's not alone in this. Let me see her. Just for a few minutes."

His smirk disappeared, replaced by that familiar stern, no-nonsense look. "Josie—"

"Please," I cut in, softening my voice. "She's sitting in there, probably feeling abandoned. Ten minutes. That's all I'm asking."

He hesitated, his eyes searching mine. For a moment, I thought he'd say no. Then he sighed, running a hand through his hair in a way that made him look far too human for his usual gruff exterior. "Fine. Ten minutes. But don't stir the pot. I mean it."

"I wouldn't dream of it," I said, my voice light, though my heart felt unexpectedly heavy.

His gaze lingered for a beat, sharp and assessing, before he finally stepped aside. "We'll see," he muttered.

By the time I made it back to Novel Grounds, the café was in full swing. Holly was still on muffin duty, and judging by the mouthwatering scents of apple, cinnamon, and pumpkin wafting through the air, she was crushing it. Customers lingered over steaming lattes, the espresso machine hissed in the background, and the usual hum of chatter filled the space. It was my version of home.

Mocha trotted in beside me, tail wagging as she sniffed every inch of the floor, clearly on the hunt for a stray crumb. Honestly, I couldn't blame her.

"Earth to Josie!" Holly's voice rang out from behind the counter. She waved a flour-covered hand, a teasing grin plastered across her face. "You've got that look again."

I blinked, snapping back to reality. "What look?"

"You know," she said, lowering her voice into a dramatic stage whisper. "The Caleb look."

I groaned, reaching for an apron. "You're imagining things."

"Oh, I'm definitely not imagining this," she shot back, her eyes sparkling. "How'd it go at the station?"

Hattie sauntered up, her timing as impeccable as always. She leaned against the counter, her expression all too mischievous. "Yeah, Josie. How did it go with Officer Broody?"

I shot her a mock glare, though a traitorous smile tugged at my lips. "He's not broody. He's just... serious. And for the record, we talked about the case. That's it."

Hattie crossed her arms, feigning disappointment. "So, no smoldering eye contact? No lingering brush of his hand against yours as he muttered, 'Be careful, Josie'?"

Holly gasped dramatically. "Oh! Or maybe a heartfelt confession that he can't stand how much he secretly admires you?"

I rolled my eyes so hard I was surprised they didn't pop out of my head. "You two have been reading way too many romance novels."

"Please," Hattie scoffed. "Real-life Caleb is basically a romance novel hero in denial. The small-town cop with a tragic backstory who doesn't realize he's in love with the quirky book café owner until it's almost too late? Come on."

"Let me stop you right there," I said, holding up a hand. "First of all, Caleb is not in love with me. Second, we didn't talk about anything personal. He just gave me his usual 'by the book' lecture."

Holly grinned, clearly not buying it. "And yet here you are, blushing like he personally dedicated a Bon Jovi song to you."

"Am not," I muttered, hiding behind my coffee cup.

"Uh-huh," Hattie said, tilting her head. "So, what did you talk about?"

"I sighed, refilling my cup of coffee to buy myself a second. "We went over some leads," I admitted, keeping my voice low as a customer walked by. "I brought up something Connie told me—about Bear Theodor blowing up at Artie a few days before he was killed."

Hattie's eyebrows shot up. "Bear? Why?"

"Apparently, Bear thought the garage was supposed to be his inheritance. Connie claims he accused Artie of swindling it from his grandfather."

Holly set down the dishtowel she'd been using to wipe the counter, her expression serious now. "That sounds like a motive to me."

"Exactly," I said, feeling a flicker of satisfaction. "I told Caleb, and he said it's worth looking into. But, you know, in his usual 'I'll handle it, don't interfere' way."

"Of course he did," Hattie said, rolling her eyes. "Because heaven forbid Josie McCarthy might be onto something."

Holly leaned against the counter, her expression turning serious. "So, Bear really thought the garage was his inheritance?"

"Apparently," I said, setting my coffee down. "Caleb's going to follow up, but..." I hesitated, glancing between them. "Bear's temper worries me. If he was angry enough to confront Artie, who knows what else he might've been capable of."

Holly's brow furrowed, and she wiped her hands on a dishtowel. "You think he could've...?"

"I don't know," I admitted. "But I have to find out. And if Bear's out fishing with Teddy, maybe I'll get some answers."

Hattie straightened, her eyes gleaming with mischief. "Oh, so you're going to interrogate them by the river? Should we pack snacks and lawn chairs for the show?"

"I'm not interrogating them," I said, shooting her a look. "I'm just... asking questions. Casually. Like a normal person."

Holly smirked. "Because you're so good at subtle."

"Hey, I can be subtle!" I protested, though even Mocha let out a soft woof like she disagreed. "You know what? I don't need this sass. I'm going, and I'll be back with answers. Or, at the very least, a great fishing story."

Hattie grinned. "Just don't scare them off, Nancy Drew. We still need you in one piece for the party."

Holly tossed a dish towel at me, "And don't go doing something

Caleb will lecture you about later. You know he will."

I caught it and threw it back at her, "Oh, he lives for it," I said dryly, grabbing Mocha's leash. "It's practically his love language."

The words slipped out before I could stop them, and both Holly and Hattie let out simultaneous gasps of delight.

"Love language!" Hattie crowed, clapping her hands.

I groaned, heading for the door before they could pounce. "Goodbye!"

"Love language!" Holly called after me, laughing.

With Mocha happily trotting beside me, I stepped out into the crisp autumn air, letting their laughter fade behind me. The square was bustling, sunlight glinting off the windows and the faint scent of wood smoke drifted through the air. It was the kind of day that made you forget, just for a moment, that anything could ever go wrong.

Holly's words stuck with me as I left the café, her playful warning still echoing in my head. *Don't do anything Caleb will lecture you about later.* Easier said than done. Between Bear's temper, Eloise's recipes, and the mounting questions churning around Artie's murder, staying out of trouble wasn't exactly easy.

When I reached the river, the scene was so tranquil I let myself relax a little. The Missouri River glimmered under the late afternoon sun, framed by sugar maples and golden oaks that were on fire with autumn color. Leaves floated lazily down to the water, their gentle landing sending tiny ripples across the surface. Mocha trotted beside me, leash slack, her tail wagging like this was just another perfect fall day. She sniffed eagerly at the riverbank.

Up ahead, I spotted Teddy and Bear on the dock. Teddy sat relaxed in his fishing vest, his line cast into the slow-moving current, but Bear was a different story. Hunched forward in his old Firefly High School hoodie, his posture was stiff, his grip on the fishing rod white-knuckled. Grandfather and grandson, side by side—surrounded by the kind of autumn beauty that should be painted in watercolors. Except this picture wasn't as idyllic as it seemed.

Mocha's nails clicked on the wooden planks as she stepped onto the dock, her nose twitching as she peered over the edge like she hoped to spot a fish. Usually, her tail would be wagging up a storm, and she'd be nudging her way into belly rubs, but not today. Her tail slowed to a cautious sway, and she gave Bear a wide berth, sensing his grouchy mood.

"Hey, Teddy. Bear," I called out, walking closer. "Mind if I join you?"

Teddy glanced up, his warm smile softening the lines of exhaustion etched into his face. "Sure, Josie. Have a seat," he said, patting the spot next to him.

Bear didn't look at me. He gave a stiff nod, his jaw tight, his attention glued to the water. Mocha padded over to sniff his leg but pulled back almost immediately, her tail dipping. I made a mental note: Mocha was rarely wrong about people.

I lowered myself onto the dock, the old planks creaking under my weight. The air smelled faintly of fish and fallen leaves. "Heard you had a bit of a run-in with Artie, Bear," I said, keeping my tone light but direct. "Want to tell me about it?"

Bear's knuckles tightened on the rod, his grip so firm I half-expected it to snap. "Yeah," he muttered, his eyes never leaving the water. "I confronted him. He stole the shop. It was supposed to be mine."

There it was—anger, raw and jagged, cutting through his words. This wasn't just frustration over a business deal. It ran deeper, like an old wound that had never healed.

Teddy sighed heavily, his shoulders slumping. "Josie, I sold the shop because I needed the money," he said, his voice heavy with regret. "But Artie... he wasn't honest about the deal. I thought I was getting enough to take care of myself and leave something for Bear, but it turned out to be less than I'd hoped."

"So, when you confronted him," I said, turning back to Bear, "you didn't know all the details?"

Bear finally glanced at me, his dark eyes flashing with resentment. "No. I thought Grandpa sold me out. Artie made sure I got nothing." He spat the words like they tasted bitter.

Teddy shook his head, rubbing the back of his neck. "I never wanted to leave Bear with nothing," he said, his voice thick with guilt. "But I've been fooled before—first by Dex, now Artie. I thought I'd learned my lesson. Clearly, I haven't."

The regret in Teddy's voice tugged at me, but I couldn't afford to get distracted. "So that's why you were so angry with Artie?" I pressed gently. "It wasn't just about the shop—it was about the inheritance."

Bear's jaw tightened further, and he turned back to the water. "Yeah," he said flatly, his voice low. "I thought Grandpa betrayed me. Artie took everything."

"And the recipes?" I asked, shifting gears. "Do you know anything about Eloise's stolen recipes?"

Bear's head whipped toward me, his expression sharp with confusion. "Recipes? What are you talking about?"

I studied his reaction carefully. "Artie was found with Eloise's recipes in his possession. If you didn't take them, maybe he did. I'm just trying to connect the dots."

Bear shook his head vehemently. "I don't care about some stupid recipes. I didn't have anything to do with that." His frustration seemed real, but Mocha was still watching him with a cautious eye, her body stiff. The tension in her stance sent another ripple of unease through me.

Teddy sighed again, his voice quieter this time. "Josie, we didn't have anything to do with Artie's murder or Eloise's recipes. We've been hurt, sure, but we wouldn't cross that line."

I wanted to believe him—wanted to believe both of them—but Bear's simmering anger and Teddy's regret didn't sit neatly together. And it bugged me.

I stood, brushing off my jeans. "Thanks for talking to me," I said, keeping my tone neutral. "I just want to figure out what really happened."

Teddy nodded, his smile kind but sad. "You always do, Josie."

As I turned to leave, Mocha stuck close to my side, her usual bounce replaced by a cautious, measured step. The sun had started its slow descent, painting the river in shades of gold and amber. The water looked calm—peaceful, even—but the tension I felt refused to let go.

Later that evening, I headed to Konstanze and Max's for our murder board session, determined to connect the dots before everything spiraled even further out of control. Their Victorian home, tucked on a quiet street in Hickory Hills, looked like it had stepped out of a storybook. The intricate trim around the windows, the antique lamps glowing softly in the twilight—it all had a charm that felt both timeless and inviting.

Inside, the warm scent of wood smoke mingled with the faint aroma of fresh flowers. The crackling fireplace cast flickering light over the room, highlighting the soft floral wallpaper and polished oak furniture. Bookshelves lined one wall, stuffed with novels that had clearly been loved, and cozy armchairs draped in tartan throws sat like loyal companions near the hearth. Emma Bridgewater ceramics—a cheerful mix of floral and polka-dot mugs and plates—stood in a carefully curated display on a rustic dresser. But it was the ceramic jug of wildflowers on the dining table, their colors a perfect match for the autumn night, that drew my eye.

The dining table itself was command central: a sprawling mess of snacks, notebooks, and our ever-growing murder board. Photos, sticky notes, and bits of red string crisscrossed in chaotic brilliance. Max was already stationed at one end, elbow-deep in a bag of pretzels, with a cookie clutched in his other hand because apparently snacking was his preferred method of brainstorming.

"Josie!" Stanzi called, waving me over with her usual flair. "Grab a seat."

"What do you say, Detective—time to catch the culprit?" Max asked, grinning around a mouthful of crumbs.

"Ready as I'll ever be," I replied, pulling out a chair. "Though, honestly, how you manage to think while inhaling half the snack table is beyond me."

"It's called multitasking," he said with a wink, popping another pretzel. "Some people pace when they're stressed; I carb-load."

Holly, Anders, Rhett, Emma, Hattie, and Dr. Emerson had already gathered around, their expressions a mix of focus and mild amusement. Holly had commandeered the cheese plate, Anders was busy rearranging sticky notes, and Hattie leaned back in her chair like she was waiting to drop the perfect one-liner. Meanwhile, Holly's dad and our steady voice of reason, Dr. Emerson, sat quietly scribbling notes, his precise handwriting filling a notepad.

"All right, folks," Max said, clapping his hands and shifting gears from snack enthusiast to strategist. "Here's where we stand: Artie's dead, Eloise's recipes are missing, and someone is working way too hard to frame her. Those things have to be connected."

"Don't forget Bear," Stanzi said, pointing to his photo on the board. "He blew up at Artie right before the murder. That alone makes him a prime suspect."

"And then there's Teddy," Hattie chimed in, gesturing to a newspaper clipping about his old garage. "He regretted selling the shop to Artie, who swindled him out of a fair deal. Resentment like that doesn't just disappear."

Dr. Emerson tapped his pen on the table thoughtfully. "Motive for both, certainly. But motive alone isn't enough—we need evidence to tie someone to the crime."

I leaned back in my chair, absently bouncing my knee. "Bear was volatile when I talked to him. He swore he knew nothing about Eloise's recipes, but I don't know. The kid's wound so tight he could snap like a dry twig."

The room fell quiet as everyone processed that.

"I've been thinking about the recipes," I said, leaning forward. "Why did they end up in Artie's garage? Did he steal them, hoping to sell them to FMR Foods?"

"Okay, but who killed him?" Anders asked, frowning as he crossed his arms. "And why? If they wanted the recipes, why not take them? Leaving them behind feels sloppy."

"Or rushed," Stanzi offered, "Maybe they got spooked. Hattie showed up, and then Josie came soon after. Whoever it was might not have had time to search for where Artie hid them."

I nodded, the timeline clicking into place. "Exactly."

Max gestured with his pretzel like a pointer. "So, about FMR Foods—what makes you think they're mixed up in this?"

"Blake," I said, my voice tightening. "He's been after Eloise's recipes for months. She told me he tried to buy them outright, but she refused. This was right after one of our volunteer meetings at Novel Grounds."

"Blake?" Rhett asked, leaning forward. "Isn't he the guy you mentioned seeing at the orchard?"

"Yep," I said, my tone darkening. "At first, I didn't realize who he was. Then it clicked. And he wasn't alone. He was with Tiffany and Dex."

That got everyone's attention.

"What's a corporate guy doing with those two?" Max asked, his brow furrowed. "And at an apple orchard, of all places?"

"Exactly," I said. "And when Blake saw me, he bolted like he didn't want to be seen. It was suspicious."

Dr. Emerson nodded, his expression grim. "If Blake's been pressuring Eloise, and now he's meeting with Tiffany and Dex, it's no coincidence. This could be corporate theft on a much bigger scale."

"But murder?" Holly asked, skeptical. "That's a big leap. Where do Tiffany and Dex fit in?"

"They're opportunists," I said. "Maybe Blake hired them to steal the recipes, but Artie found out and wanted a cut. Or maybe Artie was working with them and tried to double-cross Blake. Either way, things went south fast."

"And that bloody check planted at Novel Grounds?" Rhett added. "Were they trying to frame Hattie or just throw us off the trail?"

"Probably both," I said, frustration bubbling up. "If Eloise's recipes are this valuable, we've got to figure out why."

Anders leaned back, already pulling out his laptop. "I'll look into FMR Foods to see if they're under pressure to launch something big. If Blake's desperate, there'll be signs."

"Good," I said, "Meanwhile, I'll keep digging into Blake. If he's meeting with Tiffany and Dex in secret, he's up to something shady."

Hattie smirked. "Just don't get yourself arrested for trespassing. Caleb's patience only goes so far."

"Noted," I said dryly, though a flicker of warmth touched me at the thought of Caleb. Still, there wasn't time to dwell on that. Eloise's name was at stake.

The room settled into a focused quiet as everyone turned back to the murder board, jotting notes and tracing connections. The pieces were finally starting to form a picture, but it wasn't a comforting one. This wasn't just about stolen recipes or small-town drama anymore. The stakes were much higher, and the shadows we were chasing were darker than I'd expected.

10 brewed lies & tattered pages

LAST NIGHT, AFTER we had all gone home, I felt that time was slipping away, no matter how hard I tried to push it aside. We were so close, but the answers were still out of reach. Long after Hattie went to bed, I stayed up, hunched in my favorite swivel chair, poring over notes and scribbles until the words blurred together. By the time the clock ticked past 3 a.m., sleep felt like a distant memory, and when my alarm finally went off, I'd barely gotten two hours.

Now, standing in the café's back room, the exhaustion clung to me. The hum of the fridge and the ticking of the wall clock felt louder than usual, amplifying the heaviness in the air. Even Mocha seemed off, padding quietly by my side instead of her usual energetic pacing.

Hattie, of all people, had beaten me here this morning, which was suspicious. My sister was a late riser, notorious for rolling in mid-morning, hair askew, and complaining about how long it took to brew coffee. Today, though, she'd been waiting for me, quiet and watchful.

"You okay?" she asked now, leaning against the counter, her arms crossed, studying me like I was one of her watercolor tutorials. Her tone was casual, but the concern in her eyes wasn't.

"I'm fine," I muttered too quickly, grabbing a mug and reaching for the coffee pot like it was a life raft. Except my hands were shaking, and the mug slipped, nearly toppling before I caught it.

Hattie was faster, steadying it with one hand. "Josie," she said, her voice soft but firm. "You're not fine. You look like you're running on fumes."

I let out a sharp breath, not ready for the lecture I knew was coming. "I just need to figure this out, Hattie. Once Eloise is cleared, everything will go back to normal."

Hattie's eyebrows arched, skepticism written all over her face. "Normal? What's normal about running yourself into the ground? And dragging Holly down with you?"

Her words hit harder than I expected. "What's that supposed to mean?"

Hattie's arms tightened across her chest. "It means you've been so laser-focused on this case that you haven't stopped to think about how it's affecting everyone around you."

"That's not fair," I snapped, the defensive edge in my voice sharper than I intended. "Holly wants to help. I've been checking in with her! I told her to take a break just yesterday!"

"Josie," Hattie said with maddening calm, "you're asking, but you're not listening. Holly's exhausted. You're exhausted. But neither of you will admit it because you're both too stubborn to let anyone down."

"That's not true," I shot back, though doubt crept in even as I said it. Images of Holly's tired face, flour smudged across her cheek, flickered in my mind. "Holly's a grown woman, Hattie. If she didn't want to be here, she wouldn't be."

She leaned in, her eyes narrowing. "Holly's too loyal, just like you. She'd never leave you hanging, even if it meant running herself ragged."

The guilt hit like a punch to the gut, and for a moment, I couldn't find the words. My hands tightened around the edge of the counter, and all I could think about was how much I'd been leaning on Holly—on all of them—without stopping to notice the strain.

"You sound exactly like me the day Artie was murdered," she said softly, breaking the silence. "You warned me to slow down, to take care of myself. And now, here I am, warning you. You're so caught up in solving this case that you're losing sight of everything else."

"It's not an obsession," I said quietly, though even I could hear how hollow the words sounded. "It's focus. Eloise needs me, Hattie. If I don't figure this out, who will?"

Her expression softened, but her voice stayed steady. "Eloise needs you, sure. But not at the expense of your health—or your friendships. You're no good to her or anyone else if you crash."

The back door creaked open, and Holly stepped inside, her cheeks flushed from the brisk air. Her hair was tied in a messy bun, and she had that determined but tired look she always got after pulling a late-night shift.

"I heard you two," she said, setting her bag on the counter. Her voice was steady, but the exhaustion beneath it was clear. Mocha trotted over to greet her, tail wagging, blissfully unaware of the tension in the room.

"Holly," Hattie started, but Holly raised a hand to stop her.

"No, let me say this," Holly said firmly, her gaze shifting to me. "Josie isn't pushing me too hard. For the record, if I didn't want to be here, I wouldn't be. Eloise is family, and I'm not about to sit back and do nothing." She softened, her eyes meeting mine. "But Hattie's right about one thing—you're burning yourself out, Josie."

I opened my mouth to argue, but Holly gave me a look that silenced me.

"I can handle my part," she continued, her tone gentle but unyielding. "But you—you've barely slept, and you're running on caffeine and nerves. You're trying to do it all, and it's too much."

Her words stung, and I felt my defenses crumbling under the weight of my exhaustion. "I just... I don't know how to stop," I admitted, my voice cracking. "I'm scared. Scared that I'll let Eloise down. What if I can't figure it out? What if I fail her?"

Hattie stepped closer, wrapping me in a tight hug. "You're not going to fail her, Josie. But you don't have to do it alone. Caleb's the detective. Let him do his job and let us help you."

Holly placed a hand on my shoulder, grounding me. "We've got your back," she said softly. "But you need to trust us—and yourself—to handle this together."

I nodded, blinking back tears. The crushing weight eased for the first time in days, if only a little.

As I turned to look out the front door, I noticed a crumpled slip of paper poking out from under the front door, barely visible against the floorboards.

"Do you see that?" I asked, moving toward it with Mocha at my heels. The room fell silent as I bent to pick up the note and unfolded it with trembling hands.

My breath caught as I read the jagged handwriting:

JOSIE, YOU NEED TO KNOW THE TRUTH. ARTIE WAS KILLED BY SOMEONE YOU KNOW WELL. IT WAS ME, CHRISTOPHER THEODORE. I'M DANGEROUS.

The room seemed to tilt as the words sank in. It felt too blunt, too staged, like whoever wrote it wanted me to react without thinking. But I had to know anyway.

Without a second thought, I grabbed my coat and keys. "I need to talk to Bear," I said.

"Josie, wait—" Hattie's voice rose behind me, alarmed.

"I'll be fine," I said over my shoulder, stuffing the note into my pocket. "Watch Mocha for me."

Before they could argue, I was out the door, my pulse pounding and my thoughts racing faster than I could keep up. Taking the note to Caleb crossed my mind, but what would he do? File it under "evidence" and let it sit while we waited for something else to come along. There's no way I was going to let that happen.

The garage smelled like motor oil and dust. Sunlight slanted through the grimy windows and cut through the dust in the air. Bear was by the workbench, wiping his hands on a rag as he tinkered with the innards of an old car. He looked up when I stormed in, surprise flashing across his face.

"Josie," he said, slowly setting down a wrench like he was bracing for whatever was coming. "What brings you to Grandpa's house so early?"

I didn't bother with pleasantries. I shoved the crumpled note toward him. "This," I snapped. "I found it under my door this morning. It accuses you of killing Artie."

Bear stared at the note for a beat, then snorted a humorless laugh. "Seriously? That's why you're here?"

I blinked, thrown off by his reaction. "You think this is funny?" My voice rose. "Someone's accusing you of murder, Bear. Murder!"

He didn't flinch, his expression calm—too calm. "Come on, Josie. You know me better than that. Whoever wrote this has a sick sense of humor."

"Do I?" The words came out sharper than I intended. "Because lately, you've been... different. On edge. What's going on with you?"

Bear stepped forward, closing the gap between us. His presence felt heavier than usual, and I instinctively stepped back. "I've had a hard time," he said, his voice laced with bitterness. "That doesn't make me a killer."

"Hard time?" I held up the note, shaking it for emphasis. "The note doesn't even call you 'Bear.' It says Christopher Theodor. Do you really think that's a coincidence?"

His jaw tightened, his eyes flashing with something I couldn't quite place—anger, frustration, maybe guilt. "And that's what tipped you off?" He scoffed, a bitter laugh escaping him. "I haven't gone by Christopher in years. Everyone calls me Bear, just like everyone calls Grandpa Teddy. Whoever wrote that doesn't even know me. Didn't even spell my last name right."

I faltered for a second—he wasn't wrong. Theodor was misspelled. But I wasn't ready to back down. "Maybe you wrote it yourself," I said, frustration creeping into my tone. "Maybe this is your way of messing with me, trying to throw me off."

He grabbed a nearby ratchet, wiping it down like it was the only thing keeping his hands steady. "Messing with you?" He laughed, shaking his head. "Why would I leave a note accusing myself? That's ridiculous, even for you, Josie."

"Is it?" I pressed, crossing my arms. "Because you've been avoiding everyone. Hiding out. And now this note shows up? It's not exactly helping your case."

Bear dropped the rag onto the workbench with a heavy sigh. "You're tired, Josie. You're jumping at shadows. You're a smart woman, but you're way off base right now."

"Am I?" I countered, stepping closer. "Because everything about this feels wrong, and you're acting like someone with something to hide."

He turned away, running a hand through his messy hair. "I don't know what you want from me," he muttered, his voice quieter now. "But I'm not the bad guy here. Not in this story. Go home, Josie. Scram."

My pulse quickened, and my instincts buzzed. Scram? Really? Who even says that? But his tone wasn't just frustrated—it was defensive. He was holding something back.

Instead of letting his irritation push me out the door, I softened my voice. "Bear," I said gently, watching his body tense. "I'm not here to point fingers. I'm just trying to help. If there's something you're not telling me, you can trust me. You know that, right?"

For a moment, his shoulders slumped, like he might finally let something slip. But then his guard slammed back into place, and he shook his head. "I've got nothing to say to you, Josie. Go home."

"Fine," I said, stepping back toward the door. "But I'll figure it out. You know I will."

As I left, I could feel his eyes on me. Whatever Bear wasn't saying, it was important. And I wasn't stopping until I got the truth.

Back at the café, I sat at a table buried in notebooks, sticky notes, and my own tangled thoughts. The note, which had felt like a revelation this morning, now seemed like a taunt—a frustrating dead end that left me chasing my own tail.

Holly breezed by with a tray of muffins, but instead of her usual easy energy, she set it down with just enough force to make the plates rattle. "Josie," she said, hands on her hips, her sharp gaze pinning me in place. "You've been running yourself ragged. You're no good to anyone like this. Take a break. Clear your head."

I sighed, "I can't, Holly. Eloise is counting on me. If I mess this up—"

"You'll mess it up worse if you keep running on fumes," she interrupted, her tone sharper than usual but laced with worry. "And let's not forget how you stormed off earlier."

Her words hit their mark, guilt prickling at the edges of my exhaustion. She wasn't wrong. I'd left her and Hattie to pick up the pieces while I chased a lead that ultimately got me nowhere.

Hattie appeared, arms crossed and wearing her best "big sister disapproval" face. "We talked about this, Josie," she said, her tone clipped. "You're doing too much. I get that you want to help Eloise, but running off like you did? Not cool."

"I know," I said, pinching the bridge of my nose as my frustration and fatigue collided. "I'm sorry, okay? I just—"

"You just do whatever you want," Hattie cut me off. "You've got a café to run, a murder mystery party to plan, and, oh yeah, a team here to help you. But instead, you go full *lone wolf* the second you *sniff* out a clue."

"Okay, fine!" I threw up my hands, my voice edging toward exasperation. "I am stretched too thin. But what am I supposed to do? Sit back and wait while Eloise rots in a cell?"

"Yes!" Hattie shot back, her eyes narrowing. "That's exactly what you're supposed to do. Take a breath, let Caleb do his job, and stop running headfirst into every half-baked lead. We're all trying to help, Josie, but you can't keep acting like you're the *only one* who can solve this."

Her words hung in the air, heavier than I wanted to admit. I glanced at Holly, hoping for a lifeline, but she nodded, her expression softening just enough to make me feel even guiltier.

"Josie," Holly said gently, "we're worried about you. You've barely slept. You're juggling too much."

I opened my mouth to argue, but the look on her face stopped me. Holly rarely pushed, and when she did, it was because she meant every word.

"Look," Hattie said, her tone shifting to something closer to kind. "I'm taking these muffins to Eloise. She needs something decent to eat, and I promised her I'd check in today." She pointed a finger at me, her eyes narrowing. "You need to stay here and take care of your café. Got it?"

The logical part of me knew she was right. But the restless part—the part that couldn't stop chasing answers—was already digging in its heels. "I'll come with you," I said, grabbing my jacket before she could argue.

Hattie rolled her eyes, "Uh, no, you won't. You'll stay here and actually handle your responsibilities for once. Holly's already got her hands full, and your college crew can only do so much."

"They've got it under control," I countered, my voice edging toward stubbornness. "And if Caleb finds something out, I need to know about it."

Hattie groaned, clearly at the end of her patience. "Josie, seriously. You can't just keep—"

"I'm going, Hattie," I said, cutting her off with more firmness than I meant. "You can yell at me later."

She muttered something under her breath—probably unflattering—and snatched the basket of muffins off the counter. "Fine," she said in exasperation. "But don't expect Caleb to be thrilled when you show up uninvited."

"Wouldn't be the first time," I said with a small, tired smile, trying to lighten the mood.

Hattie shot me one last glare before heading for the door, muttering something about stubbornness being a family curse. Holly stayed behind, watching me with a mix of concern and resignation.

"You really are impossible, you know that?" she said, crossing her arms.

"Yeah," I admitted, "But you still love me."

The police station was quieter than usual, the low hum of conversation and the occasional ring of a phone filling the silence. Still, the tension in the air was as thick as week-old coffee. Caleb was in his office, hunched over, frowning at his paperwork. That frown only darkened when he spotted us.

"Oh, look," he said, standing and gesturing to us to come into his office with exaggerated flair. "If it isn't my two favorite amateur detectives." The sarcasm practically dripped off his words. "Care to explain why Bear Theodor just called me, ranting about being harassed?"

I stiffened, but before I could even open my mouth, Caleb raised a hand, stopping me cold. "Let me guess," he said, voice rising slightly. "You found something—maybe a note? And instead of bringing it to me, like I've repeatedly asked, you charged off to confront him?"

Guilt churned in my stomach, but I fished the crumpled note out of my pocket, holding it out like a peace offering. "We found this under my door this morning," I said defensively but trying to stay calm. "It accuses Bear of killing Artie."

Caleb snatched the note and scanned the jagged handwriting, his expression tightening with every word. His jaw clenched, muscle twitching. "So, instead of doing the smart thing and handing this over, you thought, 'Hey, let's go accuse someone of murder'? Solid plan, Josie."

"I wasn't accusing him!" I protested, frustration bubbling up. "I just wanted to hear his side. That's all."

"His side?" Caleb snapped, tossing the note onto his desk like it offended him. "You didn't hear his side; you backed him into a corner. He called me convinced you're setting him up, Josie."

I opened my mouth to protest, but Caleb wasn't done.

"You can't keep barging into people's lives, throwing around accusations, and then walking away like it's no big deal," he said, his tone sharp but not yelling. Caleb never yelled, but his quiet frustration hit harder. "This isn't a game, Josie. It's dangerous. You're not the only one in the line of fire here."

Hattie, ever the peacemaker, stepped forward, her tone gentler. "Caleb, we're just trying to help. You know that. We're running out of time, and—"

"I don't care about your timeline," Caleb cut her off, his voice slicing through hers. "This isn't about your deadlines or how quickly you think you can crack this. You're making it worse because you won't listen. Someone is playing you, and you're falling for it, step by step."

He turned his gaze back to me, and for the first time in a long while, I felt the weight of his frustration settle squarely on my shoulders. "Josie, you need to understand—whoever is behind this isn't just messing with you. They're setting traps. And if you keep walking right into them, you'll end up in a hole I can't dig you out of."

I swallowed hard, the sharpness of his words cutting deeper than I wanted to admit. "We're just trying to help Eloise," I said softly, my resolve faltering.

"And you think I'm not?" Caleb shot back. "If you keep going rogue, I won't be able to help anyone."

He grabbed the note and held it up before tossing it onto his desk again. "I'll get it analyzed, but don't expect much now. And this," he said, gesturing between us, "ends here. No more solo interrogations. No more rogue missions. Am I clear?"

Hattie nodded quickly. "Crystal."

I, however, wasn't quite ready to let it go. "But Caleb—"

"Josie, enough," he said, cutting me off with a tone that left no room for debate. He took the basket of muffins out of Hattie's hands, plucked one out, and took a massive bite like it was a stress snack. "Get back to Novel Grounds before you stir up more trouble. And, for the love of coffee, stay put this time."

With that, he turned on his heel and walked out, clutching the basket to his chest and leaving us standing there in awkward silence.

Hattie let out a low whistle, breaking the tension as she crossed her arms. "Well, that went about as well as I expected. I come bearing muffins, and now I'm on Caleb's hit list. Great."

She shook her head, her voice dripping with sarcasm. "Next time, remind me to just make brunch and stay out of it. You can handle the whole snooping thing solo."

I rolled my eyes, but her words stung just enough to keep me from firing back. As we left the station, Caleb's warning echoed in my mind louder than anything Hattie or Holly had said earlier.

"Well," Hattie said as we stepped into the foyer of the police building, pulling her coat jacket closed against the cooler air. "I hope this little stunt was worth it because, right now, you're on Caleb's last nerve."

I didn't respond. My thoughts were spinning faster than I could organize them. Caleb's frustration was playing on a loop in my head. He was right, and I hated it. I'd been reckless.

We stood in silence for a moment before Hattie sighed dramatically. "Okay, spill. What's going on in that over-caffeinated brain of yours?"

I glanced at her, my voice softer than usual. "Caleb's right. Someone's setting traps, and I keep walking right into them. But, Hattie… I think we're close. I just don't know what we're missing."

Her sharp gaze softened, and she bumped her shoulder lightly against mine. "Then let's figure it out. Preferably without you landing us in any more hot water."

A reluctant smile tugged at my lips. "Deal."

"Good," Hattie said with mock seriousness. "Because if Caleb bans muffins from this station, I'm blaming you."

The laugh died on my lips as my phone buzzed in my pocket. Connie's name flashed across the screen.

Hattie's teasing grin faltered. "Uh-oh. Connie doesn't usually call unless there's drama. Or snacks."

Connie's voice wavered when I answered—soft, almost fragile, starkly contrasting her usual dramatic bravado. Something was wrong.

"Connie, what happened?" I asked, already motioning to Hattie to follow me.

She hesitated on the line before saying, "I think... I think I've gotten myself in a bit of trouble, Josie."

That was all I needed to hear. Hattie and I were out the door in seconds, the quiet streets of Hickory Hills blurring as we raced toward Connie's house.

When we arrived, Connie was on her porch, but gone was her usual flair—no sweeping gestures, no exclamations about life or local gossip. She sat slumped in her chair, pale and tired, her right arm cradled in a makeshift sling.

Hattie and I exchanged a glance, her worry mirroring mine. As we climbed the porch steps, I knelt beside Connie, forcing a steady smile that I didn't feel. "Connie, dear," I said, keeping my voice light. "What's this I hear about an accident? You look like you wrestled a shrub and lost."

She chuckled faintly, "More like the shrub wrestled me. And I wasn't exactly in peak form to fight back."

Up close, the bruising on her wrist and the scratches along her arm made my chest tighten. Whatever happened wasn't a simple stumble.

"Connie," Hattie cut in, her tone a mix of anger and concern, "this isn't just you tripping over your own feet. What happened?"

Connie waved her good hand though even that movement lacked her usual energy. "Don't get all worked up. I'm fine. Just a little banged up from my misadventures in amateur detective work."

Skeptical, I said, "You're sitting here in a sling, and I'm supposed to believe this is fine?"

She sighed, looking out at the quiet street as if debating how much to tell us. "I saw Blake," she finally said, her voice dropping lower. "He was meeting some guy near the alley by that old, abandoned shop on the square. They were talking—something about a deal—but I couldn't hear much. I thought I'd get closer, maybe catch a little more." She glanced at me, a flicker of humor returning. "That was my first mistake."

I swallowed hard. "And?"

Connie shifted uncomfortably, her wince giving away more than she intended. "Before I could get close enough, a car came out of nowhere. Black, no headlights. It was barreling straight at me." Her voice wavered, the fear creeping in despite her best efforts to sound unfazed. "I barely managed to jump into the bushes. Twisted my wrist, got a few scratches, but... better than the alternative."

A chill ran down my spine, "Connie, that's not an accident. Someone was trying to hurt you."

Hattie let out a sharp breath. "You should've called the police the second it happened!"

"I didn't want to cause a fuss," Connie said, shaking her head like it was nothing. But her voice cracked slightly, "At first, I thought maybe it was some idiot not paying attention. But after hearing what you've been digging into, Josie..." She met my eyes, her own full of worry. "I don't think this was random. And that scares me."

Her words hit me like a punch to the throat. Guilt, so much guilt. This wasn't just about Connie. This was about me—my relentless poking around, my need to chase every lead. I'd dragged her into this.

"Connie, I'm so sorry," I whispered, the weight of it crushing me. "If I hadn't—"

"None of that," she interrupted firmly, "You didn't twist my arm and make me follow Blake, Josie. I've been nosy for decades, and I'll probably keep being nosy until my dying day. But..." She hesitated, her face softening. "Maybe it's time I stick to snooping around for theater gossip—who's been stealing the best dressing rooms or whose soprano isn't as flawless as they claim—instead of chasing criminals."

"You need to tell Caleb," Hattie said, her tone brooking no argument. "This isn't something to brush off, Connie. Someone tried to run you down."

Connie sighed, nodding reluctantly. "I will. But I wanted to warn you first." Her gaze shifted back to me, her expression heavy with worry. "Josie, whoever's behind this... they're not playing around. You need to be careful."

My chest tightened, the guilt mixing with frustration. Connie—bright, unstoppable Connie—had been shaken to her core. And it was because of me.

Hattie crossed her arms, her big-sister tone kicking in. "Josie, this has to stop. Caleb was right—you're being reckless, and now someone's gotten hurt."

"I know," I whispered, my voice barely audible.

"You have to slow down," Hattie pressed, her voice softening. "You're not invincible, Josie. And if something happens to you..." She trailed off.

Connie, ever perceptive, reached over and patted my hand. "She's right, you know. You're no good to anyone if you're too busy throwing yourself into danger to see the big picture."

I looked between them—Connie, bruised and tired but as stubborn as ever, and Hattie, her worry barely hidden beneath a mask of exasperation. They were both right. As much as I hated to admit it, I knew they were.

I let out a breath, my tone softening. "I'll be careful. But Connie, promise me you'll get that arm checked out—and that you'll tell Caleb everything. No skipping details."

Connie held up her good hand, her expression resolute. "Promise. Scout's honor." Then, with a wink, she added, "Though I was never a scout. Closest I got was organizing backstage chaos at the community theater."

By Saturday, I was ready to regroup—or at least try. The gang had gathered at Konstanze and Max's again, the murder board dominating the dining room. Despite the crackling fireplace and the soft glow of the lamplight reflecting off the happy Emma Bridgewater ceramics, Connie's close call and Caleb's warnings still haunted me.

Holly was busy laying out snacks—a mix of pretzels, cookies, and her famous pumpkin spice muffins because, apparently, emotional support carbs were the theme of the evening. Hattie and Rhett sifted through piles of notes and photos. Their brows were furrowed in matching concentration.

"Alright, people," Max said, clapping his hands together as he settled into his chair. "Let's solve a murder, shall we?"

I cleared my throat nervously. "Actually, y'all, before we dive in, there's something I need to get off my chest."

All eyes turned toward me. Hattie gave me a suspicious look while Holly paused mid-muffin-placement. Even Anders glanced up from his laptop.

"Remember when I jokingly said that I thought I saw Julius's ghost haunting the square?" My voice wavered slightly, and I braced myself for the incoming skepticism. "Well... it wasn't just a shadow or a trick of the light. I actually saw someone."

Konstanze leaned forward, her expression equal parts intrigued and exasperated. "You're just now telling us this?"

"I know," I groaned, throwing my hands up. "It sounds ridiculous, okay? And with everything else going on, I didn't think you'd believe it. But after what happened with Connie... I don't think it was my imagination. Someone was watching me."

Hattie folded her arms, her lips pressing into a thin line. "Josie, you do realize how shady that sounds, right? You can't just sit on information like this."

"Okay, fair," I admitted, rubbing the back of my neck. "But I didn't want to sound paranoid."

"You always sound paranoid," Hattie shot back, though her smirk softened the jab. "It's part of your charm."

Konstanze gave a dramatic sigh, waving a hand toward Max. "Well, if someone's been watching Josie, it's not paranoia—it's a lead. What do we know about this so-called ghost?"

I described what I'd seen—the shadow slipping between the trees, the faint rustle of leaves, the heavy feeling of being watched. Then I finally admitted it: I'd been chased. "I could hear the footsteps behind me—uneven, like whoever it was had a limp," I said, my voice quieter now. "At the time, I thought I was imagining things. Maybe losing it. But now…" I glanced around the room, letting the weight of my words settle. "Now I think they were trying to scare me—or figure out how much I know."

Max leaned back, munching on a pretzel as he mulled it over. "If someone's keeping tabs on you, it means we're on the right track. But it also means whoever's behind this doesn't like how close we're getting."

"Great," Hattie muttered, throwing a pointed look my way. "Because that's not terrifying or anything."

"Not helping," I shot back, though the knot in my stomach tightened further.

Anders cleared his throat from his corner, his laptop screen glowing faintly. "I've been digging into FMR Foods," he said, drawing everyone's attention. "They're mostly clean, but there's something… weird. Turns out, Artie had financial ties to a shell company FMR used a few years ago. Looks like he was either doing business with them or blackmailing them."

Rhett frowned, leaning forward. "Blackmailing FMR Foods? That's a bold move for a guy running a secondhand garage."

"And possibly a stupid one," Anders added, his fingers flying over his keyboard. "If Artie was pressuring them for money, that could've put a target on his back."

Emma chimed in from across the table. "Rhett and I talked to a few people around town—car guys, mostly. Artie wasn't exactly popular. He had a way of rubbing people the wrong way. Not just in business, but… in everything."

Rhett nodded. "Shady side hustles, bad deals, you name it. Artie wasn't above pulling strings—or stepping on toes."

Hattie let out an exasperated sigh. "Okay, so Artie wasn't a saint. We get it. But blackmail? Murder? Those are entirely different levels."

"Not necessarily," Konstanze said, sliding a thin folder across the table toward me. "I found something in Artie's past that might explain a lot."

I opened the folder, my stomach dropping as I scanned the headline:

Local Mechanic Jailed for Faulty Repairs Leading to Death.

"Artie went to prison?" I asked, barely above a whisper.

Max, setting down his pretzels, nodded grimly. "He was responsible for a crash that killed a woman and her kid. Faulty brake repairs. He served a few years, got out, and somehow swept it under the rug."

Hattie gasped, her hand flying to her chest. "And we let him work on Captain Vantastic? Are you kidding me?"

The room fell silent, the weight of the revelation pressing down on us. Artie wasn't just a shady mechanic—he had blood on his hands.

"Here's the kicker," Max added, his voice low. "The husband survived. His name's Stu Kratz."

The name landed like a grenade in the room, the silence that followed almost deafening.

"Stu Kratz," I repeated slowly, "You think he killed Artie?"

Max shrugged, but his face was grim. "If you lost your family because of someone's negligence and that someone walked free after a couple of years...wouldn't you be angry?"

Konstanze's voice cut in, calm but pointed. "Stu has every reason to hate Artie. If he's been holding a grudge all these years, it might explain everything—the murder, the threats, even Connie's close call. He could be tying up loose ends."

Anders raised a hand like a student in a classroom. "One more twist," he said, his tone grim. "Artie and Dex were in the same prison together. For two years."

The air in the room thickened as we all processed this new bombshell.

"So now we've got Dex, Stu Kratz, and FMR Foods all tangled up in this mess," I said, pacing in front of the murder board. "Artie wasn't just a mechanic with a bad attitude. He was playing a dangerous game on multiple fronts."

"And one of them finally caught up to him," Hattie added quietly.

I nodded, the knot in my stomach tightening further. "We need to find Stu Kratz. If he's the one pulling the strings."

Anders's fingers flew across his keyboard. "I'll see if I can track him down."

Max leaned forward, his expression darker than usual. "If Stu's out there, we need to find him first—before he decides to come after anyone else."

The room fell into a tense silence, the weight of the case pressing down on all of us. For the first time, I felt the full scope of what we were dealing with. This wasn't just about solving a puzzle anymore—it was about staying one step ahead of someone who was clearly willing to do whatever it took to cover their tracks.

And somehow, I had to make sure we weren't next on their list.

11 espresso shots & double-crossed plots

THE MORNING WAS BRISK AND OVERCAST as I pulled into Novel Grounds, my thoughts still spinning from everything we uncovered last night. Hickory Hills was waking up slowly, the streets quiet except for the occasional hum of a car or the distant bark of a dog. As I stepped into the café, the comforting scent of coffee, muffins, and old books wrapped around me like a warm hug. Normally, it would've been enough to calm me down, but today wasn't normal.

Today, I was going to press Dex for answers.

Inside, the café was buzzing with its usual morning energy. Holly was a blur of motion, juggling trays of pastries while also fixing up decorations for tomorrow's big murder mystery party. Her uncanny ability to multitask like a superhero made me feel slightly guilty for my less-than-stellar energy levels. Meanwhile, Hattie and Emma were battling paper streamers in the bookstore section, hanging faux cobwebs and trying not to get tangled in the process.

I tried to focus on the muffins and cobwebs, but my mind kept circling back to Artie's murder. Tiffany's smug grin. Dex's suspicious silence. There was more to their connection with Artie than either of them was letting on, and I was done waiting for the truth to conveniently fall into my lap. By mid-afternoon, I found myself standing outside Dex's house, determination pushing aside the unease gnawing at me.

His place was a mess—like it had given up on impressing anyone a long time ago. Peeling blue paint with a failed patch job of gray, a yard full of rusted car parts, and tools scattered like confetti across the workbenches—everything was coated in a fine layer of grime.

Dex emerged from the shadows of the garage, wiping his hands on an oil-stained rag. His expression shifted when he saw me—somewhere between annoyance and unease.

"Josie," he said, tossing the rag aside. "What are you doing here?"

Straight to the point. "I need to ask you a few questions," I said, my voice steady even as my nerves buzzed. "It's about Artie."

His brow furrowed, and for a split second, something flickered across his face—fear, maybe? Guilt? "I already told the cops everything I know."

"Sure," I said, folding my arms. "But I'm not the cops. Let's start with this—you and Artie served time together, didn't you?"

His jaw tightened, and he tried for casual with a shrug. "It was a big place. We weren't exactly pen pals."

"That's not the whole truth, is it?" I pressed—a shot in the dark. I took a step closer. "You two were cellmates, weren't you?"

Dex blinked, clearly caught off guard. His cocky facade cracked, and he let out a sharp breath, running a hand over his face. "Yeah," he muttered. "We were cellmates. I trusted him... stupidly. Told him all about Hickory Hills, about Teddy, about the garage. Thought I was just talking to a guy trying to get by, like me."

"But Artie wasn't just listening, was he?" I asked, my voice softening slightly.

Dex's shoulders slumped. "No. He used me, plain and simple. I told him how much I wanted to fix things with Teddy after everything I'd done. Told him how much the garage meant to me—how much it meant to Teddy. And when I got out? I found out he'd swooped in and bought it right out from under Teddy, tricking him into selling it for next to nothing."

His voice shook with anger, and his fists clenched at his sides. "I was furious, Josie. But I didn't kill him. I swear I didn't."

I studied his face, watching for cracks in his story. Anger, regret—those were real. And there wasn't that slippery edge of a lie. I believed him.

"What about Tiffany?" I asked, shifting gears. "She's got her own issues with Artie. Did she know what he did to Teddy?"

Dex let out a bitter laugh. "Tiffany? Of course, she knew. But Tiffany doesn't care about anyone unless they can do something for her. She doesn't really care about me, and she sure doesn't care about Teddy. She's not a killer, though. She's manipulative, sure. She loves playing people, but she wouldn't get her hands dirty."

Something in his tone made me pause. "Why do you stick around her, then?"

Dex's mouth tightened, and he looked away. "Because sometimes you think you deserve the mess you're in."

That hit harder than I expected, but I pushed past it. "Dex, why didn't you say anything sooner? Why not go to Caleb or even Teddy?"

He hesitated, running a hand through his messy hair. "Because I was scared, alright? Scared of what people would think, scared of what it'd do to Teddy... I've already screwed up so much. I thought keeping quiet was the best way to keep things from blowing up even worse."

I nodded slowly, letting his words sink in. There was truth there, but I could still feel something missing.

"Alright," I said finally. "But if you remember anything—anything—you come to me. Got it?"

Dex nodded, relief flickering across his face. "Yeah. Sure."

I turned to leave, but something nagged at me. "One more thing—could I use your bathroom?"

Dex blinked, clearly caught off guard by the abrupt question. "Uh, yeah. It's down the hall on the right."

"Thanks," I said, already heading down the hall. But I wasn't here for the bathroom. Tiffany's purse had been sitting on the couch, and I could see it through the opened basement door. Something about it had been tugging at me ever since.

Now was my chance.

I glanced back toward Dex. He was at his workbench, muttering under his breath as he tightened a bolt on some rusted car part. Perfect. Taking a deep breath, I leaned over Tiffany's purse, trying not to make a sound.

Receipts. Lipstick. Gum wrappers. My fingers brushed something sturdier...cardstock. My heart stuttered as I pulled it free.

One of Eloise's recipe cards.

The familiar handwriting stared back at me, the faint scent of vanilla clinging to the paper. My pulse quickened. Proof. Tiffany had stolen Eloise's recipes.

Before I could process what this meant, the sharp thud of footsteps on the stairs snapped me back to reality. My stomach lurched. Someone was coming.

I shoved the recipe card back into the purse, fumbling with the zipper before darting into the hallway, my heart pounding in my ears.

This wasn't just circumstantial anymore. Tiffany was involved—and I had seen the proof.

As I left Dex's house, the weather took a turn for the worse. The blustery autumn air clung to me, and leaves swirled in the wind like a storm of golden confetti. I zipped my jacket tighter, but the wind up here on the bluff had a bite to it—damp and bitter, promising rain. The sky hung low with heavy clouds, and the earthy scent of wet leaves filled the air—a sure sign that drizzle wasn't far behind.

The grand stone buildings of the university loomed ahead, their ivy-covered facades darkened by the damp weather. They seemed to exhale history—each stone a part of something bigger, a witness to generations of scholars, secrets, and scandals. One building stood out, its chateau-like spire reaching into the gray sky like something out of a fairytale. It's the same spire I see from the café every day like it's keeping a silent watch over the town. The scene could've been plucked straight from the pages of a gothic novel, the old-world charm of the architecture clashing beautifully with the vibrant fall colors swirling around it. The long stone pathway leading to the entrance was flanked by rain-dampened lawns and shadowed by towering trees, giving the whole place an air of timelessness.

As I pushed open the heavy wooden doors of the building, the warmth inside was a welcome contrast to the chill outside. The hallways stretched out in both directions, lined with portraits of long-forgotten scholars and intricate carvings that seemed to tell their own stories. The echo of my footsteps on the polished wood floors followed me until I reached Stanzi's classroom. I paused for a moment at the door, then stepped inside.

The room was bathed in soft, diffused light from the tall, arched windows. Outside, the rain had picked up, pattering against the glass in a soothing rhythm. The light filtered through the mist and rain, casting the room in a dreamlike glow that felt peaceful and deceptive. Beyond the glass, the wind tugged at the ivy clinging to the old brick walls, their leaves in various stages of fiery transformation from gold to crimson. The aged glass and ironwork windows seemed like portals to another time—one filled with secrets waiting to be uncovered.

Inside, the world felt far removed from the dreary weather. The semi-circular layout of tiered seating made the room feel like an intimate theater. Every detail was drenched in history, with antique brass sconces flickering on the walls, sending dancing shadows across the portraits of scholars who seemed to silently watch over our every move.

Stanzi's presence was unmistakable at the front of the room, not just in her commanding demeanor but in how her desk practically demanded attention. The aged oak piece, with its clutter of papers, leather-bound books, and that ever-present Emma Bridgewater ceramic jar filled with freshly picked autumnal wildflowers, felt like an extension of her.

One side of the desk held an open notebook, its neat, precise handwriting almost too perfect to touch, while an old-fashioned fountain pen lay discarded next to it as if she had been interrupted mid-thought. It always struck me how her space managed to be both intimidating and welcoming, a reflection of the woman herself. Above the desk, the large chalkboard still carried traces of her earlier lecture, her looping handwriting as artistic as it was meticulous, much like the woman who had written it.

Stanzi's classroom was a breathtaking mix of dark and light academia. It was a place that made you want to sit back with a classic novel or spend hours solving a mystery. With their plump floral pillows, the plush armchairs looked like they were made for sinking into, the deep leather cushions practically begging you to get lost in thought. On a side table, a collection of antique teacups—no doubt a nod to Stanzi's love for vintage elegance—sat like treasures from another time.

The whole gang was already here, scattered around the room like characters waiting for the next act. Max was draped over one of the plush armchairs, munching on pretzels. Hattie, Rhett, and Emma stood by the murder board, their expressions grim as they added more strings to the already chaotic web of suspects and motives. Holly, ever the multitasker, was balancing a notepad on her knee while sipping from one of the antique teacups Stanzi kept tucked away on a side table. Anders sat at one of the student's desks, furiously typing on his laptop like he was trying to hack into a government database.

"Alright, everyone," I said, clapping my hands to refocus the room. "Let's regroup. We've got too many threads, and they're all threatening to strangle us if we don't start connecting them. Dex didn't spill much, but he knows more than he's letting on. And Tiffany—well, she's still our best shot at breaking this wide open. So, how do we approach her?"

Max, perched in his usual armchair with his bag of pretzels, leaned back like this was just another casual brainstorming session. "Tiffany's a pro at playing people," he said, his voice calm. "She makes you believe whatever she wants you to believe. She's slippery, but even pros mess up eventually."

"She's not invincible, though," Holly added, scribbling something in her notebook. "We've already got one lead on her. Nikki overheard someone say she was near Eloise's house the night of the murder. If we can confirm that, it might be enough to put some pressure on her."

I nodded, pacing in front of the board like movement might help shake loose some answers. "And don't forget the recipes," I said, pointing to one of the notes pinned near the center. "Tiffany knew about them. I'm betting she's got more than just Eloise's muffin card in that purse of hers."

That earned a few sharp looks. I raised a hand, preemptively defending myself. "Okay, yes, I did a little snooping—again."

"Oh, for crying out loud," Hattie groaned, crossing her arms and giving me her patented big-sister glare. "Another 'bathroom break'? What did you find this time?"

"I may have noticed one of Eloise's recipe cards sticking out of Tiffany's purse while I was at Dex's house," I admitted, bracing myself for the fallout. "It's enough to prove she had access to the recipes—maybe even stole them herself."

Holly's pen froze mid-tap. Anders stopped typing, his usual poker face cracking just a little. Even Rhett leaned forward, his casual calm slipping into something closer to concern.

"You're saying Tiffany has the recipes?" Holly asked, her voice sharp.

"At least one," I confirmed. "I haven't told Caleb yet—I needed to be sure before bringing him in—but it's enough to confront her."

"And you're just sitting on this?" Stanzi asked, looking up from her notebook, her tone as precise and deliberate as ever. "Josie, if that recipe card is the key to all of this, you can't keep it under wraps much longer. Tiffany's smart, and if she catches wind that you know..."

"I get it," I said, cutting her off before she could finish the thought. "I'm not planning to sit on it forever. But I need more. If I confront her too soon, she'll twist it around or find a way to explain it away. She's too careful for me to go in half-baked."

Max frowned, setting aside his pretzels—a rare and ominous sign. "She's more than careful. If she has the recipes, it's because she knows exactly what they're worth. She's not careless, and she won't panic unless you catch her off-guard."

Before I could respond, Rhett broke in, his tone steady but laced with urgency. "Anders and I found something else. We already know Artie had ties to a shell company linked to FMR Foods. Turns out, it wasn't just shady—it was dangerous. Artie was blackmailing them. No doubt about it."

The air in the room shifted, the weight of his words settling over us like a storm cloud. "Blackmail's one thing," I said slowly, "but murder? That's a whole other ballgame."

"That's what I don't get either," Hattie said, crossing her arms and staring at the board like it might give her an answer. "Sure, Artie was shady. We've all established that. But what could he have had on FMR that would make them resort to murder?"

"More importantly," Holly added, "what did FMR need to keep hidden? It has to be something big."

"And maybe illegal," Anders said, not looking up from his laptop. "Artie was a small fish playing a big game. If he threatened to expose something that could take FMR down, murder isn't off the table."

I chewed on that. Thinking aloud, I asked, "What if it's about the recipes? Blake's been desperate to get his hands on them. If FMR is planning something shady—maybe a new product line or something—they could've needed those recipes to make it work. And if Artie found out, he could've used it to his advantage."

"That tracks," Rhett said, nodding. "If Artie tried to blackmail them and they couldn't pay—or wouldn't—it gives them motive."

"And if Tiffany and Dex were helping FMR," Max added, "it might explain why they're so tangled up in this. Maybe they weren't just helping—they wanted a cut of the blackmail money."

"Or they were scared Artie would drag them down with him," Hattie said darkly. "Either way, they're involved. And if they were willing to trash Novel Grounds and plant that bloody check, who's to say they wouldn't go further?"

The room fell quiet again, the weight of her words pressing down on all of us. This wasn't just about stolen recipes or petty grudges anymore. This was big. And dangerous.

I ran a hand through my hair, my mind circling back to Bear. "And then there's Bear," I said, the thought forming as I spoke. "He swears someone's setting him up, but he's hiding something. I can feel it."

Max leaned forward, his casual demeanor slipping. "If Bear knows more than he's saying, he's going to need a reason to spill it. He won't just volunteer information."

I nodded, though my thoughts were already shifting. No matter how often I tried to follow other leads—FMR Foods, Artie's past, Bear—it always circled back to Tiffany. She was at the center of everything. I was sure of it. But was I too focused on her? Was I missing something bigger?

"I'll track down Stu Kratz," Rhett said, cutting into my thoughts. "If anyone has a reason to hate Artie, it's him. And if he's resurfaced now…"

"We still need to find him before he finds us," Hattie finished, her voice sharp.

The words hung in the air, heavy with implication. But as much as Stu Kratz mattered, I couldn't let go of Tiffany. She was the key to all of this—I could feel it. And tomorrow, at the murder mystery party, I was going to confront her. It was risky, but it was my best chance.

12 whodunit, a double shot of drama

NOVEL GROUNDS HAD TRANSFORMED into a page straight out of a mystery novel. Dim lighting, flickering candles, and the rich aroma of chocolate and pumpkin spice mingled in the air. The shelves of books loomed like sentinels over the evening, lending a cozy, conspiratorial atmosphere to the room.

The tables, draped in crimson cloth and scattered with autumn leaves, glowed under the light of candelabras. The whole scene was bathed in a warm, golden hue, thanks to the flickering fire and the university string quartet softly playing in the corner. Every note they plucked added an air of intrigue as if we were all one wrong step away from the truth—or another murder.

Guests in costume milled about, their enthusiasm infectiously obvious. Novel Grounds' regulars had gone all out. Sherlock Holmes was deep in conversation with Miss Marple near the coffee bar, while Jessica Fletcher looked suspiciously at a group of Nancy Drews huddled near the mystery section. Even Mocha had joined in, her deerstalker cap perched at an angle, her little cape dragging behind her as she sniffed at crumbs beneath the dessert table.

"Welcome to Death by Chocolate: The Pumpkin Plot!" I announced, raising my voice over the hum of chatter. My Nancy Drew costume—complete with a yellow cardigan, plaid skirt, and vintage flashlight—helped me look the part of tonight's detective-in-chief. "Tonight, you are all detectives. Use your wits, your notebooks, and, of course, your taste buds to unravel the mystery of Poirot's untimely demise."

That earned a few chuckles as I gestured toward the "library" section, where Roy McCoy, ever the drama enthusiast, had gleefully volunteered to play the recently deceased Poirot. Roy was slumped dramatically in a plush armchair, surrounded by chocolate-covered pumpkin truffles. His fake mustache sat slightly askew, and his gray suit looked suspiciously like it had been pulled out of a thrift shop five minutes before curtain. But, to Roy's credit, he was selling it.

Before I could move on, the door burst open, and chaos blew in like a gust of autumn wind.

"Ch-ch-ch-Chip 'N Dale! Rescue Rangers!"
An entire Rescue Rangers ensemble tumbled into the café, led by Dale, whose red Hawaiian shirt flapped as he darted around, belting out their theme song at the top of his lungs.

"Rescue Rangers!" the rest of the group chimed in—Chip in a leather jacket, Gadget wielding an oversized wrench, Monterey Jack sniffing the air dramatically, and Zipper buzzing along in his makeshift wings.

Gadget marched straight up to me, all business. "Don't worry, Josie. The Rescue Rangers are on the case." She hefted her "wrench" like she was ready to crack open a safe—or a truffle.

"Well, I'm glad we've got backup," I said, biting back a laugh. "Just don't let Poirot's clues throw you off. He's known for being tricky from beyond the grave."

"Ch-ch-ch-check the truffles!" Dale sang as he spun dramatically toward the "crime scene," narrowly avoiding a stack of coffee mugs.

"Focus!" Chip barked, attempting to corral his hyperactive counterpart. "We're detectives, not tourists!"

Roy, clearly thrilled to have an audience, cracked open one eye and whispered loudly, "Check the gold-dusted truffle. It might be... a clue."

Dale dove for the tray, causing Gadget to groan and Monterey Jack to mutter about cheese. The room burst into laughter, and for a brief moment, the tension of the last few days melted away in the warmth of camaraderie and costumes.

Across the room, Sheriff Declan Sturdy, dressed as Magnum P.I. in a red Hawaiian shirt and baseball cap, strolled over, arms crossed and mock-serious. "Is that squirrel supposed to be me?" he asked, his mustache twitching as he nodded toward Dale.

Hattie, standing nearby with a pumpkin spice muffin in hand, laughed. "Maybe you should take notes. He's got more pep than you've had in years."

"Very funny, Hattie," the sheriff said, tipping his cap. "But if that chipmunk solves this case faster than I do, I'm hanging up my badge."

The lighthearted chaos of the evening was infectious, but as I scanned the room, my focus shifted. While everyone else laughed and mingled, a few people stood out—too polished, too quiet, or just plain suspicious.

Tiffany.

Dressed in a sleek black dress that screamed femme fatale, she moved through the room like she was on a runway, her red lips curving into a smile that didn't quite reach her eyes. She laughed at Hank Junior's jokes and accepted compliments on her costume with effortless charm, but there was something calculated about her tonight. Every glance, every word, felt rehearsed.

And then there was Blake Courtney, lounging near the dessert table in his sharp suit. Blake wasn't a regular at Novel Grounds. FMR Foods, the company he worked for, had a business relationship with us—they supplied some of our products—but Blake himself? He didn't have any connection to me or the café. He wasn't eating or mingling—just scrolling through his phone like he had somewhere better to be.

Every few minutes, his eyes flicked to the door, his thumb hesitating over the screen. Waiting for a message? Or someone? Whatever it was, it had him on edge. Something was making him nervous and then, some guy sidled up next to him.

I heard Blake say, "What do you want, Delany?"

My attention shifted to Dex, hunched in the corner by the bookshelf, all jittery and nervous. His fingers tapped an uneven rhythm on the table, his gaze darting between Tiffany and the door. When his eyes landed on me, he quickly looked away.

And Bear... he wasn't himself tonight either. His usual easygoing charm had curdled into frustration. He snapped at the barista when his drink order took too long, and his scowl deepened every time someone tried to engage him in conversation.

I turned my attention back to Tiffany, who caught my eye for a fraction of a second before slipping seamlessly into another conversation. My stomach twisted. She was too composed, too polished. The recipe card I'd seen in her purse flashed in my mind. What was she hiding?

"Josie!" Holly's voice broke through my thoughts as she waved me over to the coffee bar. She was dressed as a 10th Doctor, complete with a trench coat and sonic screwdriver. "We're out of cider, and someone's asking for a refill!"

"On it!" I called, but Claire swooped in out of nowhere, cutting me off like a perfectly lipsticked speed bump.

"Josie," she said, her tone oozing with polished amusement. "Is there a single square inch of this café you haven't personally managed tonight?"

She was dressed to the nines as a 1920s flapper, complete with a feathered headband perched elegantly on her blonde curls and a string of pearls long enough to lasso a horse. She practically sparkled under the dim café lights, as if she'd mistaken this for a Gatsby-themed gala instead of a cozy mystery night.

"It's called multitasking," I replied, pasting on my most hostess-like smile. "You might want to try it sometime."

"Oh, I'd love to," she said, her gaze sweeping dramatically across the room. "But I wouldn't want to deprive you of the chance to show off. You really do thrive in chaos, Josie—it's almost inspiring."

Inspiring. Almost. I took a slow, deep breath and reminded myself that Claire wasn't a villain; she was just Claire.

"It's a talent," I shot back, giving her a tight smile. "And I've had years of practice. Probably since middle school. You remember—group projects?"

Her eyes twinkled with faux innocence. "Oh, you mean when you insisted on doing all the work? I wasn't about to stand in your way back then, either. I've always been supportive like that." She leaned in closer, lowering her voice as if we were sharing some grand secret. "But seriously, Josie, if you need someone to step in and take over, just say the word. You know delegation is kind of my specialty."

I fought the urge to laugh. "And by delegation, you mean bossing everyone around while pretending it's teamwork?"

Claire gasped, one hand dramatically flying to her pearls. "Exactly! You do know me so well." She gave me a wink.

Before I could volley back, Holly's voice rang out from behind the counter, saving me. "Josie, remember, cider emergency! Can you grab another pitcher, please?"

I seized my opportunity. "Coming!"

Claire stepped aside with a flourish, clearly not ready to let me off the hook without one last parting shot. "Don't let me keep you, darling. Perish the thought that I interrupt your whirlwind of efficiency. Just let me know when you want my help—it's only a matter of time."

"Noted," I said, breezing past her.

As I reached the coffee bar, Holly greeted me with a wide grin, clearly having witnessed the whole exchange. "Claire again?" she asked, handing me the cider pitcher.

"Who else?" I said, shaking my head. "Apparently, I'm 'thriving in chaos.'"

Holly snorted, adjusting her fez. "Oh, please. Claire wouldn't know chaos if it strutted in here wearing pearls and a feather boa. She'd call it eccentric decor."

I laughed, feeling the tension Claire stirred up, start to fade. "One day, I might just let her take over—just to see how she handles it."

Holly arched a brow. "She'd probably have us all color-coded and arranged by height within the hour."

"And she'd somehow make it look fabulous," I admitted with a sigh, then glanced back at Claire. She was chatting animatedly with a group near the fireplace, her laugh ringing out like a perfectly rehearsed melody.

"She's not all bad," Holly said softly, nudging me with her elbow. "You know she'd be the first one to defend you if anyone else tried to give you a hard time."

"Yeah, I know," I muttered, feeling a begrudging smile creep onto my face. "But that doesn't mean she's going to get the last word."

Holly grinned. "That's the spirit."

On my way to the back storeroom, I caught Claire glancing my way. She raised her glass in a silent toast, her smirk more playful now than pointed. I gave her a quick nod in return. Because at the end of the day, Novel Grounds wouldn't be half as interesting without her around to keep me on my toes.

As I returned with the cider, I watched Holly behind the counter. She was in full Eleventh Doctor mode, her long coat swirling dramatically with each turn, bow tie perfectly straight, and that infectious grin lighting up her face. She twirled her sonic screwdriver like it might actually fix the espresso machine—or at least speed it up.

As I got closer, I caught the faint strains of *I Am the Doctor* playing from her phone, tucked neatly into her coat pocket. The music seemed to choreograph her every movement as she worked. She was practically dancing her way through drink orders.

"Two lattes, coming right up!" she declared, aiming her screwdriver at the machine with exaggerated authority.

I laughed as she handed me a cup with a theatrical flourish. "You really commit to the bit, don't you?"

Holly grinned wider, not missing a beat. "It's what the Doctor would do, Josie. Now, go on—there's a universe to save! Or at least a party to manage."

The café was packed, the drink line winding across the room as the hum of conversation mingled with the comforting aroma of coffee and sweet spices. Holly, Tyler, and Alexis held down the fort with the energy of seasoned baristas, even if the rush threatened to overwhelm them.

I jumped behind the counter to help, grabbing a cup and starting on *A Pumpkin Paradox*—a dark roast spiked with pumpkin and a hint of chocolate that had become an unexpected hit. Holly shot me a quick grin as she frothed milk for *A Study in Scarlet*, while Tyler worked on *Edgar Allan Poe's Midnight Mocha*, his hands moving with practiced ease.

Across the café, the party's energy thrummed around me, but my attention kept slipping. Tiffany, poised and polished in her sleek black dress, glided through the crowd like a queen holding court. Her laugh was light, her red lips curved in just the right way to charm anyone listening. But her eyes? They told a different story. Darting. Calculating.

As I handed off another *Murder on the Orient Espresso*—complete with its Viennese coffee and touch of crème de cacao—my gaze drifted to the far wall. Looking sharp in his suit, Blake was in deep conversation with the mystery guest. And then there was Dex, hunched in the corner like he wished the floor would swallow him whole. And Bear, normally, was the guy who brought the party—cracking jokes, chatting with everyone, always good-natured. But tonight? He sat at a table near the counter, scowling into his espresso like it had personally insulted him.

It hit me then: Teddy wasn't here.

Bear and Teddy were a package deal at events like this—always side by side, cracking jokes and keeping the mood light. Teddy was nowhere to be seen, and Bear's sour mood made more sense now. Had they fought? Was that why Bear looked like he'd rather be anywhere else?

Over by the snack table, Sam was quietly restocking trays of chocolate-covered pumpkin truffles. Dressed in his usual apron, he worked with the efficiency of someone who thrived on order. I caught his eye and gave him a nod of thanks. He returned a quick smile before resuming his task, restocking truffles.

The party was a whirlwind of costumes, laughter, and playful competition. Over at a nearby table, Rhett and Emma were huddled over the game clues, their costumes earning more than a few chuckles. Rhett's shaggy wig and rumpled green T-shirt were perfectly "Shaggy," while Emma, in her Scooby onesie and bright blue collar, barked enthusiastically every time they found something. I wouldn't have been surprised if they pulled out a bag of Scooby Snacks.

Holly, still in her Time Lord persona, adjusted her fez beside me, practically bouncing on her toes. "This is so much fun, Josie! Everyone's really getting into character."

I followed her gaze to Anders, leaning against a bookshelf with the kind of effortless cool that made his Sam Spade costume work. His trench coat rumpled just right, fedora tilted at an angle, and a fake cigarette dangling from his lips, he looked like he'd stepped out of a noir film. Nearby, their daughter, Nikki, was holding court in her bright yellow Dick Tracy trench coat, the addition of a drawn-on five o'clock shadow earning her extra points for commitment.

Nikki clutched a notebook tightly, pausing occasionally to scribble down "clues" with dramatic flair. Her sleek and perfect updo was a nod to her day job as a hairdresser because even while solving mysteries, Nikki wouldn't let a single strand fall out of place.

The playful energy in the room was infectious, but no matter how much I tried to focus on the fun, my thoughts kept circling back to Tiffany.

"Josie!" Holly nudged me out of my thoughts, her voice light. "Come on—don't let the caffeine mob get the best of us."

I forced a smile, handing off another cup as the knot in my stomach tightened. The café itself was a scene worthy of a mystery novel. Guests wandered through in their costumes, sipping pumpkin lattes and nibbling on Willa Mae's decadent chocolate pecan pie. The air was heavy with the aroma of coffee and sweet spices, and everywhere I turned, people were studying chocolate-covered pumpkin truffles like they held the secret to solving the night's fictional murder.

Speaking of Willa Mae, she fully embraced her Miss Marple persona, floral dress and all. She inspected each truffle like a seasoned sleuth, pausing to share her "theories" with anyone listening. Across the room, Sheriff Declan Sturdy was enjoying his role as Magnum P.I., complete with a red Hawaiian shirt, aviator sunglasses, and, of course, his signature mustache. He swaggered through the crowd, flashing his dimpled grin at anyone who passed by.

And then there was Granny Clara Belle—or "Smokin' Belle," as she was known for her legendary barbecue. She floated through the café in a dramatic old-timey gown, loudly declaring she'd "found the killer" at least five times already.

I smiled at the absurdity of it all, but my focus kept drifting. My gaze lingered on Tiffany near the chocolate bar, where she stood with Dex and Tony Castelli. She was quieter now, her posture stiff, her smiles forced. Nearby, Hank and his sons huddled together, fake pipes in hand, gesturing wildly as they debated suspects.

Then there was Bear. He was sitting off to the side, scowling into his espresso.

My thoughts were interrupted by Connie, who was fully committed to her role for the night. She was draped in frilly Victorian garb, but her arm was still in a sling, although it didn't seem to be slowing her down. Her voice rose and fell theatrically as she swept through the café, waving an oversized magnifying glass with her good hand.

"Hot on the trail of the murderer!" she announced, drawing attention as she flounced toward the chocolate bar.

I chuckled, watching her in action. Connie never did anything halfway. But then she stopped abruptly, her magnifying glass hovering over a small silver vial someone had left on the table.

She gasped loudly, holding the vial aloft like it was the Holy Grail. "Aha!" she shouted, her voice ringing through the café. "I've found something... suspicious!"

The room fell into a hush as all eyes turned toward her. Even Holly paused mid-latte pour to raise an eyebrow. "What do you think you've got there, Sherlock?" she asked, playing along.

Connie narrowed her eyes, holding the vial out in front of her with a flourish. "It's the perfect size for something nefarious—a hidden poison, perhaps?"

The college students near the bookshelves erupted into laughter, clearly enjoying Connie's theatrics, but across the room, Caleb's expression darkened. He wasn't laughing. His sharp eyes were locked on the vial, his brow furrowing with concern.

My pulse quickened. At first, I thought it was just a prop—a fun little addition to the game—but the way Caleb was looking at it made me second-guess.

"Careful with that, Connie," I said lightly, though my voice wavered. "We wouldn't want any accidents."

"Oh, my dear," Connie said with a dramatic sigh, slipping the vial into her lace purse. "An accident is exactly what we need in a proper mystery!"

The crowd applauded, cheering her on, but Caleb and I exchanged a look. That vial wasn't just for show.

Hattie was going full Miss Fisher, peppering Caleb with questions like a seasoned detective. And Caleb, in true form, was dressed as Inspector Gadget—complete with plastic limbs sticking out of his trench coat, gadgets dangling everywhere, and a spinning helicopter propeller on his hat.

It should've been hilarious—and okay, it was—but somehow, Caleb still managed to look... brooding. Intimidating, even.

I bit back a laugh. How does he pull that off?

The fedora sat low on his brow, casting shadows over his sharp eyes, and despite the ridiculous costume, the permanent scowl on his face gave him this quiet, serious presence. It was ridiculous. It was adorable. And it was very, very Caleb.

"You know, Inspector," I teased, leaning in just enough to catch a faint whiff of his cologne. Warm and familiar, like cozy fires and cinnamon rolls. Wait—did I just—

My cheeks flamed as I realized what I'd done. I froze mid-step, hoping he hadn't noticed.

But this was Caleb. He noticed everything.

His sharp gaze flicked toward me, and the corners of his mouth quirked upward in the faintest smirk. "Did you just... smell me?"

Oh no. My face went nuclear. "Very funny, Inspector," I muttered, forcing a grin and praying the floor would swallow me whole. Why does he have to smell so good?

His smirk deepened, but thankfully, he didn't press it. Instead, he glanced at the ridiculous array of plastic gadgets dangling from his costume. "Not sure these are going to help me catch a killer," he said dryly.

I swatted one of the plastic arms, sending it swinging. "Don't sell yourself short, Inspector. You never know when a go-go gadget arm might come in handy—like, say, opening a jar of salsa."

He shook his head, but there it was—that rare, fleeting smile that broke through his grumpy exterior like sunlight breaking through clouds. "Sure thing, Nancy Drew. I'll keep it in mind for the next salsa emergency."

Moments like this were my weakness. For some reason, whenever Caleb was around, I turned into a hopeless mess of teasing and terrible jokes, doing whatever I could to chip away at his broody exterior just to see that grin.

But tonight wasn't just about making Caleb smile.

Even with the café buzzing—laughter echoing through the room, guests huddled over clues, Holly waving her sonic screwdriver in full

Doctor mode—I couldn't shake the restless unease tugging at me. Tiffany glided through the crowd, polished and poised, but her movements were too smooth, her charm too controlled. She wasn't just playing the game; she was playing the room. And I wasn't leaving tonight until I found out what she was hiding.

"Caleb," I said softly, pulling him aside. His smile disappeared when he saw my expression, replaced with that familiar, no-nonsense focus.

"What is it?" His tone was quiet but sharp.

I scanned the room to make sure no one was within earshot. "Yesterday, when I was at Dex and Tiffany's... I saw one of Eloise's recipe cards sticking out of Tiffany's purse."

His entire demeanor shifted—casualness dropping away, replaced by that laser-focused intensity that made him such a good detective. "You saw what?"

I hesitated, suddenly feeling like I'd poked a bear. "Okay, I wasn't exactly snooping. It was just... there. I mean, I didn't go looking for it. But it's Tiffany, Caleb. And the card was right there."

His eyes narrowed. "So you did snoop."

"No!" I protested, though my voice wavered. "I mean... I might've peeked. But I wasn't, like, rifling through her things."

His brow arched, and the unimpressed look on his face told me he wasn't buying it. "Josie, you went to their house alone. And you snooped."

"I didn't snoop!" I said quickly, though I could feel myself starting to backpedal. "Okay, fine, maybe I snooped a little. But you have to admit, Tiffany's been acting shady! I couldn't just ignore it."

His jaw tightened. "You could've gotten hurt. Or worse." His voice dropped, the frustration in his words quiet but heavy. "You didn't think to call me? Let me go with you?"

I winced. "It wasn't like that—"

"You went into their house without backup, Josie," he interrupted, his voice calm but firm. "What if you'd walked into something dangerous? Dex and Tiffany aren't exactly amateurs. They're capable of a lot more than you realize."

"I know, I know," I said, throwing my hands up in surrender. "But I wasn't planning to snoop, I swear! It just... happened. And I couldn't wait. My gut's been screaming about Tiffany for days. Something's wrong,

Caleb."

His jaw flexed as he crossed his arms, the serious, detective-mode Caleb fully locked in now. "You should've told me. Yesterday."

"I know," I admitted, biting my lip. "But I'm telling you now. And we need to confront her—tonight."

Caleb exhaled slowly, his frustration simmering, "You shouldn't have gone alone."

"I won't again," I promised, meaning it this time. "No more solo investigating. We're a team, right? Like Cagney and Lacey…"

"Starsky and Hutch," he muttered, the corner of his mouth twitching despite himself.

"Castle and Beckett," I shot back, grinning.

He rolled his eyes, but the tension in his shoulders eased ever so slightly. "Fine. But we do this my way. No more surprises."

"Deal," I said, relief washing over me. "So… should we talk to her now?"

His gaze shifted to Tiffany across the room. She was still laughing with Tony Castelli, her polished exterior as flawless as ever. His jaw clenched.

"We need to talk to her," he said quietly.

"Yeah, let's—"

Before I could finish, Holly's voice rang out, cutting through the buzz of conversation. "Alright, detectives!" she announced, waving her trusty sonic screwdriver like a magician revealing her next trick. "It's time for the next big clue—a muffin mystery, if you will!"

Laughter rippled through the café, playful groans and mock gasps adding to the excitement as Holly lifted a tray of muffins high above her head like it was the crown jewels.

"The muffin of doom is among us!" she proclaimed dramatically. "Whoever gets the raspberry-filled one gets to stage their over-the-top death scene. So prepare your last words, people."

The tray tilted dangerously for a moment, but Bear swooped in, catching it just in time before handing it off to Sam with a grin. Laughter rippled through the café, and even Holly chuckled. "Oops!" she said with a playful shrug, then added, "Now remember, whoever gets the raspberry-filled one gets to stage their over-the-top death scene!"

"Let's get this over with," Caleb said under his breath, his patience clearly wearing thin.

But then Sheriff Declan Sturdy approached, a folder tucked under his arm and a serious-faced deputy trailing close behind. Gone was the laid-back persona he'd been wearing all evening—this was the Sheriff now, all business. His sharp gaze swept the room before landing on Caleb.

"Caleb," Declan called, motioning him over.

Caleb's jaw tightened. "Stay here," he said to me, his detective mode kicking in as he moved toward the sheriff.

Like that was going to happen.

I followed anyway, my heart thudding as Declan handed Caleb the folder. The deputy hovered nearby, glancing nervously at the crowd.

"These just came in," Declan said, flipping the folder open. "The lab confirmed it—Artie was poisoned before he was hit in the head."

My breath caught. Poisoned?

Declan lowered his voice, though the buzz of the game around us made it unlikely anyone else could hear. "He didn't die from the blunt force trauma. That wrench might've left a mark, but the poison's what killed him."

"Tiffany?" I blurted before I could stop myself.

Declan glanced at me, his brows lifting slightly, but he didn't seem surprised I was there. "We also found her prints on the wrench—though she clearly tried to wipe them away," Declan continued, his tone grim. "And given her connection to Artie…"

"Tiffany had motive," Caleb finished, his voice low but steady.

I swallowed hard, the pieces clicking into place too easily. The recipe card. Her nervous glances. The way she'd been keeping just enough distance from everyone tonight.

"She's been hiding something," I said, my voice firmer now. "Someone saw her outside Eloise's house the night Artie was killed. That recipe card was in her purse. It was Eloise's. She stole it. Probably more than one."

Declan's gaze sharpened. "You're absolutely sure about that?"

"I saw it myself," I said firmly, my voice steady despite the knot tightening in my stomach.

Caleb exchanged a glance with Declan, his expression hardening. "That's enough for an arrest."

"Agreed," Declan said, already shifting into action mode. His hand hovered near the folder tucked under his arm, a no-nonsense look on his face. "Let's move now before she can slip away."

Caleb nodded, his voice low and determined. "We'll keep it controlled. She doesn't make a scene unless we do."

Declan's lips twitched in dry amusement. "I don't know, Caleb. Drama seems to follow her like a bad perfume."

"Then we'll keep the bottle capped," Caleb muttered as his gaze swept the room. He shifted his attention to me. "Stay here, Josie."

"Not a chance," I shot back.

Holly's voice rang out again from the front of the café, drawing everyone's attention back to the muffins. "Alright, detectives!" she called, holding up a tray like it was the Holy Grail. "Who's ready for the next clue?"

The room buzzed with laughter and anticipation as the guests jostled for position around her. Standing at the edge of the crowd with Tony Castelli, Tiffany flashed one of her perfectly polished smiles, completely unaware of the storm about to descend on her.

Declan turned to Caleb, his tone sharp and decisive. "We do this now. Quietly."

Then he gave a curt nod, signaling to a deputy lingering near the door. "Let's go."

The two of them moved in unison, their focus laser-sharp as they cut through the crowd. My heart raced as I followed at a distance, my eyes locking on Tiffany. She was still laughing with Tony, her charm as effortless as ever—but I knew better.

There was a confrontation waiting to explode. And Tiffany wouldn't be laughing then.

Holly's voice cut through again, drawing everyone's attention back to the muffins. "Drumroll, please!" she called, miming a drumroll as Sam handed out the final tray. The crowd erupted into laughter, the tension in the room easing as guests eagerly grabbed muffins, trying to figure out who would be the next "victim."

Tiffany, still smiling, picked up a muffin with her perfectly manicured fingers.

"Let's go," Caleb said under his breath, but Tiffany gasped loudly before we could take a step. She clutched the muffin to her chest.

"Oh no!" she cried, her voice dripping with theatrical flair. "It's me! I'm the next victim!"

The crowd cheered and laughed as Tiffany took an exaggerated bite, staggering back dramatically. She clutched her chest, her face twisting into mock horror as she stumbled.

And then she collapsed.

On cue, Roy McCoy, still dressed as Poirot, burst into the room with his arms flailing, voice booming. "Ah! My little gray cells—they have solved the case!" He struck a dramatic pose, drawing everyone's attention. He'd been hamming it up all night, barely able to stay in character as "dead Poirot," but now was his moment to shine.

He continued, oblivious. "I was never truly dead, you see! It was all part of my genius plan to lure the killer out! Ah yes, Poirot has triumphed again—" His words faltered as his gaze dropped to Tiffany, still unmoving on the floor.

I laughed along with everyone else for a moment, thinking she was just committing to the bit.

But then she was too still. She didn't move.

Roy stopped mid-performance, confusion spreading across his face as he glanced between Tiffany and me. "What's wrong?"

The laughter faded as people began to notice her stillness. Someone muttered, "She's really good at this," but my chest tightened with a sharp pang of dread.

"Tiffany?" I knelt beside her, my pulse roaring in my ears as I gently shook her shoulder. "Tiffany, are you okay?"

She didn't respond.

"Tiffany!"

The café fell into a stunned silence as I knelt beside her. Caleb was already there, his hand brushing mine as he reached for her neck, his expression hardening with each passing second.

"No pulse," he said, his voice grim.

"Holly!" I called, my voice shaking. "Call 911. Now!"

Holly froze, her sonic screwdriver slipping from her hand, clattering to the floor with a hollow sound as the color drained from her face. "Oh, dear Jesus," she whispered, frozen. "Oh no." Her hands trembled as she fumbled for her phone.

Caleb stood, his voice sharp and commanding. "Everyone, back up! Give her space!"

Sheriff Declan Sturdy immediately stepped in, his no-nonsense authority cutting through the rising murmurs. "Alright, folks, let's clear the area. Slowly and calmly. Head toward the front door and wait there, but no one is to leave the premises." His tone left no room for argument as he gestured firmly, corralling the stunned crowd like a seasoned pro.

Slowly, the crowd shuffled away, their murmurs blending into an eerie hum. I stayed frozen, my mind racing as I stared at Tiffany's lifeless form.

Tiffany wasn't playing anymore.

Nausea twisted in my stomach as the paramedics shook their heads, confirming what I already knew but couldn't quite process. Tiffany—who I was so sure was tied to Artie's murder—was now a victim herself.

How could this have happened?

Sheriff Sturdy strode past us, his Hawaiian shirt making the scene even more surreal. "Josie," he said, his tone softening just a fraction as he caught my eye. "Let us handle this."

But I couldn't. Not this time.

13 gathering at the farmhouse

USUALLY, THIS WAS MY FAVORITE TIME OF YEAR. Missouri's woods exploded with vibrant color—golds, reds, and oranges announcing the trees' quiet surrender to winter. I loved when the town of Hickory Hills raked up all those fallen leaves and set them ablaze, the smell of smoke drifting out to my farmhouse on the edge of town. Carved pumpkins grinned from porches, and costumed kiddos roamed the streets, giggling under the weight of too much candy. The flavors of the season—apple cider, fresh-baked pumpkin treats—usually filled me with the kind of warmth that made me feel, well just, cozy. And with the holidays just around the corner, my heart always felt a little lighter, my spirit a little brighter.

The weight of the afternoon pressed down on all of us as we sat in the living room, the crackle of the fire a constant reminder of the quiet tension that filled the space. Outside, the fall fields stretched out under a pale sky, but inside, the air felt close, heavy with unspoken thoughts.

Novel Grounds, our usual post-church gathering spot, was wrapped in yellow tape, transformed into a crime scene. So here we were—my farmhouse, roast chicken still warm in the kitchen, bread cooling on the counter—but it didn't feel like home today. It felt like a holding cell, a place where answers were just out of reach.

Caleb sat closest to the fire, his arms resting on the chair as though holding himself back from pacing. His sharp features were set in concentration, the flickering light emphasizing the furrow in his brow. He was the newest addition to our Sunday coffee club. I was completely surprised when he agreed to come over after church today. Holly and Emma huddled on the couch, a blanket draped over their laps, while Max leaned against the mantel, his arms crossed and eyes fixed on the flames. Rhett stood at the window, staring out at the fields as if they might hold some kind of revelation. Konstanze, ever composed, perched on the edge of her chair, her hands clasped neatly in her lap, but her sharp gaze betrayed her unease.

The morning buzz of church was still fresh in my mind—whispers about Tiffany, glances toward me as if I'd somehow been a part of it all. The whole congregation had been abuzz with speculation. I was no closer to figuring out who had done this, and the weight of it gnawed at me.

Caleb broke the silence, his voice edged with frustration. "This doesn't make any sense, nothing about any of this is adding up." He didn't direct it to anyone in particular.

I glanced at him, grateful for his steady presence, even if his brooding intensity filled the room like a second storm cloud. I wasn't sure how to define what we were to each other, but for now, it was enough to know he was here.

Holly clutched her tea like it might anchor her, though it didn't look like she'd taken a sip. "It's hard to believe someone would do this," she said softly, her voice almost trembling. "Two murders. Two."

"And bold enough to pull one off in front of a whole room, the sheriff, and Caleb, too," Max added, his deep voice cutting in from where he stood. "Who does that?"

"They had to have been desperate," Konstanze said, her tone as calm and deliberate as ever. "Tiffany must've been silenced before she could say something she wasn't supposed to."

Holly shook her head, guilt weighing her expression down. "I made those muffins, Josie." Her voice cracked. "What if it was me? What if I..."

"It wasn't you, Holly," I said firmly, leaning over to place a hand on her arm. "The poison didn't come from the muffins. It was in that vial Connie found." My voice softened, trying to cut through her self-blame. "This isn't on you."

Caleb, who had been silent since his initial comment, straightened. "The lab confirmed it," he said. "The vial Connie found at the café last night? Traces of poison inside. Same kind that killed Artie."

The room froze. Even Rhett turned from the window to focus fully on Caleb.

"The poison came first," he continued. "Artie was already dead when he was hit on the head. And now Tiffany's dead, too. We're looking at a killer who's planned this down to the last detail."

"That vial," Max said, his brow furrowing, "how did Connie even find it?"

"She spotted it near the chocolate bar," Caleb explained. "Right around where Tiffany had been standing. Connie thought it was part of the game, but when she realized what it was, she panicked."

"Poor Connie," Emma murmured. "She must've been terrified."

"Connie isn't a suspect," Caleb said, shutting down the worry before it could take root. "She just happened to stumble across it. But finding that vial is significant. It means whoever poisoned Tiffany didn't care about leaving it behind—or didn't have time to take it with them."

"And Tiffany," I said, leaning forward, "she had to have thought Artie was still alive when she hit him." The thought hung in the air momentarily before I added, "Why else go through with it? She wouldn't have known the poison had already done its job."

Konstanze nodded slowly. "So Tiffany might not have been the only one involved. What if she was... working for someone? Someone who didn't tell her everything."

"Or," Rhett said, his voice grim, "she was being set up, just like Eloise."

The mention of Eloise sent a ripple of unease through the room. My chest tightened as I thought of her locked up, accused of a murder we all knew she didn't commit.

"She was at Eloise's house the night Artie died," I said, my voice sharper than I intended. "Someone saw her there. And those recipes? The ones that turned up at Artie's garage? Tiffany had at least one of them in her purse."

Caleb's gaze met mine, and I could see the gears turning. "She stole them," he said. "And then planted them at Artie's place to make it look like Eloise was involved."

"But why?" Max asked, his voice filled with frustration. "What's the endgame here? Why the recipes? Why frame Eloise?"

"To shift suspicion," Caleb said simply. "Tiffany wasn't working alone. Someone else is pulling the strings, and they're tying up loose ends."

Rhett frowned. "And now she's the one who got silenced."

The fire crackled in the quiet that followed, the weight of what we were uncovering settling over us.

And then Holly, as if needing to break the tension, pulled something from her pocket. "Did y'all see these at church this morning?"

I blinked at the shift in tone. "See what?"

"These," she said, unfolding a brightly colored flyer and smoothing it onto the coffee table. "Sam Keppleford's hosting another murder mystery party. A costume ball. At his house."

The room collectively stilled.

Max straightened, his expression hardening. "A costume ball? Now? After what just happened?"

Emma's jaw dropped, and Rhett muttered, "That guy's got some nerve."

"He's unbelievable," I said, leaning over the flyer. The garish colors and cheerful font made my skin crawl. "What kind of person plans a murder mystery party right after someone actually dies?"

"A distraction," Caleb said quietly, his eyes narrowing. "He's trying to distract focus from what happened last night."

Holly's brow furrowed. "You think it's more than just bad taste?"

"Sam loves being the center of attention," I said, my voice tight. "But this feels... calculated. Like he's trying to control the narrative."

Max let out a frustrated huff. "Or he's hiding something."

Konstanze tilted her head, "Do we think this is just Sam being... Sam? Or is there something more going on here?"

I stared at the flyer in my hands, the cheerful lettering and bold colors clashing violently with our reality. A knot twisted in my stomach. "I don't know," I admitted, flattening the paper on the table as if that would somehow reveal its secrets. "But I think we'd better find out."

"He's acting like Tiffany's death doesn't even matter," Rhett said, his voice low and hard. "Like it's just... some sideshow to his main event."

Max stopped his restless pacing and turned toward us, "And we've been so focused on everyone else—Tiffany, Artie, Eloise—we haven't really looked at Sam. Not closely."

Sitting cross-legged in the armchair, Hattie said, "So what's the plan? Do we go to this party?"

The room stilled, heavy with unspoken worry. I glanced around at everyone—Konstanze perched on the edge of her chair like a poised chess master, Holly clutching her mug, Rhett frowning by the window, and Caleb leaning forward in his chair, elbows on his knees.

No one spoke, the silence stretching out, pressing down on us. Finally, Caleb broke it, his voice cutting through like a blade. "We're going to that party. All of us."

His words hung in the air, and the resolve in his tone sent a chill down my spine. "But we're not going there to have fun," he continued, his gaze sweeping over the group. "We're going to keep our eyes open, stick together, and figure out exactly what Sam's up to."

Holly frowned, setting her mug down with a soft clink. "You really think Sam's involved? I mean, he's... Sam. He's obnoxious and self-centered, but a murderer?"

"He's hiding something," Caleb said firmly, his tone brooking no argument. "Maybe he's not the killer, but he knows more than he's letting on. And this party? It's either a distraction or a trap. Either way, we're not walking in blind."

Another shiver rippled through me at the word trap. My fingers curled tighter around the flyer, the glossy paper crumpling slightly under the pressure. I stared at Sam's elegant scrawl dancing across the page: *Murder Mystery Costume Ball—You're Invited!*

It felt wrong. All of it. The timing, the glitz, the audacity of it so soon after Tiffany's death. Sam Keppleford had always been a little too flashy for my taste, but this? This was beyond poor judgment.

"We're walking into the lion's den," Max muttered, arms crossed tightly over his chest. "If Sam is hiding something, he won't just hand it to us."

Stanzi said, "Then we make him think we're just there for the party. Play along. Blend in. He won't see us coming."

Hattie grinned, leaning back in her chair. "Now that's a plan I can get behind. I do love a good costume party."

"Just don't get too caught up in the fun," Caleb said, his tone dry but his gaze serious.

"Relax, Inspector Gadget," Hattie shot back with a wink. "I'll stay focused."

Despite the heaviness in the room, a flicker of a smile tugged at the corner of my lips. Leave it to Hattie to inject some levity into the moment.

I glanced back down at the flyer, my heart thudding as I traced the words again. Deep down, I knew this wasn't just another one of Sam's flashy events.

14 clues, coffee, & chemistry

ELOISE WAS FINALLY BEING RELEASED TODAY, and we all gathered in the county jail parking lot in Hickory Hills to greet her. The tension that had weighed on us for days cracked like a dam breaking when she stepped outside. At 70, Eloise still carried herself like a seasoned detective who'd seen it all. Her curly, poofy hair—normally the definition of "controlled chaos"—was now frazzled in every direction, not from heat but from stress and far too many days in a cell. Her shoulders were stiff, but her sharp eyes told the real story. Eloise might've been tired, but she wasn't beaten.

She paused, taking a deep breath of the crisp October air, as if testing whether freedom still tasted as good as she remembered. A small, almost defiant smile tugged at her lips.

"Eloise!" Holly squealed, charging forward with arms wide open.

Eloise braced herself, a chuckle escaping her as Holly practically launched into her. "Easy, Holly," she said, her voice dry but warm. "I've only got so many good bones left, you know."

The rest of us breathed a sigh of relief like we'd been holding our breath for days. Hattie stepped up next, her hug softer but no less emotional. "We've been praying for you, Eloise," she whispered, her voice trembling.

Eloise softened, her eyes warming as she gave Hattie a reassuring pat on the back. "I felt those prayers. Every single one," she said, her voice low but full of gratitude.

She pulled back, straightening her shoulders as if trying to shake off the weight of the last few days. "I'm here now," she said, her voice steady with resolve. "And I'm not done yet." Her frizzed curls seemed to puff out a little more, almost bristling at the injustice.

Rhett stepped forward next, his hands shoved into his jean's pockets. "You hangin' in there, Eloise?" he asked, his deep, easy tone laced with concern.

Eloise nodded, giving him a small but firm smile. "Takes more than this to knock me down."

Rhett grinned, his rugged features softening. "Well, if you need a day out in the woods, chopping firewood or hiking to clear your head, you know where to find me. Might even teach me how to bake while you're at it. Never too late to learn."

Eloise snorted, her smirk as sharp as ever. "Stick to woodwork, Rhett. I've tasted your biscuits."

Rhett threw his head back in a laugh, tipping his hat in agreement. "Fair enough."

Standing off to the side in her signature red coat, Stanzi nodded to Eloise. "I told you this wouldn't keep you down for long," she said; the lilt of her British-infused German accent made every word sound precise and charming.

Eloise smiled softly. "That you did, Stanzi. Thanks for reminding me."

Max approached next, his expression thoughtful as always. "Good to see you out, Eloise," he said, his gaze meeting hers. "But this isn't over."

Eloise nodded firmly. "You're right. And I'm ready."

Anders kept his distance, but he offered a brief, solid one-armed hug. "Glad you're out," he said gruffly. "But we've got to stay sharp. Whoever did this isn't done."

Eloise gave him a knowing look. "Don't worry, Anders I didn't lose my edge in there. Whoever set me up has a lot to answer for."

When it was my turn, Eloise's hug was stronger than I expected, her grip steady despite the ordeal she'd just endured. "I don't know how to thank you," she murmured, her voice quieter now, edged with emotion.

"You don't have to," I said, holding her tightly. "We've got your back, Eloise. Always."

She pulled back, her sharp eyes searching mine. "I know," she said firmly. "But this isn't over. Someone's still out there, and I'm not stopping until we figure out who framed me."

Ever the mood-lifter, Hattie looped her arm through Eloise's and gave her a gentle tug. "Come on, Eloise. We've got real coffee waiting at the diner. Not that sludge they've been giving you in there."

Eloise allowed herself to be led toward the car, though she shot Hattie a playful glance. "I'll take the coffee, but don't expect me to sit around twiddling my thumbs. This fight's just getting started."

Holly, her ever-sunny personality shining through, chimed in. "And pie! You've got to have some of Willa Mae's chocolate pecan pie. Something sweet to take the edge off."

Eloise raised an eyebrow, a smirk tugging at her lips. "I don't think pie's going to sweeten me up after all this," she quipped, though her eyes softened at their efforts to lift her spirits.

Anders, always the realist, cleared his throat. "We've still got work to do. The person who framed Eloise isn't going to stop just because she's out."

Holly shot him a warning look, but Eloise didn't seem fazed. She nodded, her expression turning serious again. "Anders is right."

Once we made sure Eloise had a ride home, Caleb pulled me aside, his expression unreadable but serious. "We need to talk," he said quietly, his tone low enough that no one else could hear. "Come by the station when you've got a minute."

I nodded, the weight of his words settling in my chest. Eloise was out, yes, but the real fight was still ahead of us. There was a murderer out there, and they weren't done.

"How long until they clear Novel Grounds?" I asked, flipping through a file Caleb had handed me without even putting up his usual fight.

Progress.

"A few more days," he said, his voice calm, but there was a flicker of frustration in his expression. "They're being thorough."

I sighed, pushing a loose strand of hair behind my ear. Every day, my café stayed wrapped in yellow tape, which meant more lost business and more unanswered questions. My leg bounced anxiously under the table, and I rhythmically tapped the pen against my notepad to channel my frustration. The clock on the wall ticked loudly, mocking me.

Caleb leaned forward, elbows on his desk, his sleeves pushed up just enough to reveal those annoyingly muscular forearms. His beautiful eyes locked onto mine. "We've got another problem, Josie."

I swallowed, feeling the familiar flutter in my stomach. Focus, Josie. Murder first, Caleb's forearms later. I cleared my throat. "What kind of problem?"

"Pressure from higher up," Caleb said, leaning back in his chair and stretching just a little too casually. "Sheriff Sturdy's getting leaned on. By Sam Keppleford."

I blinked. "Sam? What does he have to do with this?"

Caleb frowned, his jaw tightening. "Everything, apparently. He's cozying up to everyone—the mayor, the town council, the historical society. They've been fawning over him since he started restoring that old antebellum house. Now he's using his influence to pressure Sturdy to keep us off his trail."

I scoffed, sitting up straighter. "So, what, he throws around a little money, hosts a few fancy parties, and suddenly he gets a free pass to meddle in a murder investigation?"

"Pretty much." Caleb's tone was clipped, his shoulders tense. "He's made himself indispensable, and now he's got half the town wrapped around his finger. Every time we try to dig deeper, Sturdy gets pushback."

I huffed, flipping through the file in front of me. "Why does he even care about this case? What's he hiding?"

"That's what we need to figure out," Caleb said, his brow furrowing. "But it's not just about controlling the investigation. He's trying to keep us distracted. And then there's this…" He pulled out *the flyer* and handed it to me.

I stared at the glossy paper, my frustration bubbling into full-blown disbelief. "I still can't believe that he's hosting a murder mystery costume ball barely a week after Tiffany was poisoned at my café. Who does that?"

Caleb's lips pressed into a thin line. "It's not just tasteless. It's strategic."

"Strategic?" I tilted my head, trying to make sense of it. "You think he's distracting us?"

Caleb nodded. "Or testing us. Either way, we can't ignore it. Especially with the aconitine."

The word sent a chill down my spine. "Aconitine. Wolfsbane." I repeated it like it was a curse. "So the poison that killed Artie and Tiffany—it's rare. Potent. Someone knew exactly what they were doing."

"Exactly," Caleb said, his voice low. "Artie had a heart condition. The poison would've worked fast. But Tiffany? No preexisting issues. Whoever killed her was sending a message."

"Same method, same poison," I murmured, piecing it together. "The killer wanted us to see the connection. But why? What's the link between Artie and Tiffany?"

"That's the question." Caleb tapped his pen against the table, the soft rhythm punctuating the heavy silence. "Tiffany hit Artie with the torque wrench. That much we know. It was emotional—panicked. But the poison? That's something entirely different."

I leaned back, my mind racing as I tried to piece it all together. "So, what are we saying here? Tiffany thought she killed Artie, but he was already dead? And then someone else poisoned her?"

"It fits," Caleb said, his voice thoughtful. "Tiffany didn't strike me as the type to plan out something as meticulous as poisoning. She was impulsive—grabbing a wrench in the heat of the moment, panicking when she thought she'd gone too far. Poison, though? That's cold. Precise. Whoever poisoned her knew exactly what they were doing. They didn't leave room for mistakes."

"And they wanted her gone," I said softly, the realization hitting me, "She was a loose end."

Caleb nodded, his expression grim. "Exactly. Whoever poisoned Artie had a plan—keep it clean, no mess, no trail. Tiffany throwing a wrench into things—literally—wasn't part of it. And when she realized what had happened, she must've panicked. Maybe even tried to cover for herself. But she knew too much, and the poisoner couldn't risk letting her talk."

"So, Artie was their first target," I said slowly, piecing it together, "and Tiffany was just... collateral damage?"

"Could be," Caleb admitted, "Poisoning Tiffany—it feels... like she wasn't just a problem to get rid of, but maybe part of the plan all along," he ran his hand through his hair. "Oh, I don't know maybe she was just collateral damage."

I frowned, my unease deepening as I ran through the possibilities. "But why? Tiffany wasn't innocent, sure, but she wasn't exactly the mastermind here either. What's the connection? Why would the poisoner go after her next?"

"That's what we need to figure out," Caleb said, leaning forward, his voice low and steady. "Who stood to gain by silencing Tiffany? And how does it all circle back to Artie?"

I flipped through the file again, desperate for a breakthrough. My eyes landed on a familiar name. "Wait a second." I tapped the paper. "Tommy Delaney. He's Sam's contractor, right? He was at both the fundraiser and the party at my café."

Caleb's eyes narrowed. "Delaney's been practically living at Keppleford's house since the renovations started."

"And he was at both events where Artie and Tiffany were last seen. If Sam's hiding something, Delaney could be his guy."

Caleb leaned forward, his expression darkening. "If Keppleford's involved, Delaney might be his accomplice. Someone who knows the house. Someone who can move without drawing attention."

"This could be the connection we've been missing," I said, my pulse quickening. "If Delaney's involved, it explains why Sam's so desperate to shut us down."

Caleb stood, grabbing his notebook. "We need to talk to Delaney. But we can't let Keppleford know we're onto him."

"Agreed," I said, standing too. My shoulders felt lighter, "We're onto something, Caleb. This could crack the whole case."

For a moment, Caleb's eyes softened, and his voice dipped.

"You've got a sharp eye, Josie. You're good at this."

Heat rose to my cheeks, and I quickly grabbed a stack of papers to fan myself. "Well, you know, I, uh… thanks." Smooth, Josie. Real smooth.

Caleb smirked, clearly enjoying my flustered state. "You okay there?"

"Oh, I'm fine," I shot back, rolling my eyes. "Let's focus on Delaney before I die of secondhand embarrassment."

He chuckled, grabbing his keys. "Fair enough. But you're staying in the truck."

I squared my shoulders, following him toward the door. "We'll see about that."

The warehouse where Tommy Delaney stored his supplies loomed on the outskirts of town, shadowed by trees and wrapped in a creeping fog. Caleb parked the truck just outside the rusting chain-link fence, the "No Trespassing" sign hanging crookedly. The whole place screamed "bad idea," but here we were.

Caleb checked his holster before stepping out. "Stay in the truck," he muttered, his tone leaving no room for argument.

I waited exactly five seconds before slipping out of the passenger side and jogging to catch up with him. He shot me a glare but didn't say a word, which I considered a small victory.

We rounded the corner of the warehouse, the fog curling around our feet like it was alive. Everything about this place felt wrong.

"Caleb," I whispered, catching movement out of the corner of my eye. A figure lunged from the shadows, swinging a metal pipe. Caleb shoved me behind him, ducking just in time to avoid the blow.

"Stay down!" he barked, drawing his gun.

Another figure appeared, and without thinking, I grabbed a loose plank of wood and swung it at his leg. He stumbled back, cursing, and I scrambled to my feet, adrenaline pumping.

"Josie, get to the truck!" Caleb snapped, his voice sharp.

But before I could move, the men retreated into the fog, disappearing as quickly as they'd come.

Caleb lowered his gun, his chest heaving. "Are you okay?"

I nodded, still catching my breath. "Yeah. Are you?"

"Let's get out of here," he said, his voice grim. "Now."

BACK AT THE STATION...

"I told you to stay in the truck, Josie," Caleb said, pacing in front of me, his frustration radiating off him.

"I did—until we were attacked!" I shot back, my voice rising. "What was I supposed to do? Just sit there while you got hit with a pipe?"

Caleb stopped pacing, his eyes locking onto mine. "Yes! That's exactly what you were supposed to do. It's my job to protect you, Josie. Not the other way around."

"Well, too bad," I snapped, crossing my arms. "We're in this together, whether you like it or not."

Before Caleb could respond, Sheriff Sturdy burst into the room, his expression thunderous. "Caleb," he barked. "My office. Now."

Caleb sighed, giving me a look of equal parts exasperation and apology before following Sturdy inside.

I leaned against the wall, trying to steady my nerves. This case was spiraling, and I had no idea how much more we could take.

15 a whole latte lies

CALEB HANDED ME A LATTE the next morning as we sat at a table outside Novel Grounds, reviewing yesterday's notes. I took a sip and grimaced. Not terrible—but definitely not great.

"Let me guess," I teased, raising an eyebrow over the rim of the cup. "Gas station coffee?"

Caleb smirked, one corner of his mouth quirking up. "You're welcome, by the way. I even made sure they didn't hand me the pot that looked like it had been brewing since last week."

I laughed, setting the cup down with mock drama. "And yet, somehow, it still tastes like burnt hopes and dreams."

"You're spoiled," he said, shaking his head. "Not everyone can live the Novel Grounds lifestyle."

"True," I admitted, grinning. "Owning the best coffee shop in town has its perks, but it also ruins you for the sludge the rest of the world dares to call coffee."

Caleb chuckled, but his focus quickly returned to the file on his on the table. "Speaking of ruined... let's talk about Delaney."

I groaned, leaning back against the bench. "You mean Delaney and his welcoming committee? Because I'm still not over how that went. One guy tried to clock us with a pipe, and the other looked like he bench-presses pickup trucks for fun."

"Yeah," Caleb muttered, rubbing his jaw. "Not exactly the friendly neighborhood contractor."

"Okay, so Delaney and his goons are shady, but do you really think they could've been the ones to poison Artie?" I asked, leaning forward. "They don't exactly strike me as the 'subtle, calculated murder' types."

Caleb frowned, his gaze distant. "No. Poison isn't their style. They'd use a two-by-four or a fist, something messy. Delaney's crew is about brute force. That's why Tiffany's death doesn't fit them. And honestly, the poison doesn't fit Artie's murder either—not if we're saying Delaney or his guys were involved."

"Right," I said slowly, piecing it together out loud. "Poison is planned. It's almost distant. Clinical. And it's definitely cold. But Tiffany? The wrench was panic. Impulsive. And Artie was already dead when she hit him."

Caleb tapped his pen against the file, nodding. "Exactly. Tiffany panicked and thought she had killed him, but the poisoner was already two steps ahead. She wasn't the mastermind—she was a loose end."

"And now she's gone." The words left a bitter taste in my mouth. "Someone wanted to make sure she didn't talk."

"Or figure out too much," Caleb added grimly. "She wasn't just sloppy; she was unpredictable. Whoever's behind the poisoning couldn't risk that."

I folded my arms, leaning back as my mind raced. "So, where does that leave us? Delaney's crew is a distraction. Tiffany thought she was covering her tracks, but the poisoner worked in the background the whole time. And now we've got... Dex."

Caleb raised an eyebrow. "Dex? What about him?"

I shot him a pointed look. "Oh, come on. You've seen how jumpy he's been. The way he ran off with Tiffany the night that Novel Grounds was ransacked. He's guilty of something. Don't forget Connie saw him talking to Blake when she was nearly run over by that car, and we saw him with Blake at the orchard, too."

Caleb sighed, rubbing his jaw. "I've looked into Dex. He's got a record, sure, but nothing violent—small stuff. Stolen parts, chop shop connections. And as shifty as he acts, I don't think he trashed your café. Or killed Tiffany."

"Then what's he hiding?" I pressed, my frustration bubbling to the surface. "He's involved somehow. I can feel it."

"I didn't say he wasn't involved," Caleb said carefully. "I just don't think he's the poisoner. But that doesn't mean we shouldn't keep an eye on him. He knows something—probably more than he's letting on."

"Great," I muttered, my voice dripping with sarcasm. "So, add Dex to the 'suspicious but not quite guilty' list. "Fine," What about Bear, then?"

Caleb's expression darkened slightly. "Bear's been acting out. Angry. Unstable. I talked to him yesterday, and he practically bit my head off when I brought up Artie."

My stomach twisted. "You think Bear's involved?"

"I don't know," Caleb admitted, his voice low. "He's got motive— But I can't see him as the poison type either. If Bear wanted to kill someone, he'd do it with his fists, not a vial of wolfsbane."

I nodded, though unease curled in my stomach. "Still, he's been angry. Lashing out. It wouldn't hurt to dig a little deeper."

"Agreed," Caleb said, leaning back. "But we have to tread carefully. If Bear feels cornered, he's going to push back hard. And Dex? He's like a squirrel with a nut—he'll bury whatever he's hiding as deep as he can. That leaves Sam."

I sighed, rubbing my temples. "Of course it does."

"Sam's careful," Caleb said, his tone sharp with frustration. "Too careful. He's got no record, no visible motive, and he keeps his hands clean. But that's exactly what makes him suspicious. He's good at covering his tracks, and if he's behind the poisoning, he won't slip up easily."

"Oh, wait! How could I forget Blake?" I added, tapping my fingers on the table. "Let's call him Blake the Smooth Talker. Always sliding into a meeting with a smile and a scheme. Or maybe Blake the Pie Piper—because he's got his fingers in every pie."

Caleb snorted, trying to hide his amusement. "Blake the Pie Piper? Really?"

I shrugged, smirking. "Fits, doesn't it? He's always lurking around, stirring up trouble, Eloise's recipes, and who knows what else. The man practically oozes corporate charm while leaving chaos in his wake."

Caleb shook his head, though I caught the corner of his mouth twitching. "Okay, I'll give you that. He's shady. But poison? I don't see it. Blake's all about big moves and leverage, not backroom murders."

"Fine," I said, leaning forward and narrowing my eyes. "But don't tell me he's squeaky clean. You can't ignore the way he's connected to half the messes we're trying to untangle. He pressured Eloise, he's been spotted with Dex, and Tiffany wasn't exactly a stranger to him."

"He's not clean," Caleb admitted, his tone serious. "But until we've got something concrete, all he is right now is a businessman who got in over his head."

"And yet," I said, tilting my head, "he keeps showing up just enough to look suspicious but not enough to get caught." I threw up my hands. "Sam the puppet master, Dex the squirrel, Bear the ticking time bomb, and now Blake the Pie Piper," I said, my voice heavy with sarcasm. "What a lineup."

Caleb sighed, pinching the bridge of his nose. "This isn't a comedy sketch, Josie."

"No, it's a circus," I shot back. "And we're the ones trying to catch the ringleader."

Silence settled between us, the kind that's heavy with unsaid things. Caleb looked distracted, like his mind was already ten steps ahead.

"What?" I asked, narrowing my eyes. "You've got that look."

He hesitated, then sighed. "There's something you don't know."

My stomach dropped. "About Delaney?"

"About Keppleford," Caleb said, his voice low. "And the people he's connected to."

I leaned closer, bracing myself. "What do you mean?"

Caleb rubbed the back of his neck, glancing away. "Sam's not working alone. He's tied to some big names in Hickory Hills—old money, people with influence. They don't want this case dragging on, and they definitely don't want us stirring up more questions."

I clenched my jaw. "So, we're in the way?"

"Pretty much." Caleb's voice was tight, his frustration barely contained. "Sheriff Sturdy's getting pressure from all sides. Keppleford, the Chamber of Commerce, even the mayor's office. They want this wrapped up quietly."

I sat back, my heart pounding. "Quietly? Artie's dead, Tiffany's dead, and Eloise was almost convicted for something she didn't do. What part of this screams 'quiet'?"

Caleb's eyes met mine, his voice softer now. "I know, Josie. But Sturdy's got his hands tied. The people pushing him have a lot of power, and they don't care about the truth. They just want it over."

I crossed my arms, anger bubbling up. "So, what? We stop? We let them sweep it all under the rug?"

"Of course not," Caleb said firmly. "But we have to be smart about this. If we push too hard, Sturdy will pull us—me—off the case. He's already threatening to shut us down if we don't back off. Well, that's not the full truth. He has already put me on desk work."

"Desk work?"

The weight of his words settled over me like a storm cloud. Caleb was right—we were on thin ice. But the idea of backing down, of letting people like Sam Keppleford call the shots, made my blood boil.

"So, what's the plan?" I asked, my voice sharper than I intended. "Lay low? Play nice while the bad guys get away with murder?"

Caleb's expression softened, his voice dropping just enough to calm me. "No, Josie. We keep going. Quietly. Carefully. We get the answers we need without painting a target on our backs."

I huffed, crossing my arms tighter. "Fine. But if we're going to 'lay low,' you'd better have a good plan."

Caleb smirked, the faintest hint of amusement flickering in his eyes. "Always do."

I rolled my eyes but couldn't stop the small smile tugging at my lips. "Sure you do, Detective."

Caleb left me sitting silently in the morning sun, I glanced back at the yellow tape across my café. Caleb might have a plan, but the closer we get to the truth, the more dangerous things will get. I got up and crossed the street to the diner, the crisp autumn breeze tugging at my sweater and scattering golden leaves across the sidewalk.

The bell above the diner's door jingled as I stepped inside, and the warm smell of fried food and coffee washed over me, starkly contrasting the espresso and fresh muffins that usually greeted me at Novel Grounds. My café, now draped in yellow tape and crawling with cops, was locked away from me, both literally and emotionally. What was once my haven of stories and connections was now an active crime scene.

Sliding into a booth in the corner, I tried to shake off the unease. The vinyl seat felt cold and unfamiliar like I didn't belong there. I stared out the window at Novel Grounds, watching officers filter in and out of the café as if every clue I needed was just out of reach. It wasn't just my café that felt sealed off—it was the sense of control I'd clung to since Artie's death. Everything felt forbidden, closed off, unraveling.

Outside, a group of university students meandered down the sidewalk, laughing and carefree. But as they passed the café, their laughter faded. They slowed, pointing and whispering before one of them pulled out their phone to snap a picture.

For them, the yellow tape was a passing curiosity. For me, it was a constant reminder that my world had been turned upside down. Hickory Hills, my quiet town where gossip about who switched pews at church qualified as a scandal, now felt like a setting for a true crime show. And the worst part? Even though Caleb and I had only parted ways minutes ago, I already felt the weight of his absence. Sheriff Sturdy had effectively benched him, leaving me floundering without my partner in crime-solving—and, though I hated to admit it, the one person who seemed to truly get me.

The door jingled again, and Hattie slid into the booth across from me. She didn't bother with pleasantries; her sharp gaze locked onto mine like a laser.

"Alright," she said, her tone leaving no room for argument. "Spill. What's going on?"

I sighed, resting my chin in my hand. "I don't even know where to start. It feels like everything is slipping through my fingers. And yesterday…" I trailed off, the memory of Delaney's warehouse flashing in my mind—pipes swinging, shadows lunging, Caleb's voice barking orders. "Yesterday was a lot."

Hattie's brow furrowed. "I heard bits and pieces, but I want the full story. What happened?"

I leaned in, lowering my voice. "It felt like something out of an action movie. Delaney's guys weren't exactly thrilled to see us. One of them came at Caleb with a pipe, and another looked like he could crush a watermelon with his bare hands. It was terrifying." I tried to laugh it off, but even saying it out loud made my heart race.

"And yet," Hattie said, her lips quirking, "here you are. Intact. No broken bones."

"Thanks to Caleb," I admitted. "He practically dragged me out of there."

Her eyebrow lifted. "And now?"

I sighed, leaning back. "And now he's stuck on desk duty. Sheriff Sturdy reassigned him to paperwork—because apparently keeping Caleb out of the field is exactly what this investigation needs."

Hattie snorted. "Paperwork? For Caleb? That'll last all of five minutes before he loses his mind."

I smiled despite myself. "I'd pay good money to see it. But it's frustrating. We've been working together, making progress, and now he's sidelined. I feel like I will be running in circles without him."

Hattie reached across the table and squeezed my hand. "You're still in this together. You'll figure it out even if Caleb's behind a desk. You always do."

I wanted to believe her, but the knot in my chest wouldn't budge. "It just feels like someone's always two steps ahead of us. No matter how hard we push, the answers keep slipping away."

Hattie's expression turned thoughtful, her head tilting. "Maybe someone is two steps ahead. Or maybe... they're leading you in the wrong direction."

Her words sent a chill down my spine. Before I could respond, the door jingled again, and in walked Sam Keppleford, all charm and polished confidence. He waved at the regulars like he owned the place, his wide smile practically daring someone to dislike him.

Hattie's eyes narrowed. "You think Sam's involved?"

I watched as Sam made his way to the counter, his laughter cutting through the hum of the diner. "I don't know," I said, my voice low. "But he's always there. At every turn, smiling like he doesn't have a care in the world. It's... weird."

Almost as if he could hear me, Sam turned, his gaze sweeping the room until it landed on us. His smile widened as he sauntered over, his footsteps light and confident.

"Ladies!" he greeted us, his tone as bright as a summer morning. "How are my two favorite detectives?"

I forced a polite smile. "Hi, Sam. Busy day?"

"Always," he replied, as though running a multi-million-dollar business and hosting elaborate parties were minor inconveniences. "Oh, and don't forget—my costume ball this weekend. It's going to be the event of the season. Just what everyone needs after all the, uh, unpleasantness."

Unpleasantness? I clenched my jaw but kept my tone breezy. "We'll keep that in mind."

"Do," Sam said with a wink before moving on to schmooze another table. As soon as he was out of earshot, I turned back to Hattie.

"See what I mean?" I muttered. "He's too smooth. Too... perfect."

Hattie nodded, her lips pressed into a thin line. "If he's hiding something, he's doing a good job of it."

My gaze caught on someone sitting alone at the counter—Dex. He was hunched over his plate, barely picking at his food, and his expression was haunted, almost guilty. Every few seconds, he glanced toward the door like he was waiting for something—or someone.

Hattie followed my gaze. "Dex doesn't look so good," she said softly.

"No," I agreed, my stomach twisting. "And it's not just grief. He's hiding something. I can feel it."

"And Bear?" Hattie asked, tilting her head toward the other end of the diner, where Bear was snapping at the waitress over what looked like a simple mistake. "He's been wound tight lately. More than usual."

"Bear's always a little rough around the edges," I said, watching him carefully. "But this? This is different. He's on edge, like he's ready to snap."

Hattie frowned, her eyes darting between Bear and Dex. "You think they're involved?"

"I don't know," I admitted. "But I'm not stopping until we figure this out and I'm not trusting anyone that isn't us."

Hattie gave my hand another squeeze. "Then we keep digging. Like always."

Her confidence buoyed me, but my gut told me the answers we sought wouldn't come easily. I glanced back at Sam, still holding court at the counter. If he was playing us, it was time to figure out why.

"We need to be careful," I said, my voice steady. "Sam, Dex, Bear—they're all connected somehow. We just have to figure out how."

"And Blake Courtney," Hattie added, nodding toward the FMR Foods marketing guy, who was demolishing a stack of pancakes with the gusto of a linebacker. "He's always lurking, too."

I followed her gaze, my resolve hardening. "You're right. Until we know who we can trust, we trust no one."

Before I could spiral further into my own suspicions, the bell over the door jingled, and Holly and Anders stepped inside. Holly waved, her usual bright smile dimmed by the tension that had blanketed all of us since the murders. She slid into the booth beside me, sighing as Anders settled in beside Hattie with his quiet, observant nod.

"How's Eloise doing?" I asked, grateful for the distraction. It had only been a day since she was released, and while Eloise could out-stubborn a mule, I knew she wasn't invincible.

Holly's smile was small but genuine. "She's holding up, considering everything. You know Eloise—tough as nails. She was already rattling off new muffin ideas before I even got her fully settled in."

I raised an eyebrow. "She's ready to bake already?"

"Yup," Holly said, a flicker of amusement breaking through the worry on her face. "She's planning some kind of pumpkin-cranberry concoction."

I let out a low whistle. "That woman is something else."

"It's her way of coping," Holly added, her smile softening. "She just wants things to feel normal again. Baking helps her feel in control."

"Muffin therapy," I said, managing a small grin. "Not a bad strategy."

Holly chuckled. "But she's not really okay, Josie. Sometimes, she'll talk normally, and then she just... zones out. Like she's stuck, still processing everything."

I nodded, "It's going to take time. What she went through... no one bounces back from that overnight."

Holly sighed, her fingers tracing the edge of her menu. "Yeah, but she's got us. We'll help her get there."

"We will," I said firmly. "And once we clear her name completely, she'll be back in that kitchen, baking like nothing ever happened."

"That's the plan," Holly said, her voice brightening a little. "But until then, I'm keeping an eye on her. You know how she gets when she's stressed—"

"She works herself to the bone," I finished. "We'll keep her grounded."

Holly smiled, giving my hand a quick squeeze. The waitress arrived with menus for Holly and Anders, breaking the moment. Holly flipped hers open but didn't seem particularly focused on the options. I could see the gears in her head still turning.

I frowned, letting my eyes roam. Roy sat alone in his usual booth, sipping coffee and reading the newspaper like he did every morning. Reliable Roy, always dependable, always helpful. He'd been at Novel Grounds the day Artie came in... and he'd been at the murder mystery party when Tiffany was killed. Was that just a coincidence? Or something more?

And then there was Willa Mae, sitting a few tables away, chatting animatedly with another diner. She'd been at Novel Grounds the day Artie died, dropping off one of her pies like clockwork. And she'd been at the party, too. Sweet, dependable Willa Mae, who always brought me casseroles after breakups and treated every community event like her personal mission. Could she really be connected to this?

I rubbed my temples, feeling ridiculous. Get a grip, Josie. First Roy, now Willa Mae? What was next—suspecting the Sunday School teacher? Small towns have overlap. That's all this is.

"Josie?" Hattie's voice cut through my spiraling thoughts. She was watching me with a mix of curiosity and concern. "You okay?"

I forced a smile. "Yeah, just... overthinking."

Hattie raised an eyebrow, but thankfully, she didn't push.

Still, I felt like I was missing something. Willa Mae with her pies. Roy with his newspaper and friendly smile. Sam always seemed to be in the right place at the wrong time. Dex was acting like he was one bad night away from unraveling. Bear snapping at the waitress like his plate had insulted him. Were these just quirks of small-town life, or were the pieces of this puzzle staring me in the face, waiting to be connected?

Holly must have noticed my distracted expression because she nudged me with her elbow. "You're overthinking again," she said with a gentle smile. "Maybe give your brain a break?"

I chuckled lightly, shaking my head. "Just trying to fit the pieces together."

Anders, quiet until now, set down his menu and leaned forward. "Sometimes the pieces don't fit right away," he said thoughtfully. "Doesn't mean they never will."

I nodded, grateful for his calm reassurance. "You're right. It just feels like every time we get close to something, it slips away."

"We'll figure it out," Hattie said firmly, her confidence grounding me. "We always do."

16 locked in suspicion

"YOUR LIVING ROOM FEELS LIKE A SANCTUARY," Eloise said, her voice warm but edged with exhaustion as she gazed around. I had to admit, she wasn't wrong. My farmhouse had that cozy, lived-in charm that always felt like a hug you didn't know you needed—especially on days like this.

The floral couch, with its patchwork of autumn reds and oranges, sat like an anchor beneath the big picture window. Sunlight spilled in, casting soft, golden light over the room. The couch had seen everything—late-night talks, lazy Sunday naps, and more than a few tears—and now it was serving as our unofficial HQ. Beside it, a small table held a vase of fresh-cut flowers—bright orange chrysanthemums, pink dahlias, and a sprinkle of wildflowers Hattie and I had gathered from the fields. It smelled like fall in a way that almost made me forget the chaos swirling outside.

Bookshelves stretched from floor to ceiling, crammed with everything from well-worn novels to dusty trinkets collected over the years. Hattie loved to joke that if the apocalypse came, at least we'd have books on baking, botany, and survival to guide us. The other sofa, draped in mismatched throws and floral pillows, seemed to beckon, saying, Come on, sit. We'll figure this out.

But despite the comforting surroundings, tension hung in the air. Papers were scattered across the coffee table—crime scene photos, notes, scribbled theories. A giant crime board we'd put together dominated one corner, covered in strings, photos, and more unanswered questions than I cared to count.

Eloise, freshly released from jail but still as sharp as ever, was leaning against the doorway, arms crossed. Her frizzy curls seemed wilder than usual, a reflection of the chaos we were trying to unravel. "Blake Courtney," she said, breaking the silence. Her voice was as no-nonsense as ever, cutting through the low hum of conversation.

I frowned, tilting my head. "Blake? I don't know…nothing concrete ties him to the murders."

Eloise pushed off the doorframe, her detective instincts clearly kicking into gear. "Think about it, Josie. Blake's connected to everything. He's got ties to Tiffany, to Dex—and don't forget, he tried to buy my recipes."

Max, who was flipping through a stack of notes at the coffee table, looked up, intrigued. "You're saying Blake has a motive tied to business?"

Eloise nodded, her gaze steady. "Blake's ambitious, and he's ruthless in business. When I refused to sell him my muffin recipes, he got angry—unreasonably angry. If he saw Tiffany or Artie as obstacles to his plans, well…"

I sat up straighter as the memory hit me. "You're right. I remember you telling me about that. He didn't just offer to buy the recipes—he basically demanded them. When you said no, he acted like it was a personal attack."

"Exactly," Eloise said, her tone sharpening. "Blake doesn't like to hear 'no.' And if there's something bigger at stake here—something involving FMR Foods—he might've seen Artie and Tiffany as expendable."

Konstanze, pacing by the window with her usual calm precision, stopped mid-step. "And let's not forget that Josie saw him at the apple orchard with Tiffany and Dex. That meeting wasn't casual. What if they were working on something Blake didn't want anyone to know about?"

"Good point," Rhett chimed in, leaning back on the couch. "And didn't Tommy Delaney sit next to him at the murder mystery party? That didn't seem like a coincidence."

The knot in my stomach tightened. "And Connie thought she saw Dex talking to Blake the day someone tried to run her over," I added. "What if Blake orchestrated that to scare her—or worse?"

Max frowned, his hand frozen mid-note. "If Blake's framing Dex, it makes sense. He'd want to keep himself out of the spotlight while twisting the story to make Dex look guilty."

Eloise's eyes narrowed, the sharp glint in them unmistakable. "Blake's been working too hard to stay in the background. If he's behind this, he's trying to control the narrative—and distract us from what he's really hiding."

Holly, sitting cross-legged on the floor with her notebook, suddenly spoke up. "Speaking of controlling the narrative, you guys won't believe this." She held up her phone, her expression a mix of disbelief and anger. "Mindy just texted me—she works at the salon with Nikki. Apparently, Blake's been going around town spreading rumors about Dex. He's telling people that Artie and Tiffany were 'closer than people think,' trying to stir the pot."

"Why would he do that?" I asked, leaning forward.

Holly scrolled through the message, her brow furrowing. "Mindy overheard him talking to Sheriff Sturdy, too. It sounds like he's planting seeds of doubt, pushing the idea that Dex had something to do with the murders."

Eloise's lips pressed into a thin line. "Classic misdirection. If Blake's behind this, framing Dex takes the heat off him—and keeps us chasing our tails."

Max nodded, his eyes locked on the crime board. "If Artie or Tiffany had leverage on Blake—something that could damage him or FMR Foods—he'd have every reason to silence them. And if Dex is an easy scapegoat, even better."

The pieces were clicking together faster now, but it still felt like we were missing something. Blake was everywhere, tied to both Artie and Tiffany, yet he'd managed to stay just far enough out of the spotlight to avoid real suspicion.

And then, like a lightbulb flickering on, I remembered something.

"The locket," I said, almost to myself.

Holly turned to me. "What locket?"

"The one the student worker found in the café," I explained, my pulse quickening. "It was right before the murder mystery party, stuffed between the chair cushions. I didn't think anything of it at the time—it seemed like another piece of lost-and-found junk. But now..."

"Now it might not be junk," Eloise finished, her tone sharp. "It could be a clue."

"It's probably still in the lost-and-found," I said, my voice rising urgently. "I'll check first thing tomorrow."

The room buzzed with a renewed sense of purpose, but Holly's voice cut through the chatter. "Guys, if Blake's pushing this hard to frame Dex, we need to move fast. If he's manipulating the story, he's hiding something big—and he's not going to stop."

Eloise nodded, her expression fierce. "We dig into Blake's connections. Find out if there's anything linking him directly to Artie or Tiffany. And we don't let him see us coming."

I stood, adrenaline coursing through me. "We've let Blake sit in the background long enough. It's time to bring him into focus."

As I glanced at the crime board, my gaze landed on Blake's polished, perfect photo. Tomorrow, I'd dig into the locket. But soon, Blake Courtney was going to have to answer some questions—and I was ready to make sure he didn't wriggle out of them.

17 espressoing doubts

THE GOLDEN LIGHT OF DAWN stretched across the rolling hills, brushing the farmhouse with a soft, warm glow. The trees blazed in fiery reds, oranges, and yellows, their leaves whispering secrets to the cool breeze before tumbling down to skitter across the porch. The earthy, smoky scent of autumn mingled with the faint aroma of distant wood smoke, and pumpkins lined the railing like patient sentinels awaiting their big moment.

I leaned against the porch railing, inhaling the crisp morning air as Mocha stood at the edge of the porch, her nose twitching and ears perked. Her focus was fixed on a flock of Canada geese honking their way south in a perfect V, their calls slicing through the quiet morning. She gave them a long, serious stare, then padded back to me, her eyes bright and curious, as if to ask, What's the plan?

"Today's the day," I murmured, more to myself than her.

She wagged her tail like she understood, her whole body vibrating with encouragement. I crouched to scratch behind her ears. "Hold down the fort, girl. I won't be long."

Mocha barked softly, circling twice before flopping into the perfect patch of sunlight. She stretched luxuriously, like she had not a care in the world. I envied her, but the peaceful morning couldn't quite settle the buzzing urgency in my head. The locket had been pulling at me since yesterday, and I had a gut feeling it was more important than I'd realized.

I grabbed my jacket and headed down the porch steps, each crunch of autumn leaves under my boots grounding me just a little. Normally, the sound brought me joy—a small, cozy pleasure in the simple things. But today, my mind was elsewhere. That locket from the lost-and-found wouldn't stop tugging at my thoughts. Why hadn't I paid attention to it before? What if it was a clue, not just another forgotten trinket?

I tossed my jacket onto the passenger seat and climbed into my Jeep Wagoneer. The café was still taped off, a crime scene under the watchful eyes of the Hickory Hills police. But I couldn't let a little yellow tape stop me—not today.

The locket couldn't wait.

As the engine rumbled to life, I glanced back at Mocha, already dozing on the porch, oblivious to my nerves. "Lucky dog," I muttered, smiling despite myself. But as I steered down the gravel drive, the smile faded. That tugging feeling—that urgency—gnawed at me. I didn't know why, but I knew I couldn't ignore it.

I parked the Wagoneer a little farther down the street from Novel Grounds, out of sight from any too-curious eyes. The yellow crime scene tape fluttered limply across the entrance, more suggestion than a deterrent. The street was quiet, save for the rustle of leaves scraping along the pavement. Perfect.

"Just get in, grab the locket, and get out. Easy," I whispered to myself.

The crunch of leaves underfoot felt too loud, and I glanced around, half-expecting someone to pop out of nowhere and yell, What do you think you're doing? My pulse quickened as I ducked under the tape, keeping my head low. Totally casual. Just a book café owner, breaking into her own café. No big deal.

"Morning, Josie!"

I froze mid-step, my heart lurching into my throat. I plastered on a smile and turned to find Hank Junior leaning against his truck across the street, his grin easy and full of small-town charm.

"Oh! Morning, Hank Junior!" My voice cracked slightly, which was definitely not suspicious at all.

"You opening back up?" he asked, tipping his hat. "I thought the cops had it shut down."

"Uh, not yet," I said, clutching my bag tighter. "Just grabbing some... supplies."

He nodded, not even questioning it. "Alright then. Don't work too hard!"

I forced a laugh. "Wouldn't dream of it." My pulse was still racing as he waved and climbed into his truck. Way to keep it cool, Josie.

I turned back to the door, ducked under the tape, and fumbled with my keys, my hands suddenly clumsy. Why did I have so many keys, anyway? Finally, the lock clicked, and I slipped inside, shutting the door behind me as quietly as I could.

The familiar scent of coffee beans and pumpkin spice hit me, but it felt... wrong. Without the hum of customers and the clatter of mugs, the café was eerily silent. I'd never thought of Novel Grounds as anything but warm and welcoming, but today, it felt like I didn't belong. Like I was intruding in my own space.

"Get it together, Josie," I whispered, forcing myself to move.

I crouched behind the counter and pulled out the lost-and-found box, my fingers rifling through the usual odds and ends. A scarf. A textbook. An ancient pair of gloves. But no locket. My stomach clenched as I dug deeper, pulling the box onto the floor to get a better angle. Nothing.

Frustration bubbled up, and I leaned into the shelf, stretching my hand into the dark corners. My fingers brushed something cold and metallic. I froze, then carefully pulled it free. The chain was tangled, the heart-shaped locket dangling awkwardly, like it had been hiding on purpose.

There it was.

I turned it over in my palm, the small, tarnished heart gleaming faintly in the dim light. It felt so light for something that could be carrying the weight of this mystery. This little trinket was important. I just knew it.

A creak shattered the silence, and my heart shot into my throat.

"Josie?"

I spun around so fast I nearly fell over, clutching the locket like it was incriminating evidence. Caleb stood in the doorway, his silhouette sharp against the pale morning light.

"Oh, Caleb! I was just—uh—" My voice trailed off as I scrambled to hide the locket behind my back, feeling like a kid caught with her hand in the cookie jar.

Caleb raised an eyebrow, his expression unreadable. "Relax," he said, stepping inside. "We're done processing the scene. Novel Grounds is yours again."

I blinked, thrown off by the flatness in his tone. "Wait, it's... mine again?"

He nodded, not even looking at me. "You can reopen whenever you're ready."

And just like that, he turned to leave. No banter, no questions—just cold, professional Caleb. It was so abrupt, it felt like whiplash.

"Caleb, wait—don't you want to—"

"No need," he interrupted, his voice clipped. "I'm needed back at the station."

Before I could say another word, he was gone. The door clicked shut behind him, leaving me alone in the empty café, the locket still clenched in my hand.

I stared at the door, my mind racing. That wasn't Caleb—not the Caleb I'd been working with for weeks. Where was the dry humor, the quick wit? That wasn't professional distance—it was something else. Something colder. Had I done something wrong? Or was this just Sturdy's influence, forcing him to cut ties?

Maybe Caleb was just following orders, trying to keep me out of trouble. But it didn't feel that way. It felt... personal. Like a door had been slammed shut without warning, and I was standing on the other side, wondering what had just happened.

I shook my head, forcing the thoughts away. Focus, Josie. The locket was what mattered now. Whatever was going on with Caleb, I'd deal with it later. Right now, I felt this little heart-shaped mystery was about to crack everything wide open.

I pulled out my phone and quickly texted the group:

Josie: *Hey! Guess what? Novel Grounds is back open! Just got the all-clear from Caleb. Who's free to help me reopen?*

The replies came in fast:
Hattie: *About time! I'll grab Mocha and be right over.*
Holly: *Just wrapping up at the salon—be there soon!*
Eloise: *I've got muffins. See you in a few.*
Rhett: *Swamped at the woodshop, but I'll stop by later!*
Anders: *On shift, but keep me posted!*
Emma: *I'll swing by after my shift at the horse rescue!*
Konstanze: *Max and I are in class, but I'll try to come by after!*

I smiled down at my phone, a flicker of warmth breaking through. Caleb might have been pulling away, but I still had my people. And we were going to reopen this café—Sheriff Sturdy, the investigation, and Caleb's cold shoulder or not.

I shot off a quick text to the staff:

Josie: We're back in business!

Sliding my phone into my pocket, I grabbed a broom and started sweeping. The rhythmic scrape of bristles against the floor felt grounding, even if it was strange cleaning what had so recently been a crime scene. It wasn't just about tidying up—it was a small act of defiance, a promise that we were moving forward.

The familiar jingle of the bell above the door cut through the silence, and Holly walked in, still wearing her work apron. Her curls were a little frazzled, and her shoulders sagged, but her signature grin hadn't dimmed.

"Nikki can handle the rest of the day," she said, shrugging off her jacket. "What's the plan, boss?"

Hattie arrived, Mocha trotting proudly beside her. The dog didn't hesitate—she leapt onto the couch like it was her throne, wagging her tail and settling in with a satisfied sigh.

"Looks like Mocha's already claimed her seat," Hattie said, laughing as she dropped her bag by the door. She gave Mocha an affectionate pat before turning to me. "Alright, what's first?"

The unmistakable smell of warm muffins drifted through the air, and Eloise swept in, balancing a tray like a queen. "Thought we'd need a little fuel," she said with a wink, setting the tray on the counter.

I breathed in the heavenly mix of cinnamon and sugar, the scent already lifting my spirits. "Eloise, you're a lifesaver," I said, grabbing a muffin and tearing off a piece. "I swear, the smell alone is therapy."

Eloise gave a small, knowing smile but didn't say anything. Her sharp eyes were already scanning the room, as if she was cataloging every detail, every potential clue.

That was Eloise for you—sharp as a tack, even with her signature curls a little wilder than usual and shadows under her eyes from everything she'd been through. She wasn't just here for moral support; she was here to work.

"There's something I need to show you all," I said, walking to a table and placing the small heart-shaped locket down carefully, like it was the most delicate thing in the world. The group gathered around, curious.

"This was found here at the café not long after Artie was murdered," I explained. "One of my student workers tossed it in the lost-and-found, but it's been nagging at me ever since Eloise reminded us we might've overlooked something."

Holly leaned in, her brow furrowing as she studied the locket. "You think it's connected to the case?"

I shrugged, running my thumb over the cool metal. "I don't know. It's just... a feeling. But I couldn't ignore it."

"Have you opened it?" Eloise asked, her voice all business now, that NYPD detective tone kicking in.

I nodded, carefully popping the clasp. Inside was a faded photograph—a woman cradling a baby girl, both smiling as if they didn't have a care in the world. The room fell quiet as everyone stared at the tiny image.

"Do either of you recognize them?" I asked, looking up.

Hattie shook her head, her brow knit in thought. Holly squinted, but her expression stayed blank. Eloise's face shifted, her lips pressing into a thin line as her eyes narrowed.

"It's possible this is connected to someone from the party," she said after a moment. "Or even one of our suspects. Either way, we need to keep looking into it."

"Agreed," Holly said, straightening up, her voice bright with determination. "Let's figure out who they are."

Before I could respond, the door swung open, and Emma breezed in, dust clinging to her jeans from her morning shift at the horse rescue. She gave us all a wide grin, wiping her hands on her thighs.

"Hey, ladies! What are we looking at?"

Eloise held up the locket and gave her a brief rundown. Emma's smile faded as her curiosity sharpened. "Well, it's definitely worth checking out," she said, sliding into a chair. "Even if it's not connected to Artie or Tiffany, it might lead us to something—or someone—we haven't considered."

"That's what I'm hoping," I said, trying not to let the weight of uncertainty drag me down. "But I'm not sure where to start. It could be nothing, but it's been bugging me."

"It's something," Eloise said firmly. "Things like this don't show up by accident." She gave me a meaningful look, the kind that said she wasn't going to let me brush this off as a coincidence.

Hattie crossed her arms, her expression serious. "Alright, then. We're not leaving any stone unturned. If someone left it behind, there's a reason."

The wave of gratitude that swept over me was almost overwhelming. I glanced around at the group, these people who'd become my family in every way that mattered. "Thanks, guys," I said softly. "I don't know what I'd do without you."

"Probably drink bad coffee and make terrible decisions," Holly teased, nudging me with her elbow.

"Not wrong," I admitted with a grin.

From there, we fell into our usual rhythm. Holly grabbed a rag and started wiping down tables while Hattie brewed a fresh pot of coffee, the rich aroma filling the air. Eloise tidied the counter, rearranging the muffins and wiping down the register. Emma, ever the multitasker, grabbed a broom and started sweeping, humming softly to herself.

The café slowly came back to life, sunlight streaming through the windows and casting everything in a golden glow. It felt... right. Like we were reclaiming not just the space but a piece of ourselves that had been stolen by the chaos of the last few weeks.

But even as I scrubbed the countertop, my mind drifted. Caleb. His coldness earlier still lingered like a splinter I couldn't get rid of. Was it just Sheriff Sturdy's orders, or was it something more?

I scrubbed harder, frustration bubbling up. I thought we'd been working toward something—not just solving the case, but... us. Whatever us even meant. But now? He'd shut me out completely, and I didn't know why.

"Hey." Holly's voice pulled me from my spiraling thoughts. She tilted her head, studying me with a knowing look. "You good?"

"Yeah," I lied, forcing a smile. "Just... thinking."

"Well, stop thinking so hard," she said with a grin. "You'll hurt yourself."

I laughed despite myself. Maybe I didn't have all the answers, but I had my friends. And for now, that was enough.

Later that day the sun had dipped below the horizon, casting the town in a soft, golden twilight. It had been a whirlwind of a day—Stanzi and Max were off at their university classes, Rhett and Emma were wrangling Cub Scouts on horseback somewhere, and Hattie had taken her camper into the woods for an art retreat. That left Holly and me, knee-deep in papers and evidence, looking more like amateur detectives on a low-budget crime show—minus the cameras and prize money.

As for Eloise? She had barricaded herself in her kitchen, claiming she needed to "think," but I knew what that really meant: baking. By now, her house was probably drowning in muffins, scones, and enough pies to supply the town's next potluck. Everyone has their way of processing stress, I guess. Mine? Trying not to lose my mind while sifting through mountains of half-baked theories.

Holly, usually a ray of sunshine, was hyper-focused, flipping through a stack of notes with the determination of someone untangling a necklace knot. Then her phone buzzed. She glanced at the screen, and her whole expression shifted—something between excitement and apprehension.

"What's up?" I asked, sensing the knot in my stomach tighten. Holly didn't just get that look over random texts.

"It's Anders," she said, not looking up. "He's been digging into Artie's insurance policy, just like Sheriff Sturdy asked him to." She hesitated, flipping through the papers like she was trying to find the right one to show me. Finally, she stopped and looked at me. "You'll never believe who the beneficiary is."

I sat up straighter, my curiosity kicking into high gear. "Okay, who?"

"Tiffany," Holly said, her voice tinged with disbelief. "Artie made Tiffany his beneficiary."

I blinked, completely caught off guard. "Wait, Tiffany? His receptionist Tiffany? That Tiffany?"

"The very same," Holly said, setting the paper down with a little too much force. "She was his receptionist, Josie. Not his friend, not his family—just someone who answered his phones and scheduled his appointments. But here's the kicker—the policy was updated two weeks before he was murdered."

"Two weeks?" I repeated, my mind spinning. "That's... not a coincidence."

"Nope," Holly said, shaking her head. "And get this—it's not some small payout, either. We're talking a lot of money. Like, retire-in-style kind of money."

I stared at the papers, trying to make sense of it all. "Okay, so Tiffany stole Eloise's recipes and stashed them at Artie's garage—that much we know. And now we find out she's the beneficiary on his insurance policy? What was she doing, running a side hustle in extortion?"

Holly snorted, though her expression was grim. "It's looking more and more like she had Artie wrapped around her finger. She must've been blackmailing him. I mean, why else would he name her?"

I leaned back in my chair, staring at the ceiling as the pieces started shifting into place. "It makes sense. She probably threatened him—maybe with something about the stolen recipes. She could've told him she'd blow the whole thing wide open unless he made her the beneficiary."

Holly nodded. "And the timing lines up. She had the recipes, and Artie had the insurance. They must've made some kind of deal."

"Except," I said, leaning forward again, "Tiffany didn't stop there. She bashed him over the head with that torque wrench after he was already dead from the poison. Why? Was she trying to cover her tracks?"

Holly's lips pressed into a thin line. "Or she didn't know he was already dead," she said quietly.

The room fell silent as the weight of that possibility settled over us.

"You think she followed him to the garage?" I asked, my voice barely above a whisper. "Maybe she was there to confront him, or to make sure he didn't back out of their deal..."

"And then she saw him collapse," Holly finished. "She didn't know about the poison—she panicked, thought he was still alive, and grabbed the wrench."

Holly rubbed her temples, frustration flickering across her face. "It's so messy, Josie. The poison was precise and planned—someone knew exactly what they were doing. But Tiffany's move with the wrench? That was pure panic."

"She was the wildcard," Holly said, nodding slowly. "And now she's dead too. So whatever she knew—whoever she was working with—it died with her."

I picked up the locket sitting on the table, turning it over in my hand. "Unless," I said softly, "she left something behind. A clue. A connection."

Holly's gaze sharpened, her attention locking onto the locket. "You really think this is tied to her?"

"I don't know," I admitted, running my thumb over the cool metal. "It's too strange to ignore—something about it feels important."

Holly leaned in, inspecting the locket with a mix of curiosity and suspicion. "We know she was sneaky. Manipulative. If anyone had a backup plan or a secret, it'd be Tiffany."

I nodded, flipping the locket open to reveal the tiny, faded photograph inside. "But who are they?" I murmured, staring at the image of a woman holding a baby.

"Do you think Artie knew them?" Holly asked, tilting her head.

"Maybe," I said, my voice trailing off. "Or maybe Tiffany did."

Holly sighed, leaning back in her chair. "Between this locket, the insurance policy, and the stolen recipes, there's too much overlap to ignore."

"Exactly," I said, "And now that Tiffany's gone, we're back to square one. Whoever poisoned Artie and Tiffany is still out there, and we're no closer to figuring out who they are."

Holly's phone buzzed, breaking the tension. She glanced at the screen and frowned. "It's Anders. He found something else. Apparently, Artie had a second safe deposit box—one that no one knew about."

My eyebrows shot up. "A secret safe deposit box? That's new."

"Yeah," Holly said, already typing a reply. "And guess whose name was on the access list? Tiffany's."

I felt my pulse quicken. "So whatever was in that box... Tiffany knew about it. Maybe she was using it to blackmail him."

"Or," Holly said, her voice turning grim, "maybe someone else was using both of them. If Tiffany thought she was in control, but someone bigger was pulling the strings..."

The idea sent a chill down my spine. "Then they set this whole thing up and made sure both Artie and Tiffany ended up dead."

Holly nodded, her expression hard. "And if we don't figure out who it is, they're going to get away with it."

I leaned back in my chair, the locket still clutched in my hand. "Then we'd better get to work."

I picked up the small locket from the table, turning it over in my hand like it held all the answers. "Maybe this ties into it somehow," I murmured, more to myself than Holly. "Artie had a fight with Tiffany that morning at Novel Grounds. I overheard bits and pieces—he threatened her, said something like, 'You better hold up your end of the deal.'"

Holly's eyes widened. "He what? Josie, why are you just now telling me this?"

"I didn't think it was important!" I said defensively. "At the time, it just sounded like... workplace drama. But now?" I shook my head. "It does feel important."

Before we could spiral too far, Holly's phone buzzed again. She glanced at the screen, and her face fell. "I've got to go," she said, her voice tight with urgency. "It's my brother. He's in the hospital."

My stomach dropped. "Oh no, Holly. Go—don't worry about this. Just text me when you can, okay?"

She nodded, giving me a quick, tight hug before rushing out the door. And just like that, I was alone again, surrounded by stacks of papers and unanswered questions.

I sighed, turning my attention back to the locket. I'd been fiddling with it all day, but now it felt heavier—like it was holding a puzzle that I couldn't solve. Absentmindedly, I popped the clasp open and shut, open and shut, until—click.

I froze as a hidden compartment popped open.

Inside was a faint dark, earthy, and slightly spicy scent. My breath caught in my throat. This wasn't just a forgotten trinket. I snapped the locket shut and bolted to the sink, scrubbing my hands furiously as my mind raced. Could this locket have held the poison? Had it been part of the plan all along?

Back at the table, I grabbed my phone and snapped a quick photo of the locket, sending it to Eloise with a simple message: Found this. Could be big. Smells almost licoricey and kind of like absinthe. Thoughts?

The room was eerily quiet as I sat there waiting for a reply. My mind wandered—of course, it wandered to Caleb.

His distant, cold attitude earlier had left a sting. We'd been working together for weeks, and I thought we were... something. Partners, at least. Friends, maybe. But the way he brushed me off, like I was just another problem he didn't have time for—it hurt.

Knock, knock.

I jumped, nearly dropping the locket. My heart raced as I peered through the window.

It was Caleb, standing on the porch, looking... conflicted. His usual confident demeanor was gone, replaced by something heavier.

I opened the door cautiously. "Caleb?"

"We've got a problem," he said, his voice low and steady. "Sheriff Sturdy's decided to move forward with Eloise's trial. He thinks the evidence is solid enough."

My chest tightened. "But it's not. We know it's not."

"I know," Caleb said, his tone softening. "But he's under a lot of pressure. And without any other viable suspects..." He trailed off, his jaw tightening.

I hesitated, then blurted out, "I found something." I held up the locket, my voice rushing. "It has a secret compartment. I think this is where the poison was hidden."

Caleb's eyes widened as he gently took the locket from my hand. "We need to get this analyzed," he said, his voice suddenly urgent. "This could be the break we've been waiting for."

He started to leave but stopped at the door, turning back to me. His expression softened, and for a moment, the cold distance from earlier melted away. "You shouldn't be doing this alone, Josie," he said quietly.

I blinked, my heart catching in my throat. "I'm not alone," I said, though it sounded more like a question.

Caleb's gaze held mine for a beat longer than necessary. "We'll get the bad guy," he said, his voice firm but almost... tender. "Don't lose hope."

And then he was gone, leaving me standing in the doorway with a locket in one hand and a whirlwind of emotions in the other.

Whatever was happening between us—whether it was work or something else—it was as tangled as the mystery we were trying to solve. But for now, I had a clue to chase. And that would have to be enough.

18 grinding down the truth

The next morning, dawn's soft, golden light filtered through the curtains, casting long, delicate shadows across the room. Outside, the yard was a patchwork of autumn colors—rich oranges, deep reds, and the occasional burst of yellow. The honking of geese flying south echoed faintly in the distance, and the cool, crisp air clung to the porch, carrying the earthy scent of fallen leaves and damp earth. It was the kind of morning that made you want just to *be*, to let the stillness wrap around you.

I wrapped my hands around my coffee mug, savoring the familiar comfort of its warmth, and stepped onto the porch. The quiet of the early hour felt like a gift, a brief moment of peace before the day truly began. I took a deep breath, letting the freshness of the air settle my nerves as I gazed out at the trees, their branches gently swaying in the breeze.

Mocha, ever the morning companion, trotted up the porch stairs and nudged my leg with her nose. Her tail wagged, thumping against the wooden boards as she gave me that look—the one that said *it's time to go inside, now.*

"Alright, alright," I murmured with a smile, scratching behind her ears before I opened the screen door. She trotted in, hopping onto the floral couch, already curling up in her favorite spot for her morning nap. Lucky dog.

The porch swing creaked softly as I pushed it with my foot, coffee steaming in my hands and a blanket draped over my shoulders. The world was calm, painted in shades of early morning gold, but my thoughts were anything but. Sleep had been elusive, chased off by the relentless buzz of questions about the case—and Caleb. Mostly Caleb.

Mocha snoozed on the couch, her chin resting on the back cushion. Every so often, she'd sleepily crack one eye open to peer out the window as if making sure the outside world was still behaving before drifting back to her doggy dreams. She had the right idea, relaxing like there wasn't a schemer in sight. I sighed, pulling the blanket tighter around me just as my phone buzzed on my lap.

Holly: Tom's stable now. It was minor. Can't wait to tell you about it. :) See you later today!

Relief poured over me. Thank goodness her brother was okay. That was one less thing to keep me up at night. Setting the phone aside, I smiled, but the sound of tires crunching on gravel pulled my attention to the driveway.

A sleek, black Mercedes eased into view, so shiny it reflected the soft sunlight like a mirror. My grip on the coffee mug tightened. Mocha, ever the watchdog, perked up and let out a low growl, her nose twitching as she sniffed the air.

And then he stepped out.

Blake Courtney.

I knew him right away—FMR Foods' smarmy marketing guy with the smooth-talking charm of a politician and the ethics of a used-car salesman. He always seemed to pop up at the worst times, from spreading rumors at the Curl Up and Dye salon to cozying up to town officials. I'd been meaning to track him down, but I guess he decided to save me the trouble.

Blake adjusted his jacket, and his polished shoes crunched against the gravel as he surveyed the scene. His sharp eyes flicked over the barn, the pumpkins on the porch steps, and the pecan trees swaying in the breeze.

He looked as out of place as a tuxedo at a barn dance.

Mocha growled again, jumped off the couch, and pressed her nose to the screen door. Her tail stiffened, and her body language screamed, "I don't trust this guy one bit."

"Knock, knock," Blake called, rapping his knuckles on the porch post with a practiced grin that made my skin crawl.

I rose from the swing, coffee cup still in hand. "Morning," I said, keeping my tone neutral. Mocha let out another low growl, and I let her outside on the porch with me. She sat at my feet, and I gave her a quick pat on the head.

"Josie," he said, flashing a business card like we were in the middle of a high-stakes corporate deal. "Blake Courtney. FMR Foods. You might've heard we're interested in Eloise's recipes."

Oh, I'd heard all right. I crossed my arms, leaning against the porch railing. "Eloise's recipes aren't for sale, Mr. Courtney. She's been pretty clear about that."

His grin didn't falter, but there was a flicker of annoyance in his eyes. "Of course, of course," he said, his tone as smooth as butter on hot biscuits. "I just thought I'd stop by for a friendly chat. Small towns thrive on community, don't they?"

I resisted the urge to roll my eyes. "Is that what this is? Community outreach?"

Blake chuckled and brushed imaginary lint off his jacket. "Well, you know how small towns are. People love to talk. And lately, I've been hearing some... interesting things about Eloise."

My stomach tightened, but I kept my face steady. "What kind of things?"

"Oh, just whispers," he said, lowering his voice like he was sharing a secret. "Small-town gossip. You know how it is. People speculating about her involvement in... unsavory activities. I'm sure you've heard the rumors."

Unsavory activities? My jaw clenched, but I forced a calm tone. "I haven't heard anything like that. Sounds like whoever's talking doesn't know Eloise very well."

Blake tilted his head, his grin sharpening. "You'd be surprised what people say when they're under a little pressure. Sometimes, truths—or half-truths—slip out."

And there it was—the veiled threat. He wasn't just here to spread rumors. He was here to discredit Eloise and make me feel like we were fighting a losing battle.

"I know Eloise," I said firmly. "She's a good person. And if you're here to stir up trouble, you're wasting your time. I don't scare that easy."

Blake raised his hands in mock surrender, his grin never wavering. "Hey, I'm just doing my due diligence. If Eloise has nothing to hide, then no harm done, right? But if things... escalate, sometimes it's better to be proactive. Get ahead of the story. I'd hate to see things get worse for her—or for you."

My pulse quickened, but I refused to let him see me flinch. "You've said your piece. Now, if you don't mind, I've got things to do."

Blake's smile tightened, but he didn't argue. Instead, he slid his business card onto the porch railing and took a step back. "Just a friendly conversation, Josie. You know how to reach me if anything... changes."

I didn't reply. I just watched as he turned and strode back to his Mercedes, his expensive shoes tapping against the wooden porch. He climbed into the car, threw me one last glance through the window, and drove off, leaving a cloud of dust in his wake.

As soon as the car disappeared down the road, I let out a long breath. Mocha nudged my leg, her nose cool and reassuring against my hand. I picked up the business card, stared at the crisp black lettering, and flicked it into the nearest flowerpot. "Well, Mocha," I muttered, scratching behind her ears. I guess I don't need to track him down anymore."

I sat in my office at Novel Grounds, staring at the scattered notes and scribbles spread across my desk. The smell of fresh coffee lingered faintly in the air, but it wasn't doing much to wake up my brain. Blake's smug grin kept replaying in my mind. He'd said just enough to plant seeds of doubt, but not enough to make me believe him. That was the game he was playing—control through whispers. I wasn't buying it, but I also wasn't underestimating him. Not with Eloise in his crosshairs.

There was a soft knock at the door before I could spiral into another round of overthinking. "Come in," I called, half-expecting Holly or maybe

Caleb.

Instead, it was Eloise, balancing a tray of muffins. The smell of cinnamon and nutmeg wafted into the room like a warm hug. Curled under my desk, Mocha perked her head up at the scent, her nose twitching in approval.

"Thought you might need a little pick-me-up," Eloise said, setting the tray on the desk with a wink. She was in her usual baking uniform—flour-dusted apron, sleeves rolled up. And her hair? It was as much a part of her personality as her sharp wit and no-nonsense demeanor: an unruly halo of silver curls frizzing in every direction.

"You always know exactly what I need," I said, smiling despite the tangle of thoughts still buzzing in my head.

Eloise sank into the chair across from me, smoothing her apron. Her eyes swept over my desk, taking in the clutter of notes, photos, and my abandoned coffee mug. "You've been burning the candle at both ends again," she said lightly, though her tone had an edge of concern.

I shrugged, leaning back in my chair. "There's a lot to burn."

She gave me a knowing look. "I heard Blake was sniffing around this morning."

I nodded, setting down my pen. "Yeah, he showed up unannounced and tried to play mind games—talking about 'gossip' and how you'd better watch your back. He's fishing, Eloise."

Eloise let out a dry chuckle, but her gaze sharpened. "Oh, I know Blake's type. Thinks he can throw his weight around with a fancy suit and a slick smile. But if he thinks he can intimidate me, he's barking up the wrong tree."

I grinned a little. "You handled him last time just fine, but I thought you should know. He's escalating. This isn't just about recipes anymore."

Eloise leaned forward, folding her hands neatly. "Of course, it isn't. Recipes are only part of it—Blake's the kind of man who doesn't just want to win. He wants to own. If he's poking around again, it means he hasn't found the information he's looking for and likely he's getting pressure from someone else."

I paused, her words sinking in. "You think he's working for someone?"

"Josie, people like Blake don't make their own moves," Eloise said, her voice firm and steady. "They take orders. Someone local with a real stake in this is behind all of this mess. You're looking at the wrong end."

That gnawed at me. She wasn't wrong—Blake had the polished veneer of a middleman, not a mastermind. "So who's pulling his strings?" I muttered.

"That's the question, isn't it?" Eloise said, breaking off a piece of muffin and popping it into her mouth. "But you've got good instincts. What's your gut telling you?"

I sighed, staring at the notes scattered in front of me. "I keep circling back to Artie and Tiffany. Their connection feels like the key. Artie updated his insurance policy two weeks before his death, naming Tiffany as the beneficiary. That's not random. And Tiffany—well, we know she stole your recipes. That had to be part of it, but..." I trailed off, the pieces still refusing to fit together.

She tilted her head, her sharp eyes studying me like I was a crossword she was halfway through solving. "Someone wanted Artie dead, and Tiffany... Tiffany was a loose end. She was greedy, sure, but that doesn't explain everything."

"Tiffany was there that morning," I said, my voice picking up speed as the memory clicked into place. "Tiffany, Dex, and Artie all came in for coffee. I think she saw something, Eloise—something that put her in danger."

She leaned forward, her elbows on the desk. "What did she see?"

I shook my head. "I don't know yet. But that morning, Artie had a sandwich from Dex, muffins from Sam, and coffee from Tyler. We can rule out Tyler—he wouldn't have poisoned Artie. That leaves Dex and Sam. And..." I hesitated, the thought dawning on me. "If Blake wanted your recipes and thought Artie had them, maybe he got involved, too."

Eloise arched an eyebrow, her expression turning skeptical. "Blake? You think he poisoned Artie?"

"Maybe," I said, my mind spinning. "Artie had your recipes, and Blake wanted them badly enough to harass you. It's possible he saw Artie as an obstacle."

Eloise didn't look entirely convinced, but her face darkened, her hands tightening slightly around the edge of the tray. "Blake's not above scheming to get what he wants. But poisoning someone? That's a different level."

"It's all connected," I said, frustration bubbling up. "Artie's murder, Tiffany's death, Blake's interference—it all ties back to those recipes. But the why... that's what's missing."

Eloise let out a small sigh and reached across the desk, resting her hand on mine. "Josie, you're close—I can feel it. But you're leaving people out. You're narrowing in too fast, and that's not like you. You've got the right instincts. Don't get tunnel vision."

"What do you mean?" I asked, blinking at her.

"You're focused on Blake right now, which makes sense—he's a loud, shiny distraction. But don't forget about Dex," she said firmly. "He's been acting jumpy ever since this started. And Sam? The guy's as slippery as they come. He's throwing that costume party like it's business as usual, barely a week after Tiffany's death. Doesn't that seem off to you?"

I leaned back, her words sinking in. "You're right. I've been so focused on Blake that I've sidelined them."

"Exactly," Eloise said, her voice growing sharper. "Dex had access to Artie that morning. He's a good kid, but good people can get desperate. And Sam? He's too smooth. Anyone who acts like this whole thing isn't touching them is hiding something."

"So you're saying I need to dig deeper into both of them—Dex and Sam. See if they've got connections I've missed."

Eloise nodded. "That's exactly what I'm saying. Don't get distracted by Blake's bluster. He might be involved, but he's not the only one who had something to gain. Dex, Sam, Blake—start pulling their threads. See where they unravel."

I stared down at the notes again. "You're right. I'll split my focus—Blake's just one part of this. I need to figure out what Dex has been hiding and keep my eye on Sam."

Eloise smiled, a flicker of pride in her eyes. "Now you're thinking like a detective. You've got this, Josie. And don't forget—Caleb might be frustrating, but he's still in your corner. Talk to him. He's got resources you don't."

I nodded, her steady confidence bolstering me. "Thanks, Eloise. I mean it."

She stood, brushing muffin crumbs off her apron and grabbing another muffin from the tray. "You're not alone in this, Josie. You've got me, Hattie, Holly—even Mocha. And Caleb. Lean on us when you need to."

I smiled as she headed for the door. "What's next on your list?" she asked, her voice lighter now, like she was daring me to take the next step.

I straightened in my chair, the weight in my chest lifting slightly. "First, I'm going to figure out what Dex has been hiding. Then, I'll see what I can dig up on Sam. And I need to talk to Caleb—figure out what he's found with the locket."

Eloise grinned, pausing in the doorway. "Good plan. Now get to work. I'll be here if you need me—or more muffins."

As the door clicked shut, the room felt brighter and a little less heavy. Mocha stirred by my feet, wagging her tail as she looked up at me, her soft brown eyes full of encouragement.

"Alright, girl," I said, scratching behind her ears. "Time to follow those instincts."

She gave a soft woof, and I laughed. Eloise was right—Dex, Sam, Blake. They all had secrets. And I wasn't stopping until I uncovered them.

19 storm in a coffee cup

October 30th, Evening

HATTIE WAS STILL CAMPING in the woods with her art students, leaving the house quieter than usual. Outside, the sky sagged low and heavy, dark clouds pressing in with the promise of a storm. I curled up in my favorite overstuffed armchair—the kind that hugged you back. A plush rug was spread out beneath me, warm under my toes, and the fire crackled softly in the hearth, casting golden light across the room. It was exactly the kind of evening meant for cozy mysteries, not living one.

Mocha snoozed at my feet, her head resting on my legs like the world's softest weighted blanket. She let out a tiny sigh, and I stroked her fur absently, my mind wandering.

The quiet would've been perfect—if not for the storm gathering in the pit of my stomach. My phone buzzed on the side table, cutting through the stillness. I glanced over at the screen. Holly.

Holly: Meet me at the Old Silo. Urgent.

I sat up, the weight of the words hitting me immediately. Holly wasn't one to use "urgent" lightly.

"Really, Holly? The silo?" I muttered, typing back a quick reply.

Me: What's going on? Are you okay?

No response.

I tried calling her, but it went straight to voicemail. My stomach tightened. What could possibly be so urgent that she'd drag me to the Old Silo?

The silo, once a postcard-worthy spot for romantic picnics and lazy summer afternoons, had long since lost its charm. Now, it was just... creepy. A forgotten relic with rusted ladders and stories whispered around campfires. I'd avoided the place for years, and not just because I have a thing about heights.

I glanced down at Mocha, who blinked up at me sleepily, her ears twitching in half-hearted curiosity. "Stay here, girl," I murmured, giving her a quick scratch behind the ears. "I'll be back soon."

Sliding into my boots, I grabbed my jacket and keys, bracing myself as I stepped out into the chill of the October night. The storm was getting closer, the air thick and electric.

As I started the Jeep, I muttered to myself, "This better be good, Holly."

The drive out to the Old Silo was unnervingly quiet. The wind whispered through the brittle cornfields, the once-vibrant stalks now dry and yellowed with the season's change. Even the zinnias that had lined the roadside earlier in the fall were drooping now, their heads bowed as though they knew something I didn't.

I tried calling Holly again. Still no answer.

By the time the silo came into view, my nerves were frayed. The towering structure loomed ahead, its weathered brick exterior glowing faintly under the eerie light of the stormy sky. The charm it once held was long gone, replaced by a sense of foreboding.

I parked near the edge of the field, gravel crunching under the tires. Holly's car was already there, parked at an awkward angle. Relief and dread hit me all at once. She was here. But why wasn't she answering her phone?

Stepping out of the Jeep, I tightened my jacket against the wind.

The air was thick and humid, and the silence pressed in around me.

"Holly?" I called, my voice carrying out into the field. No response.

The Old Silo stood like a sentinel, its rusty ladder clinging to its side like a bad idea waiting to happen. I glanced around, hoping to catch a glimpse of her, but there was no sign of movement. Just the dry rustle of corn stalks swaying in the breeze and the occasional creak of the silo in the wind.

The place felt... wrong.

"Holly?" I tried again, louder this time.

Nothing.

I circled the base of the silo, running my hand along the rough, cold surface of the bricks. The door was locked, and there was no way in from the ground. That left the ladder.

I stared at it, dread curling in my chest. Heights weren't exactly my thing, and that ladder looked like it hadn't been touched—or maintained—since the early '90s.

"Come on, Josie," I muttered, steeling myself. "It's just a ladder. You've climbed one before."

The wind whipped around me, carrying with it the faintest sound of... was that a voice? My breath caught.

"Holly?"

The sound was faint but unmistakable, coming from above. My stomach sank. She was up there. Of course, she was.

I grabbed the first rung, slick cold metal from the damp air.

Climbing the ladder was as terrifying as I'd imagined. The wind howled around me, and each step creaked under my weight, the rusted rungs groaning in protest. Halfway up, I paused, clinging to the ladder as the storm's first rain drops began to fall.

"Holly! Are you up there?"

A faint reply floated down. "Josie! Hurry!"

Her voice was thin, barely audible over the wind, but it was enough to push me forward.

When I reached the top, my hands were shaking, and my heart was racing. I pulled myself onto the platform, rain pelting my face as the storm broke overhead.

"Holly?" I shouted, my voice barely cutting through the storm's chaos.

Lightning split the sky, illuminating the scene for a single, harrowing moment. My breath caught in my throat.

A figure stood at the edge of the platform—not Holly.

He was tall, shadowed, and unmistakably wrong.

"Who's there?" I called, my voice trembling.

No response. The figure shifted, stepping closer.

"Where's Holly?" I demanded, trying to keep the rising panic out of my voice.

The figure stepped into the light, and for a moment, I thought my heart might stop. The tattered remains of a Confederate soldier's uniform clung to him, frayed and filthy. Mud streaked his face, and his eyes burned with a wild, unnatural intensity.

My rational brain screamed that this was impossible. But in that moment, nothing felt impossible.

"What do you want?" I asked, barely above a whisper.

He didn't answer. Instead, he raised something gleaming—a rusted sword. Its blade flashed in the lightning, jagged and menacing.

I stumbled back, nearly slipping on the rain-slick platform. My mind raced, trying to make sense of what I was seeing.

"Holly!" I shouted again, desperation turning my voice shrill.

Thankfully there was a door at the top of the silo. I hurried towards it. The figure advanced, silent and deliberate, his grip tightening on the sword. I teetered dangerously on the edge of the first step, and when my foot caught on the slippery boards, I went sprawling onto the staircase landing. The silo yawned open beneath me, its dark depths promising a quick and unpleasant end if I fell.

The figure loomed above, the wind whipping at his tattered uniform.

"Why are you doing this?" I gasped, clawing at the slick wooden planks to pull myself upright.

A cold laugh echoed through the storm, sharp and cruel. "You don't even know, do you?" His voice was jagged, as if it hadn't been used in years.

He stepped closer, each movement deliberate.

I scrambled back, my heart pounding so hard it felt like it might burst. My hands slipped on the wet surface, but I managed to claw my way to my feet.

"Where's Holly?" I tried again, my voice cracking.

No answer. Instead, he raised the sword. The air hummed with menace as he lunged toward me.

I ducked just in time, the blade slicing through the air where my head had been moments before. A scream tore from my throat as I raced down the staircase, rain blurring my vision and adrenaline driving my legs.

Lightning lit up the interior of the silo, and when my vision cleared, he was closer. Much closer.

I tripped on an uneven step and went sprawling again, crashing into an old piece of rusted machinery. Pain shot through my arm as I felt the jagged edge of something sharp slice into my skin. Blood began to seep down in thin, crimson lines.

I clutched my arm, panic bubbling to the surface. "No," I whispered, barely able to catch my breath.

But then something unexpected happened.

The figure froze.

His sword lowered slightly, and his movements turned jerky, almost uncertain. His eyes darted to my arm—specifically to the blood running down it.

His breathing grew ragged, almost panicked. He shook his head, stepping back as though the sight of my blood physically repelled him.

"What...?" I muttered, watching him in disbelief.

The man—ghost?—seemed to unravel in front of me. The wild intensity in his eyes dimmed, replaced by something almost childlike. He shook his head again, muttering, "No... no..." His voice cracked, full of fear.

I blinked, stunned. Was he afraid? Of me?

No. Not me. The blood.

He stumbled back, dropping the sword to his side. His pale face twisted in horror as he backed away, retreating into the shadows of the silo. Without another word, he disappeared.

The sudden silence left me breathless.

I slumped against the cold brick wall, clutching my bleeding arm. My mind whirled, trying to process what had just happened. He wasn't a ghost. He wasn't some supernatural phantom. He was real.

And he was afraid of blood.

I forced myself to my feet, my legs trembling beneath me. Whatever had just happened, one thing was clear: this wasn't just some Halloween ghost story. Someone had lured me here, and that someone had a very real, very dangerous plan.

I stumbled down the last few stairs, desperate to get out of the silo and into the open air.

But before I could reach the door, a shadow moved in front of me. My heart lurched, and I braced myself, ready to fight—until the figure stepped into the light.

"Holly!"

Relief flooded my chest as she stumbled toward me, her face streaked with dirt and fear.

"I got out," she panted, her voice shaking. "That... that thing shoved me in a crate. I managed to break free, but..." She trailed off, her eyes darting around the dim interior.

I grabbed her shoulders, steadying her. "Thank God you're okay. But we need to get out of here. Now."

"The doors are locked," she said, her voice tight. "I tried. Both the base and the top. We're stuck."

My stomach sank. Lightning flashed again, and the storm's fury raged louder than ever.

"Then we'll find another way," I said, trying to sound confident, even though my stomach was doing flips.

Deep down, I knew we were in trouble.

I pulled out my phone, hoping for a miracle, but the signal bar taunted me with a big, fat zero. Of course.

Leaning against the cold brick wall, I slid to the ground, utterly drained. "Jesus, please help us get out of this place and protect us," I prayed softly, my words barely above a whisper.

Holly sank down beside me, brushing dirt from her jeans. "In Your Precious Name, we ask these things, amen," she added, giving me a small, tired smile.

I nodded, managing a weak grin. "Thanks for the backup."

She grinned faintly, but her brow furrowed. "Josie, why are you here? Not that I'm not thrilled to have company right now, but this whole setup..."

I tilted my head. "That's funny—I was going to ask you the same thing."

"I got a message from Tyler at the café," she said, crossing her arms. "He said you left a note asking me to meet you here because you'd cracked something on the case. Sounded urgent."

My stomach dropped. "Holly, I didn't send that message. I've been home with Mocha all night."

Her face darkened. "Figured something was off when Julius the Ghost stole my phone and locked me in a crate." She jerked a thumb toward the stack of crates nearby. "What's going on, Josie?"

I blinked at her. "Sorry—you got what?!"

"Yeah, he tossed me in there like a sack of potatoes," she muttered, shaking her head. "Oh, and I'm guessing he used my phone to lure you here?"

I pulled out my own phone and handed it to her. "I got this message from you."

She read aloud, "'Meet me at the Old Silo. Urgent.'" Her eyes met mine, wide with disbelief.

I exhaled slowly, the pieces clicking together. "We're getting too close to the truth. Whoever this guy is, he's desperate. And clearly, he's not afraid to get his hands dirty."

"I just wish our phones worked in here," Holly said, glaring at hers like it had personally betrayed her.

"Yeah, me too," I muttered.

I stood, brushing dust from my hands. That's when I spotted it—a narrow door hidden behind the stack of crates.

"Holly," I said, my voice hushed.

She followed my gaze. "No way..."

We hurried over, and I fumbled with the latch. My hands were slick with blood from the cut on my arm, making the handle even harder to grip. Finally, with a groan of rusty hinges, the door creaked open to reveal a narrow, spiraling staircase leading down into the unknown.

"Oh, good," Holly deadpanned. "Because this night wasn't creepy enough already."

I shot her a look. "You want to stay here with the rats instead?"

She shuddered. "Nope. The rats and I had our quality time earlier. Lead the way."

I swallowed hard and stepped onto the staircase, my phone's dim light barely cutting through the darkness. Holly followed close behind, muttering under her breath about horror movie clichés.

"Seriously," she said, her voice echoing in the narrow space. "Creepy tunnels, flickering lights, shadows that move on their own... We're one jump scare away from a Hollywood deal."

"Don't forget the storm outside," I added dryly.

"Oh, right. Add that to the list," she said, shaking dirt from her hair.

Despite the tension, her grumbling made me smile. "Any other complaints you'd like to file while we're here?"

"Actually, yeah," she said, her tone lighter now. "I still owe you the story about Tom landing himself in the ER."

I glanced back at her, eyebrows raised. "Now? You want to tell me now?"

"Yup," she said, her grin breaking through the tension. "Either I laugh, or I cry, and crying's not on my to-do list tonight."

I couldn't argue with that. "Alright, spill. What happened?"

"So," she began, laughter already bubbling under her words, "Tom got stuck in the washing machine."

I nearly tripped on the uneven ground. "I'm sorry—what?"

"You heard me," she said, giggling now. "He was trying to grab a sock from the bottom and managed to wedge himself in there. Arms stuck, legs sticking out—it was a whole thing. And since his phone was out of reach, he had to wait for his wife to get home and find him yelling for help."

I couldn't help it—I burst out laughing. The absurdity of the story cut through the fear like a ray of sunshine. "No way. And he had to go to the hospital?"

"Oh, yeah," Holly said, snorting. "They had to cut part of the machine to get him out. He's fine—just a bruised ego and a couple of scrapes. But the look on his face? Priceless."

"Poor Tom," I said, wiping tears of laughter from my eyes. "That's... that's amazing. I needed that, Holly. Thanks."

"Anytime," she said, grinning. "I figured we could both use the distraction."

The laughter eased some of the weight pressing down on us as we descended further into the tunnel, and thankfully, my arm had stopped bleeding. The air grew damp and heavy, the walls pressing closer with every step. The flickering light from my phone barely cast strange, shifting shadows that made my skin crawl.

"This must be how he disappeared," I said quietly, my voice swallowed by the oppressive air. "It's no ghost, Holly. And did you see how he reacted to the blood?"

"Yeah," she whispered, her voice tight. "Whoever he is, he's hiding behind that 'ghost' act. But why would he be afraid of blood?"

I didn't have an answer, but the question gnawed at me.

Finally, up ahead, a faint glow broke through the darkness. A dusty curtain hung over the tunnel's end, barely stirring in the stale air.

"Please let this be the way out," Holly muttered, her voice tinged with both hope and dread.

I pushed the curtain aside, revealing a staircase leading to an attic-like room. As we climbed, the air grew thick with dust and mildew. At the top, the sight of us waiting made my stomach drop.

The room was cluttered with forgotten relics—a cracked porcelain doll, a rusted gramophone, stacks of yellowed papers, and, in the corner, a partially open trunk.

Inside the trunk was a tattered Confederate uniform with a wide-brimmed hat and bandana.

My blood ran cold. "Holly," I whispered, barely able to speak. "We need to leave. Now."

Holly didn't move. Her face had gone pale, her eyes locked on the room around us. "Josie," she murmured, her voice trembling. "What is this place?"

I followed her gaze, my stomach tightening as I took it all in—a mounted deer head sitting askew on a shelf, an old suit of armor, yellowed papers, the torn and moth-eaten costumes draped over an old trunk. Every inch of the room screamed secrets and neglect. Outside, the storm wailed through the cracks in the walls, the wind carrying with it an ominous moan that sent shivers racing down my spine.

Holly's breath hitched. She raised a trembling hand and pointed to the far wall. "Josie..." Her voice dropped to a shaky whisper. "Look."

I turned, my heart pounding as my eyes landed on the source of her fear.

There, propped against a stack of old crates, was a sword—its blade caked with dried, dark stains. Blood. It wasn't just any sword; it was the sword, the one the so-called ghost had wielded at the silo. The image of it slicing through the air, inches from my face, flashed through my mind, and I instinctively took a step back.

For a moment, all I could do was stare, my chest tightening with panic. But then, curiosity clawed its way through the fear. Slowly, cautiously, I moved toward it.

"Josie, don't—" Holly started, but I waved her off.

I knelt by the sword, hesitating before picking it up. My hands closed around the hilt, expecting the weight of cold steel, but instead...

"It's light," I murmured, my voice laced with confusion.

"What?" Holly edged closer, peering over my shoulder.

I turned the sword over in my hands, the realization hitting me like a lightning bolt. "Holly," I said, looking up at her. "It's fake."

Her jaw dropped. "Fake? What do you mean fake?"

I held it up, shaking my head in disbelief. "It's a prop. Plastic, painted to look real." I tapped the blade against the edge of a crate, and it gave off a hollow, unimpressive clink.

Holly stared at the sword like it had personally insulted her. "Are you telling me the ghost who chased you around with this thing was swinging a toy sword?"

"Apparently," I said, still turning it over in my hands. "It looked real in the dark, but this... this is just for show."

She let out a short, incredulous laugh. "Oh, great. So now we've got a theater kid ghost on our hands?"

"Not a ghost," I corrected, my mind racing as I set the sword down. "A person. Someone who wanted us to think it was a ghost. This was all staged, Holly. The outfit, the sword—it's part of some twisted performance."

Holly ran a hand through her hair, frustration and disbelief written all over her face. "Okay, but why? Why go through all this trouble to scare us?"

I stood, brushing the dust off my hands. "To keep us away from something. Someone's trying to throw us off the trail."

The storm outside seemed to howl in agreement, the wind rattling the loose boards on the walls. Holly hugged herself, glancing around the room. "Okay, so this isn't a ghost. Great. But we still don't have a way out of here, and I'm not loving the idea of sticking around for an encore performance."

"The tunnel's a dead end," I said, glancing toward the way we'd come. "But there has to be another way."

We split up, frantically searching the room. My hands skimmed over dusty bookshelves and old furniture, looking for anything out of place. That's when I spotted it—a small, hidden lever tucked behind a stack of brittle, yellowed books.

"Holly, over here!"

She rushed over as I gripped the lever and gave it a firm pull. A loud, metallic clunk echoed through the room, followed by the creak of hidden hinges. A section of the wall swung inward, revealing a narrow passageway beyond.

"Well, would you look at that," Holly said, her voice a mix of relief and sarcasm. "Secret tunnel number two. Because the first one wasn't creepy enough."

I flashed her a tight smile. "Ready for round two?"

She rolled her eyes but motioned for me to lead the way. "After you, Indiana Jones."

The passageway opened into a dimly lit corridor lined with faded portraits. The figures in the paintings stared down at us with cold, unblinking eyes, their expressions frozen somewhere between disapproval and disdain.

"This is officially the creepiest scavenger hunt I've ever been on," Holly muttered, glancing over her shoulder.

We moved quickly but quietly, the plush carpet muffling our footsteps as we descended a staircase at the end of the hall. At the bottom, a massive front door loomed before us, its brass handle tarnished with age. Holly reached it first, yanking it open with a creak that echoed through the empty house.

The cool night air hit us like a splash of water, and for a moment, I just stood there, taking in the drizzle of rain and the faint glow of the moon. We'd made it out.

But then, a chilling laugh echoed from somewhere within the house.

I froze, my heart lurching in my chest. Slowly, I turned to look back at the darkened doorway.

Holly's voice was a whisper, barely audible over the patter of rain. "Josie, what is it?"

"I know whose house this is," I said, my stomach twisting, "and he was afraid of blood."

Her eyes widened. "Wait—who?"

And then it hit her. I saw the realization flood her face, her eyes wide as saucers. "Wait—Josie," she stammered, grabbing my sleeve. "This is Sam's house. We're at Sam's house."

At that moment, a shadow shifted in one of the upper windows. My breath caught as I looked up, spotting a dark and unmoving figure watching us from the second floor.

"Holly," I whispered, my voice tight. "Run."

I didn't wait for her reply. I grabbed her arm and took off, pulling her with me as we bolted across the muddy field. The rain had turned the ground slick, and my boots slipped with every step, but I didn't dare slow down. My heart pounded like a drum, drowning out the sound of my own ragged breathing. The figure in the window didn't follow, but that didn't make the feeling of being chased any less real.

The Jeep came into view, and I fumbled with the keys as we reached it. "Get in!" I hissed, throwing open the driver's side door and climbing in. Holly slid into the passenger seat, slamming her door behind her. I locked the doors with trembling hands, the click of the locks barely easing the panic still clawing at my chest.

We just sat there, catching our breath, rain pattering against the windshield. My hands shook as I grabbed my phone and dialed Caleb, the screen slick with rainwater. He picked up on the first ring.

"Josie, where are you?"

"Caleb," I said, my voice breathless but urgent. "We're at the Old Silo. Sam trapped us, but we got out. And I know what Tiffany saw. She saw Sam poison Artie."

There was a pause, and then Caleb's voice came sharp and tense. "Josie, listen to me. You need to leave. Now."

"Caleb, you're not hearing me," I said, my voice rising. "Sam poisoned Artie; he doesn't know we're onto him. This is our chance—"

"Josie," he interrupted, his voice firm but laced with concern. "This isn't your fight. Go home. Now."

I tightened my grip on the phone. "It is my fight, Caleb. Artie was poisoned at Novel Grounds. Tiffany was killed at my café. This is personal. And we're not backing down."

I glanced at Holly, who gave me a determined nod. This wasn't over—not yet.

20 masquerades & macchiatos

Halloween Night

SAM'S ANTEBELLUM MANSION rose before us, glowing with an almost otherworldly charm. The golden light spilling from its tall windows made the massive red-brick structure look warm and inviting—if you didn't know better. But I did. Beneath the grandeur, the house seemed to pulse with a quiet tension, as if it were alive and waiting for something to happen.

"It's like it knows we're here," I muttered to Holly as we climbed the slick stone steps leading to the grand entrance.

Holly adjusted her masquerade mask nervously, her fingers fidgeting with the satin ribbon. "Yeah, well, let's hope the house doesn't eat us whole," she whispered back.

The mansion's towering white columns framed the front door, their cracked bases bearing silent witness to decades of history. Massive oak trees lined the property, their fiery leaves shivering in the night breeze. Somewhere off in the distance, an owl hooted, its mournful call only adding to the eerie vibe. I glanced over my shoulder, feeling the weight of the night pressing down on me.

Inside, the house was a stage. The sweeping staircase, polished to a high shine, curled gracefully to the second floor, its dark wooden banisters catching the flicker of chandelier light. The air was thick with the scent of beeswax polish, aged wood, and the faint tang of old secrets. Guests in elaborate costumes floated from room to room, laughter and conversation bubbling around us like champagne.

"Quite the production," Caleb said, stepping up beside us. Dressed as Sherlock Holmes, complete with the deerstalker hat and magnifying glass, he surveyed the room with sharp, wary eyes. "Sam didn't cut any corners."

"No kidding," Holly muttered, her gaze darting around the crowd. "This party's doing its best to scream 'normal,' but we all know better."

"Exactly," I said, lowering my voice. "Stick close. If Sam's got something planned, we're not giving him the chance to catch us off guard."

Rhett and Emma approached us next, Rhett grinning like a kid at a theme park in his Regency-era suit. "You've outdone yourself, Josie," he teased, tipping his hat. "When the drama starts tonight, let's hope it's all scripted."

Emma rolled her eyes but smiled at me. "You've got this," she said softly, her confidence steadying me.

I glanced up at the massive chandelier hanging above us, its crystals shimmering like stars. If only the light could chase away the shadows clinging to the edges of the room.

From her perch on the grand staircase, Connie stole the show. She was dressed as Scarlett O'Hara—specifically that Scarlett, from Carol Burnett's famous curtain-rod skit. The brass rod jutted out from her shoulders, the green velvet gown cinched dramatically with a valance draped over her head like a bonnet.

"Well, darlin'," she drawled in a perfect Southern parody, waving theatrically to the crowd, "ain't no party like a murder mystery party!"

Guests burst into laughter, her performance temporarily easing the tension in the room. Even I couldn't help but chuckle.

"She really committed, huh?" Holly whispered, nudging me.

"She always does," I replied, smiling despite myself. If only all the drama tonight stayed on Connie's level.

As the laughter faded, I spotted Sam moving through the crowd, his smile polished to perfection, his Southern charm dialed up to eleven. He greeted each guest as though they were the most important person in the room, but his movements were too precise, too controlled. He wasn't hosting a party—he was managing it, orchestrating something far more calculated.

"Look at him," Holly murmured, her eyes narrowing as she watched Sam shake hands and laugh easily with a group of guests. "He's loving this. Playing the role of the perfect host while pulling who-knows-what behind the scenes."

"Let him enjoy the act," I said, keeping my gaze steady on him. "It won't last."

The crowd drifted toward the massive brick fireplace, its roaring flames crackling like a living thing. The hearth was nearly large enough to walk into, its aged bricks blackened from decades of use. Teddy stood near the fire, his scarecrow costume illuminated by the flickering light. The straw sticking out from his sleeves gave him an almost ghostly quality, like he belonged to the mansion more than the party.

"This place gives me the creeps," Teddy muttered as we joined him. He tugged at his straw hat, his eyes scanning the room with barely disguised unease. "Feels like it's hiding something."

"It probably is," Caleb said, his tone dry. He straightened his deerstalker hat and gave Teddy a look. "But we're here to find out what."

Bear, towering beside his grandfather in a Viking costume, let out a low chuckle. "You're perfect for this setting, Grandpa. Gothic novel vibes and all."

Teddy shot him a half-hearted glare but cracked a smile. "If I disappear tonight, you'll know why."

"You won't disappear," I said, trying to sound confident. "We're all sticking together."

Despite the camaraderie, the tension in the room continued to thicken, clinging to the air like humidity before a storm. Smokin' Belle sidled up next to me, her black dress glittering faintly in the firelight. She leaned in conspiratorially, her voice low.

"Y'all aren't seriously gonna eat or drink anything here, are ya?"

I shook my head firmly. "Not a chance."

"Smart," she muttered, her eyes scanning the room.

The heavy velvet drapes by the windows stirred as a breeze snuck in, carrying the scent of rain and wet leaves. The rich gold fabric glowed faintly in the firelight, but even their beauty couldn't lighten the mood.

This wasn't just a party. It was a stage, and we were all players in Sam's twisted production. Every mask in the room, every burst of laughter, every clink of a champagne flute felt like part of a script—a script written to distract us from the truth lurking in the shadows.

Caleb reappeared beside me, his jaw tight, his eyes scanning the room like he was already ten steps ahead. "It's time," he said, his voice low but steady. "You ready for this?"

I nodded, my pulse quickening. "We're ready."

"Please be careful. My team and I will be waiting for you at the end of the tunnel. We've got men surrounding the silo. And Stanzi and Max will be flanking you."

His gaze lingered on me, a flicker of concern breaking through his calm exterior. "Be careful," he said quietly, his voice softer now. "If anything doesn't go to plan just pull back. No risks, Josie."

I gave him a tight smile, more for his benefit than mine. "We've got this."

As Caleb disappeared back into the crowd, I turned to Holly. Her hands trembled slightly as she adjusted her mask, but the determination in her eyes matched my own.

"We need to find that hidden room," I said, my voice steady despite my nerves. "Sam will follow us. We know he will."

Holly nodded, her voice barely above a whisper. "Let's end this, Josie."

And with that, we melted into the crowd, the mansion's walls closing in around us like a curtain falling on the final act.

I led the way up the grand staircase, each creak beneath my feet loud enough to set my nerves on edge. The chandelier's soft glow overhead felt too bright, like a spotlight we couldn't escape. My heart hammered in my chest, every beat reminding me that Sam was somewhere behind us—and he'd follow soon enough—that much I was sure of.

Konstanze and Max fell into step beside Holly and me, their presence grounding me as we wove through the opulent corridors.

"We're with you, Josie," Stanzi murmured, her voice calm and steady. "We won't let him get the jump on you."

"Thanks," I whispered, though my nerves felt anything but steady.

We reached the hidden bookcase and slipped into the secret room. It was just as we'd left it: dim, dusty, and oppressive, like the past was alive in this place and didn't want us there. I held my breath as I scanned the room—the relics, the uniforms, the crates.

Then I saw it.

"Wait," I whispered, freezing in place. My eyes locked on a potted plant shoved into the corner, half-hidden in the shadows.

Dark, slender stalks rose from the soil, their delicate purple flowers glowing faintly in the dim light. Wolfsbane.

The world seemed to tilt as the realization hit me. I'd seen pictures of it in the hours of research Caleb and I had done—beautiful, dangerous, and utterly lethal. One touch could be deadly.

"Holly," I murmured, crouching down. My voice was tight, my breath shallow as I pointed.

She knelt beside me, her own breath catching. "Is that...?"

"Wolfsbane," I confirmed, my voice barely above a whisper. "This is it. This is what killed Artie. And Tiffany."

Her eyes darted nervously around the room as she stood up, like Sam might step out of the shadows any second. "Why would he just leave it here? It's practically a smoking gun!"

I stood, my gaze shifting to the Confederate uniform still folded neatly in the dusty trunk. The sight sent a chill through me. This was it. Showtime.

"Holly, look," I whispered, pointing to the uniform. My voice carried just enough urgency to draw out anyone listening.

Her gasp was perfectly timed. "Sam," she said, loud enough to carry, "he's been behind this all along."

A faint creak cut through the silence, and I stiffened. Holly's wide eyes darted to mine just as the hidden door swung open at the far end of the room.

Sam stepped in, his silhouette looming in the doorway, framed by the dim, flickering light. He closed the door behind him with a slow, deliberate click, his polished smile as cold and sharp as the chill in the air.

"Well, well," he drawled, his voice calm and smooth, like he was hosting us for tea. "It seems you've stumbled onto my little collection. I hope you're enjoying yourselves."

Every muscle in my body tensed. I glanced at Holly, whose trembling hands gave away her nerves. Sam stepped further into the room, his movements deliberate, calculated.

"You've been busy, Josie," he said, his voice dripping with mockery. "Digging where you shouldn't. Asking the wrong questions." His eyes flicked to the wolfsbane, and his smirk deepened. "You're clever, I'll give you that. But tonight... tonight, the game ends."

Holly edged closer to me, her breathing shallow. "We know what you've done, Sam," she said, her voice shaking but loud enough to sound defiant. "It's over."

Sam's chuckle was low and menacing, sending a chill down my spine. "You think you've got it all figured out, don't you?" he said, stepping closer. "But you have no idea what's coming."

Before I could react, Sam lunged. His hand clamped around my arm like a steel trap, and a gasp tore from my throat as he yanked me toward the corner of the room. His grip was iron, dragging me toward an old chair tucked in the shadows.

"Let go!" I hissed, twisting in his grasp, but he was stronger than I expected.

My mind raced, adrenaline flooding my system. As we passed the display stand with the suit of armor and the battle ax, instinct kicked in. I grabbed the weapon and swung the blunt end with all my strength, catching Sam squarely in the chest.

He stumbled back, a grunt of surprise escaping him as he collided with the edge of the desk. His grip on my arm loosened, and I yanked myself free, setting the ax back in place with absurd precision—because apparently, I was still me, even in a life-or-death situation.

Sam recovered quickly, his eyes blazing as he lunged for me again. His hand locked around my wrist, his face inches from mine. "You think you're clever, don't you?" he growled, his voice low and full of venom.

I met his gaze, refusing to look away despite the fear. "You're scared, Sam," I said, my voice steady even though my heart was racing. "You're losing control."

His eyes flickered—just for a moment. A crack in the mask.

"You don't know anything," he spat, but there was a tremor in his voice now.

I leaned in slightly, forcing myself to hold his gaze. "We know enough. Artie. Tiffany. The wolfsbane. It's all coming together, Sam. And soon, everyone else will know, too."

His grip faltered, just for a split second, but it was enough. I wrenched myself back, putting space between us. "It's over, Sam," I said, my voice sharper than the fear pounding in my chest.

For the first time, I saw something crack in his expression—not anger, not that smug arrogance he always wore like armor. It truly was fear.

Holly stepped forward from the shadows, holding a knife. Well, calling it a knife was generous—it was one of those dull props from the costume trunk, but she gripped it like her life depended on it. Sam's eyes darted toward her, and that cruel smile curled his lips again.

"You're kidding, right?" He let out a sharp laugh, grabbing my arm again and tightening his hold on my arm until pain shot through my shoulder. "What are you gonna do, Holly? Wave that thing around and hope I faint from boredom?"

Holly's hand trembled, but she didn't back down. Her face was pale, but her voice was steady. "Let her go, Sam," she said, each word deliberate.

Sam's laugh darkened, a low, menacing sound that echoed through the room. "Oh, I see. You want to play the hero now?" He cocked his head, mocking her. "Go ahead. Stab me. Come on, Holly. Be the big, brave savior. Do it!"

Her hand wavered slightly, the blade shaking in her grip. I could see the fear in her eyes, the sheer weight of what he was daring her to do pressing down on her.

Sam moved fast, grabbing her wrist before she could react. His grip twisted the knife toward his side, the fake blade pressing against his shirt. "Do it!" he spat, his voice a low hiss.

"No!" Holly gasped, struggling against his hold, but Sam was too strong.

The knife sank into his side—or so it seemed.

Holly froze, her face a mask of horror. "Oh my gosh. Oh no. Did I just—" Her voice broke, her breath catching in her throat as the room went deathly still.

And then Sam laughed.

Not just a chuckle—a full, dark laugh that made my stomach turn. He yanked the knife away, holding it up to show its harmless, rubber tip. "You thought you stabbed me, didn't you?" he sneered. "It's just a prop, Holly. Just like this whole thing. A game."

Holly's face drained of color as she stared at the knife. "I—I thought..."

Sam shoved her hard, sending her stumbling into a pile of old costumes. She landed awkwardly, fabric tangling around her legs as she scrambled to get up, but her face stayed fixed in stunned disbelief.

"See?" Sam said, turning back to me with that twisted grin. "It's all fake, Josie. Everything. Just a fun little game for me, and you're the entertainment."

"Yeah, I don't think your audience is laughing," I snapped, trying to pull away again.

His grip tightened like a vise, and he yanked me closer, his face inches from mine. "You're not going anywhere," he growled, his voice low and menacing.

"Your charm is really wearing thin, Sam," I hissed, trying to mask the rising panic in my chest.

Before I could twist away, Sam dragged me toward the hidden entrance to the tunnel. "Let's take this somewhere private," he said, shoving me through the narrow opening.

"Holly!" I screamed, my voice raw with desperation.

She was still pulling herself free from the pile of costumes, her hands grasping at the fabric tangled around her feet. "Josie!" she cried, trying to scramble to her feet.

But it was too late. Sam shoved me hard into the tunnel's opening, and I stumbled onto the narrow stairs, the cold, damp air rushing over me like a slap. Darkness loomed ahead, swallowing me whole as I tumbled further inside.

Behind me, I heard Holly's voice echo faintly, frantic and determined. "I'm coming, Josie! Hang on!"

But Sam blocked the entrance, and the shadows closed in.

21 dark roast, dark secrets

WITH GRIM DETERMINATION, I struggled against Sam's iron grip as he dragged me toward the hidden passage leading back to the silo. Holly's voice echoed faintly from somewhere behind us, shouting for help, but it was swallowed by the dark, suffocating silence of the tunnel.

"Why, Sam?" I asked, forcing steel into my voice even as fear made my stomach churn. "You're such a 'fun guy'—always hosting parties, flashing that charming smile. Why go through all this? Was it just an act?"

He snorted, bitter and sharp. "You wouldn't understand," he muttered, his grip tightening painfully on my arm. "None of you ever could."

His words hung in the air, heavy with something raw and unspoken. Anger, yes—but also grief. I could hear it in his voice. Whatever this was, it was personal. It always had been.

"Try me," I pressed, hoping to keep him talking. If I could buy a little more time, maybe Caleb and the others were already closing in.

Sam stopped walking, his flashlight casting jagged shadows along the damp walls. His eyes flashed with something dark, and I saw another crack in the façade—a man haunted by whatever he'd done.

"It was never supposed to go this far," he said quietly, almost as if he was talking to himself. His voice broke, and when he looked at me, his expression teetered between desperation and regret. "Artie, yeah... Artie had to die. But Tiffany..." His breath hitched. "I didn't mean to—I didn't want to. She didn't give me a choice."

My pulse quickened. He wasn't just a killer—he was unraveling.

"What do you mean, Sam?" I asked softly, my voice steady despite the panic rising in me. "Why didn't you have a choice? What did she do?"

His face twisted in anguish, and he let out a hollow laugh that sent chills down my spine. "She figured it out," he said bitterly. "She saw me that morning... saw what I did to Artie. At first, she didn't understand, but later—" He broke off, his voice turning cold. "She tried to blackmail me, Josie. Blackmail me. Like I was some kind of fool. But I couldn't let her ruin everything."

My mind raced. Tiffany had seen him. She must've known. But what had she seen? "What did she see, Sam?" I asked, pushing. "What did you do to Artie?"

He hesitated, his expression flickering between defiance and guilt. "You already know," he finally said, his voice soft, almost a whisper. "I poisoned him."

The confirmation hit like a punch to the gut, even though I'd already suspected it. Hearing it from his mouth made it all too real. Sam had been planning Artie's death for a long time.

And then it clicked.

"Stu Kratz," I whispered, the name landing heavily between us.

His jaw tightened, and his expression darkened. "Took you long enough," he muttered, a bitter edge in his voice.

I swallowed hard, piecing it all together. The newspaper clipping Konstanze had found. The tragic car accident. Stu Kratz's wife and baby had been killed when the brakes on their car failed. Artie had done the brake job. He went to prison for it, but that clearly wasn't enough for Stu.

"You're Stu," I said, the realization sinking in. "You changed your name, started over. But Artie... when he got out—"

Sam—Stu—laughed bitterly, cutting me off. "Do you have any idea what it's like to lose everything?" he snapped, his voice raw. "My wife. My baby girl. Gone. Because of him. And what did he get? A few measly years in prison? That wasn't justice. That wasn't enough."

His grip loosened slightly, and I saw the tears welling in his eyes now, carving trails down his face. "I thought I could move on," he said, his voice cracking. "I thought I could start over, leave it all behind. But then Artie walked free. Free, Josie. After everything he took from me."

My throat tightened as I stared at him, the weight of his grief and rage pressing down on the air around us. "Stu," I said gently, trying to keep my voice calm. "I'm sorry for what happened to your family. But killing Artie—it didn't bring them back. It just created more pain. And Tiffany…"

His face twisted with anguish. "I didn't mean to hurt her," he said, his voice trembling.

"How?" I asked, my voice barely above a whisper. "How did you do it? How did you poison him?"

His lips curled into a grim smile, and for a moment, he seemed almost proud. "The locket," he said simply. "It was my wife's. The one thing I had left of her and my little girl. I kept it with me always. Inside the clasp, there was a hidden compartment. Just a few drops of the poison—enough to coat a muffin. Artie never suspected a thing."

My blood ran cold. The locket. The one we'd found in the lost-and-found. It hadn't just been a clue—it was the key to everything.

"I lost it that day," he admitted, his voice tinged with frustration. "It slipped out of my pocket during the chaos. I searched everywhere for it. I even trashed Novel Grounds trying to find it. But when I couldn't, I had to throw you off the trail. That's when I planted the check."

"Hattie's check," I said, the memory slamming into me. "You framed her."

He nodded, his expression almost casual, as if it were the most logical thing in the world. "I needed you to look anywhere but at me. And it worked, didn't it?"

I stared at him, a sick feeling twisting in my gut. "It worked," I admitted, the words tasting bitter.

Stu stepped closer, his flashlight casting eerie shadows on the walls. His voice dropped to a low, dangerous whisper. "But you didn't stay off the trail, did you, Josie? You just couldn't leave well enough alone. That's why I left you the note about Bear. That bought some time."

The air between us felt heavy, the weight of his confession pressing down like a storm cloud ready to break. I took a shaky breath, forcing myself to hold his gaze. "And now what, Stu? What's your endgame?"

His grip on my arm tightened like a vise. "The same as it's always been," Stu said coldly. "I'm just fighting a wrong. Artie killed my family and took my future away from me."

And with that, he yanked me deeper into the tunnel, the shadows swallowing us whole.

My mind raced, adrenaline surging as I tried to think of a way out. "The locket had their picture," I said, my voice quieter now. "Your wife and baby…"

Stu stumbled, just for a second. "They were everything to me," he murmured, his face twisting with pain. "Artie took them from me, and no prison sentence could make up for that. So I waited. I waited until he got out. And then…" His voice hardened. "I made sure he paid."

The raw emotion in his voice sent a chill down my spine, but I pressed on. "And Tiffany?" I asked. "How did she figure it out?"

He barked a laugh—cold, sharp, and bitter. "She saw me," he hissed. "That morning, I slipped the locket back into my pocket after poisoning the muffin. At first, she didn't know what it meant. But Tiffany—she was clever, conniving. She put it together." His jaw clenched, anger and regret flickering in his expression. "She threatened to expose everything unless I gave her what she wanted."

"What did she want?" I asked, keeping my voice steady despite the knot forming in my stomach.

"She wanted money. Power. Control over Dex." His lip curled in disgust. "She didn't care about Artie or me. She just wanted to climb higher." He spat the words like venom. "I couldn't let her destroy everything. So, I poisoned her too. It was easy—I was handling the food at the murder mystery party."

My stomach turned. I could picture it too vividly: Tiffany scheming, and Stu—desperate, unraveling—deciding that murder was his only way out.

"So, you killed her because she got in your way," I said softly, the weight of it sinking in.

"She didn't give me a choice," Stu snapped, his voice raw.

We kept moving, the tunnel growing colder, narrower. Every step echoed, the sound bouncing off the damp walls like whispers of everything Stu had done.

"You don't have to do this, Stu," I said, trying to keep my tone calm. "It doesn't have to end this way."

His laugh was hollow, devoid of anything human. "It already has," he said, dragging me forward.

But then, something shifted. His steps slowed, his breathing hitched. I glanced up and saw his face—a flicker of hesitation, of uncertainty, crossing his features. He wasn't as sure as he wanted me to believe.

"Stu," I said, keeping my voice gentle. "It's over. You've done what you set out to do. But this? Taking me? It won't fix anything. You've already lost so much—don't lose yourself completely."

He looked at me, his eyes glassy with grief. For a moment, I thought I'd gotten through to him. But then his expression hardened again, the rage snapping back into place like armor. "You don't get it," he growled, his voice shaking. "You'll never get it."

A sound broke through the tension—movement behind us. Footsteps. My heart leapt. Caleb. He was close.

Stu didn't notice—he was too caught up in his own turmoil. "It's not over," he said, his voice dropping to a whisper. "Not until I finish this."

And then Caleb's voice rang out, clear and commanding. "It's over, Stu."

Stu froze. His grip on my arm tightened briefly, then faltered as he whipped around. Caleb emerged from the shadows, his flashlight cutting through the dimness, casting sharp angles across his face.

"Let her go," Caleb said, his voice steady and firm. His eyes locked on Stu like a hawk zeroing in on its prey. "This ends now."

I could feel the weight of the choice hanging in the air. Stu's hand trembled, his fingers loosening on my arm as he seemed to deflate.

"You don't understand," Stu said, his voice barely above a whisper. "They were my family."

"And you think this is what they would've wanted?" Caleb shot back, his tone sharp but not unkind. "Look at what you've done, Stu. Look where this has taken you. It's over. Let her go."

Something in Stu broke. His shoulders sagged, the fight draining out of him as he let his hands drop to his sides. Slowly, he raised them in surrender, his expression a mix of defeat and sorrow.

Caleb moved swiftly, cuffing Stu's hands with practiced precision. As he led him toward the exit, Stu kept his gaze down, his steps slow and heavy.

I stood frozen, my heart pounding as I watched them disappear down the tunnel. Relief and exhaustion hit me all at once, leaving me weak-kneed. It was over. But instead of triumph, I felt a strange emptiness.

"Josie." Caleb's voice was soft, pulling me from my thoughts. He was back, his flashlight casting a warm glow across my face. His eyes searched mine. "Are you okay?"

I nodded, though the ache in my chest said otherwise. "Yeah," I said quietly. "Just... a lot to take in."

"We'll figure out the rest," he said, his voice steady. "Tiffany, Artie—everything. But you're okay, and that's what matters right now."

His words were a balm, steadying me as I took a deep breath. "Thanks, Caleb," I said, managing a faint smile.

Before I could say more, footsteps echoed behind us. I turned to see Holly, Max, and Stanzi rushing toward us, their faces pale but determined.

Holly wasted no time wrapping me in a tight hug. "You're okay," she whispered, her voice trembling with relief.

"I'm okay," I assured her, squeezing her back. "It's over."

"Not completely," Stanzi said, her sharp gaze cutting through the moment. "There's still more to unravel."

I nodded. She was right. Tiffany's motives, the full scope of Stu's actions—there were still pieces of this puzzle left to put together. But tonight, we'd taken a major step forward.

As we stepped out into the cool night air, the stars above seemed brighter, sharper. I let the crisp breeze wash over me, clearing my head.

"We'll regroup tomorrow," I said, turning to my friends. "We've got more work to do."

They nodded in agreement, and we began making our way back to the cars. Tonight, the darkness had been heavy, but tomorrow, the light would shine brighter. Together, we'd finish what we started.

22 steaming ahead, case closed

THE AROMA OF FRESHLY GROUND COFFEE mingled with the sweet scent of apple-cinnamon muffins, wrapping the café in a hug of cozy warmth. The clinking of cups and hum of the espresso machine blended with chatter and laughter, filling Novel Grounds with a lively buzz. Sunlight poured through the windows, streaking the wooden floors with golden light. It was everything I loved about my little book café—well, except for the espresso machine acting up again.

With a loud hiss, it shot out another rogue puff of steam, cloaking the counter in a fog that sent Logan, one of my student baristas, into a coughing fit.

"Boss!" he called out dramatically, waving a hand in front of his face. "It's like a coffee sauna in here. Am I supposed to charge extra for that?"

"Fix it before we have to add 'fog hazard' to the menu!" Hannah shot back, rolling her eyes as she slid a latte across the counter.

I chuckled as I darted to open the windows, letting in a crisp breeze to clear the steam. "Let me know when it starts spitting espresso instead of air. Then we'll charge double."

As the fog dissipated, so did my stress. The café was alive with life—friends, family, and regulars filled the space, chatting about anything from local gossip to last night's Halloween party at Sam's mansion. It felt like my world was finally back to normal, though "normal" was always a loose term around here.

Stanzi and Max waved as they left, arms loaded with coffee and muffins, ready for a full day of teaching. Holly, manning the display case, turned to me with a worried look. "I was so scared for you last night, Josie," she said, her voice quieter than usual.

I gave her a soft smile. "I know, Holls. But thanks to you texting Caleb, help got there in time. You always have my back."

Caleb, leaning against the counter nearby, shrugged like it was no big deal. "Took longer than I wanted to get there," he said, his tone gruff but his eyes soft. "Glad I made it when I did."

Holly added, "We all knew what he was capable of, but still… seeing you in that situation was awful."

I reached over and squeezed her hand. "I couldn't have handled any of it without you all. Seriously."

Before I could get too sentimental, Rhett and Emma breezed in, arms full of donations for the café's charity drive. Emma beamed as she dropped a box of wrapped gifts into the bin. "I love this year's cause, Josie!" she said, practically bouncing with excitement. "It's so fun shopping for all these kids!"

Rhett placed a hand on her shoulder. "Don't let her fool you—she almost bought out the toy aisle. She's not allowed in that section alone anymore."

Emma swatted his arm, laughing. "Some people have no Christmas spirit!" She dropped into one of the comfy armchairs by the fire with Hattie and started chatting. Rhett grabbed his usual coffee order and gave me a wink. "Glad everything's okay, Josie. I'm off to the woodshop—tell Emma not to donate the whole house while I'm gone."

I laughed as he left, just in time for Eloise to walk in, her silver curls frizzing slightly in the cool air. "Josie," she said with a triumphant smile, "I knew you'd figure it out. You always notice the details."

"Thanks, Eloise," I said, a warmth blooming in my chest. "I'm just glad we cleared your name."

My baristas chimed in from the counter. Tyler gave me a thumbs-up. "Great job, boss!"

"You nailed it," Logan added with a grin. "And you didn't even let the espresso machine explode—major win."

"Yet," Hannah said with a smirk. "Let's not jinx it."

The front door opened, and Connie burst in, wearing a turkey hat with flapping wings. "I heard there was an after-party last night, and I wasn't invited?" she declared, feigning outrage. "I'm devastated, Josie!"

I laughed, shaking my head. "Next time, Connie. I promise."

Dex slipped in behind her, looking sheepish as ever. "Josie," he began, his voice low, "I messed up. Big time. But... thank you for not giving up on me."

I met his gaze, my tone gentle but firm. "Just make better choices from now on, Dex."

He nodded, his expression earnest, then glanced across the café. His eyes landed on Teddy, who sat quietly by the fire, flipping through an old book.

"I think there's someone I need to talk to," Dex said.

Teddy looked up, his expression softening. "I'd say so, son."

They stepped aside, voices low but clear enough for me to hear Dex's quiet, "I'm so sorry."

I smiled to myself as I watched them talk. It was a start—a step toward healing for both of them.

Caleb appeared at my side, leaning casually against the counter. "Well, Miss Meddling Detective," he said with a playful grin, "you did it. Solved the mystery. How's it feel?"

I raised an eyebrow. "Still grumpy, huh? One of these days, Caleb, you're going to give me a compliment without turning it into a dig."

He smirked, the corner of his mouth tugging upward. "That's your problem, Josie. Always where you don't belong."

"Oh, I'm sorry—would you prefer I hadn't solved the case?" I shot back, crossing my arms.

He shrugged. "You've got me there. But one of these days, you're going to give me a heart attack. You know that, right?"

I tilted my head, teasing. "Aw, Caleb, I didn't know you cared so much."

He rolled his eyes, but I caught the flicker of warmth behind them. "Don't get used to it," he said, though his tone was softer now. "Seriously, though—you did good, Josie."

For a moment, the noise of the café faded into the background as I let his words sink in. "Thanks," I said quietly, a rare moment of sincerity slipping through. "It's not just about solving the case, though. It's about protecting the people I care about. That's what really matters."

He nodded, his expression thoughtful. "Yeah. And you're pretty good at that, too."

Everything felt normal again. Or, at least, as normal as it could be after the chaos of the past few days.

Hattie, who had been sitting quietly by the window with her drawing pens in hand, gave me one of her signature warm smiles. "You've come a long way, Josie. We're all so proud of you."

"Thanks, Hattie." I looked around the café, my heart full as I took in the faces of my friends and neighbors. "And thanks to all of you—for believing in me."

Eloise, perched on her favorite stool near the counter, smirked knowingly. "So, what's next for you, Detective Josie? Another mystery brewing already?"

I chuckled, shaking my head. "Who knows? But if there is, I'm ready for it."

Just as the café started to settle into a post-lunch lull, the bell above the front door chimed, slicing through the cozy hum of conversation. The room seemed to collectively pause as a tall woman in a sharp black suit strode in, her posture so rigid she looked like she'd been carved from marble.

"Oh, great," I muttered under my breath. "Cassandra Drake."

Emma, who had been leaning against the counter beside me, followed my gaze. Her eyes narrowed. "What's she doing here?"

Cassandra's presence had the kind of weight that made people unconsciously straighten up. Her dark hair was pulled into a sleek ponytail, and her eyes swept the room like a hawk surveying its prey. Her professional smile was polite but stiff, and there was a controlled intensity about her—like she was trying very hard to keep a lid on something simmering just beneath the surface.

Her gaze landed on me and Emma, and she made her way over, her heels clicking sharply against the wooden floor.

"Josie. Emma," she said, nodding to each of us. Her voice was smooth, almost pleasant, but there was a storm behind her eyes. "Good to see you again, though I wish it were under better circumstances."

"Cassandra," I said, standing to meet her. "This is... unexpected."

"Unexpected for me too," Emma muttered under her breath, crossing her arms.

Cassandra ignored the comment, her focus entirely on me. "I'm here regarding Blake Courtney. I want to formally apologize on behalf of FMR Foods for his actions."

Emma raised an eyebrow, her tone skeptical. "Blake? Really?"

Cassandra's jaw tightened ever so slightly, but she nodded. "Yes. Blake overstepped his authority and let his ambitions get the better of him. His actions were unethical and completely unauthorized by the company."

Emma snorted softly. "That's putting it mildly."

If Cassandra heard, she didn't acknowledge it. Instead, she pressed on, her tone crisp and measured. "Blake led us to believe Eloise would sell her recipes. He even exaggerated progress to our investors and internal teams. When Eloise declined, he panicked and made poor choices—choices that violated company policy and basic ethics. As soon as we uncovered the full scope of his behavior, we terminated his employment."

The café fell quiet as her words sank in. I studied Cassandra's face, looking for cracks in her polished facade. She was good—calm, professional, and controlled—but I could see the irritation flickering in her eyes. Blake had clearly left a mess, and she wasn't thrilled about cleaning it up.

Eloise, who had been sitting with her arms tightly crossed, finally spoke, her tone icy. "So you're saying all of this—every lie, every scheme—was just Blake? FMR Foods had no clue?"

Cassandra didn't flinch, though her composure seemed to tighten by a fraction. "That's correct. Blake acted alone. He let his desperation for success cloud his judgment. This is not how FMR Foods operates."

Eloise narrowed her eyes, her skepticism palpable. "And Tiffany? How does she fit into this?"

Cassandra hesitated—a brief pause, but enough for me to catch it. "Tiffany overheard discussions about Blake's pressure to secure the recipes. She realized his career hinged on getting them and... used that information to blackmail him. She demanded favors in exchange for her silence."

Emma leaned closer, her voice low but pointed. "So you're saying your company had no idea any of this was happening?"

Cassandra met Emma's gaze head-on. "None," she said firmly. "Blake hid everything from us. It wasn't until we launched an internal investigation that we discovered the extent of his actions."

Eloise shook her head, her frustration evident. "I find it hard to believe a company like yours wasn't keeping closer tabs on someone like Blake."

Cassandra inhaled deeply, her expression softening slightly. "I understand your hesitation, Ms. Jackson. And I don't blame you for being cautious. But we've taken steps to ensure this never happens again. FMR Foods values our relationships with small businesses, and we hope to rebuild your trust."

Eloise didn't budge. "Let me save you some time. I'm not selling."

Cassandra's lips pressed into a thin line, though her tone remained polite. "We respect that. We're no longer pursuing your recipes. My only goal today was to apologize and make it clear Blake's actions don't reflect our company's values."

Her apology was genuine, but I could tell it wasn't going to win Eloise over. Damage like this wasn't easily undone.

After a moment of silence, Cassandra straightened her blazer and nodded once. "Thank you for your time. If there's anything further we can do to make amends, please don't hesitate to reach out."

With that, she turned and walked out, her heels clicking in the same sharp rhythm as when she arrived. The door swung shut behind her, and the café seemed to let out a collective breath.

Emma broke the silence first. "Well, that was... anticlimactic."

"Good riddance," Holly added, wiping down the counter with a little extra force.

Eloise, still sitting stiffly, finally relaxed her posture. "I don't trust them," she said flatly. "But at least they know I'm not someone to mess with."

I smiled, pride swelling in my chest. "That's for sure."

Caleb, who had been standing near the back, stepped forward with his arms crossed. "So... think that's the last we'll hear from them?"

I shrugged, glancing toward the door. "For now."

As if on cue, the door chimed again, and a stranger stepped inside. He was tanned, with a rugged, beach-weathered look that screamed "not from around here." His sharp eyes scanned the café, pausing briefly when they met mine. Something about his measured gaze sent a ripple of unease through me.

He held a worn envelope in his hand, its edges frayed like it had been handled a thousand times. I couldn't help but wonder how far it had traveled—and why it was here now.

"Who's that?" Holly muttered beside me, leaning in.

"No idea," I whispered, my curiosity already working overtime.

The stranger's eyes lingered on me for just a moment longer before he moved toward the counter, blending into the café's hum of conversation and clinking cups. I had the distinct feeling this wasn't the last time I'd see him.

Before I could dwell on it, the café pulled me back into its warm, familiar rhythm. The espresso machine hissed, sunlight streamed through the windows, and the smell of apple cinnamon muffins filled the air. Despite the lingering mystery of the stranger, peace settled over me. This was my world—friends, family, and the small-town challenges that kept life interesting. But at our table, the air crackled with the thrill of finality as Caleb laid out the last pieces of the puzzle.

"So let me get this straight," Eloise said, her hand slicing through the air for emphasis. "Blake's master plan unraveled because Tiffany out-schemed him, and Sam was quietly orchestrating a revenge campaign the whole time?"

"Pretty much," Caleb replied, his lips curving into a wry smile. "Blake was trying to save his skin, Tiffany was scheming her way to the top, and Sam? He was playing the long game—one poisoned muffin at a time."

Emma's eyes widened, a mixture of disbelief and fascination. "And here I thought Sam was just the charming guy who brought deviled eggs to potlucks. Turns out he was moonlighting as a villain straight out of Agatha Christie."

"Unhinged," Holly declared, her nose wrinkling in distaste. "I don't think I'll ever look at a muffin the same way again."

"You're welcome," I teased, though the exhaustion in my voice betrayed me. "Consider me your official Muffin Taster if it'll help you sleep at night."

Eloise shot me a pointed look, her no-nonsense demeanor firmly in place. "Breadcrumbs or not, you saved my business and my reputation. Don't downplay it."

"Fine," I relented with mock defeat, raising my hands. "I'll take a muffin as a thank-you. Maybe two."

"Make it three," Holly added with a grin.

Caleb leaned back in his chair, arms crossed, a faint glimmer of amusement in his eyes. "So," he began casually, "what's next for you, Josie? Another murder to solve? Or are you finally taking a break?"

I smirked, leaning forward. "Oh, Caleb. Trouble has a way of finding me, break or no break."

"True," he said dryly. "But maybe next time, skip the part where you end up in life-or-death situations. My blood pressure's starting to resent you."

As laughter rippled around the table, my gaze drifted toward the door. The stranger from earlier was leaving, his weathered envelope still clutched in hand. Just before stepping out, he cast another glance my way. The moment lingered just long enough to set my curiosity buzzing.

Holly nudged me with her elbow. "What's his deal?"

"No clue," I murmured, watching the door swing shut behind him. "But something tells me we haven't seen the last of him."

The café's comforting hum carried on around us, but Caleb leaned forward, his voice dipping low. "Speaking of loose ends," he began, his tone tinged with regret, "we were wrong about Delaney's warehouse."

I frowned. "Wrong? About what?"

"About Delaney being tied to Sam," Caleb clarified, his jaw tightening. "Turns out, Delaney and his crew weren't working with Sam at all. Sam used their construction company for a few projects, but that was the extent of it."

My stomach churned as his words sank in. "So, they weren't doing Sam's dirty work?"

"No," Caleb said, shaking his head. "They were tied to Artie."

"Artie?" I blinked, surprised.

"Yeah," Caleb continued, leaning forward, elbows resting on his knees. "Delaney and his goons were on Artie's payroll. He'd hired them for under-the-table jobs—shady construction deals, stolen materials, that sort of thing. When Artie was murdered, everything they'd been working on collapsed. That's why they came after us."

"So they weren't protecting Sam's secrets… they were protecting their own business," I muttered, the pieces clicking into place.

"Exactly," Caleb said grimly. "They panicked. They thought we were digging into Artie's dealings. When Artie was killed, they were left holding the bag—and they didn't know if we were there to expose them."

"That's why they attacked us at the warehouse," I said softly. "They were scared."

"Desperate," Caleb corrected. "They had no idea how deep Artie's trouble went, and when he died, their livelihoods went up in smoke."

A heavy silence settled over the table as we processed this new layer of Artie's tangled web. He wasn't just a victim—he'd been pulling strings in the shadows, dragging Delaney's crew down with him when the whole thing unraveled.

"And now?" I asked quietly. "What happens to them?"

"They're facing charges," Caleb said simply. "Assault, obstruction, conspiracy to cover up Artie's mess. They weren't innocent, but they weren't part of Sam's bigger plan either. Just another casualty of Artie's bad decisions."

I let out a slow breath, the weight of it all pressing down on me. "So, it's over now?"

Caleb met my gaze, his voice soft but certain. "Yeah. It's over."

Holly tilted her head, her curiosity piqued. "What about Tiffany? How does she fit into all this?"

"That's where things get tricky," Caleb admitted. "Tiffany thought she killed Artie. She hit him with the torque wrench," Caleb explained, "but by then, Artie was already dead. Sam had poisoned him earlier with the muffin."

Emma's hand flew to her mouth. "She thought she killed him? That's awful."

Caleb nodded. "And in her panic, she started framing Eloise, stealing recipes, and blackmailing Sam to cover her tracks."

I jumped in, "yeah, she blackmailing Sam. He told me that last night."

"Yeah," Caleb said grimly. "She figured out he poisoned Artie and used it to try to get what she wanted. But Sam wasn't about to let her hold that over him."

"And that's why he poisoned her muffin," I said softly.

"Exactly," Caleb confirmed. "He couldn't risk her blowing his cover."

Holly shook her head in disbelief. "This feels like something out of a bad soap opera."

"You're not wrong," I said, exhaustion settling over me.

Just then, Mandy Morrison appeared at our table, clipboard in hand, her smile as bright and calculated as ever. "Well, well, if it isn't Hickory Hills' resident sleuths!" she trilled. "Now, are you signing up for the pickleball tournament or what? It's going to be very competitive this year."

I blinked at her sudden shift in tone. "Pickleball?"

"Yes, pickleball," Mandy said firmly, her pen poised. "It's a matter of town pride."

I exchanged a look with Caleb, a slow grin spreading across my face. "Why not? Who knows—maybe there's another mystery waiting for us on the court."

Caleb groaned, rubbing his temples. "Josie, don't jinx it."

"Too late!" Holly quipped, grabbing the clipboard and scribbling our names.

And just like that, life in Hickory Hills carried on, filled with laughter, the scent of freshly brewed coffee, and the promise of whatever adventure waited around the corner.

THE END... FOR NOW.

THANK YOU FOR READING!

DO YOU WANT MORE OF JOSIE AND THE GANG?

Wondering what mystery will unfold on the pickleball courts? Sign up for my newsletter to receive updates and sneak peeks, and receive **"Pickleball Peril,"** a free novella where Josie and her friends find more than just competition waiting for them on the court—available only to subscribers!

Sign Up Now and Get Your Free Bonus Short
CarolynMaplewood.com

STAY TUNED FOR THE NEXT THRILLING ADVENTURE IN JOSIE'S JOURNEY!

Here's the first chapter of Josie's next big holiday adventure. Enjoy!

1 claus for concern

The Hickory Hills town square was alive with the sights, sounds, and scents of the annual Christmas market. The iconic white gazebo stood proudly in the center, twinkling with fairy lights, its roof dusted with snow. Every summer, the town gathered here for the beloved "Dance of the Fireflies," where the gazebo glowed with magical light as fireflies danced in the warm evening air. But today, it was the backdrop for the festive chaos unfolding during the winter season. Twinkling lights draped over stalls, holiday music filled the air, and the smell of freshly baked goods and spiced cider wafted through the crowd. It was the perfect setting for some holiday cheer, but little did anyone know trouble was lurking.

My nephew Zeke was back in town for Christmas break, home from his first semester at the University of Alabama. While football was his main focus, his real passion—our shared passion—was rare collectibles. And today, he was all about the coins.

We were manning our booth in the "Unique Gifts" section of the market, tucked under a sprawling white event tent that stretched across the square. The tent, the kind used for weddings and large outdoor events, housed rows of handcrafted goods, baked treats, and one-of-a-kind items from local artisans. Twinkling string lights draped along the ceiling added a festive glow, while the scent of cinnamon and pine filled the air, mingling with the chatter of shoppers. The towering county courthouse stood in the background, its clock tower looming over the market like a quiet guardian, as it had for generations.

Zeke was in his element at our booth, showcasing our collection of rare and antique coins. His eyes lit up as he explained the history of each piece to curious passersby, his enthusiasm drawing them in like moths to a flame.

"Look at this one, Aunt Josie," Zeke said, holding up a particularly shiny coin. "It's from the early 1800s!"

"That's a beautiful piece," I said with a smile, ruffling his hair—despite him now being much too tall and old for that. He grinned, the same sheepish look he'd had since he was little.

"Maybe if football doesn't work out, I'll be a professional coin collector," he joked.

I laughed. "I'm sure Alabama fans would love to hear that their star freshman is ditching football for rare coins."

We were in the middle of chatting when my phone buzzed in my pocket. It was Caleb, the town's deputy—and lately, my reluctant partner in solving mysteries.

Caleb: *There's a new guy at the café who is acting really shifty. Beachy type. I'm keeping an eye on him, but I'd feel better if you were here.*

Josie: *You got this.*

My curiosity was piqued, but I tucked the phone back into my pocket. This was a Christmas market, not the time for chasing after shady strangers. Besides, Tyler, Logan, and Hannah had everything under control at Novel Grounds, along with a few extra student workers eager to make some holiday money. Caleb's paranoia was unnecessary—between my regular staff and the eager college kids, the café could handle the holiday rush just fine.

Still, something here was already catching my attention—a Santa who didn't seem quite as jolly as the season demanded. My instincts prickled. Suddenly, a commotion broke out near the market entrance. I saw the man in a Santa suit stumbling through the crowd, drawing confused laughter and concerned whispers. But my instincts told me something was off—his erratic movements, the way he clutched the sack slung over his shoulder, the furtive glances he threw around.

"Zeke, stay here," I said firmly. "I'll be right back." I dialed Caleb on my phone.

I slipped through the crowd, keeping my eyes on the man in the Santa suit. He was now arguing with Willa Mae, his voice rising in agitation.

"I didn't steal anything!" the man protested. "I swear!"

"Then why are you acting so suspicious?" Willa Mae snapped back. "What's in the bag?"

My pulse quickened as I drew closer. The sack Santa carried looked far too lumpy to be filled with gifts. I approached, trying to keep my tone casual.

"Is everything alright here?" I asked, my gaze shifting between Willa Mae and the man in the Santa suit.

The man's eyes flicked to me, his grip tightening on the bag. "No problem, lady," he muttered, his voice shaky. "Just a misunderstanding."

Before I could press further, another shout rang out from a nearby booth. "Stop! Thief!" A shopkeeper pointed directly at the man in the Santa suit.

Without warning, he bolted, pushing through the crowd with surprising speed.

I didn't waste a second. I called Caleb. When he picked up, I shouted into the phone, "Caleb! Santa's running your way toward Novel Grounds!" I was already in motion, weaving through the bustling crowd, my heart racing as I tried to keep that flash of red in sight.

Caleb, who had just been at the café and was patrolling the other side of the market, was already moving. I spotted him just ahead, weaving through the crowd. With one quick, practiced motion, he intercepted the fleeing Santa, tackling him to the ground.

The crowd gasped, forming a circle around them as Caleb wrestled the sack away from the man. Inside, we found a stash of stolen goods—including some of Willa Mae's pies and rare coins from our booth.

"You've got some explaining to do," Caleb said, hauling the man to his feet.

The man muttered under his breath, but before he could say anything more, the security guards for the event arrived to take him into custody. "Hey Caleb," the tall one said, "we'll detain him until the officers on duty arrive to take him over to the station." Caleb handed him over to the guards, but I couldn't shake the feeling that this wasn't the end of the mystery.

As the crowd began to disperse, I walked back to the booth with Caleb beside me.

"Nice work, Josie," he said, his usual gruffness softened with a hint of a smile. "Looks like you saved Christmas."

"Just another day in Hickory Hills," I replied with a grin, though my thoughts were already racing ahead.

When I got back to the booth, Zeke and I were sorting through the recovered items. Something strange caught my eye as I placed a coin down on the table. Another coin was lying there, mixed in with our usual collection, but it wasn't one of ours. I frowned, picking it up and turning it over in my hand. It was intricately designed, covered with strange symbols that didn't match anything in our collection—or anything I'd ever seen.

"Zeke," I called, motioning him over. "Take a look at this."

Zeke leaned in, studying the coin closely, his brow furrowing. "I've never seen this one before. It's... different."

Different indeed. I slipped the coin into my pocket, my mind buzzing with curiosity. It hadn't been in our collection earlier—so how did it end up on the table? A nagging sense of unease crept in. This wasn't just a case of petty theft—there was something bigger at play. And I felt this mysterious coin was only the beginning of a much larger puzzle.

I glanced at Zeke, who looked just as puzzled as I felt. "I think I'm going to have to drop by Hickory Hills University's Archaeology Department and have them take a look at this," I said, slipping the coin deeper into my pocket. "Something tells me this coin has a story we're not ready for."

Get ready for more twists, turns, and cozy mystery fun in the next book!

About the author

Carolyn Maplewood grew up in a small town in Missouri, and she still calls it home—just like the fictional characters in her cozy mysteries. She's an unabashed fan of classic 80s TV shows like Murder, She Wrote and Scarecrow and Mrs. King. Carolyn brings a touch of that nostalgic charm into her own writing. She's never met a cozy mystery she didn't love, and she crafts stories filled with quirky characters, sweet romance, and intriguing puzzles that'll keep you guessing until the end.

Autumn is Carolyn's favorite season, and you'll often find her soaking up the beauty of fall with her trusty Goldendoodle by her side, a cup of coffee in hand, and her mischievous cat curled up nearby. Whether it's the crunch of leaves underfoot or the smell of firewood in the air, she's in her element when the world is blanketed in shades of orange and gold.

Carolyn writes the kind of stories she loves to read—packed with small-town charm, quirky characters, sweet romance, and, of course, a deliciously puzzling mystery. So, grab a cup of coffee, settle in, and escape to the heart of her charming, small-town mysteries.

Printed in Great Britain
by Amazon